Branded
Strand Brothers Series Book 1

Lora Ann

Strand Brothers Series

Book 1
Branded

Book 2
Bound

Book 3
Broken
Coming Spring 2015

Acknowledgements

Honestly this is the hardest art for me. I always worry I will leave someone important out. It truly takes a village to bring a book to fruition, so without further ado, let me shout out to some exceptional people.

First and foremost none of this would be possible without my Lord and Savior. Thank you, Jesus, for showing me what love truly is and for giving me this passion to write, along with all the other amazing gifts you so freely offer.

Of course the love and support of my family also help make this possible. To my husband who puts up with all the "extra" people in my head, I love you so much and thank you for all that you do. You mean the world to me.

To my lively and wonderful sons: you each hold a piece of my heart and I love you all more than you can fathom. Thank you for putting up with me and always understanding, "give me just a few more minutes to finish this," means mom's in her 'cave.'

Licensed Private Investigator and Behavioral Analyst, Virginia Braden, I could never fully comprehend the criminal mind without your expertise and advice. You are an incredible lady, and I am privileged to call you friend. I love you, girl.
Please check out Virginia's website:
http://www.StillTheySpeak.com

There is a special group of ladies who are the ultimate cheerleaders for my work. They tirelessly went over each draft of Branded without complaint. Ladies, I couldn't have done this without you. I love each of you like a sister. Jenn, Heather, & Angela, from the bottom of my heart—thank you!

This next group helped me catch many of my errors during the proofreading process, and I couldn't do this without them. Here's to: Debbie D-R, Stephanie M., Kayla L., Nicole I., as well as Jennifer M., Heather B., & Angela S.

Dedication

In loving memory of my grandmother, who taught me love is worth the fight.

Grandma G, even though you've been gone eleven years now, the lessons you taught me and your love for the Jesus has never been forgotten. I will see you again. I love you.

There is a time for everything, and a season for every
activity under heaven:
a time to weep and a time to laugh, a time to mourn
and a time to dance

Ecclesiastes 3: 1 & 4 (NIV)

Prologue
Aimee

What on earth was I thinking when I agreed to go to this charity masquerade ball? Some of the most wealthy and influential people would be in attendance. *Seriously! I need to have my head examined.* "Alright now, just breathe, you can do this," I whispered to my reflection in the mirror. I turned myself every which direction to get a good look at the dress I was wearing. Renée had really outdone herself putting it together for me. When I placed the mask on for the full effect, I realized there was no way anyone would recognize me. Not that I ran in such circles; however, this was a staged event for me. An opportunity to see if I had what my—hopefully soon—employer was looking for. I stepped out of my room to get the final approval from my best friend, Renée.

"Girl, you're going to knock their socks off." She exclaimed, "You look amazing!"

On a long exhale, I released the breath I'd been holding. "Are you sure?"

"Hell yes, I'm sure."

I ran my hand down the full skirt of my gown. It truly was a magnificent dress—emerald green in color with gold edging. I felt like I'd stepped back in time. The mask matched perfectly. While there was no question I was feeling beautiful, my nerves were frayed. "Ren?"

"Yes."

"I'm not sure I can do this."

She walked over to tuck a tendril of my hair behind my ear. "Hey. It's only escorting. You've been clear that you want no part of the other *business*. Relax. They're going to love you. You have the look men want—sexy yet innocent."

I scoffed, "My hips are too wide, and my boobs are too large."

"My point precisely. Men like something to hold on to."

I smacked her arm. "Renée!" Then I reiterated, "I'm not going to prostitute myself."

Her lips thinned. "So, I'm a whore?"

Oh, shit. "No." I inhaled deeply before I clarified, "That's not what I meant. All I mean is that, that side of the business isn't my cup of tea. You know I'd never judge you."

Her entire body relaxed. "Sorry, Aims. I know you don't."

Truth be told, the lure of the money was quite intoxicating. And I would be a liar if I said I hadn't thought about it. My only hang-up was married men. Strange, I know, call it my own sense of morals, but there were just some lines I refused to cross.

"Okay, now." Renée explained, "You'll meet Ann and Jack around eleven-ish. They'll either give you the go ahead or turn you down."

I still had a hard time grasping it was a brother and sister team that ran the escort service. But according to Renée, they were fair-minded and knew what men of such caliber required. So if I was turned away, it was nothing personal. Still, I really needed the money desperately. With my dad fighting cancer, there was not a dime left for me. And I had run up an astronomical amount of student loans. Bottom line, this was my best bet to pay them off quickly *and* help out my family. Renée brought me back to the here and now when she said, "Remember, midnight. You make sure you're out of there."

I couldn't stifle the giggle. She raised an eyebrow at me. "Oh, come on." I clarified, "Even you have to admit it is rather Cinderella sounding."

She grinned, "Then, by all means, find yourself a very rich Prince Charming."

I rolled my eyes. "Ha! Surrrrre. I'll make that my top priority."

My phone beeped with an incoming message. I read the screen and turned to her. "Car's here."

She kissed my cheek. "Go get 'em, girl."

I waggled my fingers on the way out. "Ta-ta."

*****

I focused on breathing and tried to keep my heart rate under control. There was no point in showing up soaked with sweat while I panted like I'd just run a marathon. I gave myself a mental pep talk: *You can do this, Aimee. No worries. Everything's going to work out fine.* If I could only believe it was true. I considered praying but then thought that wasn't such a great idea. Yes, I was only applying for an escort position; however, I knew God was fully aware of just how tempting the offer was to take it a step further. *Right, nix on the praying.* When the door to the limo opened, I was pulled from my musing. I stepped out onto a red carpet. Luckily, I was no one of significance or with anyone important; hence, the focus was on others that arrived at the same time. Thank goodness.

I was gathered swiftly into the throng and rushed inside. While I took in my surroundings along with all the marvelous attire, a waiter passed by with a silver tray of champagne flutes. I grabbed one and took a sip. In a matter of moments, I was swept onto the dance floor where one gentleman after another danced with me. I eventually needed a break and excused myself to the nearest powder room.

Upon my return, I did my best to observe—all to no avail. A deep voice whispered in my ear. "May I have this dance?"

A chill of awareness instantly shot up and down my spine. I swallowed the lump in my throat and fought the urge to lean into whoever he was. "Yes," I huskily replied. *What the hell is the matter with me?* Never have I had such a reaction to a man. He stepped around me. Once I was in his arms, we began to waltz around the dance floor. He was extremely tall, and his broad shoulders stretched the fabric of his tux deliciously. I ran my tongue over my bottom lip. He didn't miss the motion. Due to the full mask he wore, I couldn't get a good look at his face. But I could see his eyes, which were a brilliant light blue. They reminded me of a glacier: sharp, intense, and very observant. There really wasn't anything else visible on him. I did notice his hair appeared to be blond, maybe a shade or so lighter than mine, and long enough that he could tie it back with a black leather thong. Everything about the man screamed danger, so, of course, I was drawn to him like a moth to a flame. Confidence radiated off of him in waves. I was immediately reminded of how you could tell a man made love by the way he danced. Although I was not delusional, this man would not make love. No. *He* would fuck. The thought made me wet. All of a sudden, I became aware of several things at once: He inexorably danced me into the shadows while Michael Bublé sang, "I've Got You Under My Skin." The actual performer was there live, and, honestly, I

4

couldn't imagine a better song for how I felt at that moment. The next thing I knew, he had pulled me through a door I never noticed before.

I looked up at him and inquired, "Where are you taking me?"

His lips curved up slightly as he replied, "Somewhere quiet."

Oh, my word. I had let a complete stranger drag me away from everyone and everything. And damn, if the idea didn't excite me more. You would think I'd be a bit more concerned about my safety. For all I knew, this guy was an axe murderer. Yet, for some reason, I completely trusted him. I knew he would never hurt me physically. Although I was quite sure, the man had left more than one broken heart in his wake.

We slipped into a small library/office. The room was dimly lit; thus, I reached over to turn on a lamp sitting on a side table.

"Don't," he murmured.

I really wanted to know how his voice truly sounded. So far, the few words he had spoken were all whispered; therefore, I couldn't hear it clearly. I did catch a slight rasp with a hint of some kind of accent but nothing discernable. Gah! The man became more frustrating by the moment. I heard the door lock, and then he was in front of me. He caressed up and down my sides, nibbling along my neck. I leaned to the side to give him better access, all the while I made little mewling noises.

He suckled the tender spot just below my earlobe. "Tell me to stop if I've misread the attraction between us," he demanded.

No way in hell I was doing that. The electricity was arcing between our bodies with a mind of its own. Instead, I begged for more. "Please."

I felt his smile along my throat. "Right

answer," he groaned. Meanwhile, I began to explore his body. I managed to push the jacket off his shoulders, as he tugged the bodice of my gown over my breasts. With his teeth, he worked the lace of my bra out of the way and then laved my nipple. The man had a wicked tongue and knew just how to use it. He gently scraped the sensitive peak with his teeth, causing me to moan. "So responsive," he purred. I reached up to draw the mask from his face when he stilled my hands. "No," he commanded. "Let's leave them on."

I growled out of frustration. In response, he decided to lavish attention on my other nipple. I was beyond hot and bothered. I *wanted* this man deep inside me. "More," I demanded.

With that, he eased me onto the sofa. He reached under my dress and traced his fingers under my panties. "You're ready for me." His finger dipped inside my core.

"Yes." Was the only coherent thing I managed to say.

Another finger joined the party while his thumb began to draw slow, exquisite circles around my tight nub. I was going to come if he kept that up for much longer. All of a sudden he stopped, and I actually whined. "Patience, little one," he instructed. I bit my lip in an attempt to hold back my protest. As his fingers continued to explore my body, he leaned back on his heels. "I can't decide where to taste you first. Should it be here?" He ran the pad of his thumb across my bottom lip, and I could taste my essence. "Or should I kiss these lips?" His finger teased my cleft before he traced up to circle the bundle of nerves at the top. *Oh, fucking, my!* I arched my hips. "I agree," he confirmed, and then his mouth was there at my center—licking, sucking, and nipping. While I rode his face, I tugged his head tighter into me. The man knew his way around a woman's body. And, let's be honest here, there was nothing hotter than a man who enjoyed going down on a woman. My orgasm hit ferociously. Before I could come down off the first one, his fingers were inside me coaxing the second.

Once I regained some semblance of composure, he released himself into his hand. Holy shit. He was very large *there* as well—thick, long, and incredibly swollen. I was not convinced he would fit. He pulled out a condom and ripped open the package with his teeth. As he slid it over his impressive penis, his fingers were, once again, sliding in and out of me. He placed the head of his cock into my entrance, and I moaned in pleasure. Slowly, he inched inside me. Just when I thought he couldn't go any further, he grabbed my ass and lifted. After he fully seated himself, he held still for a moment. "You're so damn tight," he growled as his eyes closed.

I wrapped my legs around his waist to get even closer, which caused him to groan. Then, he began to move. It didn't take long for me to catch on to his rhythm. As I predicted, he began thrusting harder and faster. His hips slammed into my butt with enough force to rock the sofa back. I worried someone could hear the thumping. But there was no way I would stop him. My climax was building, and I knew this one would be even more intense than the other two. He didn't fail me. My eyes rolled back as the orgasm hit, and then with one more powerful thrust he followed.

As our breathing began to regulate, I stroked my hands across his expansive chest. "You are amazing."

He pulled out and said, "You're the astounding one."

I watched as he removed the condom, tied it off, and put it in his pocket. Then, he stuffed his still semi-erect sex back into his pants. He handed me my panties and watched as I put them back on. Once we were back to rights, he hauled me into his hard body and kissed me senseless. When he pulled away, I was once again breathless. He held out his hand to me and walked over to the door. We stepped out of the room hand in hand.

*****

I turned towards him and queried, "Are you going to tell me your name?"

He shook his head. "And ruin the mystery? Never."

"But… if I don't know your name and you don't know mine, how will I see you again?"

He half-smiled. "I'll find you, little one," he promised.

"Mmm." I pointed out the obvious. "You don't even know what I look like."

"Now that's half the fun."

Once we reached the ballroom, he pivoted towards me and drew my hand to his lips, where he kissed my knuckles. "Till we meet again."

I stood there dumbfounded. Before I could say another word, he turned and left. The synapses finally fired in my brain. Oh, hell, no. He was not leaving here until I knew who he was. I searched frantically; however, I was unable to tell who was who in the sea of masks. I reached the door to the outside but couldn't see in the dark. I slowly pivoted and then scanned the room urgently. It was useless. He was nowhere to be found. I noticed the song playing was "We'll Meet Again" by Johnny Cash. How ironic. I shook my head to clear the fog and then stepped outside.

*****

I walked to the line of limos. When I heard my name, I turned around to see a couple striding towards me. The woman stuck out her hand. "Hello, Aimee. I'm Ann. And this is Jack," she introduced.

I shook hands with both of them. "How do you do?"

Jack asked, "Were you going to leave without speaking to us?"

Crap. I'd completely forgotten why I was here. "I'm sorry. I wasn't able to locate you, and it has been a long night." Okay, yes, I was lying. I hoped they didn't figure that out.

Ann smiled, "No worries, my dear. We just wanted to welcome you."

Well, now I really felt bad. "Thank you." I smiled. "When would you like me to start?"

They both grinned. "We'll be in touch," Jack answered.

Ann replied, "Expect a call on Monday." They turned to walk back inside. She looked over her shoulder and called, "Have a good night, Aimee."

I responded, "You as well. Again, thank you."

With that, I found my limo driver holding the door open for me. I crawled into the backseat and closed my eyes. On the drive back to my apartment, all I could think of was my mystery man. How would he ever find me? More importantly, that had been the best sex of my life, so, how was I supposed to go on like nothing had ever happened? I inhaled deeply and could still smell him on my dress. The memory of his hands, his mouth, on my body brought forth an ache deep inside my core. *Ah, hell, I'm in serious trouble.*

Chapter One
Aimee

Five years later.

Talk about a rock and a hard place. How had my life come down to this? I grabbed the note I received yesterday and, once again, read the ominous threat any fool could see.

Aimee darling,

You will agree to be my wife this evening at six o'clock sharp! I will neither accept any delays nor will I put up with you running away from me again. Now that I have your full and undivided attention you will do the following:
Cancel your airline ticket for San Francisco.
Explain to Renée you've changed your mind.
Call your parents and give them the good news.
Meet me at the Delmont to greet my constituents. This will be where we make our wonderful announcement.

Yours always,
—C

Damn the man! There was no use taking this note to the police. One, the threat was not spelled out. And two, half of the force was in cahoots with the senator. Well, crap! This was just one huge clusterfuck of epic proportions. Would he hurt someone I loved? More than likely. Not that I thought any of them were in physical danger, per se. But he could make their lives a living hell if he chose. Could he destroy my plans for the future? Without a doubt. Had I overlooked some obvious solution to this nightmare? That'd be a no. I groaned loudly and rubbed my face with my hands. Never in a million years did I want to be tied to such a horrid man. Why I ever got involved in the first place still baffled me. I knew why actually but was ashamed to admit it— even to myself. How stupid. I'd made my bed, so fate deciding I needed to lie in it really shouldn't shock me. I couldn't just sit here and sulk. Right now, I needed my best friend. Maybe she'd have some insight into this debacle. If you want to get down to the bare bones of the situation at hand, Renée was truly at the center of it all. No, in truth, that wasn't quite fair—I'd made the decision. She was only responsible for offering me a solution to my financial woes. *Ah, hell. I need out of my head for a few minutes.* With any luck, together we could figure out a way for me to be free of Senator Caleb Reynolds. I threw the note in my purse and then walked out of my apartment with purpose. Come hell or high water, I was not marrying that man!

*****

Renée opened the door, took one good hard look at me, blew out an exasperated breath and asked, "What'd he do now? I thought you told him to pound salt."

I shook my head. "I've done everything I can think of to make it clear I don't wanna marry him. Yet he still insists. And now this…" I handed her the note before I sat down heavily on her couch. "You tell me, what more I can do?"

"Shit."

That truly did sum it up. "Got that right." I buried my face in my hands. At this point, crying and/or screaming didn't seem like enough. So when I began to laugh manically, it shouldn't have surprised me.

Renée more than understood me. She wrapped her arm around my shoulders and stated, "The man is freakin' delusional."

One of the things I loved most about my best friend was her ability to hit the nail right on the head. I was finally able to squelch the uncontrollable laughter. "I'm open to suggestions."

She shrugged. "I don't have any."

"Great. So what're you saying, I have to marry the asshole?"

She stood and began to pace. "What the hell is his game, anyway? I mean, you've told him no for the past three months now. Yet he continues. This little gem"—she held up the note for emphasis—"is just asinine."

I couldn't agree more. Still, there didn't appear to be any solution. Sure, I could once again refuse; however, my gut told me he would make good on his warning. Not one single person I cared about was safe from his powerful reach, which meant he had me—there was not a damn thing I could foresee that'd stop him. My eyes began to burn with the tears I'd attempted to tamp down.

Renée looked over at me and comforted, "Oh, hey, none of that. The dickhead just isn't worth it."

I really did try to smile, but my mouth just

wouldn't cooperate.

She knelt in front of me and held my hands in hers. "Listen. Go ahead with this thing tonight." I gasped as my eyes widened. She continued, "Shh, girlfriend. I didn't say you were going through with it. I'm simply saying, for tonight appease him. In the meantime, I'll do a little investigating. Maybe there's something we can find on him, so you can flip the tables."

I nodded. Because, at that moment, words just wouldn't come.

She tried to make light of things. "Wear that awesome silver cocktail dress with the shimmer-y Jimmy Choo's. At least that way, all eyes will be on you the entire night."

While I rolled my eyes at her, I queried, "What good will that do?"

Her face was fierce when she replied, "He won't be able to lay a finger on you."

It was a valid point. In the year that I'd been involved with Caleb, he'd threatened to strike me more than once. But he never followed through. Although I began to realize, pushing him too far might have dire results. And like I said before, he was well connected. Not that I was making any excuses for his behavior, but, the fact remained, in my business getting knocked around really was nothing new. All any of my clients had to say was: "I got a little rough during sex, and she enjoyed it."

I sighed heavily. Never did I think I would become a high-priced call girl. Really? What little girl dreamt of such a thing? When I started five years ago, it was going to be short term—and I was only going to *escort*. Yeah, right. Let's face it; the money was too good to walk away from, not to mention my parents really needed the financial help that I had no other way of obtaining. My only true hang-up was that I in no way wanted to be with married men. I learned quickly I didn't have to be, and, well, as the saying goes, "When in Rome…" Yep, I've made a huge mess out of my life. Where did all of my hopes and dreams go? *Oh, hell, no! I refuse to go down that road. What's done is done.* Time to pull up my big girl panties and face the big, bad wolf. Um…maybe a red dress would be much more appropriate for this evening. I inwardly chuckled.

Renée stood and walked into the kitchen. A couple minutes later, she returned with a shot of whiskey. "Here's to liquid courage."

I raised my glass and affirmed, "Hear, hear." In one gulp, my glass was empty. "Thanks for trying to help me out, Ren. I do love you."

"Yeah. Yeah. What's not to love?" She preened. Her face became serious when she said, "We'll figure this out, Aims. Don't worry about tonight. You'll be fine, I promise."

My lips curved up slightly. "From your lips to God's ears. I'll text you when I get home. If you don't hear from me, call in reinforcements."

When you were in the kind of business we were in, you had to have someone looking out for you. Renée and I had been each other's safe call since college. I knew if she needed to, Blade would be brought in. The fact that he was Renée's brother helped immensely. What didn't help was that he was a mean son-of-a-bitch. You did not want to piss that man off. His name said it all. It was his gang name, and he still lived up to the rep. He scared the living daylights out of me; however, the knowledge that he'd take care of whatever or whomever we needed him to was comforting.

*****

I arrived at the Delmont around five thirty that evening. Caleb spotted me instantly. I was swept into his side tightly before I said, "Hello." By the feel of his tense body, I knew this would be a night to tread lightly. He was in no mood to hear the word no. Quite frankly, I was in no mood to fight with him. My decision to be subservient tonight would serve me well. I'd obviously learned a few tricks of the trade— so to speak—when to take the upper hand with a man and when to speak only when spoken to.

Once he finished his conversation with one of his cronies, he turned to me. "You will obey me, Aimee," he ordered. "I'll be damned if you refuse me publicly. Are we clear?"

I kept my eyes on the floor and softly answered, "Yes, sir."

While he stroked my back, he praised, "Good girl."

I mentally rolled my eyes at him and then flipped him the bird. Please! BDSM was not my thing or his either. He just liked control of any and every situation. I honestly had no problems with that. I was drawn to commanding men, as well as gorgeous ones. Once you got past the whole "do as I say or else" persona, you realized he was quite charming. With his dark brown hair and chocolate eyes, plus, his lean, athletic build, you had yourself one nice piece of man candy. He ought to come with a warning to all ladies: Look out! No wonder the man held a seat in the senate at the tender age of thirty-eight. He had a charisma that drew you in. There really wasn't a woman who could resist his thousand-watt smile. Even I had fallen victim, until he slowly began to reveal his true self. Now, the man gave me the heebie-jeebies. Something was off. But after a year, I still couldn't figure out what it was.

By six the party was in full swing, with Caleb

and me taking center stage. In true Caleb fashion, he commanded the crowd. After his spiel, he got down on one knee. "Aimee, my dear, you are my light. I cannot imagine another day without you being my wife." He held my hand a little too tightly as he popped the question: "Would you do me the honor of marrying me?"

There were "ooohs" and "aaahs" throughout the room. For full effect, a single tear ran down Caleb's cheek. Oh, please! I had to hand it to him, he was good. My bottom lip trembled out sheer terror, albeit the effect was magnificent. Even Caleb thought it was from the proposal. I quietly answered, "Yes." When he dipped me over his arm and kissed me, I was more than surprised. There was triumph in his eyes once he pulled away. This was definitely an oh, shit moment. How would I get out from under this train wreck? I felt like a wild animal that had just been trapped. As cold sweat trickled down my spine, I chanted to myself: *I will not pass out. I will not pass out.* Nothing helped. Once we were off stage, I politely excused myself. "I need to use the powder room. I'll be back in a few minutes."

I turned to walk away when his firm hand landed on my shoulder. "No tricks, Aimee," he warned. "I'll be waiting for you."

As I tried my best to smile, I fought off a cringe. "Of course, darling," I said in a saccharine tone. Meanwhile my brain screamed, "Run! Tell him to take a flying leap and run like hell." If only, that was even a possibility.

Once I rounded the corner, my pace quickened. I was nearly sprinting towards the ladies' room when—bam—I ran into a wall of muscle. *Crap! It's probably one of his damn henchmen.* I looked up and up and up through my eyelashes. Finally, I saw the face of the giant I'd bumped into. My goodness, he was freaking gorgeous! He was not only tall but big all over. I was thoroughly convinced that shoulders like his belonged on a football field, not in a hotel corridor. His massive hand came up to steady me so I wouldn't fall on my butt. There was a rough, raspy sound. "Are you all right?"

Oh my! The sound was his sexy as hell voice. I stammered, "Um…yes. Yes, I'm alright."

His lips curved up slightly on one side. "You seem to be in a hurry."

Wow. That hint of an accent of his was unbelievable. I smiled, "Just need to pee." *OMG. Did I just say that?!* The odds of me saying anything intelligible around this man were slim to none. "I'm s-sorry. I can't believe I just said that."

He chuckled low in his throat. I swear if he did that one more time, I would have an orgasm. "No need for apologies," he countered. "When you have to go, you have to go." He motioned with his hand towards the restrooms. "Please, don't let me keep you."

"Right. Excuse me."

I darted into the ladies room and then leaned against the wall. I just met a god. And I needed to hurry, because I really wanted to talk to him some more. Fact was, I actually did need to pee. Ironic. Once I had myself put to rights, I walked back into the hallway where *Thor* was glaring at my intended. *Oh, just shoot me now.* They appeared to know one another, nonetheless their voices were terse, and the tension was thick between them. For whatever reason, I stepped in the middle. But I wasn't there more than a moment. Caleb yanked me to his side with enough force to knock me off balance. And that was when the heel on my brand-new, lace-up Jimmy Choo's snapped. I shoved him with both hands. "What the hell, Caleb?"

He squeezed my upper arm so tight I knew I'd have a bruise. At that moment, I caught a movement out of my peripheral vision. A fist came back, and I knew what was about to happen. Or, so I thought. Before *Thor* could make contact, four huge secret service men were on him. Caleb shoved me into action, pushing me up the hallway while I struggled to help my rescuer. I filled my lungs with air to scream, but Caleb's hand was quicker—clamping over my mouth so snug breathing became difficult.

He roughly shoved me inside a room, all the while I struggled for air. I fell to my hands and knees, gasping. My lungs burned. And it took me a few moments to catch my breath. Then, I heard the door lock. I looked up from under my hair and saw Caleb had drawn his foot back to kick me. I quickly rolled out of his way, which only managed to piss him off more. For the life of me, I couldn't figure out what he was doing. I mean, yes, he had threatened to hit me before, but never had he followed through with it. My gut told me that was not the case this time. I beseeched, "Please, Caleb. I'm sorry. I'll do whatever you say."

He twisted my hair around his fist. "You're damn right you'll do what I say." He unfastened his slacks and slid them along with his boxers to his knees. "Open your mouth," he commanded.

I was complying when the door flew in with a loud *thud*. And there stood, in all of his muscular glory, my protector. Caleb fumbled to pull up his pants, but he wasn't quick enough. *Thor* landed a roundhouse kick to his solar plexus, followed by a dead-on right hook to his jaw that sent him a good two feet across the floor. He sprawled face down with his pants still around his ankles so his ass was bare for all to see. Under different circumstances, it would've been funny. A large hand gently reached under my arm to help me up. As I stood, the once beautiful, red chiffon tiered dress slid off my shoulder where the strap had been torn. *Uh...when'd that happen?* I tried to at least keep my breast covered. All of a sudden, an extremely large suit coat was placed around my shoulders. *Thor's* finger grazed tenderly under my chin to raise my face up so our eyes met. As a tear escaped, I murmured, "Thank you."

The pad of his thumb caught it. "Hey, now," he comforted, "It's okay. I'll take care of you." With that vow, I was tucked safely under his arm.

As we left the room, the secret service guys arrived. One of them asked, "Mr. Strand?" *Thor* tilted his head over his shoulder and commanded, "Take care of that."

*****

I was quickly taken to a limo where my protector steadily assisted me into the back. We sat in silence for most of the drive. While I appreciated the quiet so I could pull myself together, I needed to text Renée. "Do you have a cell phone I can use?"

"Sure." He handed me his phone. As I began to type my message, I inquired, "Where are you taking me?"

"My place," he replied.

My text read: **I'm safe. Not home. Will explain tomorrow. A.**

Since I wasn't using my cell, I hoped she realized it was me. I passed the phone back over to him when it vibrated with a text. He read what was on the screen aloud: "Where's your cell? No worries. Talk to ya later." He quirked a brow at me. "Did you want to answer the question?"

I shook my head. "She knows I'm okay." I affirmed, "That's all that matters."

"Indeed."

I glanced back over at him. "What's your name?"

He reached over and placed his hand on mine. "Nik."

Puzzled, for a moment, I tried to figure out how I knew that name, and then it hit me. "As in business mogul, ex-heavyweight UFC champion, Nik Strand?" I could hear the awe in my voice. Did he?

He inclined his head. "Yes."

Holy crap! I turned my hand so I could lace my fingers with his. "I'm Aimee Taylor."

He chuckled low and squeezed our hands together. "Nice to meet you, Aimee."

Chapter Two
Aimee

There was no rhyme or reason as to why this man felt so familiar to me. As we walked into his penthouse, I studied his face. His bone structure would make a sculptor cry with joy, but I knew I'd never seen him before tonight. Or, had I? That was the confusing part of it all. Also, it didn't escape my notice he was inspecting me as well. So I shouldn't have been surprised by the extraordinary heat that passed between us when he placed his hand on the small of my back to lead me further into the room. I'd felt the waves of attraction before, but this was more—as if my body recognized his. Where did I know him from? I mean, sure, everybody knew who he was. Still, there was something else I couldn't put my finger on.

He stepped away, and, for some unknown reason, I felt bereft. He offered, "Would you like something to drink?"

Ah, I could orgasm from his voice—which was laced with a barely there accent—alone if he kept talking. Again, there was a hint of familiarity I couldn't quite place. I replied, "I'd love a brandy."

He approached the sideboard and prepared my drink. The man was sheer perfection—all sharp lines and hard muscle, not to mention *huge*. He must still work out a lot for his body to look like that. My fingers itched to run through his glorious mane, which was at least six shades of blond. Women paid a high price for hair like his. When he returned to sit next to me, I got my first good look into his eyes. My goodness, they were glacial blue, intense and shrewd. Reality hit, this was a man who got exactly what he wanted when he wanted it. No questions asked. *Hmm…I'd only ever seen irises like his once before. Interesting.*

I accepted the drink he handed me. "Thank you for everything."

There was a ghost of a smile on his perfectly etched lips. Heavens, the man was pure masculine perfection. I wondered what his face would look like with a full megawatt smile. I was willing to bet it would be panty dropping. I held the sifter in my hand and tried not to stare at him. He gently removed my glass and set it on the coffee table. With his fingers stroking my jaw, he turned my face towards him. "Why don't you tell me how you know Reynolds?" He spoke Caleb's surname as an expletive. There was definitely some bad blood between the two.

Instead of answering his question, I asked one of my own. "What happened to make you hate him so much?"

His steely gaze held mine. Unbidden, an image of a Viking came to mind. Fierce. Powerful. Oh, this man was a force to be reckoned with. And God help me, I was more than a little turned on. He countered, "I asked first."

Yes. Yes, he did. "Point taken," I conceded. I looked down at my hands for a moment and willed myself to spit out my story. I knew once I did, he would want nothing to do with me. I reached over for my glass and downed the rest in one gulp. His eyes widened in surprise. I replaced it on the coffee table and squared my shoulders. "He was my client."

"Client?" he inquired, "What business are you in?"

Inhale. Exhale. "I'm a high-priced call girl."

His brows hit his hair line. "Say what, now?"

That would've been funny if I wasn't so damn attracted to him. "A prostitute," I clarified.

"I know what a call girl is, sweetheart," he snorted.

Shit! I didn't mean to insult him. "Sorry." I confessed, "I had no intentions of insulting your intelligence."

That earned me a slight curve of his lips. "I'm not insulted," he acknowledged, "However, I am confused. What was the proposal all about?"

I stood and walked back over to grab the decanter of brandy. I was going to need more alcohol for this conversation. I returned back to the sofa and offered, "Refill?"

He nodded and held up his sifter. After I filled both glasses, I sat back down and took a healthy swallow. I continued, "I haven't been with anyone else in six months."

"Because he paid you to be *only* with him?"

"Yes. He asked me to marry him three months ago, but I refused. Obviously, he didn't give up. He finally found a way to get me to capitulate."

The room temperature dropped a good fifteen degrees. I hugged myself tightly, rubbing my hands up and down my arms. Then it hit me, the chill was coming from him. His gaze was hard as ice, and his voice was laced with violence. "He threatened you?"

"You could say that."

He glared at me. "How?"

I eased away from him before I answered, "The usual. Career, family, friends—basically anything that means something to me." He was flabbergasted, but that didn't stop his inquisition. "He knows your real name?"

"Yes. I never used an alias because I wasn't living a double life. I did, however, use a different last name strictly for protection. Though, he eventually learned my real one. But how are you aware that's common practice in my line of work?"

He dubiously replied, "I wasn't born yesterday, Aimee."

"Fair enough. The point is, I was trying to get out and start my career. I had a sweet job lined up in San Francisco. I never intended to do this long term. I always had a plan."

He graced me with a genuine half-smile. *Fuck. Me.* It was the kind of smile that would make any woman do anything he asked of her, and she would do so just to please him. I had to wonder what kind of damage a full smile that reached his eyes would do to me, or anyone else of the female persuasion. I actually lost my train of thought. *What were we talking about?* "And your plan was?" he prompted.

Oh right, now I remembered what I was saying. "I'm going to own and operate at least one hotel and resort."

He leaned back with a smug expression on his face. "Do tell."

"My degree is in business and hotel management. Unfortunately, I need some hands on experience before I dive right in. So, I was going to work for a small five star hotel in San Fran to get my feet wet. They were fully aware of my plans, and the agreement was to meet with the silent partner at the end of the year. If all went well, I'd own my first hotel."

"Which hotel?"

"The Fairmont."

"You don't say. I find this information interesting." He steepled his fingers in front of his mouth. "You said 'was,' not are. What changed?"

What was that look about? I could not read his face, but I had a feeling he knew something I didn't. *Grr!* "My instructions from Caleb were to cancel all of my arrangements. Therefore, I had to inform my prospective employers there had been a change in plans."

"I see."

"Yes, well." I sighed heavily.

"Was he specific in what he would do to your family and friends?" he inquired.

"Not really. I mean, let's face it; he could make their lives a living hell if he chose to. I can't live with that. I won't. So really, what choice did I have?"

"Is your family aware of your present job?"

"It's not my *job* any longer. I'm serious about leaving it all behind and starting over, which had been my intention all along. I was only going to escort. But then my dad lost his job, and that meant no insurance to pay for his chemo. They needed money, and I wasn't about to tell them where it was coming from. It would break their hearts."

"Why escorting?"

"Student loans. And my dad was diagnosed with cancer." I sighed. "My best friend talked me into it." I hoped it didn't sound like I had just blamed Renée for my circumstances.

He only nodded, deep in thought. "I can help you," he declared.

I was not expecting that. Honestly, I was growing skeptical. What if he offered to *hire* me? Yes, I was more than attracted to him, but I was no longer hiring myself out. That chapter of my life was over—the end. "How, exactly?"

Again with the half-smile—*Dear Lord*—he replied, "Marry me."

"Excuse me? Look, this is the twenty-first century. A woman doesn't get married because some asshole threatens her. Come on! That's just absurd."

Well, that did it. Now he was furious. He stood up so fast I thought he was going to knock over the sofa and me with it. Then he began to pace while he growled, "I'm fully aware of the century, Aimee. The point is, that 'asshole' can wreak havoc on your life like you've never seen. You cannot ignore him and hope he'll go away. You need protection, and I can provide it. It's really that simple," he apprised.

Now I was angry. "First off, don't talk down to me. I'm not a child. I'm obviously aware he can ruin my life. That was why I had agreed to stay with him in the first place. I have plenty of money to hire my own protection. I damned sure don't need *your* help, Mr. Strand."

He grabbed my upper arms. "Yes, Ms. Taylor, you do *need* me."

"You know what…Piss off!" I broke free of his grasp and marched over to the elevator to push the call button. The door opened immediately.

I heard Nik bellow, "Aimee. Get your ass back in here, now!"

As the doors slid closed, I flipped him off. Just who did that man think *he* was? I would figure this out myself. I was sick and tired of these powerful, commanding men telling me what to do with my life. They could all go to hell.

*****

Once I reached the lobby, I had the doorman call me a cab. A short time later, I arrived at my apartment building and went straight to Renée's. I didn't want to be alone, and, quite frankly, I needed some girl time.

She opened the door in her pj's with her sleep mask pushed up on her forehead. "Hey, girl. What's up?"

"I'll tell you in the morning," I proclaimed. "Can I crash on the couch?"

"Of course you can," she replied.

As I made myself comfy, she gave me a huge hug. "It'll all work out for the best, Aims. You'll see."

I scoffed, "No, Rens. It won't. But I don't wanna talk 'bout it now. I love you."

She shook her head. "Silly girl, you need to have some faith. I love you, too. Sweet dreams," she called as she padded towards her bedroom.

All night, I tossed and turned. Everything that'd happened in the last twenty-four hours replayed through mind. "Have faith," Renée had said. She really had no idea how fucked up my life truly was. Worst part, it was my own doing. Life really did suck.

Chapter Three
Nik

Holy hell. Was she that delusional? Caleb was one mean son-of-a-bitch. I should know. I'd had him in and out of my life for almost twenty years now. Fate had apparently decided that yet another woman was to be the object of both of our affections—or obsession, depending on how you'd like to look at it. *No, I refuse to revisit the past.* So, what to do with a problem like Aimee? I was beginning to see she was fiercely independent. Not that I didn't understand. I had been doing things my way for quite some time. I wouldn't take kindly to someone deciding to take control over my life; therefore, I couldn't blame her. Problem was, I had to have control of anything and anyone involved in my life. Whether she liked it or not, I fully intended for her to be very engaged. She needed my protection, and I had the means to provide it tenfold. However I wasn't a fool. Aimee would not capitulate easily. No, I fully expected a challenge— one that I had every intention of rising to. She really had no idea whom she was up against.

I poured myself another two fingers of Courvoisier and sat down in front of the fire, contemplating my next move. The idea of marriage terrified me, and, honestly, I wasn't cut out for intimacy. Yet I had to have Aimee close. It didn't make sense to even me, so how did I convey it to her? *Fuck. What was I doing? I cannot marry again.* I furiously stood, threw the glass at the rock fireplace and then stormed into my home office.

I grabbed the phone and punched the numbers so hard on the keypad I was surprised it didn't crack. A deep timbre voice answered, "Hello."

"Get over here, now," I ordered.

"Why, Nik, so nice of you to call," he mocked.

My brother thought he was funny. "Shut the hell up, Alex."

He chuckled, "I'll be there shortly."

I slammed the handset back into its cradle and then sat there staring out the window. As memories tried to resurface, I shoved them back into their box inside my mind. I would not allow myself to go there. *I refuse!*

A short while later, Alex sauntered into the room. "To what do I owe this pleasure, brother dear?"

"Sit," I commanded.

He smirked. "Domineering as always, I see."

"I didn't call you here to bust my chops." I clarified, "I need some advice."

He sarcastically replied, "Awesome. How may I assist the almighty Nik Strand?"

"Fuck you," I said with no heat. My brother knew how much his opinion mattered to me.

He laughed, "No, thanks. I'm really not into that sort of thing. Besides, incest is illegal," he pointed out.

"Hardy har har. You're so damn funny," I sardonically proclaimed.

"I do my best." He ran his hand through is hair. "What's going on, Nik?"

"I met a woman."

His brow arched. "Well, that's not so surprising. Considering, you don't date the same one twice."

"I don't date, period," I asserted.

"Yes, I know." His look betrayed his concern for me.

"Here's the thing, Alex." I leaned forward and steepled my fingers in front of my mouth. "She's engaged."

"Not like that has ever been a deterrent to you before."

"True." I added, "But there's more."

"Do tell."

Such a smartass. "She's engaged to Reynolds." I held my hand up to silence him. "It's being forced on her, Alex. She in no way wants anything to do with him."

"Then, why?" I could see the confusion in his eyes, not to mention the worry etched in his face. Caleb was bad news for me, and Alex knew it.

I took a deep breath before I explained, "He's threatening her."

"Ah, hell!"

"Now, you understand?"

He pushed back from the desk and stood. Then he began to pace. "This is bad, Nik. Really bad."

"You don't think I know that? Why do you suppose you're here in the middle of the night?"

"Oh, I know you're fully aware of just how fucked up this is. Question is, what're you planning to do about it?"

"Hence, the reason I called you."

"You want legal advice?" he inquired.

I countered, "Is there anything she can do legally?"

He shrugged. "Depends."

My ire was up. "Expound, please."

He shook his head. "Did he actually threaten her? Or was it perceived? If actual, was it verbal or written?"

"What the...? Look man, I need your expertise, not your legal mumbo jumbo."

He had the audacity to laugh. I growled. He sobered up and deadpanned, "I'm not trying to be difficult."

"Point taken. Then, let's assume all of the above. What can she do about it?"

"If verbal, file a police report. If written, again, file a report with the note. If perceived, she's shit out of luck. Gut instinct does not hold up in a court room."

I ran my hand through my hair out of pure frustration. "You and I both know that a woman's sixth sense is spot on nine times out of ten."

"True," he agreed. "Yet, it still won't hold up. What do you think you can do for her?"

I grumbled, "I offered to marry her myself."

"Say, what?!" he passionately exclaimed.

I sighed heavily and then elucidated, "I can provide 'round the clock protection for her. Although I highly doubt she will consent to it."

"Why not? She seems to understand that Caleb's trouble."

"Yes. But she doesn't see the complete danger involved. Get this...she thinks he'll only go after her reputation, career, family and friends. She has no concept that *she's* the one in danger."

"While I get that he'll take whatever means possible to get her to comply with him, how would her reputation matter?"

Dammit all. Here goes nothing. "She's a call-girl."

"Is this a joke, Nik?"

I laughed with no humor. "I wish."

"Fuck me." He ran his hand along the side of his jaw. "She's in way over her head."

I couldn't put into words how much I appreciated that my brother didn't even bat an eye at the fact I just shared Aimee was a prostitute. This was one of the many reasons why I loved him so much. He also understood that Senator Caleb Reynolds had a notorious reputation for "bringing prostitutes to justice," as he liked to call it. It was just *this* side of legal what he'd been known to do with ladies of that profession. For years we've been waiting for him to make a mistake, because truth be told, I had a gut feeling there was more to it than what we knew. And he was good, damn good, at covering his tracks. "Yeah, you could say that."

"Marriage, Nik? Can you even do that again?"

"I don't know. But I can't see another solution." I implored, "Can you?"

There was a pregnant pause before he finally sighed and shook his head. "No. I'm sorry, I don't see another alternative. I wish to hell I did, for your sake."

I bowed my head in defeat. "Me too, little brother." I lifted my head and made eye contact with him. "Me, too."

Alex stood and began pacing. "What if I help? What if E helps out as well? With your connections, surely you could round up some bad MOFOs. There must be another way, Nik."

While I appreciated his faith in me, and our youngest brother, E, I didn't see that as enough of a diversion for Reynolds to keep his distance from Aimee. Plus, he comprehended my issue with marriage. Damn it all to hell, what was I going to do? My emotions must have played across my face— something I normally didn't let happen unless I trusted you— because he suddenly clasped my shoulder and proclaimed, "Talk about a serious case of history repeating itself."

I nodded and affirmed, "Got that right, brother."

"Do you think…?"

I cut him off. "Don't," I growled.

Surprised by my abruptness, he assuaged, "Hey. I didn't mean to bring her up. Sorry."

The "*her*" he referred to was my late wife, Rachel. *Shit. Fuck. Damn…I can't think about her. Not now. Not ever.* Some things needed to stay buried. I ran both of my hands through my hair. Even though I still loved Rachel, I was exigently drawn to Aimee. There was no explanation for why. It just was. Something elemental existed between us, as if my body recognized hers, though I didn't recall ever meeting her before tonight. Still…? I appeased, "'S alright, Alex."

"No, it's not. I'm truly sorry."

I squeezed his shoulder. "Change the subject. Please."

He quirked a brow. "You still haven't dealt with it, have you?"

"Shut up, Alex."

"Fine," he reconciled. "As for this mess with…?"

"Aimee," I provided.

"Ah, yes. Aimee. If you really don't think all three of us can keep her safe, then you're right, marriage is your only solution."

When I answered, "Let's try it your way first," I surprised myself.

His jaw dropped in shock. "Are you actually saying I'm right?"

I grumbled, "Don't let it go to your head." I poured another drink and slammed it back in one hard swallow.

He stepped towards me with his hand out for my glass. "How many of these have you had?"

"Don't start," I cautioned.

"I'm not," he hedged. "Why don't you go lie down for a while? Get some rest. Maybe things won't look so bad later this morning."

"Can't hurt," I conceded.

After that, I left the room.

As I made my way down the hall, I stripped off my clothing. My mind was in turmoil. One thing was for sure, I was willing to avoid marriage if possible. Although, the thoughts of Aimee writhing beneath my straining body were something I couldn't seem to keep at bay. No matter the outcome, I *wanted* her.

And what I wanted—I got.

Chapter Four
Aimee

I crept out of Renée's place, as quietly as I could, and froze when I saw the mountain of a man leaning against the wall next to my apartment door. I thought Nik was huge until I laid eyes on this guy. If I'd ever wondered what Goliath from the Bible must have looked like, there was no longer a question in my mind—this was him. To say I felt tiny would've been a monstrous understatement. All of a sudden, approaching my place didn't seem like a good idea. I turned and beat feet back to Renée's.

Once I slammed the door, she yelled, "Aims?"

"Yeah," I confirmed, "It's me."

As she shuffled into the living room, she exclaimed, "What the?!"

"Sorry. I didn't…I mean…Crap," I stammered.

She padded into the kitchen. "Hold that thought. If I have to play detective here, I need caffeine."

There was no way I could answer at the moment. I joined her for a much needed cup of coffee. When I reached for a mug, I hoped that my trembling hands didn't give me away. Lucky for me she was still half-asleep and grumpy; therefore, she hadn't noticed until she spun around to grab the milk.

"Hey. What's goin' on? You're shaking."

Double crap. I explained the strange man standing outside my apartment. Her stride was purposeful as she headed out the door. Then I heard her in the hall as she interrogated, "Who the hell are you?"

That was Renée. She wasn't afraid of anything. Ever. Which most of the time, seriously worried me; however, at that moment, I was grateful for her fearlessness. A rumble answered, "Who's askin'?"

"Why should I tell you anything?" she shot back.

"Ditto," Goliath retaliated.

She huffed, "Look, buddy. Why are you standin' out here in front of my best friend's apartment at freaking eight thirty in the morning? Either you've been hired to be here, or you're up to no good. Which is it?"

"You Aimee Taylor's friend?"

"Again, who's asking?"

"Steve. I'm here under Mr. Strand's directive."

"Who?"

I heard the confusion in her voice, for she had no idea who Nik was. I cleared my throat. "Renée, 's okay. I've got it."

She spun on me. "The hell? You were shaking like a leaf a few minutes ago. Now you've got it? Start talking, Aimee, or I swear…"

I held up my hand to silence her. "Trust me." I inclined my head so she would fully comprehend what I attempted to convey to her silently.

"Fine," she sighed and stepped around me to go back inside her apartment. But I knew my best friend; she would hover by the door to make sure I really was all right. I approached *Goliath*—I mean,

Steve—and introduced myself. "I'm Aimee Taylor." I
held out my hand to shake his.

As he grasped my hand, he affirmed, "Steve
Thompson, ma'am. I'm your body guard."

"Body guard? I didn't hire a protection
detail."

He smiled, which was alarmingly bright. He
truly was easy on the eyes. "No, ma'am. Mr. Strand
assigned me to you."

"Nik hired you for me?"

"I already work for Mr. Strand." Steve
confirmed, "He sent me here to keep an eye on things
until he arrived."

I blew out a long breath. "How did…?"

I never did get to complete my inquiry
because the man in question prowled to my side.
Whew, even the man's gait was hella sexy. *Oh boy,
I'm in so much trouble.*

Nik addressed, "Thank you, Thompson. I'll
take it from here."

"Sir." Steve gave him a deferential nod. "Did
you want me to wait for you here or the car?"

"If you wouldn't mind keeping an eye on
things out front, thank you."

"Affirmative, sir. Let me know when you're
ready."

With that he left. And I stood there in the
hallway with the most audacious man I'd ever met.
That was saying something. I fluctuated between
extremely pissed off and grateful. I settled for
somewhere in the middle and queried, "Nik, what's
going on?"

He grasped my elbow and ushered me through
my front door. *Wait! How's my door open?* As we
stepped inside, I abruptly stopped. "What? How?" I
stood there in absolute shock. My apartment—the one
place that I could be me. My sanctuary had been

completely destroyed. I gasped, "Oh, my…Who? I-I don't…" I took in the sight completely befuddled. "Why would someone do this?"

Nik grabbed me by my upper arms and moved me against the wall. Then he took a protective stance in front of me and withdrew a gun from an ankle holster. He glanced over his shoulder and commanded, "Stay." He began to case my apartment. His gaze missed nothing. If I hadn't known better, I'd think he was law enforcement. After he performed a thorough search, he returned. He replaced his gun back in its holster and held out his hand to me. "Come."

Still unsure how I felt about him barking orders at me, I took his hand. I would think about it later. At that moment, I clutched his hand firmly and obeyed, letting him lead me through my once beautiful space. Nothing appeared to be salvageable. But, then again, that could've been my mind playing tricks on me. With lack of sleep and my emotions high, I wasn't firing on all cylinders. When we reached my bedroom, I froze in utter horror. After a beat, I screamed, "NO!!!" The word **WHORE** was spray painted on the wall and my bed. Everything had been slashed to bits or broken beyond repair: my clothes, shoes, books, and bedding. There wasn't a thing left untouched from the hatred. I ran to the toilet and heaved. Nik crouched beside me and held my hair back with one hand. With the other, he soothingly stroked up and down my spine. "Don't worry," he appeased. "I'll find out who did this. I'll handle it," he vowed.

Of that I had no doubt. He would not only find the person responsible, but he would hold them accountable. A shiver passed through me. Heaven help the person who did this when Nik got his hands on them. I didn't know him well, at all. Yet, even I could tell he was a powerful being that demanded respect. Absolute authority. You did *not* cross this man. Since my tooth brush was nowhere to be found, I rinsed my mouth out in the sink. *Seriously, my toothbrush! For what purpose, exactly?*

"Are you all right?" Nik asked.

"I have to go." I walked into my living room and over my shoulder demanded, "Call the police, please."

He nodded and replied, "Done."

*****

I proceeded to Renée's with Nik hot on my heels.

"What the hell's goin' on?" Renée inquired.

At that point I snapped, no longer able to contain the emotion that had been building up since the first moment I laid eyes on my apartment. The dam broke. I fell to my knees and sobbed. Renée rushed over at the same time Nik knelt in front of me.

Nik leaned in so he was speaking in my ear. "Hey, now." He reassured, "You're going to be fine." I reached up and clasped my hands behind his neck, letting the tears continue to fall. "Shh, baby," he comforted, "I've got you."

There was a knock at the door. "I've got it," Renée announced.

As two police officers stepped into the apartment, I pulled away from Nik. I felt cold without his warm body against mine. I wrapped my arms tightly around my middle and answered their questions. When all was said and done, I found myself barely able to stay awake. Exhaustion was taking its toll on me. I leaned heavily into Renée. She looked over at Nik, who hadn't left my side through the entire ordeal. He was silent the whole time the police officers were there, but it was his presence I appreciated most.

Renée took charge. "She needs to rest. Don't worry; I'll take care of her. She can stay here."

Nik responded with a resounding, "No. Until we know who's behind this, she'll be safer with me."

She exhaled. "While I can't argue that your place is safer—probably tighter security than Ft. Knox—does she really know you?"

I cleared my throat. "Um…I can speak for myself. Thank you."

Renée smirked, "There's my girl. Wondered where you'd been."

I smiled, "Up yours."

She laughed. Nik sat there and brooded for a moment before he chimed in, "Aimee. It'd be best for you to stay with me until we figure out who did this to you."

I could neither argue nor did I have the strength to. I was terrified whoever had done such a malicious act on my apartment would return to do the same to me. I shook with fear so Nik coiled his arm around my shoulders. I glanced up at him and nodded my acquiescence.

Renée grabbed my hand and stared at me intently. "You sure about this?"

I softly replied, "Yes."

She stood. "Okay, then."

Nik joined her and assured, "I won't hurt her. Thank you, Renée. I'll make sure she calls you after some much needed rest," he promised.

She squared her shoulders and warned, "You make sure you don't. If you harm her in any way, I'll kick your ass."

He slightly grinned. "That, I don't doubt."

Nik reached down to help me to my feet and then pulled me into his side for support. I couldn't explain it to myself or anyone else. There was just something about *him* I trusted. I knew he would always protect me. Odd, that. Yet not only my body seemed to recognize him, my entire being somehow knew *this* man was *mine*. *Oh, I am definitely in over my head.*

Chapter Five
Nik

We entered the penthouse, and I immediately led her towards one of the spare bedrooms. It was a crucial error on my end. How did I expect myself not to touch her when she was under the same roof? The smell of her lured me to her side. As I opened the door for her, I informed, "You can sleep here in the guestroom." She was so weary I wasn't sure she'd make it to the bed. When she stumbled over her own two feet, I clutched her elbow to keep her from faceplanting onto the floor. My God, she was beautiful. I had to divert my gaze before I did something impetuous.

Her eyes were heavy as she curled up under the covers. As I turned off the lamp on the nightstand, she grabbed my hand. "Stay. Please?" she slurred.

Oh, hell no. I did not have the strength for that. I brushed my fingertips along her cheekbone. "I'll be right here, little one," I reassured. "I'm not going anywhere. Rest, now."

She mumbled, something like, "Only one man has ever called me 'little one.' "

I smiled and whispered, "Sleep sweet." I shut the door, not quite understanding why she had shared that information. *She's very tired and probably has no idea she said it*, I chastised myself mentally. A woman like her should be loved and cherished, not debased and ignored, which was exactly what would happen if I gave into my impulses. I could not have a functioning relationship with a woman. I knew that. I was fully aware of my failures, and how much I was capable of hurting her. My past alone was enough to make any woman run, screaming.

*****

I stepped into my home office and was surprised to see Alex lounging on the sofa against the wall. As I entered, he looked up and greeted, "Nik." Then he inquired, "You want to start explaining why she's here?"

I scoffed, "Hell no."

His perfect brow arched. "Really? Because I think you need to."

I proceeded to tell him everything that had gone down since he'd left me in the wee hours that morning.

"Shit."

"Yeah. That about sums it up." I ran my hand through my too long hair. "Here's the thing, my gut tells me this was not a chance break-in."

"You think it was done to scare her?" He rubbed the stubble along his jaw line. "Maybe to send some kind of message? Has she threatened to leak information on her clientele?"

"No. Not that I'm aware of. I really don't think she'd do something like that. She just wants to move on with her life. Put this chapter behind her," I inferred.

He leaned forward. "You don't say. How exactly was she planning to do that?"

I folded my arms across my chest. "What're you hinting at?"

"Nothing." His eyes widened.

I shook my head. "Sorry. No offense, I thought you were accusing her of pulling a Heidi Fleiss."

He chuckled and assured, "None taken, brother."

"Are you laughing at me for some reason?"

"You don't see it, do you?"

I sighed in exasperation. Alex could talk a person in circles for hours if you didn't nip it in the bud. "See what?"

"You're defending her, wanting to provide protection, already." He shrugged. "I've never seen you this intense over a female. It's interesting, to say the least," he intoned.

I flipped him off and then stood. "Did you need something else?"

"Nah," he teased, "Just enjoy watching you squirm."

"Knock it off, Alex." I declared, "I've had enough."

"Damn. You've got it bad."

I growled, "Leave."

He stood while he shook his head. "I'll be back later," he advised as he left me alone.

*****

I did have it bad, and it was beyond what I thought if my brother could pick up on that. Images of Aimee invaded my mind every waking moment. Honestly, she starred in my dreams as well. I couldn't seem to stop, and this was only after twenty-four hours. I'd only felt this tied up in knots over a woman once before. Never quite like this, though. I would not go down that road again. The connection with Reynolds was even more confusing. Downright

disturbing, actually. In both instances, he had a valid
reason for being involved. But dammit, there was a
gut feeling I could not shake no matter how hard I
tried. This was not a coincidence. And by God, I
planned on getting to the bottom of it.

I poured myself a glass of Jameson and
pondered for awhile. I must've dozed off. I awoke to
tender fingers stroking my temple. I clenched them
too tightly as I exclaimed, "The hell!?"

"I'm s-sorry," she stuttered. "I didn't mean
anything by it." She tried desperately to pull her hand
away, but I wouldn't let her. Instead I glared at her,
causing her to swallow hard. "I just…" she hesitated.
"I'll go."

"No," I growled and then tugged her onto my
lap. She fell ungracefully. The look of shock made
me chuckle, which ticked her off.

"Don't laugh at me," she commanded in
haughty tone that made me itch to put her over my
knee.

I flexed my hand to resist. She squared her
slender shoulders, inadvertently raising her beautiful
breasts to my hungry gaze. I licked my suddenly dry
lips. As she watched my mouth, her eyes darkened. In
anger or desire? I couldn't quite tell. *Only one way to
find out.* I pulled her to my chest and felt every
luscious curve of her body pressed against mine. Shit,
now I have a hard on. "You do not tell me what to
do," I asserted roughly due to my sexual frustration.
"Are we clear?" Damn, sometimes I could be a real
asshole.

She stared at me, not sure if she should stand
up to me or back off. I was curious to know her
buttons so I prodded, "Answer me."

She shoved me and tried to stand. I wouldn't
let her. It was good to know she had a feisty side.
True, I generally liked my women submissive and

solicitous to my needs and wants. Yet there was something intriguing about her. As in, she wouldn't put up with my shit. And that was a major turn on. I was even harder now. I knew she felt it against her stomach where I held her captive. When she wriggled to try and get away from me, an unbidden groan from deep in my throat escaped. Ah, hell. If she showed an ounce of interest, I would end up taking her here and now. *No, that can't happen!* I grasped her upper arms, not too hard but enough that I had her attention. Her eyes widened. "I'm waiting," I declared.

Emotions played across her face: fear, anger, and lust. She lifted her chin defiantly. "Yes, sir," she retorted.

Fuck me. Of all the things she could've said. I pushed her off my lap and quickly adjusted myself. We needed to hammer out some things, so I softened my voice and began, "Listen. Until we know who's behind the ransacking of your place, I'd like for you to feel comfortable staying here. You're my guest."

Her brows rose. "Really? 'Cause you seem pissed off that I'm here." She glanced away. "I didn't mean to invade your space."

I stood and placed two fingers under her chin, raising her face so she'd look at me. "Go on," I coaxed.

She closed her eyes to break contact. I wanted to shake her lightly to get her to open them again, but I resisted. After a beat, she looked at me directly. "You looked so sad in your sleep." She disclosed, "I wanted to comfort you. That's all."

Could she see into my soul?—well, the pieces that were left—was it possible she understood me a little? "Why?"

She pulled her face away and then walked across the room to look out the window. "You seem lost," she whispered, "I know how that feels." Oh man, did she have me pegged. Instinct told me to rush over and hold her tight. However, male pride reared its ugly head. "You're wrong," I insisted. As I stepped over to the side bar to refill my glass, I offered, "Would you like something to drink?"

"No, thank you. I'm good."

I gulped what was left of the fiery liquid and then refilled it again. Dammit, my hands were actually trembling. *What is it about her?* I turned to stare at her back. She was all curves, with an ass that begged for my hands. It was not the first time I'd felt lust for a woman. I'd had plenty of women of all shapes and sizes; though, I didn't usually go for blondes. *"Because no woman compares to Rachel,"* the little voice in my head whispered. *Shut the hell up!* I began to pace while I conveyed, "It shouldn't take long for the investigation to be completed."

She turned around and queried, "Do you think they can figure out who did it?"

I didn't lie to her. "No. I don't."

"Oh," she gasped. Once she collected herself, she asked, "Then why exactly am I here?"

Good fucking question. "I wanted you to feel safe," I replied.

She held my gaze. "Why would that matter to you?"

I strode towards her. When I rounded the desk, I set my glass on it. I took a hold of her shoulders and honestly answered, "I don't know."

Her head was tilted back due to our significant height difference. "I see."

Now that shocked me. "You do?"

She reached up to hold my biceps, which flexed under her long, slender fingers. "You feel that?"

How could I not? The air crackled with the sexual energy coming off both of our bodies. But there was something else, too, and it scared the hell out of me. As I pulled back, I dropped my hands to my sides and clenched my fists. "We're attracted to each other. Doesn't mean anything," I stated. But I didn't know if I said that for her benefit or mine.

"If that's the way you want it, fine," she acknowledged.

She sashayed across the room to the door. I stood there and admired those gorgeous hips in motion. What would they feel like underneath mine as they arched up to pull me deeper inside her? *STOP! We are not going to tap that.* My self-control was at its limits. I was a goner if she spun around and offered the invitation. She glanced over her shoulder. "Too bad." She added, "We could be really good together," as she closed the door.

A woman who knew and accepted her sexuality—not to mention wanted me as much as I wanted her—had just walked out of my office. I barely restrained myself. Truth was, I could not deny myself much longer. I poured myself another drink and hoped the investigation was complete by morning. Otherwise, I would have one helluva case of blue balls. I could do this. I *would* stay away from her. *Liar.* Could and would. Once Aimee Taylor returned to her apartment, and her life, I would keep my distance. Yeah, right. Who was I kidding? If only, I was that strong.

Chapter Six
Aimee

Did I just proposition the most gorgeous and dangerous man I had ever met? Yes. Yes, I did. OMG, what was I thinking? First off, I'd never done such a thing before in my life. Men simply wanted me. I'm not conceited. I simply knew how to work my God given assets to the best advantage. Granted, my body would fit in better in a different era. However, I was always pleasantly surprised by how many men liked a curvy woman. I remember being so concerned with that when I chose to escort. I thought men this day and time preferred svelte bodies. Or even athletic ones. No amount of working out was going to get rid of my butt. I could give J. Lo a run for her money. And my rounded size double Ds were not the result of surgical enhancement. I always felt my hips were too wide, but they did seem to balance the package. The only two things I really liked about my body were: my tiny waist and shoulder-length natural blonde hair. Of course, Nik's hair was much longer than mine, but my color was darker with more gold in it. None of that mattered at the moment, point was, I'd offered myself and was shot down. That hurt. More than I was willing to admit, even to myself.

As I stepped into the shower, I reevaluated where I went wrong. Maybe it was him? Gah, I didn't know the answers. What I did know was that I wanted him with a ferociousness that terrified me. It wasn't just his looks. Even though he was by far the most striking man I had ever laid eyes on. I wasn't kidding when I referenced him to Thor. He was tall—probably six-foot, four-inches or more—and his shoulders were massive. I wanted to run my tongue along every hard, heavy muscle on his big body. He was a masterpiece, with angles and planes on his rugged face. And sculpted lips that made a woman beg for them to be anywhere on her. There was no mistaking the danger and power that radiated off him. I loved successful men. They all had such pull, like gravity itself.

Once I sat on the bench inside the shower, I instantly remembered that look in his eyes—the one that disclosed vulnerability for just a moment. He was broken somehow, and that was what really drew me to him. How did I thaw him? He gave a whole new spin on the quote "Island unto oneself." I wanted more than his body. I wanted to know the man inside. I felt connected to his wounded soul, as if I had known him for years. Maybe, I was seeing my other half. I didn't know what it was, but I needed to find out.

I was startled when a deep male voice called out, "Hello. Everything okay in here?"

I swallowed the lump in my throat and answered, "Yes." I entreated, "Give me a few moments, please."

"No problem."

There was a red silk robe hanging on the back of the bathroom door. I ensconced myself in its luxury. The lining was soft terrycloth and I nearly moaned from the pleasure of my body encased in such extravagance. I padded into the guestroom and stumbled a bit when I saw the man lounging in the arm chair by the fireplace. He was just as magnificent as Nik. When he stood, it became obvious he was just as tall, yet leanly muscled. He wore his hair short in a classy GQ style. Everything about him screamed urbane and money. The look he gave me was peculiar, as if he had just seen a ghost. He recovered quickly before he spoke, "You must be Aimee. I'm Alex, one of Nik's younger brothers." Oh, his cultured voice was melodic. Unlike Nik's, which had that dark rasp. Though they both shared that hint of an accent I still couldn't place. I held out my hand. "Nice to meet you, Alex."

He smiled and there was an adorable dimple on the left side of his mouth. Wow, I had no doubt this man could have any woman he wanted. Where his older brother was enigmatic and brooding, he was laid back and charming. I was going to need a cold shower when he left. Too bad I wasn't drawn to *this* brother—he would've been better for my overall wellbeing. He took my hand with masculine grace and brought it to his lips for a soft kiss across my knuckles. Goodness, these Strand men were enough to make a woman melt. "I hope you don't think I'm being presumptuous," he stated. "I wanted to meet you on my own without Nik standing guard, if you know what I mean?"

I chortled, "Actually, I do." I waved my hand in a motion for him to sit back down. I took the chair across from him. "He can be a bit intimidating," I acknowledged.

"Don't let him frighten you," he professed.

"I'll try. Not an easy task, considering he vibrates with restrained violence."

"Yeah, well, there is that," he confirmed with a smile. As he sat up straight, he held my gaze with his beautiful cornflower blue eyes behind a sexy pair of tortoiseshell glasses. "He won't hurt you. I hope you know that."

Maybe not physically, but I wasn't so sure about emotionally. I had a feeling Nik could absolutely break my heart if I let him in. I had no words so I simply nodded and pulled my robe a little tighter around me for security.

"I've made you uncomfortable," he proclaimed. "I apologize." Sincerity laced his voice.

"It's not that." I glanced over at the fireplace and mustered up the courage to ask him questions regarding Nik. Finally, I turned my head back towards Alex. "Can I ask a few questions?"

He held his hands out. "By all means, I'll do my best to answer."

"Nik is a former UFC heavyweight champion?"

He grinned, "Yes. That's common knowledge, Aimee. What do you really want to know?"

"Well, how did he go from that to successful mogul?"

"He has always been good with money. Also, he has an MBA."

"Doesn't surprise me, although, it still doesn't make sense." I could see the confusion on his face, so I spelled it out. "How did he get the money to start up a company?" I raised my shoulder in a slight shrug. "I mean, did your parents have a lot of capital?"

"Why all the financial questions?" he probed defensively.

"I meant no disrespect." I waved my hand around the room for emphasis. "I was just trying to figure it all out."

He rubbed his jaw with his forefinger and thumb contemplatively. "I see where you're going with this. You think most cage fighters come from rough backgrounds?"

I nodded emphatically. "In my experience,

they do. Have I missed the mark with Nik?"

"No, not at all. As a matter of fact, you're spot on. However, this isn't my story to share. You need to ask him yourself," he affirmed.

I appreciated his loyalty to his brother, even if it frustrated the hell out of me. "Fair enough, Alex."

He reached for my hand and clasped it in his. "Was there anything else?"

At that moment someone coughed. We looked up at the same time to see Nik leaning against the doorjamb. He looked confident and relaxed, but his eyes gave away the storm raging inside him. "Are you finished talking behind my back?"

Alex stood with ease, not at all intimidated by his enormous, pissed off brother. "We're good," he said. As he walked through the door, he cuffed Nik on the shoulder.

*****

Once Alex was gone, Nik stepped into the room. "Did you need to know something?"

I twisted the belt on my robe around my hands —a nervous habit of mine. I tried to hold his gaze, but it was no use. "I didn't mean to intrude on your personal business. I apologize if I have upset you."

He scoffed, "Bullshit. You had every intention of wringing out every drop of information you could from my brother." He sauntered over to me and crouched down in front of my chair. "For the record, he's my attorney. He won't tell you shit that isn't a matter of public record, sweetness."

Oh, the man infuriated me *and* set me aflame with desire. *How does he do that?* "I was trying to learn more about you. Forgive me for giving a damn," I snapped.

When I stood, he had to lean back on his

haunches. Wow, the fantasy that played through my mind at such a visual. This man was beyond trouble. I needed to stay far, far away from him. I paced across the room then spun and asked, "Why are you here?"

He chuckled darkly. "I live here."

I sighed in exasperation. "No. What I mean is, why are you in this room with me?"

He stood. "There are detectives here to see you."

I shook my head to clear my thoughts. "You couldn't have told me that from the get go?"

He shrugged his big shoulders. "I could have. I just didn't." He strode towards me, and I took a step back. "Get dressed," he commanded over his shoulder at the doorway. "They're waiting." Then the door closed.

Grr. I wished I had something to throw at the stupid door. Better yet, at his head. Oh, the man was pushing all my buttons. And I would be lying if I didn't admit; he was turning me on. Big time.

*****

I put my clothes back on, sans panties—since that always grossed me out to put on dirty underwear after I was clean—and walked into the living room to meet the detectives. Once introductions were fulfilled, we got down to business. I learned that they, Detectives Michaels and Reeves, had no idea who had broken into my place, which wasn't at all a huge surprise. I knew they had done their job, but, still, I felt uneasy. I inquired, "Do you think whoever it was will return?"

Reeves answered, "Can't predict that, ma'am. If they do, you've now made a paper trail. That's always important in prosecuting, if it comes down to that."

"Alright. Is there anything else I should do?"

"Yes, ma'am," Michaels replied. "Don't go back to your apartment until it's been cleaned up."

Well, duh. As if I would want to step foot in there again with it looking like a tornado had hit it. Plus, I didn't want to see that horrid word—albeit fact—written across my stuff.

Reeves pulled me from my reverie. "Do you have some place to stay?"

I was pretty sure Renée would let me crash with her. Of course, there was a reason we were no longer roommates; however, a few days wouldn't kill either one of us. "Yes. Thank you for asking."

When Detective Reeves smiled, I realized he was an attractive man. I glanced down and caught a glimpse of the wedding ring on his left hand. *Ah, a very married good-looking man.* "Stay aware, Ms. Taylor. Make sure you don't go anywhere alone." I heard the concern in his voice and was touched.

Then Nik replied, with a resounding, "I'll see to it myself, Detective Reeves. Thank you for your time. If you need to reach Ms. Taylor, she'll be here," he announced.

WTF? Was he joking? There was no way I could spend another night in the same space as Nik Strand! I just stared at him while Alex showed the detectives out. As soon as they were gone, I responded, "No. I'll go call Renée. I will not stay *here* with you."

He prowled forward and grabbed my upper arms firmly. "The hell you won't."

I tried to pull away, but he tightened his grip. He hadn't hurt me, per se.

Although Alex didn't see it that way as he asserted, "Get your hands off her, Nik."

Nik growled low in his chest as he dropped his hands to his sides. He was looking at me when he spoke to his brother. "I didn't hurt her," he affirmed.

Alex's brows rose. "Aimee?"

I held Nik's gaze as I answered, "I'm fine, Alex. He didn't harm me."

Alex walked over to me and placed his hand on the small of my back. I reverted my gaze to his when he queried, "Do you want me to stay?"

I shook my head. "No, thank you. I'll be fine."

He nodded, "All right, then. I'll be in the other room if you need me, just yell." With that he sauntered out of the room, but not before I saw the look that passed between them.

While Nik stroked his hands up and down my arms, which he had clutched earlier, he looked at me intently. "Did I hurt you?"

"No. You didn't." I stepped away from him so I could think clearly. "Why do you want me to stay here?"

"It's safer."

That was true. But I had a feeling there was more to it. "Nik?"

"Yeah."

"What aren't you telling me?"

He sighed. "Sit down, Aimee."

Well, crap. I just had to ask. As I sat on the sofa, he joined me, turning his body so he faced me directly. "I think Reynolds is behind this."

Okay. Truth was, I'd thought the same thing. But I had disregarded it because he wouldn't do something so petty. *Would he?* "Why do you think so?"

"I've seen him do something similar in the past."

"Really!" Now this was news to me so I questioned, "To whom?"

He glanced away. "Doesn't matter. Point is, until we know for sure you're better off here."

I had no argument. Or maybe, I just wanted to stay close to him for a little while longer. Which was really a bad idea, the man was wreaking havoc on me. I needed to leave. Instead I acquiesced, "Okay. But *only* until I get my place back in order."

His lips curved up in a sexy half-smile. "I'll take care of it in the morning."

"Oh, no. That's not necessary. I'm sure insurance will cover it."

"It's already being handled, Aimee."

"Well, then." I was shocked silent for a moment. Then I held out my hand and said, "Thank you."

He took my hand in his and lightly stroked my inner wrist. "No problem."

I would never know what might have happened, for at that moment, Alex walked back into the room. "Nik," he announced, "We *need* to talk." His voice held a seriousness that I had no doubt he used in the courtroom.

Nik inclined his head towards the door and then met my gaze. "Excuse me, Aimee."

Once Nik and Alex were absent from the room, I was left to contemplate just what the hell I was doing.

For the record—I didn't have a clue.

Chapter Seven
Nik

Once Alex closed the door to my home office, I demanded, "Tell me."

"No, Nik. You're the one who needs to start spilling his guts," he retorted.

I spun to face him. "Enlighten me, Alex. What am I supposed to convey, exactly?"

"Please. As if you have no idea why I brought you in here."

"I really don't have a clue. You need to elucidate." Annoyed, I walked over and poured myself a drink.

Alex shook his head in disapproval. "You've had enough," he asserted.

"Shut up." To make my point perfectly clear I added, "I don't need you mothering me."

"Fine," he incensed. "It's your liver." He began to pace the office. "Mind telling me what the hell you were thinking when you had your goons perform an illegal search of a senator's private residence?"

Ah, the interrogation begins. I nonchalantly shrugged one shoulder. "Hunch."

"Come on, Nik, work with me here," he implored. "What were you searching for?"

I raised my brows at him. I swear he had his

head so far up his ass he was going to find his lungs any second! "Evidence." I fought like hell not to add the "duh."

"Last time I checked, you were not the police." He shoved both hands through his hair in exasperation—*family trait, that.* "Do you realize you could have gone to jail if you were caught?"

I shrugged. "But I wasn't."

Alex stormed across the room, got right up in my face and hissed, "Stupid, bastard. What if I had not been alerted? Were you *ever* going to tell me?"

I glared into his eyes. To this day I couldn't handle anyone—not even my brother—in my personal space. Flashes of the prison yard went through my mind in rapid fire: me, bloody and damned near unconscious; L.D. stepping in at the last moment before I became Rex's bitch; the initiation with my blood, sweat, and tears. Adrenaline roared through my veins as the need to fight—to win at all costs—tried to take hold. I shook my head to clear it and growled, "Back the fuck off. Now."

Alex realized instantly what was going on with me. He stepped back and put his hands up in surrendering fashion. Then he apologized, "I was out of line. Sorry, Nik."

I nodded, needing a minute to get my act together. Shit! I could've hurt my brother, my best friend, just now. I fought hard not to hurl. *What the fuck is wrong with me?* After thirteen years, one would think I was past all of that. Truth was, some things never leave a person—especially survival instincts. "It's done," I assured. "Don't worry 'bout it."

He scoffed, "You're a real piece of work, my brother." He sat down hard on the sofa against the wall and stared off into the distance for a moment. I knew he was preparing to say or ask something difficult, so he was mentally bracing. Ah, hell. I didn't want to hear it. He looked up at me and queried, "Nik, why would you suspect Caleb broke into Aimee's apartment?" I shot him a wary glance. "I knew it!" he crowed as he stood up abruptly. "You do see it, don't you?"

"Don't," I warned. There was no way in hell I wanted to have this discussion.

He clapped my shoulder and noted, "This can't be easy. But, surely, you haven't missed the resemblance."

I cautioned, "Enough, Alex," as I stepped away from him. If he wasn't careful, I would lay him out.

"Will you ever let yourself grieve properly?" He laughed with no humor. "You have to quit blaming yourself, Nik."

I clenched my fists so tight at my sides the knuckles were white. "Not what a jury of my peers said," I snarled.

Alex admonished, "Rigged and you know it, so don't throw that crap at me."

I grunted, "You have some nerve," before I sat down and rested my elbows on my knees.

"I know you've been to hell and back." *Still there, Alex.* "I also know I want my brother whole, not this," he waved his hand over me, "husk."

"Ha!" I corrected, "Don't you mean asshole?"

He sat down next to me and said, "While you have ass like qualities, I know somewhere in there is my brother."

"No. He's not, Alex. The sooner you come to terms with that, the better off you're going to be."

"Talk, Nik. If not to me, then someone— please. You've got to move past this."

"Un-fucking-believable! Just how do you expect me *not* to still love her?"

"I don't," he stated. "But she's been gone for a long time. Do you really think she would want this for you? She would want you to be happy."

"I can't ever be happy," I mumbled. "I'll never love another."

He quirked a brow. "Really? 'Cause you sure as hell desire that pretty woman in the other room."

"Desire is not love," I countered. "Sure, I want to fuck her, but I'm not going to love her."

"Keep telling yourself that, Nik," he remarked before he stood and walked out of the room.

*****

I rubbed my face with both hands. Alex was right, I did desire Aimee. More than I wanted to. Sure, I could have sex with her, and it would be damn good. But fall in love? Not going to happen. Ever. What my brothers failed to comprehend was that I no longer had a heart. I'm the ruthless bastard I was known for. The boy my brothers remembered was buried fifteen years ago with his beautiful wife. The shell left behind was a cold-hearted son-of-a-bitch who didn't give a damn. I grabbed the glass sitting on the end table and chucked it across the room. When it connected with the wall, I took little pleasure in the sound it made. I needed outta here—to get out of my head for a while.

I stalked down the hallway and ran right into five-foot, two-inches of luscious woman. *Gorgeous.* Like Alex, I thought she looked a lot like Rachel. However, as I truly studied her, I realized she only resembled my late wife slightly. Their height was the same, as well as their golden blonde hair and baby doll face. But that was where it ended. Rachel had been pixie-like and dainty; Aimee was curvy and delicious.

Her mesmerizing grayish-green eyes held mine as she asked, "Is everything all right, Nik? I thought I heard something break."

Every ounce of my being screamed at me to haul her closer and kiss her breathless. What the hell?! I hadn't kissed a woman on the mouth since Ra—*that's a lie. There was that mystery woman at the masquerade some five years ago.* I ran my tongue over my bottom lip at the memory. Why was I remembering that night so clearly all of a sudden? The only other woman I had allowed myself to taste and she still haunted my dreams. Aimee reached up and rubbed her fingertips along my stubbled jaw. "I want you," she purred.

No, do not go there. Back away now! I reached down and traced her cheekbones. "You don't. I'm no good, Aimee."

She took a step closer and whispered, "Neither am I." Then she reached down and stroked my cock through the heavy denim. "I'm not asking for anything emotional here. Just sex."

I swallowed hard. *Dear God, I'm not going to last another minute. Do something, please!* "I'm s-sorry," I stammered before I turned and beat feet out of the penthouse.

*****

The nightclub was hopping, not to mention the seductive dance music—which did not help my present state. Definitely, not one of the smartest decisions I had ever made; however, I really needed to speak to my youngest brother, E. I sat in the V.I.P. section and was instantly served a scotch on the rocks. The cocktail waitress, Mindy, greeted, "Here you go, Nik. Let me know if I can get you anything else?"

I watched her hips sway seductively, not missing the invitation she had just offered. I smiled slightly, maybe that was just the cure I needed. It wasn't long before E joined me. We sat back to enjoy the go-go dancers. They were not strippers, just dancers providing entertainment. No, the no holds barred entertainment took place on the lower level. There, a man could get lost in the eroticism. *Nope, not going there.* As soon as my drink was finished, Mindy supplied another. This time I was given a peek down her shirt. Ah, hell. I really needed to get laid, quickly. I shifted to relieve the pressure in my jeans.

E didn't miss a thing. "See something you like, brother?"

I shot him a wry glance and admitted, "Yeah. But that's not going to solve my dilemma."

He chuckled, "Since when does bedding a woman ever *fix* a problem?"

"True. Generally speaking, it's asking for trouble."

He threw his head back and laughed. "Nah, Nik. You just need to tap the right one."

Oh, I had the right one sitting in my penthouse asking me to. I looked at E sincerely. "I need your help."

He sat up instantly. "'Sup?"

I confessed, "I'm in over my head, E, and I have no idea how to get out of the mess I helped create."

He leaned back and inquired, "This have anything to do with the beauty staying at your penthouse?"

Ah, so Alex *had* talked. Figured. Nothing was sacred between my brothers. They meant well, and I knew they loved me, but sometimes I wished they'd keep their damn mouths shut. "I swear you two are like a couple of old biddies. You gossip way too much."

He snorted, "Fuck you and the horse you rode in on." There was no heat behind his oath.

I smiled though I knew it didn't reach my eyes. Crap, I couldn't remember the last time I truly smiled or laughed. Pathetic. The closest I'd come to a genuine smile was with Aimee. Maybe Alex was right, perhaps it was time to let Rachel go. My heart screamed in protest, as if Rachel herself was saying, "I'll never let you go." God, I missed her so much. Hard to believe she had been gone for nearly fifteen years now. The image of her broken body suddenly flashed before my eyes. To this day, her last words continued to haunt me: "I love you, Niky." I squeezed my eyes tight, refusing, yet again, to shed one tear. I was brought back to the present when E stated, "You have to let go."

Shit. He knew me too well. I retorted, "Really? Like dad? Can you honestly tell me you've let him go? What about mom?"

When E shook his head, I noticed his eyes were suddenly very bright with moisture. "Point made," he conceded.

I nodded, knowing that was a low blow. We had lost our dad to a tragic accident when E was only eleven-years-old, and then our mom to a heart attack nearly ten years ago, which left just the three of us. If it wasn't for my brothers, I would have never survived this long. "Hey, E, I'm an asswipe. I shouldn't have brought them up."

He held my gaze intently. "I get that you can't ever *really* let go, but you have to move on, Nik. You can't keep living in the past or blaming yourself. What's done is done."

Didn't Alex almost say the exact same thing? It was not like this was the first time they had said these things, just ironic they were on the same page at the same time. Crap. This was not how I envisioned my conversation with E tonight. I conceded, "You may be on to something there."

He smiled, "So, what's going on with the blonde bombshell shacking up with you?"

"She's not shacking up with me," I replied exasperated. "She's in trouble."

"And you're her white knight in shining armor?"

"Hell, no. If anything, I'm the dark knight."

He chuckled at my remark and then addressed, "You really think Caleb did it?"

Geez, what didn't Alex share? "Yeah, I do. It has his stench all over it."

"You would know better than anyone. After the shit he pulled with Rachel, you'd recognize the signs."

That was no lie. Caleb Reynolds stalked Rachel for the year and a half I was with her. He had probably been at it much longer than that, but she had never put it together. Besides, there was no proof even if he had. He had been completely obsessed and thoroughly convinced I'd stolen her away from him. Now there was Aimee, who had an uncanny likeness to Rachel, and, once again, I was involved. The whole thing had disaster written all over it. For the best interest of everyone, I should put Aimee on a plane and let her move on with her life. Yeah, well, as if I could let her go now that I found her. *What the…? I am not getting involved with her!* I would simply make sure Reynolds backed off, and then I would send her on her way. Simple. "Thanks, E. I think I have a game plan."

His brow arched. "Mind sharing?"

I smirked, "I'll clean this mess up, make sure Caleb doesn't bother her again, and commission her to go on with her plans."

His eyes widened. "Who're you kidding? You *want* her and you know it."

While that was a statement of fact, it didn't mean I would act on it. "I'm not known as a cold-hearted bastard for no reason. I *can* and *will* control myself."

He grinned and quipped, "Are you trying to convince me or yourself?"

I shoved back from the table and stood. "It's only a week at the most. I'm not some green boy who can't keep his dick in his pants."

E raised his glass in salute. "Keep telling yourself that, my brother."

I could hear his laughter over the din of music as I strode away. I would show him and Alex, too. *Yeah, right, I'm going to enjoy watching you fail*, the little voice in my head mocked.

Chapter Eight
Aimee

Grr! The man was a darn yo-yo. One minute, I could
see desire—hell, I felt the evidence against my
stomach—in his eyes. The next, he pushed me away.
What the heck was that "I'm no good" about?
Nonsense. As if a prostitute was good? Really! What
parallel universe was he from? After he shut me
down, one thing was certain: I would not stick around
for an encore. He could go screw himself. *I'm done.*
With anger propelling me, I stormed out of his
humongous penthouse and made my way home.

*****

As I unlocked the door to my apartment
building, I couldn't help but be reminded of how
different Nik's and my life were. He was accustomed
to luxury in the extreme. While I lived well, there was
no comparison. I had done my best to put away every
cent I could to buy my first hotel. The only other
place I put my money was in Dad's doctor and
hospital bills. I could easily live in a high-rise with a
doorman for security, but I was happy in my
brownstone in the Upper West Side. No, it was not
Fifth Avenue, but it'd been my home for five years.
Now, more than ever, I knew I'd made the right

decision to leave Manhattan and move across country. California was definitely on my radar. With the San Francisco deal pushed aside, maybe it was time to check into San Diego, Lake Tahoe, or Napa Valley. Guess I would see where fate led me.

I approached my apartment and quickly realized I couldn't enter. Instead, I used my key to Renée's place. *That's funny, the lights are on but she's nowhere to be seen.* "Ren!" I hollered, "You here?" There was no answer, which was very odd. She didn't believe in wasting electricity. I decided to go check her bedroom. All of a sudden, there was a heavy knock at the front door as a deep male voice roared, "Aimee! Open the damn door."

Crap! How did Nik figure out where I was? "No!" I bellowed.

"Either you open up or I'll break the fucking thing down. You have till the count of three." Was he serious? Then I heard him counting, "1…2…" Well, that answered my question.

Before he finished, I yanked the door open. "What the hell are you doing here?"

He stood there with a menacing look on his face, add to that his thick arms crossed over his massive chest, and I was terrified. I took a step backwards. I'm not stupid; I knew when to back away from a furious man. And this one, in particular, was beyond that. I actually rubbed my hands over my arms due to the icy waves his body produced. *Oh, he's pissed off.* "Why'd you run from me, Aimee?"

"I…uh…well, I…" I stammered—unable to complete a thought, let alone a sentence. *Geez, what have I gotten myself into with this man?* He arched a brow at me, as if to say, "I'm listening." Finally, I found my voice. "I wanted to stay here. I was uncomfortable at the penthouse."

With a firm "Bullshit," he called my bluff.

Ah, hell. How could I tell him the truth? As if I would ever confess to being hurt by his rejection. So I suggested, "You don't have to take my word for it. I think my actions speak very clearly," I huffed and spun around to walk away from him.

He wasn't going to put up with that. Therefore, he firmly grabbed my arm, turned me around and commanded, "Never turn your back on me." His gaze was intent, and his grip insistent. I wasn't in pain, exactly, but I wasn't comfortable either. When I tried to pull away, he wouldn't let me. "Are we clear on this, Aimee?" I stared him down. Who did the man think he was? I did not take orders from anyone, especially *him*. "Answer me," he demanded.

As I stood my ground, I titled my chin up in defiance. "Fuck. You."

He hauled me against his hard body. "Watch it," he warned. "You're on thin ice with me right now. Don't make me take you over my knee," he threatened.

What the?! And why did that sound so hot? I'd never been into pain for the sake of pleasure. When I say pain, I mean the hard core kind like Renée was into. Not my thing, at all. I scoffed, "As if."

Next thing I knew, I was lying across his lap, and he was actually spanking my butt. It was not pleasurable. It hurt! "Ow," I complained. He only struck harder. "Okay, enough. Dammit." When he released me, I was fighting back tears. Immediately, I stood and backed away from him. My eyes blazed into his as I scolded, "That was uncalled for." He had some nerve. The man wouldn't have sex with me, yet he'd spank me. Appalling. *Why I oughta find something big and heavy to clock him with. Asshole!*

While he approached me, he declared, "I

warned you. Next time, you better remember I don't make idle threats."

"You are a Neanderthal."

"Maybe. But you will respect me."

"Oh, like you revere me? Let's be clear here, *Nik*. Touch me like that again and I'll find a way to retaliate. Are we clear?" It was not a threat; it was a promise.

His demeanor softened, as if suddenly he admired me. "You had me worried sick. I can't very well protect you when you take off like that." He ran his hands through his long hair. A sign of frustration I was becoming familiar with. "Are you okay? I never meant to hurt you," he stated sincerely.

"I'll be fine." For emphasis I rubbed my butt, silently telling him that it did *indeed* hurt.

At least he had the good sense to wince. "I'm sorry, Aimee," he apologized.

Just as I was about to fire off a sassy retort, we heard something break in the bedroom. Both of us took off at a full sprint and abruptly halted at the sight we'd come upon. Surely my eyes deceived me, that couldn't be my best friend laid out on the floor. Could it? When she moaned and reached up for the nightstand, I realized it was her. "Renée?" I squeaked, "Honey, what happened?"

Nik grabbed my hand when I reached for her. "Hold on a sec. Let me check something first."

I stared at him dubiously. What was he thinking? My best friend was lying there semiconscious and needed help. "Why?"

"I'll tell y'later. You can touch her as soon as I'm done." I watched in horrific fascination as he scanned the area for—evidence?—clues, like he'd done when my apartment had been ransacked. Bewildered by what I was witnessing, the man came across as a thug sometimes, then, at other times, he was as observant as an investigator. Yet, another piece of the puzzle that was Nik Strand. How I wanted to fit it all together so I could see the complete picture. Complicated didn't even begin to define him. When Renée groaned again, I held my hand above her blood soaked head and looked up at Nik, silently begging him to let me touch her. "Go ahead." He nodded his head for emphasis.

I was eternally grateful as I mouthed *Thank you*. I swept Renée's hair to the side. "Hey, Ren. I'm here," I reassured. "Don't move, okay? We're going to get you some help." I fought back my hysteria while I watched her try desperately to open her beautiful hazel eyes. She couldn't due to the swelling. They were already a horrid blackish-blue. My heart broke for her. She had been through so much for a young woman of twenty-seven. It just wasn't right this had happened to her.

Nik glanced up, pocketed his cell phone and announced, "An ambulance is on its way."

"Hear that, sweetie? Help is coming," I assured. "You just hang on for me, okay?" She reached over and squeezed my hand. Unable to hold them back any longer, tears slid down my cheeks. All of a sudden, I was engulfed by incredible heat when a huge corded arm wrapped around my shoulders. Grateful for his support, I was no longer angry with Nik. Whenever my life was in tatters, he was always there to rescue me. *Sure seemed that way*. How could you not appreciate such a quality? I leaned my head into his shoulder and absorbed the comfort he provided.

The firm knock at the door broke the bond we'd been forging. He stood and stated, "That'd be EMS." He walked out of the room, and I couldn't help but feel bereft by his absence. Renée moaned again in pain, and I suddenly felt guilty. Something inside of me knew, somehow, this happened to her because of me. I backed away to let the medics do their job. As they loaded her onto the stretcher, Nik said, "Come on. I'll take you to the hospital."

There was no way I could speak at that moment, not with anxiety and guilt digging their claws into me. I nodded in acquiescence and leaned on him when he put his arm around me, once more. Yet again, appreciative for his strength and presence.

*****

On our way to the hospital, Nik queried, "Does Renée have any enemies? Someone that'd want to hurt her?"

I shrugged. "Old ones." Then I firmly replied, "No. I don't know of anyone who'd do that to her."

"What'd you mean by old ones?"

I heard the inquisitiveness in his voice. How much should I share about Renée's past? I figured honesty was best. "Her brother's in a gang. She had a rough upbringing, but that was a long time ago."

"Do you think this has anything to do with him?"

"No, I really don't," I concluded.

"Why's that?" he questioned.

"Well, honestly, she keeps her distance from him." I turned to face him. "He's only around when she needs him. Otherwise, they don't really have a relationship," I answered.

"I see," he said contemplatively. I suddenly had a sick feeling deep in my gut and began to shake uncontrollably. He squeezed my hand. "Hey. Are you okay?"

I bit my lip hard, tasting blood. "It's him, isn't it?" I whimpered.

"We don't know that for sure." He didn't even

pretend not to understand whom I meant—for which I was grateful—but it didn't change the fact Caleb was sending a message. No matter what Nik had said about not knowing for sure; I knew. And his message was loud and clear: Return to me *or* else. I shuddered at the thought. How was I going to get away from that man? More to the point, how would I protect the ones I loved *from* him? "Don't let your imagination get away from you, Aimee," Nik said, pulling me from my reverie. "Once we know for certain, then, we deal with it." He'd parked the car and tugged me into a hard embrace. "You're not alone," he vowed. "I'll do whatever I have to, to keep you safe."

I whispered, "Okay." Still not understanding the pull between us, I hugged him back. "Thank you, Nik."

He pulled back and lifted my chin gently. "It'll all work out. Trust me?"

Ironically I did, which made no sense considering I didn't know this man. Yet, I did. It was beyond confusing. I decided to be truthful and responded with a definite, "Yes. Yes, I do trust you."

He rested his forehead against mine. "Thank you," he murmured.

With that, we left the car and proceeded into the hospital.

Chapter Nine
Nik

Hate was too weak a word for how I felt about hospitals. The smell alone was enough to make me turn tail and run. Hard. Fast. As far away as I could possibly go. All of a sudden, I was *there* all over again: The five security guards wrestling me to the ground. The doctor screaming, "Stop! Before you permanently damage your arm!"—which had already been broken. The gut wrenching howling as they informed me, "dead on arrival. Baby could not survive outside her mother's womb." Every finite detail of the worst night of my life played through my mind in HD Technicolor. Somewhere in the haze between past and reality, I heard a soft voice.

"Nik? Can you hear me? Come back, you're scaring me," Aimee confessed. She grabbed my face with her hands and tugged me down to her. "Hey, I'm right here." She reassured, "I won't leave you."

I blinked furiously and attempted to get my bearings. "What...?"

She held my gaze. "Do you know who I am? Where you're at?"

"Aimee." Then I paused as I tried to assimilate my location. When I answered, "Hospital," I felt the blood drain from my face.

"Yes. Do you remember why we're in the

hospital?"

I shook my head as cold sweat trickled down my back and my palms became clammy. With a jolt of recollection, I realized what was going on. I pulled her hands away from my face and replied, "Renée. Is she all right?"

Aimee narrowed her eyes at me. While she avoided my question, she inquired, "What was that?"

I feigned innocence. "What are you talking about?"

She didn't buy my act for a second. With her hands on her hips, she responded, "Don't pretend you don't know what I'm talking about it."

Man, she was even more beautiful when she was angry. But there was no way I would confess to anything. I held my ground with a nasty, "Drop it," as I walked away from her. I didn't plan to go far; just needed some space to get my shit together. Dammit. This was neither the time nor the place for a meltdown. I took several deep breaths to calm myself down. Aimee didn't need this crap. No one did. My memories were things of nightmares.

When I heard her gasp, "Oh no," I turned suddenly and made a beeline to her side, then wrapped my arm around her shoulder.

She leaned against me for support when the doctor informed, "We're sending her down for a CAT scan now. Once that's completed, we'll put her in a room."

"Will I be able to see her?"

"Yes. As soon as we've finished everything, you can go in to see her."

Aimee politely replied, "Thank you, doctor."

I pulled her into a full embrace while she cried. "She'll be fine," I comforted. "Yes, she'll be bruised and sore, but, otherwise, okay. Don't worry."

She glanced up at me with doleful eyes. "How

do you know it's nothing serious?"

"If it is, then, we'll deal with it," I affirmed. "Would you like to go get something to drink while we wait?"

She nodded.

While we sat in the waiting room, Aimee finally asked, "Are you going to tell me what happened when we arrived here tonight?"

I sat there contemplating whether it was a good idea or not to air my dirty laundry. However, there was just something about her that made me want to share a little part of myself. "Officially, I have PTSD," I acknowledged.

At that revelation, her eyes widened. "Oh."

"Yeah. 'Oh' about sums it up."

"Is it from an injury during your fighting days?"

Damn. I did not want to talk about this. "No."

She arched her beautiful brow. "Are you planning to expound here? Or leave it at that?"

Shit. She was not going to let this go. A part of me admired her tenacity. It was refreshing to have someone call me on the carpet when I shut down. No one had in years. My brothers just left it alone when I got like this. Wise of them actually, because the truth was, I'd tear them a new one if they tried. I swallowed past the lump in my throat and answered, "It was an accident many years ago."

She cocked her head to one side. "You were injured?" she asked with compassion.

"Yes." I doubled up my fists preparing for the rest of her inquisition.

"Severely?" she continued to query.

"No," I replied abruptly.

As she began to fit the pieces together, she nodded, "I see. Someone you loved was," she speculated.

I stood and through clenched teeth confirmed, "Yes." I began to walk away, but then suddenly turned. While holding her gaze intently, I blurted, "She's dead." After I dropped that lil' piece of info, I stepped outside for some much needed air.

*****

What the hell was wrong with me? I was supposed to be here for Aimee, not reliving the night Rachel and my unborn daughter died. Talk about six kinds of fucked up. She would want more details with the bomb I just detonated. And I, in no way, had any intentions of playing twenty questions. I stepped to the side of the building and leaned back against it, as I tried to get the images—which refused to die—out of my head. *Shit. It's a friggin' lost cause*. As I kicked a soda can, as hard as I could, I watched it sail through the air and land with a significant *thunk*. That felt good. I ran both hands through my hair and marched back inside. Aimee needed me to be a man. Not a pussy.

When I stepped around the corner, I saw her. Her lost look almost undid me, right there. Even if I could have stopped myself, at that moment, I wouldn't have. I hauled her against my body and held her tight. *What is it about this woman?* On some visceral level, I recognized her. *Why?* Not to mention there was just something about her that made me want to protect her from all harm. Once you added the undeniable attraction, you had one hell of a cocktail.

Heady.
Tempting.
A force to be reckoned with.

I ran my hand down her spine and rested it at the small of her back. The urge to kiss her was unbearable. Again, it didn't make sense. I did *not* kiss on the mouth. *Well, not any more, that is.* There was only one exception I'd made to the rule, and I had vowed to never repeat it. That kiss had been like no other. And I knew, no matter how hard I tried, I would never find another woman who could bring me to my knees like that. Not even my lovely wife had been capable, and I had been head over heels in love with her. I inhaled sharply as Rachel's memory danced through my mind. There wasn't a moment I didn't miss her or wish like hell it'd been me that had died that night.

I carefully pulled away from Aimee, fighting not to let a tear escape. Since that night, I hadn't let myself cry for Rachel. And I refused to succumb now. I cleared my throat and asked, "You okay?"

She attempted a watery smile. "Sort of."

"Wanna talk 'bout it?"

"No." She shook her head for emphasis. "I just want to sit down for a moment."

I led her over to some chairs. While she closed her eyes and rested, I held her hand. It wasn't long before a nurse informed her she could go in to see Renée. I glanced up at her. "You go ahead without me. I'll be here when you're finished," I promised.

She nodded, "Thank you."

*****

While I sat there with my elbows on my knees, I let the memories I'd held at bay flow. For whatever reason, instead of Rachel, the night of a particular masquerade invaded. To this day, that night was unforgettable. My mind had begun to play tricks on me. I could swear it was Aimee from the night a few years past. How could that be? At the time, I had been in Chicago on business. Since the hosts were friends of mine, and I attended every year, I had a standing invitation. Therefore, I had not been placed on the guest list. I shook my head to clear it. Nothing made sense anymore.

Then, the recollection of spanking Aimee's gorgeous ass came unbidden. Crap. What a colossal mistake that'd been. Yet, I couldn't seem to contain myself. I was furious she had run; subsequently, worried sick something awful had happened to her. When she defied me, I lost it. I had never done anything like that before. It did not help my hand still tingled with desire to do so again. Although this time, not out of anxiety or frustration. Damn. How could I continue to avoid taking her? I adjusted my painful erection. I was going to end up a patient with the worst case of blue balls ever recorded. I stood and began to pace.

After I got my overactive libido under control, I sat back down and attempted to form some kind of plan. Time passed while I waited for Aimee to return. I had a pretty good idea she was right about Reynolds being behind the attack on Renée. Question was, how did I prevent him from getting to Aimee? Not to mention those she cared about. Since the last time I had dealt with his obsession, he'd escalated. With Rachel he had done things differently. Probably due to the fact he was much younger then, and she'd been his first. Who knew how many women he had stalked since? We'd never been able to prove it years ago. Now, he had so much wealth and power at his fingertips. Truth was, he could get away with murder. I knew it. He knew it. So what to do? First thing, was to get a security team together quickly. I decided to make some calls.

I had just ended my call with Alex when

Aimee returned to my side. I looked into her weary eyes and inquired, "How's she doing?"

She yawned before she answered, "Sleeping."

"I take it you'd like to stay here with her?"

"Yes, please," she confirmed.

I nodded while I assisted her into a chair. "Wait here."

"Thank you, Nik."

I held her hand for a moment. "No big deal." Then I went to make overnight arrangements for her.

One of the nurses, Liz, was kind enough to assist me with getting Aimee a cot placed in Renée's room. While she set everything up, I went to get Aimee. Who was sound asleep in the chair where I'd left her. Not having the heart to wake her, I picked her up and cradled her close, then walked back into the room. When she mumbled something indecipherable and nuzzled my chest, I about lost it. *Dear God, she's perfect like this.* I wanted nothing more than to kiss her luscious lips. But I knew better; instead, I gently kissed the top of her head as I laid her down on the cot. I tucked the blanket around her and then stepped out into the hall with the nurse.

"Will she be all right there?" I asked.

Liz confirmed, "Yes, Mr. Strand."

"Do I need to do anything else tonight?"

"No, sir. You've taken care of everything." I knew she referred to the fact I had paid for Renée's private room. "Go home and rest." She assured, "I'll watch over both of them."

"Thank you, Liz. I'll leave as soon as security makes it up here."

"See you in the morning, then." She turned and left.

A few minutes later, my head of security, Ray, arrived to watch over Aimee and Renée. He confirmed that Jim and José were also on site. Once I concluded with my team all was well, I headed home for the night.

Chapter Ten
Aimee

The next morning, I awoke on a small cot. As I stretched and searched the room, my gaze instantly fell on Renée. She looked so small—quite a feat, considering she was nearly five-foot, ten-inches tall—lying there broken. Tears slid down my cheeks. If I didn't know that was my best friend, I would not have recognized her. Her face was a mottled mess. Both eyes swollen, one of which I knew she wouldn't be able to open for a few days. Her lip was split as well. *Poor baby.* I wanted to hug her, but I was unsure where it was safe to touch her. At least her leg had only been broken in one place, the left fibula. She'd heal relatively quickly, for that I was grateful. She began to stir and barely managed to crack open one eye. "Hey," I greeted with a watery smile.

She croaked, "Where am I?"

I grabbed her hand and held it as I replied, "Hospital."

She swallowed and winced when she licked her bottom lip. I reached over to the side table for a glass of water. After I helped her with a much needed drink, she asked, "Why am I here?"

"Oh, Ren. I really hoped you could tell me what happened," I replied.

She blinked in confusion so I relayed what I

knew. "We found you in your bedroom. You have a concussion, two black eyes, a split lip, bruising all over your face, and a broken leg."

She looked down at her leg and grimaced when she tried to move it. "No cast?"

"You got lucky there." She shot me a disbelieving look. I clarified, "What I mean is, it's your fibula, no cast required."

"Alright." She inquired, "So who beat the shit out of me?"

I shrugged and acknowledged, "We don't know."

She held my gaze so incessantly I had to look away. Of course, she knew my tell. "But you have an idea," she suggested.

Still unable to look at her—*how do I admit this is all my fault?*—I nodded.

"Caleb?" she speculated.

Holy crap! How does she do that? Her instincts were always spot on. I admitted, "We think so."

"Look at me, Aims." I did as she ordered. "Who's 'we'? You keep saying that."

I licked my dry lips and confessed, "Nik and I."

Her eyes widened. "Nik? Start talking, girlfriend."

I brought her up to speed—well, mostly; I wasn't ready to share *everything*. I'd left out the intimate, or lack thereof, details. Although no one could ever accuse Renée of stupidity; hence, her next question shouldn't have surprised me. "Have you slept with him yet?"

"Uh…well…" I stuttered. Then squared my shoulders and unashamedly answered, "Actually, no, I haven't."

"You don't say."

Thankfully, at that moment, we were interrupted by Keshaun. He swooped into the room and began to gush all over her. I politely excused myself. *Phew! That was close.* But I knew Renée, all too well. This wasn't the end of the discussion. Not by a long shot.

*****

As I rounded the corner, I ran smack dab into a slab of muscles. Goodness, the man was stacked. And I would be lying if I didn't own up to the fact; I wanted nothing more than to run my tongue over each and every one of them. I glanced up while I licked my bottom lip as the erotic image passed through my mind. Nik watched my tongue intently and mirrored my action. I exercised vehement control not to jump him, right there, and greeted, "Hi."

"Hey. How're you?"

"Better, thanks."

"And Renée?"

"As well as can be expected. She's with her"—*crap, what do I call Keshaun?*—"boyfriend." There, that sounded a whole lot better than sub. I highly doubted Nik would understand their relationship. Hell, I had a hard enough time with it. I mean, how did a big, handsome, famous basketball player let a Domme beat him with various implements while restrained all for the sake of pleasure? *Whatever. To each his own.* Their relationship was between them, and while Renée was a Dominatrix by trade, he had never paid for her services. I shook my head to clear the mental image.

"You alright?" Nik stood there with his eyes narrowed. *Ah, hell, don't tell me he has the same uncanny gift as Renée at knowing what I'm thinking.*

"Sorry. Was just trying to clear my head," I

acknowledged.

It wasn't a lie, per se, but I was pretty sure he didn't buy it; however, he remained courteous. "Did you sleep well?"

"Actually, it wasn't quite as awful as you would think. Once again, thank you."

"No problem." Then he asked, "Would you like to have breakfast with me?"

I smiled, "Yes, I would."

*****

As we perused the menu, Nik commented, "I hope you don't mind this café instead of the hospital cafeteria." He made a face like he'd just tasted something vile.

Couldn't say I blamed him. No one ever enjoyed hospital food. *Blech!* I grinned, "No. I don't mind, at all."

His lips turned up slightly. Never had he graced me with an actual smile that reached his eyes. He'd come close, and that had been heart pounding. *Will I ever see his amazing lips in a megawatt smile?* The thought made me squirm, because I *knew* it'd be panty dropping. *Oh my.* I fanned myself mentally. He held my gaze—no doubt, trying to figure out what I was thinking. "Penny for your thoughts?" he purred.

Holy crap! Surely he didn't know. "Um…just trying to make a selection," I replied.

He shot me a knowing look. *Ah, hell.* "Riiiight. You only had food on your mind."

Not like I was going to claim my indecent musings. "Yes." I asked innocently, "Was there something else I'm supposed to be considering?"

He nodded and half-smiled—*good heavens, that mouth!* "If that's the way you wanna play this, Aimee."

The timing couldn't have been more perfect when our server asked, "What can I get for you?"

I looked up at her. "I'll have the Spanish omelet and a cup of coffee, please."

She turned her attention to Nik. When he glanced up at her, she blinked rapidly. Her lips parted as her breathing increased. *Good, at least it's not just me he has that effect on.* The man was handsome personified—by no means an actor or model attractive, more like rugged and untamed and a wild kind of good-looking. That *did* things to a woman. He answered, "I'll have the same but with a short stack of pancakes on the side. Coffee as well, thank you."

She paused a moment too long and then turned to leave. I shook my head at him. "You have no idea, do you?"

His brows rose. "'Bout what, exactly?"

I grinned wryly. "Your effect on women."

He actually looked astonished. "Come again."

"Please! You can't be that oblivious."

He steepled his fingers in front of his mouth and admitted, "I have no idea what you're talking about."

Why was that so hot?! He wore humility well, and damn, if it wasn't a huge turn on. My mouth was suddenly dry. I wanted him. And I had no clue how to make that happen. I knew he was attracted to me. No one could ignore the awareness that arced between us; even now it was a force to be reckoned with. I decided honesty was best. "You're a very attractive man, Nik. There's not a woman in here that hasn't checked you out."

His eyes conveyed his bewilderment. "Really?" He shrugged. "Can't say I've ever noticed."

Now I was the surprised one. "How is that, exactly? All you have to do is look around."

He did just that. His gaze finally returned to mine, and there was something there that hadn't been a few moments ago. Anger? Jealousy? Why would he feel either one of those? "What I see is every man in here eyeing you in a most licentious way," he clarified. "It's very disturbing." His voice was too quiet.

Oh, dear. He was pissed off. I glanced to my left, and the man sitting there made a very base gesture. *As if.* Nik tried to stand, but I grasped his hand. "No, don't. Please?"

"That was uncalled for," he snarled.

I didn't disagree; however, I knew nothing good would come out of Nik calling the guy on the carpet. "It was," I concurred. "But the slimeball isn't worth the effort."

"I can't agree with that." He stood and walked over to the dickwad. He leaned down and said something that caused the man to wan. Next thing I knew, the jerk stood next to our table and apologized profusely. I accepted graciously and watched as the guy made his exit.

A part of me was flattered Nik stood up for me, while another part was furious he'd done precisely what I had asked him not to do. I went with anger. "You have some nerve!"

He blinked a few times, as if he couldn't understand my ire. *Really*?! "Do I, now?" he responded dryly.

Oh, the man was so infuriating. I stood to leave. He grabbed my upper arm firmly—it *just* didn't hurt. "You haven't eaten. Sit," he commanded.

Oooh, he was so dang bossy. However, I didn't want to make a scene; therefore, I sat. Once I took a deep, calming breath, I addressed, "Look. While I appreciate you defending me, I can fight my own battles. I don't need your help. Capiche?"

He held my gaze incessantly until eventually he stated, "I won't concur to that. Let it go."

Exasperated with the whole situation, and the man before me, I realized we were at an impasse. It really wasn't worth the fight. Plus, he had protected me once again. "Thank you," I said reluctantly.

When our food arrived, I dug in with gusto. To say I was famished would be an understatement. He finally acknowledged my gratitude. "You know, you're welcome. It hasn't gone unnoticed you have quite a knack for finding trouble."

I placed my fork beside my half-eaten omelet and held his gaze for a beat. "Maybe. But honestly, I don't have honor that needs protecting. The gesture is kind, yet completely uncalled for." I held my hand up to stop him from interrupting. "Having said all that, I am grateful for all of your assistance these past few days."

He swallowed. "About that."

Ah, shit. What now? I sighed, "Go on."

"Reynolds isn't going to stop. You know that, right?"

"Yeah, I do."

"Until we get the situation under control, I would like for you to stay with me."

"C'mon, Nik. That's just ridiculous."

"Is it?"

I nodded emphatically. "We can't stay in the same location. Surely you realize this."

His eyes blazed. "Why?"

"Because...this thing"—I waved my hand between us for emphasis—"it's not going away. If anything, it's only growing with intensity."

He shrugged. "Doesn't mean we have to act on it."

I almost spat my coffee all over him. So, this was the way he wanted to play it. I'm not going to lie,

I wasn't happy with his declaration. But I'd be damned, if I would tell him that. As coyly as possible I assessed, "Alright. Deal. No physical contact, whatsoever."

"Works for me," he concluded.

With that he stood, and we walked back to the hospital in an awkward silence. Who was I kidding? The desire between us was its own entity. Before too long, it would rear its head. And then what?

Chapter Eleven
Nik

I shot a sidelong glance at Aimee, and I had to admit, there was no misconception about the sexual awareness between us. However, if she thought I lacked self-control, she was sadly mistaken. One of the lessons learned, thanks to the school of hard knocks. Moreover, I'm an impassive SOB. She had no idea who she was up against. I mentally smiled— sad, but true, I hardly ever genuinely grinned at anyone. Of course, until recently, there never really was much of a desire to. *Odd, that.*

She broke the uncomfortable silence. "I'm going to go check on Renée. You're welcome to leave. I'll be staying until she's released."

Like hell. I glowered at her and grumbled, "That's not a good idea."

She had the good sense to take a step backwards. "Whether you agree or not doesn't really matter." She faced me and squared her exquisite shoulders. "I'm staying. Deal with it," she added petulantly.

I shook my head, vacillating between awe and fury. While she exasperated the living shit out of me, she also stirred a longing I had no wish to examine too closely. Not to mention grown men had pissed their pants under my glare of disdain. And there she stood defiantly telling me off. Kiss her or put her over my knee? *Yeah, right, as if either were truly options.* I held my ground and tried for reason. "My security is top notch, but this is a public place. If someone wants to get their hands on you, there's not much we can do to prevent it," I pointed out the blatantly obvious and then added, "Surely, you can see that." Big mistake! I swear I saw steam rise off her body. Damn, should've remembered how sensitive a woman could be.

She didn't disappoint me. As she stamped her tiny foot for emphasis, she snapped, "How dare you insinuate I'm stupid or helpless, Tarzan!"

"Ah, name-calling. Bit childish, don't y'think?"

When she raised her hand to slap my face, I caught it mid-swing. "Careful," I warned, "You don't want to piss me off." The memory of spanking her in Renee's apartment made my other hand twitch at my side.

She didn't miss it when I noticed comprehension dawning in her eyes. *Yes, she remembers as well.* She attempted to jerk her hand out of my grasp—which I wouldn't permit—and hissed, "Let me go."

I yanked her closer and growled, "No. Not until you hear me out."

After she bobbed her head in acquiescence, she patronizingly said, "Go ahead."

Ah, what I would like to do to that smart mouth of hers. "All I'm trying to say, is that Reynolds won't stop now that he has your attention. He's biding his time, Aimee," I cautioned.

She shuddered. Good, she needed to understand the danger. "I don't doubt you're right," she professed. "But I've told you before; I can take care of myself."

Alright, that pissed me off. "Yes. I can see

that." I added sarcastically, "You've done such a great job of it so far."

Instead of the retort I expected, her shoulders hunched forward in defeat while she looked down at her shoes. *Oh, hell no. This, I do not want*. I placed two fingers under her chin and lifted her head up so she would have to hold my gaze. "Listen." I softened my voice. "He's a powerful man with a lot of money and influence. He'll stop at *nothing* to get what he wants." She fought back the tears that threatened to fall. And while I may be a cold-hearted bastard, I couldn't stand knowing I was the one to cause such a reaction. I pulled her into my chest and comforted, "Hey now, you're a strong woman. Don't let a prick like Caleb scare you."

She mumbled, "No, I'm not, Nik." She glanced up at me as tears streamed down her lovely, rounded cheeks and confessed, "I'm terrified he's going to win."

Before I did something stupid and kissed the moisture from her face, I put some space between us. I kept my hands on her shoulders and reiterated, "I *will* protect you."

Out of desperation, she shook her head. "I just don't see how you can do that." Her voice was soft and defeated, which tore at my soul—*or what was left of it*.

I vowed, "I will do whatever's necessary."

Her eyes widened. "You wouldn't…?"

I chuckled darkly. "Don't worry, little one." Her head popped up with bewilderment on her face. I swallowed hard—*what'd I say to cause such a look?*—and continued, "I'm not going to do anything illegal."

That seemed to mollify her. She stepped out of my hold. "Let me go check on Renée. Then I'll go home with you," she stated while she turned and walked away.

*****

Shit! What a clusterfuck. I ran my hands
through my hair and began to pace. It wasn't long
before the idea I'd once had to fix this problem
resurfaced. Marriage. Really, what other choice was
there? Yes, I could hire a top notch security team to
watch over her twenty-four/seven; however, Reynolds
was crafty, and it wouldn't take him long to hire his
own henchmen to get around me. As it was, a team
watching over her family and friends until he found a
new obsession would be necessary. Would he find a
new one? Or could Aimee be looking over her
shoulder for the rest of her life? I didn't know. Rachel
died, end of story. Caleb had no choice but to move
on. *Like me—if you call this husk of a man moving
on.* I shook off the morose thoughts bouncing around
in my head. Time to man-up and do what needed to
be done. I had to convince Aimee this was the best
solution. Right, who was I kidding? Marriage wasn't
exactly something I ever wanted to do again. Surely
she'd want hearts and flowers. Romance was not in
my vocabulary. *It was once*, Rachel's voice
whispered in my mind. *Yeah, maybe, but not
anymore.* Let's face it, I was screwed. Yet there were
no two ways about it, this was the answer. I strode
with determination and went outside to make a call.
Yeah, this was happening whether we wanted it to or
not.

*****

When I returned to the corridor outside of
Renée's room, my eyes alighted on the scene playing
out. Aimee was having a heated debate with one very

tall, very famous basketball player. Holy shit! Keshaun Fields stood there arguing with her. *About what, exactly? Only one way to find out.* I strode towards them and possessively wrapped my arm around Aimee's shoulders. It didn't go unnoticed by either one of them. She raised her brows at me. *What the fuck* written across her lovely face. I bit back a chuckle and squeezed her tighter. I looked up at Keshaun, which unnerved me, considering I'm a big guy. I stand six-foot, four-and-half-inches, and I was not accustomed to looking up at many people. All six-foot, nine-inches of him radiated hostility. I held my ground and challenged, "Problem here?"

As Aimee shook her head in denial, Keshaun glowered. Finally he spoke, "This is between me and her. Butt out."

Hell, no. Did he just say that? The dickhead obviously didn't realize who I was. I firmly pushed Aimee behind me and then stood toe to toe with Fields. "Beg pardon?"

He studied me for a moment, taking in all two-hundred-and-forty pounds of solid muscle that faced-off with him. Aimee placed her small hand on my shoulder and whispered, "Nik." I leaned down to hear her. "Everything's fine here." She continued, "Keshaun and I simply disagree on what's best for Renée. He won't hurt me."

Not convinced of that, I stared at Fields— hard. He didn't back down, which impressed the hell out of me. "Does she have it right?" I asked, "Or do you and I need to step outside?"

He snorted, "I'd never harm blondie. She knows that."

Aimee squeezed my hand. "See? 'S all good," she declared.

Once more, I appraised Fields and then glanced back at her. "I'll just be over there with Ray."

I inclined my head in the direction of my security guard.

She nodded. Then, her and Fields began to walk down the hall while deep in conversation.

*****

Ray had not seen any action that day—*no surprise, there*. Reynolds wasn't stupid enough to try anything in public. A fact that didn't sit well with me, for experience told me he was waiting for an opportunity to arise. We had to be one step ahead of him, diligent in our mission to keep everyone safe. Although there was no doubt in my mind Aimee was his target. The sooner I married her, the sooner she would be safe from him. Hopefully she would see that. However, I was getting to know her pretty well; she would not take this lightly. Just like I knew she'd blast me for the incident with Keshaun a few minutes ago. Aimee Taylor was definitely not a damsel in distress. She was already furious she needed my help. A proposal of this magnitude would be met head-on with her determination and tenacity. What I needed to find was her Achilles' heel. I decidedly opened the door to Renée's room. Time to get some answers.

I approached with gentleness and made myself known by rubbing her hand. One eye blinked several times before focusing. The other, was swollen shut. I greeted, "Hello."

"Hi," she responded back.

"Do you remember me?" I inquired as I took a seat in the chair next to her bed.

"Yeah. Nik, right?"

"That's me," I confirmed.

"So, she told you?"

Hold on, told me what? "Not sure I know what you're talking about."

She blew out a breath. "Figures. That girl doesn't wanna accept the danger she's in."

No joke! "Tell me something I don't know."

She attempted to smile but then winced from the pain in her lip. "Listen. I shouldn't betray her trust. However, she *needs* you. Stubborn girl won't admit it though."

I sort of chuckled and sort of snorted, "Reynolds is behind this."

"Got that right. Asswipe had his goons send Aimee a message via me." She waved a hand over her body for emphasis.

"Any words involved?" She had definitely piqued my interest. And I had a whole lot of respect for her, knowing that she loved Aimee enough to keep this part from her.

She snarled, "Oh, yeah." She attempted to imitate the thug's voice that attacked her. "'Tell Aimee, either she marries Caleb or else.' "

"Douchebag."

"Couldn't agree with you more."

"Don't worry about her." I apprised, "I have a plan."

"Do you, now?"

I actually did half-smile at that. "Yeah. She won't like it," I warned.

"We'll make her," she scoffed. "Lay it on me."

I took a deep breath and said, "I'll ask her to marry me."

"Oh, shit! Look handsome, that ain't gonna fly with her."

I leaned forward. "Sure it will. You're gonna help me convince her it's for the best."

She attempted to nod but I could see the pain the motion caused. "I didn't say I disagreed with you. It would be for the best." She added, "But honestly,

I'm not sure we can make her see that clearly."

I shrugged. "Clearly or not, it's the right answer."

"Okay. I'll do what I can." She acknowledged, "Just know, you're in for an epic battle."

"I'm a champion when it comes to a good fight." I patted her hand.

"Good thing."

All of a sudden, Keshaun reentered the room. My sign it was time to leave. I glanced back down at Renée and asked, "Wish me luck?"

She softly laughed, "Baby, you need prayer, not luck."

I nodded, "True."

Keshaun floored me when he held out his hand. "My apologies for earlier."

I shook hands with him. "Forgotten."

Then, I headed back out to find Aimee and braced myself for the fight that was about to ensue. I knew full well I didn't want a bride any more than she wanted to be one. "Life's a bitch…" For some reason, I just couldn't bring myself to finish that quote.

Chapter Twelve
Aimee

As Keshaun stepped inside Renée's room, I went to the ladies' room—not missing Ray's watchful eyes following me. It was unnerving to have security everywhere I went. Could I live with this for the rest of my life? No. Question was, how to evade Caleb? The phrase "in over your head" instantly came to mind. Crap. That was me in a nutshell. Either I marry the ogre or he'd harm those I loved. Seriously, what options were left? Nik could not continue with the constant surveillance. Caleb would eventually figure out a way around it. The one saving grace was that he didn't know my parents' last name. Yes, Taylor is my legal name, although most knew me by Lockhart— which had been assumed for privacy. Nonetheless Bill's my stepfather—and the man I'd called Daddy my entire life—hence Mitchell being my mother's married name. Point was, no one but immediate family knew any of that. Reason was, my biological father, Mark Taylor, had been killed in a car accident when my mother was three months pregnant with me. She married Bill right before I was born; therefore, their identity was safe from prying eyes. I felt very grateful knowing they would be out of harm's way. Now it appeared, after the incident with Renée, Keshaun would protect *his* woman. So really, I only needed to worry about myself. *Caleb's beyond dangerous*; the little voice in my head reminded me. Yes, I did know that. Along with the obvious, no one was really secure if Caleb put his mind to it. Great. Back to square one.

After I finished my business and returned to the hallway, I spotted Nik casually leaning against the wall with one shoulder. *Dang, he's hot*. When would I be unaffected by his looks? *Never*. I shook my head to clear it and then approached him. He appraised me for a moment before he asked, "Everything okay?"

"Fine. You ready to leave?"

He straightened to his full height and placed his hand on the small of my back. Electricity shot through me. I glanced at him in speculation, which caused him to remove his hand. Phew! At least he remembered our no contact vow, because I was in no mood to argue with him at the moment. He waved his hand for me to walk in front of him and requested, "Shall we?"

"Sure thing."

*****

We approached his fancy sports car—*what on earth is this thing?* Ever the gentleman, he opened the passenger door and assisted me into the very low to the ground automobile. Once he gracefully sank his large body behind the wheel, I inquired, "What kind of car is this, anyway?"

Nik actually half-smirked. OMG! "A McLaren MP4-12C," he replied with not a little awe in his voice.

Boys and their toys. Although I must confess, it was kind of cute to see his face all lit up like that. "You really are the quintessential multimillionaire, aren't you?"

He cocked a brow. "Do you expect me to apologize for that?"

I shrugged one shoulder. "Not really."

He bobbed his head once. "Good."

He whipped through the frenetic New York City traffic like it was nothing, handling the car like a professional. Once we arrived at the parking garage for his penthouse, my knuckles were white and cramping. On our way up in the elevator, I pivoted towards him. "Mind if I ask you something?"

He held my gaze intently. "You can ask."

I nodded and theorized, "But it doesn't mean you'll answer."

"I'll try," he ceded.

Really, what more could I ask for? Well, actually—"Will you tell me the truth?"

He looked affronted. "I'm not a liar, Aimee."

"Fair enough." I gathered my thoughts for a minute. We had arrived in the foyer before I spoke, "What happens now?"

"We need to talk 'bout that," he hedged.

Shoot! That didn't sound good. I took a fortifying breath and asked, "When?"

He escorted me into the kitchen and held out a barstool for me at the breakfast bar. "Are you hungry?" he evaded.

I raised my eyebrows and pointed that fact out, "You're dodging my question."

"No. I'm getting ready to fix myself a sandwich." He countered, "I was being polite."

"Oh. In that case, yes, I am hungry."

As he prepared the sandwiches, he queried, "What would you like to happen at this stage of the game?"

"Not sure I'm following you here," I admitted. "Could you elaborate, please?"

"Yes. Well, you don't want to marry

Reynolds, correct?"

"Definitely not!" I vehemently responded.

He paused, stroking his jaw with his forefinger and thumb. "Can't say that I blame you there." He sat down and placed a plate in front of me. "How long do you think you'd need security?"

After swallowing, I answered, "I just don't know. I mean, I'd like to think he'd give up and move on, but I already know that's not likely."

He gave me his full attention. "How'd you know that?"

I sighed, "Because he's been actively pushing marriage for over six months now."

"Shit."

"Yep. That about sums it up."

Once we finished eating, he put the dishes in the sink, sat back down, and poured both of us a glass of white wine. Hmm, it was delish. Curious to know what kind it was, I glanced at the bottle to see. Huh, I'd never had Grüner Veltliner before. His inquisition continued, "No offence, but why has he been pursuing the issue?"

"None taken." I shrugged. "I'd like to know that myself."

His chiseled face was pensive and forlorn as he silently sat there for a few moments. I wanted more than anything to take that horribly sad look away. This man had some deep wounds, and I was unsure if there would ever be true healing for him. That morose thought brought tears to my eyes. He misunderstood and comforted, "Hey, now. I thought you weren't offended by my questions." With the pad of his thumb, he wiped the moisture away and implored, "Please, don't cry."

I knew I couldn't very well confess the tears were for him. So I said, "I'm okay. Just a little worried."

"About what, exactly?"

"Well, he hurt Renée to send a message to me. Although we have no proof, we know he destroyed my apartment. What's next, Nik? What more is he capable of?"

For a moment, his eyes widened in surprise— *wonder what that's about*—then he recovered quickly and murmured, "More than you realize."

I stood and walked over to the floor to ceiling windows overlooking Central Park. The view was amazing. Once I gathered my thoughts, I pivoted towards him and stated, "I need to know."

He joined me and offered to refill my glass. Afterwards he asked, "Know what?"

"Don't be obtuse. You know I need to understand how much danger I'm in."

A myriad of emotions played across his face: pain, sorrow, bitterness, denial, and hopelessness. Each and every one of them caused my heart to fissure. There was nothing I wanted more than to wrap my arms around him. To reassure him that love could conquer all of this and more. Somehow, deep inside, I knew he would not accept my compassion. He was so lost, a prisoner in a cell of his own making. How could I free him? Especially when he did not seem to want freedom. *Oh, Nik.* He held out his hand for me and commanded, "Come. I'm gonna need a stronger drink for this conversation." I didn't miss the grimace on his face.

All of a sudden, I wasn't sure I wanted to know.

*****

As we entered the living room, he motioned for me to take a seat on the massive oversized couch, and then he walked across the room to turn on an incredible sound system. The song that began to play was a bit confusing at first. It sounded as if it were an old radio broadcast—*something about war?* Fitting. Then, the most incredible music began: a combination of heavy rock, an orchestra, a choir, and the most haunting voice I'd ever heard singing lead. Mesmerized by the song, I sat utterly still and listened. Nik approached with crystal rock glasses full of amber liquid. He stared down at his contemplatively. The music held us captive. When it began to replay, I realized he had it looped. I glanced over at him as he sat beside me and inquired, "What is this song?"

He turned towards me and acknowledged, "Our Solemn Hour." He took a drink and then continued, "The band is Within Temptation. In this recording, they are accompanied by the Metropole Orchestra and the PA'Dam choir."

"OMG!" I exclaimed. "Her voice is incredible."

"Yes, I agree. Sharon den Adel is amazing."

"But we're not sitting here to discuss music," I sighed.

The corner of his mouth rose slightly. "No. We're not." He finished his liquor and set the glass down on the coffee table, then faced me once again. "I first met Caleb Reynolds just before my senior year in high school. He was a lifelong friend of my late wife, Rachel."

His words from the hospital immediately came to mind *"She's dead."* Now it all made sense: his turbulent emotions; the post-traumatic stress disorder—the *she* he had referred to was his wife. Dear Lord, how long ago did this happen? And where did Caleb fit in? *Listen to the man, Aimee.* He continued, "At least she had thought he was her friend. Once I entered the scene, it didn't take long for him to reveal his true colors."

I arched a brow but didn't interrupt him. He proceeded, "See, Rachel and Caleb's parents had hoped they would eventually date and marry one another. But once I stepped into the picture, things changed." My eyes widened, still, I let him speak. "Rachel never, ever thought of Caleb as anything but a friend. Unfortunately, Caleb saw her as much more. Well, I s'pose you can see where the story is heading."

Yes. Yes, I could. However I wanted him to go on. He took my silence as his cue and resumed, "Anyway, Reynolds became more and more obsessed with her. The closer she and I became, the angrier he got. Before long, the stalking began. It appeared innocent enough to the onlooker, yet we knew it was anything but. Needless to say, once we were married, his threats escalated. I had finally convinced her it was time to take our concerns to the police; however, she died before she had a chance to do so."

So many questions bubbled through my mind. This was the most I'd ever heard him speak, though I could tell it'd taken its toll on him. The first thing I did was reach over to squeeze his hand. "I'm so sorry."

When he jerked his hand away, I was shocked and not a little wounded. "Don't," he hissed.

What the hell? Why wouldn't he accept sympathy? As if he read my mind, he clarified, "I do not deserve any of your pity."

Pity! What was wrong with him? "Nik..." I paused before I continued, "It isn't pity I feel."

Odd, he didn't seem to be feeling grief regarding Rachel. If I had to put a name to his expression, at the moment, it would be dispassionate. *Huh?* Then both of his brows rose, he obviously didn't believe what I had just conveyed. He hesitated,

104

"What, then?"

Wow, he had really closed himself off from any empathy whatsoever. I wondered why that was. "I know what it's like to lose someone. That's all," I confessed as I wiped away my tears. Every time I thought of my cousin, Cheryl, the grief hit again.

With a flat voice he queried, "Who?"

What a difficult man. I recommenced, "My cousin Cheryl." When he didn't say anything, I forged on, "She was as close to me as a sister. So when she took her own life, I thought mine was over, too." There was no controlling the sob that caught in my throat. He patted my knee for comfort. *See, he's not without emotion—just damaged.* The act gave me courage to go on, "She tried to tell me. But I was sixteen, and none of us knew what signs to look out for." I swallowed the large lump caught in my throat, not wanting to rehash this. Then I realized he felt the same way. At that moment, I clearly heard the lyrics to the song still playing in the background: the question of breaking free from chains hanging in the air between us. Wish I had the answer to that.

I took his hand in mine, needing contact— some form of connection. When he gazed into my eyes, something shifted. He leaned in, but instead of placing his lips on mine, he kissed me right below my ear. To give him full access to my throat, I tilted my head to the side. The invitation was accepted. Ah, his mouth was hot and wet. Once he began to lick up and down the tendons of my neck, I was lost and wanted *more*. So much more. I tried to reciprocate, but he wouldn't allow me to. Already panting with need, I noticed his breathing was heavier as well. At least I knew he felt it, too.

He nuzzled my nose with his and breathed, "Marry me, Aimee."

I was instantly pulled from my sensual haze.

WTF?! "Excuse me?"

"Do I really need to repeat myself?" he asked rhetorically. "It's the only way to insure your safety," he explained. "I know you recognize that."

"This is insanity," I blurted out. To reiterate that fact, the lyrics once more played loud and clear about how it was all around us. Ha! How was that for rhetoric?

"Maybe." He countered, "Doesn't change anything." No, the irony wasn't lost on him either.

I stood and walked away, needing space and time to think by myself. As I paced down the hallway, over my shoulder I called, "Give me a few minutes, will you?"

He nodded in agreement, which ended our conversation—*for a while at least.*

I opened the door to the guestroom I was staying in. That was the last thing I ever expected from Nik Strand. Sure, he had proposed before, but I knew he didn't want to follow through with it. But *this* time something was different, as if he had decided there was no other way. So how could I say yes? My subconscious pointed out, *how can you not? You want him.* And there lay the crux of my answer.

Chapter Thirteen
Nik

Holy shit! Did I actually just propose? Yes, that had
been my plan. But it wasn't supposed to be so easy to
do. No, it should've been the hardest thing to ask.
Instead, reality kicked me in the teeth. Bottom line, I
wanted her to be *mine*. Fuck. That wasn't right. Those
feelings should not exist. "I'm not supposed to care,"
I mumbled under my breath. With my head in my
hands, I sunk down onto the couch and fought like
hell to keep the tears at bay. Over and over in my
head I told Rachel, *I'm so sorry, baby. I'm sorry.* My
heart ached and guilt overwhelmed me. How could I
betray Rachel this way?

I didn't know if I sat like that for a few
minutes or a few hours, so when Aimee approached
and greeted, "Hey," I startled.

I ran my hand over my face and hoped there
was no trace of moisture there. I responded, "Hi," and
patted the cushion beside me. She took the hint and
sat down. Shock instantly shot through me when she
clutched my hand in hers.

She confided, "I've been thinking."

Ah, hell. She was going to fight me on this.
As much as I wanted her to say yes, I also wanted her
to say no. *How messed up is that?* "Come to any
conclusions?"

"Yeah, I did."

Damn. Here goes. "What are they?"

She took a fortifying breath and acknowledged, "You're right. It is the best answer to the problem."

I sort of chuckled. "Is that a yes, Aimee?"

She bit her bottom lip. Heaven help me, but that was hot. At the moment, I wanted to run my tongue over her mouth before I delved deep inside to explore. *Where do these thoughts keep coming from?* Again, I was struck by familiarity. As if I already knew how she tasted. Impossible. She glanced up at me and answered, "Yes."

The desire to sweep her onto my lap and kiss her senseless was almost my undoing. Somehow, I mustered every ounce of self-control and stood, then strode over to the bar and called, "Would you like a drink?"

In disbelief she shook her head and observed, "I just agreed to be your wife. And you're asking if I want a drink? What the hell, Nik?"

Ah, should've known that temper of hers wasn't far off. I fought the smile that threatened. Her feistiness was a huge turn on. I adjusted myself, as discreetly as possible, before I walked over with a bottle of champagne and offered her a glass. Next I held mine to hers and expounded, "Yes, to celebrate."

As our flutes *clinked* in a toast, she regarded me sheepishly. "Sorry 'bout my outburst."

"'S all good." I took another drink before I proceeded, "Listen. I'm not expecting you to be my wife in the biblical sense. Only on paper."

She actually looked affronted. "What the...?!" She stood and began to pace the room. "Expound, please?"

"I meant what I said," I reiterated, "We'll be married on paper only."

She spun around and marched right up to me. While she pointed her slender finger at my face, she growled, "Seriously? You expect us to be married for what"—throwing her hands up in exasperation—"months, years perhaps? And we won't share a bed. Is that what you're saying?"

Well, yeah. I thought that'd make her happy. Obviously, I was mistaken. "We don't love each other." *At least, you don't love me*. I wasn't so sure about me loving her. Which was just beyond fucked up, I *couldn't* love her. Or could I? Dammit. It was never going to work if I didn't get my head on straight.

She blinked her eyes furiously. Was she crying? *Way to go, Nik*. "Maybe not yet. But later…Well, we could eventually, right?"

I could hear the hope in that question. Time to quash it, so I lied, "No."

She gasped, "You won't even give us a chance?"

I can't, Aimee. Don't you see that? If I allow myself to love you, or worse, you love me, something bad will happen. It always does. "Many marriages don't have love involved. It's nothing new," I pointed out.

"Omigod! Do you really expect me to be caught in a loveless marriage for the rest of my life?" She was appalled, and honestly, so was I. What the hell was I thinking? She hissed, "So no sex? Am I supposed to live without it forever? Or find it elsewhere?"

Now that pissed me off. No way would I let her give that sumptuous body to another man. "Sex and love are not mutually exclusive. *You* of all people should know that."

She stamped her foot. "Did you just call me a whore?" she screamed.

What a frustrating woman! I had not called her that. How could she think such a thing? I snarled, "I would never call you something so vile. How dare you accuse me of such?"

"How dare I? Oh, Nik, you are beyond exasperating!"

"Me? Woman, you aggravate the hell out of me." With that, I turned and left the room. But I heard the glass shatter, along with her sobs. I knew I should turn around. Comfort her. At the very least, talk to her and share my thoughts. Not. Going. To. Happen. *I really am a bastard.*

*****

I needed to calm down, so I took a shower. Every cell in my body cried out for Aimee's. There was nothing I wanted more than to shove her against the wall and take her. No other woman had ever stirred my emotions like she did. Well, the exception was the beauty from that masquerade. Something about the masked goddess had called to me on an elemental level. I had to have *her.* Kind of like now. Who was I kidding? I was fighting a losing battle. If it were simply lust, I would act on it. Yet even in this agitated state, I knew it was more. Knew, I couldn't live with just one time. No, if I had sex with Aimee, I'd only want more. So, the solution was not to do anything stupid. *Yeah, right. Stupidity has never stopped you before.* As the visions of the masquerade played through my head, I stroked my enormous erection. Hell, I didn't know I could swell to this size. What was the connection between that one night from my past and Aimee? How could two different women cause the same reaction? Why had my wife not had such an effect on me?

This was exactly what I needed—release. I

poured more body wash into my hands and allowed myself the escape. As I pumped myself harder and faster from base to tip, I thought I heard a sigh. My eyes popped open as I tried to see through the steam on the shower door. Then I froze, literally, with my dick in my hands, as I recognized the figure watching me. *Aimee.* I held her gaze and began to stroke again. Without breaking eye contact, I grunted as I came harder than I ever had in my life. The orgasm wouldn't stop as I continued spurting the shower door and walls over and over again. *Holy shit. At this rate I won't have any left.* She stood there blatantly aroused, watching. The lust dancing in her eyes made her appear to be a goddess standing there before me. One pleased with the effect she had. *Minx.* Fine, I could play.

Once I cleaned myself up, I shut off the water, grabbed my towel, stepped out of the shower, and, without pause, stalked towards her. After I dried off, I clasped her waist and lifted her onto the vanity. I ran my hands through her hair and fisted it. Then I pulled her head back and ravaged her throat with my lips, tongue, and teeth. I continued to taste her until she was breathing rapidly. In response, she rubbed her body against mine like a cat in heat. *Fuck. Yeah.* When she arched her back, I could feel her nipples harden through her blouse and bra. Unable to resist such an invitation, I took one of them into my mouth. All the while she begged for more. Against her breast I whispered, "Take it off. All of it."

There was no hesitation as she bared herself to me. And I could do nothing else but step back and admire the beauty before me. "Lovely," I purred, "So damn perfect." Once more, I zeroed in on her voluptuous tits. They were enough to make a man weep with joy. There was no other choice, homage must be paid. Under my assault, her head thrashed back and forth. She was close, so close, but I didn't want to bring her this way. My fingers traveled down to the dripping crevice between her thighs. As I stroked her clit, she moaned deeply. "That's right, Aimee. Come for me." I circled the bundle of nerves again with my thumb and entered her hot core with two fingers. While my hand was busy between her legs, I once again laved, first one, and then the other nipple. I used my other hand to hold her in place by the waist and gave her no choice but to accept all I had to give. After a few moments, she broke apart. Damn, her detonation was spectacular. A smug, *yeah, I did that* echoed through my mind. And I had every intention of doing it again when we both heard:

"Oh, sorry."

Shit. Why was my brother here? Without taking my eyes off Aimee's I said, "Give me a minute, Alex."

He stammered, "Yeah…okay…I'll wait for you in the study."

Once he left, I asked, "Are you all right?"

Aimee's face was flushed a beautiful shade of pink. Unsure if it was from embarrassment or pleasure, I wrapped a robe around her. She finally answered, "I'm fine."

I walked into my bedroom and grabbed some sweats and a t-shirt from my dresser drawer. She stood in the doorway. As I passed her, I stroked her cheek. "We'll talk later, okay?"

"Alright." She turned and padded away.

I couldn't help but wonder what in the world I was going to do now. Like I had predicted, once I had a taste of her, I wouldn't want to stop. Damn it all to hell.

*****

Alex sat pensively on the chair in front of my desk with a scotch in his hands. Hell, this did not look good. After I filled my own glass, I took the chair next to him. "Lay it on me."

He shook his head. "I didn't realize the two of you had gotten so close."

I shrugged. "Neither here nor there. Talk to me."

He was affronted. "Don't give me your I-don't-give-a-crap attitude, Nik."

"You really wanna go there?" I snarled while giving him a baleful look.

He squirmed under my heated gaze and put his hands up in a surrendering fashion. "All I'm sayin' is you care." As I leaned forward, he wisely pushed back as far as possible in his seat. "You don't want to, but you do," he bravely stated.

Damn. I wasn't ready to own up to anything. My head, my heart, and my body were in knots over Aimee. I couldn't. No, wouldn't voice a thing. Not until I had some ounce of control back. Funny, self-control had never been an issue for me. Probably the reason why I was so good at business. Knee-jerk reactions weren't in my repertoire. *Until Aimee. You have no control around her. Oh, shut the fuck up*, I told myself. I stood and then strode across the room. After a beat, I finally proclaimed, "You're not here to discuss my love life."

"So, you admit to having one?"

For Pete's sake! "Why do you give a rat's ass?"

He gave me an are-you-shittin'-me look. "Because I love you, my brother. I thought that'd be obvious," he snorted.

Ah, hell. I loved him as well. But he knew I wouldn't say it. I crossed my arms over my chest and softened my voice. "It is. Tell me why you're here."

He chuckled, "Still can't admit to your feelings, can you? Not even for your own family. Sure hope Aimee knows what she's getting herself in to."

No, I couldn't. Every time I shared my emotions, I lost that person. I wouldn't risk my brothers' lives or anyone else's, ever again. For whatever reason I shared, "She agreed to marry me."

"No, shit. Congratulations, Nik!" he exclaimed as he walked over and clasped me on the shoulder.

Shame welled up, hot and heavy, along with a side of guilt. Not an easy mix to swallow. "It's not like that, Alex," I cautioned. "She needs protection from Reynolds. That's all. Just an agreement," I pointed out.

He smirked, "You keep telling yourself that."

I growled in response.

"Easy there, big guy. Reynolds is actually why I'm here," he announced.

That got my attention. "Is he, now?"

"Yep. I had a little chat with one of his goons. He was most forthcoming," he smiled.

Arrogant bastard. While my brother was a damn good attorney, he knew how to toe the line. He continued, "Let's just say, a certain business deal will go in his favor tomorrow."

Yes, I'd taught him well. "Learn anything new?" I inquired.

"Nope. Just confirmation on what we already had knowledge of."

"Fuck. When will the asshole mess up so we can catch him red-handed?" I asked exasperatedly.

"Your guess is as good as mine on that one, Nik," he replied.

My fist doubled up at my side. The need to handle things with brute force was tangible.

Alex didn't miss my inner turmoil. "He's going to screw up," he assured. "And when he does, we'll be waiting."

"Damn straight."

For emphasis we knocked knuckles.

He tossed back the rest of his drink, clapped me on the back, and headed out the door. On his way out he said, "I'll let you get back to business." Then he winked.

I called, "Alex?"

As he turned around, I flipped him off. Jerk-off actually laughed while he walked away. I stood there with a ghost of a smile on my face. *You will not pussyfoot around this*, I told myself as I worked up the courage to go talk to my future bride. For whatever reason, there was *purpose* in my stride when I walked down the hall to her room.

Chapter Fourteen
Aimee

After I had just experienced the best orgasm by a man's hand, I was a bit revved up. Soooo ready for more. If he could finger that well, how spectacular would his mouth be? Or, better yet, his cock? Geez, I needed a cold shower. Although thoughts of a shower brought back the image of Nik masturbating. Dang, that was hella hot! Sure, I'd seen plenty of men stroke-off, but there was something primal in his exhibition. I hadn't meant to walk in on him like that. Furious with the way he'd left the room; my intentions had been to tell him to forget it. I wasn't going to marry him, after all. Yet when I saw all of that hard, rugged maleness in the throes of self-pleasure, I *had* to watch. Of course, watching only made me want to join the party. When he prowled out of the shower, I knew I was a goner. Everything about the man screamed sex, especially, the dagger tattoo over his heart. Next time, I would trace it with my tongue.

I had only ever met one other man that had such an effect on me. Visions of that one amazing night at the masquerade played through my mind. It really was unfortunate I had left town only twenty-fours afterwards, which hadn't been on the agenda. However, Ann and Jack needed to move their business. Pronto. So naturally I tagged along with Renée, who would always follow the brother and sister team. To her they were a lifeline—the reason she wasn't selling herself on the streets.

In a matter of a few short weeks, I had learned of Daddy's cancer. As if that hadn't been a big enough blow, then his company decided to downsize and let him go. After twenty years of service, they just wished him well. No way would an escort job cover surgery and chemo. But that was all water under the bridge. I couldn't—no, wouldn't—regret my decision. *Now I'm caught in this pickle.* Marriage to Nik was a whole lot more inviting than to Caleb. At least there was attraction between Nik and me; also, deep in my soul, there was familiarity. Over time we could fall in love, if he'd only allow himself to feel. Of course that was the elephant in the room, Nik's lack of emotions. Maybe I could help him open up? *Possibly. But odds are you'll get hurt. He's a mess.* Yes, he was—yet worth the pain if I could somehow reach him.

All of this reverie wouldn't change what had just happened with Nik. There must be some way to crack through the walls he had so expertly built. From what I could see, he loved his brother. I was willing to bet he loved the youngest one as well. So he was capable, even if he refused to acknowledge it. How did I reach him? We had a connection; I simply needed to tap it. Perhaps physically was the way. Whether he admitted to it or not, sex could bring people closer together. It was the reason I had to be so careful in my previous *job.* To keep the emotions and mental bonding out of it was complicated. Could I now purposely let myself do what I'd spent five years avoiding? To save this man, I'd do whatever was necessary. Nik. Was. Worth. It. *At what price? You're going to lose your heart over this one.*

Probably. Yet sacrifice was all about that. Shoot, I had already begun to lose it to him. There was no stopping it. When the end came, hopefully, I would survive. Because let's face facts, inevitably he would push me away.

As if on cue, he appeared in my doorway. "How're y'doin'?"

With a smile I answered, "Good."

His lips curled up slightly. "Glad to hear it." He ran a hand through his incredible mane. "Listen, I'm sorry 'bout Alex's interruption."

"Seriously, it's okay. Although…" I sashayed towards him, figuring now was as good a time as any to seduce him. The sooner I had him, the better. When I approached him, I ran my hand up his gloriously hard chest and purred, "I would really like to get back to where we were before the disruption."

"Uh…" He cleared his throat while I watched him make up his mind. "About that. I shouldn't have done it."

"Which one?" As both memories hit me full force, I licked my lips.

By the look in his eyes, he remembered, too. "Both," he rumbled, not out of anger but sexual tension.

If he spoke long enough, I would orgasm. His voice was just that sexy. "Why's that?"

"I shouldn't have let you watch me," he admitted. "And I damn sure shouldn't have touched you."

"I walked in on you. I'm the one who needs to apologize," I confessed while I stroked his huge shoulder. "As for the other"—standing on tip toes and leaning in close enough for my lips to touch him—"I want you to do it again. Now," I whispered.

Before my hand could cup his magnificent manhood, he clasped it. "No. It won't happen again," he asserted.

What the hell? Was he serious? "Are you trying to tell me you're not attracted?" I let my gaze roam over the very spot I almost touched a moment ago. Oh, yes, he was aroused. Not to mention there was enough electricity between the two of us to light up all of Fifth Avenue. *No, I don't buy it.*

"Of course, I want you. That's fairly obvious," he declared. "But I'm choosing not to act on it."

"So, we're back to marriage with no love, as well as no sex. Correct?"

With his lips in a tight, thin line, he gave me a curt nod. "That's the way it has to be."

"Horseshit!" I threw my arms in the air and marched across the room. Once I was out of slapping range—because trust me, I wanted nothing more than to slap him silly—I pivoted around and exclaimed, "Hypocrite! You have fucked more women than I can count. Odds are, you've had more partners than I have. Your reputation of one-night-stands is phenomenal. You're a damn legend in this city. So don't you *dare* tell me it's best this way," I huffed.

He shrugged. "That may all be true. However, it doesn't change a thing."

I yanked open my robe and let it fall to my feet. Desire flared in his eyes as his erection actually grew more. He was interested, yet held himself back. Therefore, following my instincts, I began to stroke my breasts, rolling and tugging my nipples until I let out a moan. All the while I held his heated gaze to let him know I was thinking of his hands on my body. Then, I ran my hands down my body until I reached the apex between my thighs and dipped into my wet folds. His jaw tightened as his nostrils flared. No doubt he smelled my arousal.

"Lay down," he commanded, "Spread your legs wide."

Hell, yes. As I continued my self-exploration, I stepped backwards till I hit the edge of the bed. He strode forward, moving with animalistic grace. I assumed he would climb on the bed along side of me. I thought wrong. Instead, he fell to his knees at the end of the bed and tugged me downwards. Once my most private parts were at his eye level, he placed my heels on the edge while he pushed my knees as far apart as possible. With his chin resting on his folded hands, he announced, "Continue."

I paused for a moment. Did I really want to give him a show? Oh, hell yeah, I did. Without any more thought, my fingers began to work my sex. Since it was *his* show, he decided to call the shots. "Slower. Yeah, like that. Circle your clit for me, but don't touch the center."

O-M-G! This was beyond erotic. To prove my point, my hips writhed of their own accord.

He continued, "Use your other hand. Put your middle finger inside your core. Now, push in and pull out. Faster," he growled, "Add your ring finger. Harder."

I moaned loudly. And before I could hold back, I pled, "Please. I need to come."

"Not yet," he pronounced. "Easy. Move slower. Don't you dare touch the center of that swollen bundle of nerves."

I had never wanted to orgasm so bad in all my life. Then, he decided to blow over my sensitive womanhood. "Ah…Nik, I can't."

"Shh," he soothed. "Yes, you can. Take those two fingers and turn them up. Find your g-spot. Do not rub it," he ordered.

I did what he asked and bucked when my fingers came in contact with my oh-so-happy spot. I hissed, "Now?"

"Soon, baby," he assured.

I groaned in frustration. Bastard actually chuckled low in his throat and went on with his torture. "Remove the finger on your nub. Keep the other two inside you. Trace your secretions back over that muscle just below your entrance." *Damn!* "Keep stroking. Now, turn those two fingers up and rub that special spot." My eyes rolled back from the intensity. "Yes, like that."

He held me on the edge and refused to let me fall over. Just when I thought all hope of climax was over, he said, "With the hand inside you, use your thumb and rub your clit. Don't come," he demanded.

I swear the man was demented. My back bowed off the bed. He grabbed my ankles to hold me in place. "Again, stroke your g-spot."

My head began to thrash back and forth as he continued, "Faster. Harder. Push your thumb down on your clit. Now."

As I came in wave after wave, drenching the bed, I screamed. Still, I couldn't wrap my brain around the fact I'd done this to myself. Sure, I've pleasured myself in front of many clients, but never like that. Never had anyone directed what I did to my own body. There were no words for it. Nik released my ankles and pushed my body up the bed by my hips. While I lay there in post-orgasmic bliss, he grabbed the duvet. Once he'd seen to my comfort, he turned to leave. I mumbled, "Give me a few minutes. I'll be ready for you."

With a poignant look, he stood there for a moment and then commented, "No, I'm good. Get some sleep."

I wanted to argue with him. But the fact remained; I was spent—too wiped out to even speak again. I rolled over and began to slip into slumber, as he shut off the lights and closed the door.

My last coherent thought was, next time, Nik.

Your.
Turn.

Chapter Fifteen
Nik

What had I just orchestrated? Never had I been so domineering with a woman. Hell, usually I didn't care. Even though the women I'd been with had always climaxed. The least I could do. Yet, I had rules: like no kissing on either set of lips. Too damn intimate. Over the years I'd only made one exception, with no plans to do so again. Like most men, I loved to watch a woman manipulate herself into complete bliss. There was no opposition for her to use toys, either. Whatever she needed to achieve pleasure, I was cool with. But *this* experience was beyond the pale. *My God...after that, how do I keep myself from returning to Aimee tonight?* No matter how you looked at it, I was screwed six ways to Sunday.

When E rounded the corner, I'd never been so grateful to see him. He did not miss my state of upheaval. Astute. Plus, no doubt, he could smell Aimee on me. I sure could, inhaling deeply to luxuriate in her heady scent. My mouth actually began to water. *Shit!* Some kind of release was necessary. I locked eyes with my brother and directed, "Gym."

He chuckled, "Weights? Or are we going to have a go at it?"

Over my shoulder I asked, "Aren't you

worried I'll mess up that pretty face of yours?"

"Hell, no. Bring it," he taunted.

"Let's do this, then."

One of the things I loved about my youngest brother was his willingness to fight me anytime, anywhere. He was good, too—could have done well in the UFC medium-weight division. But his tastes ran to the extreme—of the kinky sort. He always found women willing to let him do all sorts of erotic acts to them. How was beyond my comprehension. Fact was people all over the world practiced in the lifestyle, which was how his clubs were so successful. Usually he trained others, rarely participating anymore. According to him, he'd grown bored with a lot of it. Still, I didn't buy it. My brother was not the type to go "vanilla." He *needed* a submissive. This phase wouldn't last long. And Heaven help the woman he unleashed all that pent up Dom frustration on. Sure hope she had some training; otherwise, I worried he might hurt someone from too much exotic sex.

Due to the direction my mind had taken me, E got in a fantastic side kick and knocked me on my ass.

"You may wanna get your head in the game, Nik," he gibed.

"Go ahead, keep talkin' smack," I mocked and then retaliated with a roundhouse, followed by three jabs and an upper cut to the jaw.

He stumbled backwards. "That all y'got?"

Smart ass. We had a great spar. I won, barely. As we mopped up the blood and sweat from the mat, he inquired. "So...Wanna tell me who I smell all over you?"

"Nope," I countered.

He shook his head. "No worries. I think I figured it out."

"You don't say."

He laughed. "I take it Aimee's still here?"

No sense in denying it. "Yeah, she is."

He nodded his head and asked, "Any news?"

"Alex and her best friend, Renée, confirmed it was Reynolds," I replied.

"Crap! What now?"

I shrugged my shoulders. "I marry her."

His eyes popped open wide as his jaw dropped. He opened and closed his mouth several times before he spoke, "Seriously?"

"As a heart-attack," I confirmed.

"Fuck." *Yeah, that about sums it up.* His eyebrows rose as he questioned, "So you decided to sample your future bride?"

"More or less."

Before we finished cleaning up, he clapped me on the back. "Well, then, I s'pose congrats are in order. Set a date, yet?"

"Nah. I need to talk to her about that." I began to walk towards the living room. "It needs to be soon."

*****

Aimee approached from the far hallway, as if our talking about her was a summons. She looked irresistible in my robe. Her rumpled hair fell over her eyes, which she tucked behind her ear. Then she realized someone else was with me and gasped, "Oh. I'm sorry. I didn't know anyone else was here."

I had to fight the urge to walk over and kiss her. Instead I introduced, "Aimee, this is Ev, my youngest brother. Ev, this is Aimee." I almost added: my fiancée.

He gave me an arch look—*yeah, he saw the resemblance*—before he held out his hand to her.

125

"Nice to meet you, Aimee."

As she shook hands with him, she responded, "You, as well."

I cleared my throat. "So, E was just asking me when the big day was."

"Well, I don't know." She cocked her head to one side. "Does it need to be soon?"

"Probably best," I hedged.

E chimed in, "Will you have a church wedding?"

Crap. I really hadn't thought about it. However, Aimee should have whatever she wanted. I held her gaze and affirmed, "I'm good with whatever you decide."

She shrugged one shoulder. "We'll see. I want Renée to be my maid of honor, so we need to wait until she heals from her injuries."

While I didn't want to wait, she'd made a fair point. "No arguments, here."

She had the look of surprise on her face, but she covered well. "Thank you. Also, I need to contact my parents. They'll want to be there, as well."

Shoot. I'd forgotten about that. Problem was, there wasn't any guarantee Reynolds wouldn't do something to prevent the wedding. Therefore, when I said, "We should have the wedding in your hometown," no one was more shocked than me.

"Really?!" A smile played on her lips.

Well, it hadn't been the plan, but I could see it made her happy. "Yes, really."

A full scale grin lit up her beautiful face. She was breathtaking. She walked over and hugged me, hard. "Thank you, Nik," she whispered.

E coughed. I shot him an irritated look. Then he addressed, "Congratulations, Aimee. I'm so happy for you and my brother."

Asshole! I mouthed over her head. He actually

had the gall to wink. I disengaged from Aimee's embrace and went to get a bottle of water. When I returned, E was talking to her. "Do you want a big wedding, Aimee?" he inquired.

"Not really," she replied.

Phew, that was good to know. I handed E some water and confirmed. "Once the details are hammered out, I'll let y'know."

"Works for me," he said before he took a long pull from his bottle. After he wiped his mouth with the back of his hand, he declared, "'S getting late. I better get home." He waved on his way to the foyer.

Aimee called, "See you soon, Ev."

"Yes, you will." He gave her his megawatt smile.

Little shit's gonna pay for that one.

*****

Once he was gone, I turned to her. "Been a long day. I'm hittin' the hay."

"It has," she confirmed as she stepped in front of me. But I wouldn't allow her to wrap her arms around me. The hurt in her eyes was something I didn't want to see again anytime soon. Yet, there really was no way around it because I knew I couldn't have a real marriage. As I escorted her to the guestroom, I put my hand on the small of her back. When we arrived, I held the door open for her and proclaimed, "This'll work out, Aimee, I promise. It won't be all bad. You'll see."

She shook her head. "You're one stubborn man, Nik. But you should know, I won't give up," she warned and then closed her door in my face.

I had to wonder, just how long could I keep up the façade that I didn't want her as much as she wanted me? I was already a helluva mess. My self-restraint wouldn't hold forever. *Then, what?*

Since sleep was out of the question, I decided work would be best. I didn't know how long I sat and stared at my laptop screen. But it eventually registered through the cobwebs in my brain; the spreadsheets weren't going to make sense tonight. As I poured another glass of brandy and contemplated the shit fest that had become my life, I wondered, for the millionth time, how sex wasn't going to be part of my marriage. *As if.* Aimee had been right; we couldn't live without it permanently. Again, the idea of another man near her raised my hackles. Big time. And the thought of lying with another woman made my stomach churn.

Once again, my mind shifted gears. For a hundredth time that night, I wished Rachel could give me insight. She'd always had a way of expressing things so I saw it from every perspective. If she had lived, she would have been a great partner in my business as well as my life. Unfortunately, she had been taken far too soon for us to see our dreams manifest. Of course, at the time, being a CEO of my own company had never been on my radar. *God, I miss her.* Once more, I fought the water works—which generally happened when I thought of Rachel. The fact it was because of *me* that she was no longer here drove the knife deeper into my heart. As I rubbed the dagger tattoo on my left pectoral, I tried to ease the pain of that night from my mind. It was no use. I pulled my guitar out of the closet. While I sprawled on the couch, the tune that was so familiar drifted through the room. The haunting melody came straight from my shattered soul.

> *Where do I go?*
> *Now, do I go?*
> *You took my heart and soul*

When you left me here
All alone

How do I go on?
Do I go?
You were all I ever loved
Now you've left me all alone

Where do I go now?
How do I go on?

I'm on my knees
I'm begging please
Angel, please come back to me

Where do I go now?
How do I go on?
You took my heart and soul
When you left me here
All alone

I'm on my knees
I'm begging please
I'm on my knees
I'm begging please

Angel, please come back to me

Chapter Sixteen
Aimee

Unable to find a comfortable position, I tossed and turned. Somewhere in my dreams was a song I couldn't place. Heartbreaking. How could so much torment be locked into something so beautiful? I cried and cried. I wanted nothing more than to wrap my arms around his wounded soul. Yet, in my dream state, I couldn't locate him. The man's voice growled in pain, which caused my soul to howl. I needed to find *him*—searching frantically through the penthouse, all to no avail. I awoke with a start and wiped my eyes. What was that dream—maybe nightmare was a better term—about? There was no music playing; thus, it must've been in my head. How strange. But that voice had been oddly familiar. What had awakened me? Before I could figure it out, I heard the soft strains of a guitar. I pulled on the robe Nik had let me borrow and padded out into the hall. *Let my quest begin.*

*****

The source of music didn't take long to find. Somehow, Nik's voice and the man's in my dream were one in the same. He sat on the couch in his study and strummed a tune I recognized; "Walk Away."

Wow, his deep and raspy voice added something new to the Linkin Park song. Did he sing that particular song because he liked it? Or was it a message? Surely, he didn't mean me. We were only just beginning. When he looked up and stopped playing, the question popped out of my mouth. "Is that how you see *our* future?"

His gaze dropped. It was all I needed for a confession. I queried, "So, you plan to walk? Or you think I will?"

He snorted, "It's inevitable, Aimee."

Oh, he was willing to talk. I asked, "How so?"

He blew out a heavy breath. "Have you Googled me?"

No point in denying it. "Yes, I have."

"Learn anything?"

"Nothing I didn't already know," I hedged.

His jaw tightened. "Expound, please."

"You're CEO of a multimillion dollar company, although I'm not sure exactly what you do."

A ghost of a smile played across his lips. Would I ever see him actually smile? "I buy out companies and/or properties that are in financial trouble."

I inclined my head. "Then you sell them to the highest bidder." I shouldn't judge him for that. Everyone had a right to make money.

He raised a brow. "Sometimes. But mostly, I help restructure them to be profitable."

Well, that changed things. "Thus, you don't *only* rescue damsels in distress."

He shook his head. "You're a far cry from needing to be rescued."

"How do you figure?"

"You're strong." He laid the guitar aside and patted the seat cushion next to him. I sat and pivoted towards him. He did the same, which brought us knee to knee. "Truthfully, you don't need me."

How wrong you are, Nik. I did need him. "But that's *not* true."

"Sure it is." He shrugged one heavily muscled shoulder. "You have all the right contacts to take care of yourself."

Really? "If that's the case, then why are we getting married?"

"Because Reynolds is like a bad rash, he won't go away with only one application of ointment."

I sat up straighter. "Are you saying he'll still be an issue even once we're married?"

"Yup," he confirmed.

Holy crap! "So why marriage?"

He ran his hand over his face and mumbled, "Hell, if I know."

"What'd you just say?"

He covered up the statement as he reasoned, "If you're my wife, it'll be harder for him to get a hold of you."

I hadn't missed his fabrication. "Don't *ever* lie to me."

He looked perturbed. "I'm not. The fact of the matter is, you're safer being married to me."

"Not about that! Before, you said 'hell, if I know.' "

"I don't have to explain myself." He stood and began to pace. "You *need* to marry me. That way, it'll be harder for him to try anything."

"Why would he bother?" This was what I couldn't understand. Sure, Caleb had been persistent. But if I left New York, he'd eventually give up. "It's not like I'm the only woman on the face of the earth."

He ran a hand through his hair. "True. But how long will that hold him at bay?"

Now I stood, placed my hands on my hips and stated, "Doesn't matter. He can't cause mortal damage. His career would be over. And he wouldn't risk that," I pointed out.

Nik countered, "You sure?"

Exasperated with where the conversation was going, I shouted, "Oh, please! Did he kill *your* Rachel?" Huge mistake! I shouldn't have ever mentioned his late wife. Pain, longing, anger, and several other awful emotions played across his rugged face. *Gee, I'd caused that.* At that moment, I wanted nothing more than to comfort him. Therefore, I stepped in front of him and apologized, "I'm sorry."

He glared at me and scoffed, "To answer your question: no, that's all on me."

Confusion caused my brows to lower, as I queried, "Come again?"

He didn't answer. Instead he walked away from me, and didn't stop until he faced the window behind his desk. "Rachel is not up for discussion. Ever," he growled.

Shoot. Now he was pissed off. "Okay," I reassured and then added, "For now."

"Go to bed, Aimee," he ordered.

Whoa, talk about whiplash. The man could change subjects faster than his sports car could reach sixty MPH. "Maybe I don't want to," I countered.

He calmly set his glass down on the desk and strode out of the room. *Oh, hell, no.* I followed him out. "Don't walk away from me, Nik."

He spun and gripped me by the shoulders. "It's settled," he demanded. "We're getting married. I don't have to like it, and neither do you. But it's happening. Now, leave me. The. Fuck. Alone."

With that he stormed away. And I was left standing there to ponder: What in heaven's name was I going to do about the situation at hand? Then it hit me, I'd handle this. After all, it was my mess. Nik seemed to think I was strong. Time to find out just how tough I really was. One thing was for certain, I wouldn't marry a man that couldn't love me. Therefore, I needed to clear the air with Caleb and move on.

* * * * *

After a much needed shower, I dressed and snuck out of the penthouse. No easy task with the armed security Nik had hired. Yet somehow I had managed. I beelined to the airport and bought my ticket for a five thirty in the morning departure to D.C. Caleb and I were going to come to an agreement. I purchased a coffee and hit shuffle on my iPod. While I waited to board the airplane, the song "Before It Began" by Olivia Somerlyn began to play. Appropriate. Although I knew this thing with Nik could never work out, a part of me felt bereft. In such short amount of time, the difficult and complicated man had worked his way under my skin. Doubtful, I would ever truly erase our short time together. Driven to distraction, no one was more surprised than me when suddenly Senator Caleb Reynolds sat down next to me.

He reached over and pulled my ear buds off. "Going somewhere, my dear?"

It just kept getting better and better. *Not!* "Why are you here?" I asked while I shut off my iPod and put everything back in my purse.

He smiled in that cheesy politician way and pointed out, "I could ask you the same question."

Well, I wanted an audience with the man. No time like the present. "We need to talk," I asserted.

"I agree. Why don't you come with me?" He motioned towards the exit.

Funny, but that door didn't lead back through airport security. Red flags went up instantly, along with some serious bells ringing. Maybe Nik's paranoia had rubbed off. No way was I going anywhere with Caleb. Better to be safe than sorry. "I'm fine right here."

He inclined his chin but didn't argue. "As you wish."

I nodded, "How do I get you to take me at my word?"

He gasped, "Aimee. Are you insinuating that I called you a liar?"

Oh, he was good. I'd give him that. "No. Not at all, Caleb," I responded innocently.

He ran the back of his fingers along my cheek. For some reason, it gave me the heebie-jeebies. I fought to control the shiver down my spine. "Glad to hear that. You know I'd never harm you." *No, dammit, I don't know that!* "Tell me you're not afraid of me," he insisted.

I couldn't do that. All of a sudden, I became very aware of the danger he presented. Best to be honest, so I confided, "I can't."

He clucked, "I see. How can I ease your fears?"

While I held his gaze, I squared my shoulders and answered, "Let me go."

He shook his head. "I was hoping it wouldn't come to this."

Wait a minute! Who did he signal with two fingers? All of a sudden, a hard hand firmly grasped my upper arm. Then Caleb warned, "You will leave with Mr. Jones without any drama. Clear?"

Damn. Now what do I do? I looked frantically around for *anyone* who could help me. However there was no one. Double damn! *Think, Aimee. Think.* I came up empty. Then I recollected hearing somewhere, the moment you left crime scene A and went to crime scene B you were as good as dead. *Lord, a little help here, please.* Nothing. Once again, I came up empty handed. Not to mention I was out of ideas. Great. What now? I was forced to my feet and joined by, yet another, monster of a man. Through the exit I noticed earlier, I was escorted out of the airport. There, a heavily tinted Escalade waited on the ramp. *OMG! Not only am I going to die, no one will even realize I'm gone.* I could be missing for hours before it was reported. If ever. By then, there'd be no clues as to where I might be. Hell, at least I could try and fight. I dug in with my heels and shouted, "Get your hands off me!"

A burly arm came around my waist and lifted me into the vehicle. The driver calmly pulled away and drove towards a side exit gate. Where were they taking me? *Oh, Nik, I'm so sorry I didn't listen.* We drove off into the predawn horizon. And all I could think was, *I didn't even get to say goodbye.*

Chapter Seventeen
Nik

Something wasn't right. I bolted from my bed, trusting my gut instinct. Crap. This wasn't good. I grabbed a pair of jeans, yanked them on and then stepped into the hall. I began to search the penthouse. For what, I didn't know. When I reached for the door to the guestroom Aimee occupied, tiny hairs on the back of my neck stood at attention. Before I entered, a sick feeling came across me. As I walked inside, I looked for her. There was no sign of her or her purse. Not good. Right then and there I knew she was gone. How had she left the premises without my team noticing? Time to find out.

While I marched into the living room, I called my lead security guy on duty. "Where is she?" I hollered, "What do you mean you have no idea!" I tried my best to hold some sort of composure as I dangerously whispered, "You and your team have two minutes to get your asses up here." I almost threw my cell phone across the wide expanse of the room but, at the last minute, realized she might try to call. This was all kinds of FUBAR.

As I paced with restless energy, I replayed the last time we had spoken. She actually left me. Problem was, I couldn't really blame her. Who wanted to be shackled to a loser like me? Now she was in danger. For that I had no doubts. Caleb would seize the opportunity. Damn. Didn't she know that? I mean, why would I insist on marriage if I thought he wasn't a very real threat? *She doesn't know you, Nik.* No, no one did. I kept everyone at arm's length and refused to show any emotion—never permitting my heart to get involved. *What heart?* Yeah, that was an issue. God damned me long ago for my sins. There was no coming back from it. The elevator opened and out stepped three huge guards—though, none of them were quite as big as me. I barked, "Well?"

José held up his hands in a surrender gesture and inquired, "When did you notice her missing?"

I ran both hands through my hair and answered, "'Bout five minutes ago."

He stalked towards Ray's office while the others followed in his footsteps. What was he…? Ah, right, security cameras. Duh. I hoped to hell they gave us some clue as to where she was. Otherwise…*Nope, not going there*. José pulled me back to reality. "There, sir." He was pointing to the screen.

Sure enough, it was Aimee climbing into a taxi. "Can we get a bead on the cab company?" I queried.

At the same time, one of the other guys, Lee, asked, "How 'bout a number?"

Good thinking. I knew I liked working with them.

"Well, would you look at that," José said.

"What do y'know," Lee chimed in, "Looks like we found both." Before I could give the directive to call the company, George was on it.

A couple of minutes passed before he ended the call. George nodded, "Got it."

"And?" I bit out.

"LaGuardia," he answered.

She got on a plane. Going where? Dammit.

She just *thought* the spanking I'd once given her hurt. When I got my hands on her, so help me. I grabbed a shirt on my way out of the penthouse. José was right beside me. "We'll find her, sir. Don't worry."

Easier said than done.

While we scoured the airport, I was more than a little surprised to see Caleb. He was reclining in the First Class Lounge. With a cup of coffee in hand, he inclined his head once our eyes met. SOB. I wanted nothing more than to beat the ever-loving shit out of him. Right. Now. My blood was set to boil. Every muscle in my body poised to strike. There was no point in attempting civility. I didn't give a rat's ass who overheard us or saw us together. "Where the hell is she?!" I whispered dangerously.

"Ah, Nik," he greeted. "So nice to see you again. Please, join me."

"Cut the crap, Reynolds."

His elegant brow arched. "Now, now. Is that the way you greet all of your old friends?"

I growled, "We were *never* friends."

He mocked, "Acquaintances, then."

"Whatever." I held his gaze insistently. "Tell me what you've done with her."

"Why, Nik," he said haughtily. "How could you ever falsely accuse me?"

I flexed my hands, fighting hard the urge to wipe the smug look off his aristocratic face. "Do not play coy with me," I warned.

"Or what?" His eyes widened.

Fuck. It took all I had to hold myself together. But getting arrested would not help me find Aimee. I sneered, "Talk."

"Now see, there's your problem. No diplomacy, whatsoever."

I cracked my knuckles and squared my shoulders.

He held his hand up in a surrendering fashion. *Pussy!* "Am I to assume you are inquiring about the lovely Ms. Taylor?"

"You know damn good and well that's who we're talking about."

He chuckled, "No need for expletives, Nik."

Man, I loathed this guy with every fiber of my being. My skin crawled just being in his presence. "You bring out the best me," I countered.

He smiled, "Yes, well. Rest assured, I mean her no harm."

Bullshit! He was obsessed with her; however, I couldn't very well point that out. Could I? No, best not to show my hand at this point in the game. "Then tell me where to find her."

"I give you my word, I'll return her shortly."

His word wasn't worth crap. But, at the moment, he had me by the balls. "She won't marry you," I stated.

"That remains to be seen. I admit, I handled things in the wrong fashion. However, I plan to rectify that."

How? "I swear, Reynolds, you harm one hair on her head and I'll make you pay."

His eyes widened. "Are you threatening me?"

"Not at all."

Just then, his cell phone chimed. "One moment, please," he said before he answered it. "Yes. How is our guest? By all means, put her on the phone." He grinned wickedly at me. "Ah, Aimee dear, I do hope your ride was most pleasurable." I could hear Aimee cursing in his ear. "I see. Well, that's impossible at the moment. Once we have conversed in person, I will happily return you to Mr. Strand, here. Yes, he's sitting in front of me as we speak." He handed me the phone. "She would like to speak with you. Briefly," he cautioned.

Yeah, fuck that. "Aimee? Are you all right?" Even I heard the concern in my voice. Could she?

"I'm so sorry, Nik," she apologized. "I just wanted to talk to him. I didn't think…"

No, she didn't. But that was neither here nor there. We needed to get her away from him safely. "Hey." I reassured, "We're good." Reynolds motioned for his cell. "I have to go. I'll see y'soon," I promised her.

Her voice trembled as she said, "Okay."

I returned the cell to Reynolds. "Here y'go."

He nodded with approval. What I wouldn't give to throttle him. *Get it together, Nik. She's at his mercy.* Yes, she was. He began, "Aimee, my dear, I'll be there shortly. Decide what you would like for breakfast." With that he ended the call. She was somewhere close by. Where would he have her? He looked up at me. "See. She's unharmed."

For now. "What do you want with her?"

He shrugged one shoulder and replied, "I want her to agree to be my wife."

Like hell. For whatever reason, I had a gut feeling there was more to it than that. I barely held it together as I acknowledged, "That's her decision. Only hers."

Both of his brows rose. "But, of course."

I'd had enough. I stood and vowed, "One hair on her head, Reynolds, and you'll wish you'd never met me."

He laughed without humor. "I wished that a long time ago."

My fists doubled of their own accord. José approached in the nick of time. I inclined my head, then pivoted and strode away.

Once out of Reynolds' hearing range, I asserted, "Tell me you found her."

"We have a make and model on the SUV she

left in," José confirmed.

"Any leads?"

"Not yet."

Damn. "What now?"

"You're not going to like what I have to say," he cautioned.

"Probably, right. Hit me."

"Go home and wait."

"Hell, no," I countered.

"Very well," he ceded. "Let's see if we have a lead."

*****

As we climbed into the back of my black Mercedes SUV, George acknowledged, "We have a location."

"Go," I growled.

I had no idea where we were going or if we could rescue her. All I did know was that she needed to be safe. I couldn't bear the thought of the alternative. My anxiety shown through as I barked, "Drive faster."

Chapter Eighteen
Aimee

With plenty of time to ponder this epic mistake, my thoughts continuously returned to Nik. Though he didn't sound angry with me over the phone, my sixth sense told me he would be once he knew I was safe. Couldn't really blame him, I was furious with myself. *What am I going to do if Caleb won't release me?* Not going there. Surely after letting Nik speak with me, he wouldn't try anything. Would he? Trouble was, I just didn't know. This waiting around crap was bound to drive me insane. As if on cue, the door opened and in strode Caleb. Hard to believe I ever thought he was handsome. When I looked at him now, the visage of a rat was clear as day. How had I missed the evil that undulated out from him? Out of self-defense I stepped back. Guess it shouldn't have surprised me. I mean, the last time we were in a hotel suite together he attacked me. My self-preservation instincts were working overtime at the moment.

His brows arched as he studied my stance and demeanor. He motioned with his hand as he announced, "Have a seat, my dear. We have much to discuss."

Crapola. The last thing I wanted to do was play nice-nice with the douchebag. *Really. What choice do you have?* I sat as far away from him as possible. "Why am I here, Caleb?"

"We'll get to that in a moment." He removed his suit coat and loosened his tie. "Have you decided on what you would like for breakfast?"

I raised an eyebrow at him and proclaimed, "Not hungry."

"You need to eat." With that, he picked up the phone and placed a room service order. Once finished, he sat at a respectable distance. Huh, luring me into false security? "First off, how are you?" he inquired.

Seriously! Like he cared? "Cut the act," I demanded. "You don't really care one way or the other."

He scoffed, "You're wrong about that, Aimee."

What was his game? I snorted, "That why you attacked me the last time we were together?" Ha! He actually blanched. Good.

He nodded, "I owe you an apology for that. My emotions were running high"— holding his hand up to stop my interruption—"however, that's no excuse for my behavior."

"Whatever." Should I bring up the ransacking of my apartment? What about the attack on Renée? Was it wise to show my hand at this point? "You wanted to speak in person. So, talk," I insisted.

He chuckled, "Yes, well. I do believe you wanted to converse with me as well, correct?"

A fact I'd made clear earlier—no need to lie about it now. "Yes."

He waved his hand and announced, "By all means, ladies first."

Lady? Yeah, right. Lady of the evening was more like it. Before I responded, I pondered. I needed to do this just right, I held his gaze. "Why did you harm Renée to give me a message?"

"You ran from me. To my adversary, *no less*," he sneered slightly, yet his voice remained calm. "If she'd cooperated, she wouldn't have been hurt," he stated reasonably.

I knew I couldn't very well argue with him on that. Renée wasn't exactly known for her conversational skills. Especially if someone she loved was in danger. She would go to her grave before she'd rat you out. Loyal to a fault. None of that changed the fact: He'd threatened me via my best friend. No way would I let him get away with it. I squared my shoulders, lifted my chin and asserted, "'Marry you or else.' Wasn't that what your thugs told her?"

He had the decency to appear chagrined. *Please*. "I do believe I have been misrepresented."

"You don't say," I added with mock dismay.

"No need to be facetious," he scolded.

Just who did he think he was? He was the one who had Renée beaten-up as a form of communication. "You have some nerve!" I accused, "She would not be in the hospital if it hadn't been for you. Do not play innocent."

He apologized, "I am sorry she has suffered as a result of a poor judgment call. Rest assured, I have fired the men involved in that unforeseeable incident."

Well, that was news, but didn't change the fact it'd happened. Nor that it was under his orders. He obviously thought I was gullible. "Doesn't change the outcome—your men, your responsibility."

He ceded, "You may be right about that. Although I am sorry she was injured. I'll make sure her hospital bills are covered. Along with that she'll receive income until she's able to work again."

"Why would you do such a thing?" I asked incredulously.

"As you pointed out, it is my albatross. I do not slack on my obligations," he affirmed.

Duh. What kind of politician would he be if he did? The fact that all the ones I had been involved with were two-faced shouldn't have changed a thing. I mean, looking out for numero uno was the code in D.C. Well that, and—you scratch my back, and I'll scratch yours. I was more than ready to leave that life behind me. "Fair enough," I abdicated. "However you need to understand—I. Will. Not. Marry. You."

"Why is that, exactly?" he inquired wholeheartedly.

Never forget he's acting sincere, I reminded myself. Nevertheless, I owed him honesty on this. "I'm not in love with you."

He chuckled, "But…"

I held up my hand. "There's no but. And before you say love has nothing to do with marriage, let me be perfectly clear, I won't *ever* love you."

He placed his hand over his heart. "You wound me."

I rolled my eyes. "I cannot be married to a man I have no hope of ever loving."

"Ouch!"

"It may sound cruel, but it's the truth."

He nodded, "Point made. I only wanted the reason."

Now *that* I did not buy. Nonetheless, there wasn't any point in arguing with him. If it could end amicably, then, by all means, I was for it. "Nothing more?"

We were interrupted by room service. I took the respite offered. For I knew he would drop an H-bomb sooner or later. In order to prevent his hounding, I ate half a slice of toast, couple bites of eggs, and a piece of bacon. Grateful for the coffee, I sat and waited for the shoe to drop. He did not disappoint.

"You were correct. Love is neither needed nor wanted for me to be married to you."

I set my mug down. "What's in it for you? My previous occupation would ruin you."

"Are you willing to sacrifice your reputation?"

I contemplated that. Not worried about me, per se, more concerned with my parents. If the fact that I'd been a call-girl got out to them, they would be devastated. Truth be told, that was probably what I would have to do in order for him to leave me alone. I stared at him intently. "Yes," I answered unwaveringly.

"Well, then," he gasped.

No doubt, I had shocked him. Yet his cunning knew no bounds. "I hope it doesn't come to that."

Something had changed. He had the strangest look in his eyes, as if a veil had just been lifted. And he was...? There were no words for his expression. After a beat, he revealed his true self. "You. Lying. Bitch."

"I beg your pardon."

All of a sudden, the table and all its contents went flying. He reached for my throat. I had barely dodged his hands before I ran towards the door. "How *dare you* pretend to be someone you're not," he bellowed.

No clue as to what he was talking about, I pled, "Caleb? I don't understand. What are you talking about?"

He roared, "Shut the fuck up!"

On cue, there was a knock at the door. Then I heard my savior's voice. "Open the door, Aimee."

Nik. Oh, thank God! I reached for the knob but was shoved out of the way. I screamed, and that was when the door flew open. I tucked myself into a ball to avoid being hit by said door as I rolled out of the way. This time there was no fight. Before I could blink, Caleb was in a choke hold. Nik assisted me up to my feet. "Are you all right?" There was concern etched in his eyes.

"Yeah." I added, "He didn't touch me." By the look on Nik's face, I realized that statement saved Caleb's life.

He pivoted. "Get him out of my sight."

José escorted Caleb out of the room. But not before he declared, "If I ever see you again, I will kill you for impersonating *her*."

What. The. Hell. I had no clue who "*her*" was. I shook my head as shivers traveled up and down my spine. That look in his eyes was going to give me nightmares for the rest of my life.

Nik's gaze traversed between us. Once Caleb was out of sight, he queried, "What did he mean?"

I sank to my knees. "I have no idea." My voice trembled.

"Hey. Let's get you out of here." He reached down and lifted me into his arms. I folded in on his muscular chest, needing the comfort and warmth his body provided. I had never been so terrified. Plus, I knew beyond a shadow of doubt Caleb meant what he had said. Annnnnnd didn't that just suck.

*****
Caleb

Un-fucking-believable! The audacity of that wretched wench pretending to be someone she was not. She'd pay for that. I grabbed my phone and placed a call to my right-hand man. "Joe? Yeah, I need another one. Right. I should arrive in D.C. this afternoon. Uh-huh, same location. You know the drill."

Just what I needed to let off steam, some crack-whore no one would miss. Easy pickings, they came a dime a dozen. And I knew full well what was in store for her. With that knowledge, I rubbed my growing erection. It'd been awhile since I'd *played*. Yes, I was looking forward to it. Still, the need to teach Ms. Taylor a lesson was at the top of my to-do list. How, exactly, would I go about it? Strand would make sure to keep her well-guarded. Hell, wouldn't surprise me if he went ahead and married her himself. That was what I'd do in his position—which meant, I had my work cut out for me. Good thing I loved a challenge. If there was a way to kill two birds with one stone, I'd have it made. And wouldn't that be a dream come true. The bastard had escaped my last attempt. Next time, he wouldn't be so lucky. No, I'd learned a few tricks in the past few years. Quite frankly, taking a life was as easy as taking candy from a baby, even if the prostitute I was with wasn't high.

Where there's a will there's a way.

I sat in my private jet and pondered all the possibilities. To plan murder took time and effort. *Like the last time you went after Strand?* Shut-up! I lacked experience then. All of a sudden, Rachel ethereally appeared next to me—like so many times before—she smiled at me and declared, "I believe in you, Caleb."

I held her hand. "No worries, baby. I promise you, I'll take care of everything."

I closed my eyes and envisioned our life together. This was precisely what we needed to be happy forevermore. Nik must die. And so did the trollop who had impersonated my beautiful Rachel.

*****

Aimee

Curled up in Nik's lap, I felt protected. Not just due to his size—which did help immensely—no, it was also his compassion and sense of honor. He tried so hard to keep his walls up. "Let no one in" was his motto. But every now and then, I got a glimpse of the wounded man inside. I only wanted to know more of *him*. As I snuggled in close, I could feel the electricity humming between our bodies. I wanted him like never before. Would he let me breach his barriers this time? There was only one way to find out. Before I could put the moves on him, the SUV unfortunately came to a stop. After a beat, the door opened. He easily climbed out with me in his arms and whispered, "Let's get you inside and comfortable, okay?"

"Sounds good to me," I murmured into his chest. Heavens, he smelled good. And I knew once the opportunity presented itself, I *would* have this man.

Totally and completely.

Chapter Nineteen
Nik

Every cell in my body screamed at me to take Aimee straight to my bed and have my wicked way with her. This close, with her scent all around me, I wasn't sure I could resist much longer. My arousal was downright painful. Fact was, she didn't need this right now. She was almost attacked, again. Although this time, something was off with Caleb. Things were about to go DEFCON 5 before I walked into the hotel suite. What set him off? Why was he convinced she was impersonating someone else? For that matter, who? No, the last thing I needed to do was act on my lust. I had to admit, if only to myself, I was losing not only the battle, but the desire to stay away from her. It was only sex. So, why shouldn't I act on it? She wanted me as much as I wanted her. We're consenting adults. What was the harm? *Because you're half in love with her already, idiot. What happens when you give in? Where will that leave your precious memories? How could you betray Rachel that way? Besides, doesn't Aimee deserve all of your heart?* No matter what, I couldn't give her something I no longer had. That would be beyond unfair. *Who says life's fair?*

I was thankful Alex and E were here. With their help, we could work out a strategy to keep Aimee safe. Not to mention she really should rest.

And I needed some distance from her. I walked into the guestroom and placed her on the bed. I attempted to smile. "My brothers are in the other room. Get some rest." I clasped her hand for reassurance. "We'll talk later, okay?"

When she tugged on my hand, I had to take a step closer. She stretched upwards and kissed my cheek. "Thank you, once again." She pulled back and let go of my hand. "I'm not sure I would've been able to handle Caleb by myself." She shook her head. "No, that's not true. I doubt I would've left there in one piece if you hadn't shown up when you did."

"Glad I could be of some assistance," I acknowledged.

She half-smiled. "Yeah, I'm feeling rather grateful at the moment."

Oh, hell no. You will not ask her to show you how much. I swear, around her I seemed to have only thoughts of sex. Not good. I was a grown man, not a teenage boy. I *could* and *would* control my lust—even if it killed me. I assured, "I'll be here for the rest of the day if you need me." With that, I closed the door and strode into the living room where my brothers sat, waiting.

* * * * *

In desperate need of a drink, I hit the bar across the room first.

Alex inquired, "Everything all right, Nik?"

At the same time E chimed in, "'Sup, brother."

I shook my head to clear my thoughts. They were daylight and dark. Unsure of what that made me, I replied, "No. This has become a clusterfuck. I don't have any idea what's going on here." I squared my shoulders and said something I thought I'd never say. "I could use some help from both of you."

That got their attention. Alex instantly stood. E leaned forward on the sofa with his elbows braced on his knees, held my gaze intently and said, "Tell me what you need."

Alex nodded as he approached, clapping me on the shoulder. "Anything," he vowed. "I'll help in any way I can."

I knew I didn't deserve their loyalty. As I began to pace, I took a gulp of the fiery liquid out of the glass I held and then laid my cards on the table. "Here's the deal. Caleb went bat-shit on Aimee today." Alex's brow furrowed, as E stood. I began to fill them in on the events of that morning. Once they were up to speed, E claimed, "He won't touch her. What's your plan of action?"

I chuckled without mirth. "Time to take a trip to the altar."

He whispered, "Fuck me."

Yeah, that about summed it up.

Alex was far more level headed on the issue. "Marriage will definitely make any attempt to harm her more difficult. I think the sooner you say 'I do' the better."

No, shit Sherlock. I wasn't exactly whistling Dixie here. "It'll happen ASAP," I affirmed. "But what I can't put my finger on, is who does Caleb think she's posing as? Something just doesn't add up here." I took a deep breath to fortify my next confession. "She's not the only one in danger."

Alex sat down and stroked his jaw thoughtfully. "What makes you suspect that?"

I threw my hands up. "Hell, if I know. Call it a hunch."

"Hmm."

E glanced over at him. "Whatcha got, Alex?"

"Well, I can see where Reynolds would think

Nik is a threat as well."

Yup, my thoughts exactly. E then voiced our cooperative thought, "Wouldn't be the first time."

"No, it wouldn't," I confirmed. "See the dilemma?"

Alex glanced up at me as he concluded, "If he gets a chance, odds are, you won't survive."

E piped up, "Wait! Was it ever proven Nik was the intended victim in the accident?"

Alex had suspected that for some time. I stalked away to stare out the window and was suddenly there all over again: I remembered frantically pumping my brakes. Rachel's screams as the deer stood in the middle of the road and stared into the headlights; the storm which had blocked nearly all visuals. How the brakes refused to catch as the car careened out of control and down the embankment, finally coming to an abrupt stop against the huge pine tree with a sickening *thunk*. God, I couldn't do this. Yet my brain refused to snap back into the present.

E called, "Nikko. Nik, can you hear me?"

I braced my hands against the floor to ceiling glass, panting. I fought the urge to scream and nodded once, hard. Alex and E came up on the either side of me; then, both of them placed a hand on each of my shoulders. Alex soothed, "We've got you."

E affirmed, "Always."

I continued to focus on breathing while I let the images pass. Once I had my act together, I mumbled, "Thanks." Then I carefully disengaged from their hold. Their unfailing love never ceased to humble me. Even now, I couldn't process it. Someday I hoped I could voice my love for them. *No, you can't. If you do, they'll die.* Would they? Or was that just fear talking? Aimee's presence was messing with not only my body, but my mind as well. Normally emotional crap didn't even hit my radar. Truth, my apathy knew no bounds. So why, suddenly, did I want to embrace them and tell them what they meant to me? I needed another drink, so I went to the bar for a refill.

Alex inquired, "Do you need me to make arrangements with the justice of the peace?"

"Nah," I replied. "Aimee deserves to have her wedding in her hometown. As soon as she lets me know the whens and wheres, I'll have my assistant, Jamie, work out the details."

E's brow quirked. "You're actually having a wedding?!"

I understood his reaction, and was not a little surprised at myself that I'd suggested such a thing. "Yeah," I confirmed. "She deserves some form of normalcy. Plus, there will be a level of comfort for her where she grew up, don't y'think?"

"It's a great idea," Alex approved and then shot me a peculiar look. "Are you sure *you'll* be all right?"

Hell no! Yet there wasn't really another option. For whatever reason, I wanted Aimee to have her special day. Forget the fact it was a marriage in *name* only. No way was I prepared to dive into the whys of the feelings that were stirring deep within me. Just was. I craved to provide for her in any way possible, as well as protect her. And the possessiveness I felt was only growing stronger with each passing minute.

"So, who's your best man?" E smiled.

I shook my head and answered, "I can't very well choose between the two of you."

Alex shrugged. "I'm cool with E having his turn."

I sighed heavily. How had I forgotten Alex was there at Rachel's and my wedding? Though, he wasn't eighteen at the time so he couldn't be my best man—well, official witness. I asked, "No hard feelings, Alex?"

"None whatsoever," he assured. "We're good."

I walked over to E and clapped his shoulder. "You asked for it."

His grin was downright contagious. I actually cracked a smile at the same moment Aimee stepped into the room. With an odd expression, she stood there staring at me. If I didn't know any better, I'd swear she wasn't breathing. I looked to my brothers for some sort of insight. E shrugged his shoulders while Alex strode over to her and asked, "Everything all right, Aimee?" When he laid his hand on her upper back, I actually growled. E's surprised look made me aware of just how loud I'd been. Alex immediately dropped his hand, all the while Aimee blinked hard several times.

She finally took a deep breath. I was right, she had been holding it. Why was that? "So, the wedding's still on?" she asked as she held my gaze insistently. I nodded. Then, she shocked the hell out of me when she asserted, "Were you planning on asking me? Or do I have a say?"

Whoa! What'd I miss here? Alex and E politely left the room to give us some privacy. I stalked towards her and queried, "Didn't we already settle this?"

She threw her hands up in exasperation. "Really?!" she exclaimed as she began to pace. "A wedding isn't a business agreement!" she yelled.

"I beg to differ," I countered.

"You would," she huffed as she pivoted to face me. "In case you missed something, I *left* you this morning."

I growled, "Yes. And you see where that got

you."

She marched up to me and began to poke my chest with her forefinger. "I'm fully aware of my error. *But* it doesn't mean I'll go through with this farce of a wedding."

I grabbed her by the shoulders and hauled her up against me. "It's the only way to keep Reynolds away from you," I warned.

"You're hurting me," she cried.

Instantly I let her go, but I didn't step back. Neither did she. "Surely you can see this is the only answer," I imparted.

She shook her head in denial, yet I could see it in her eyes—she was quickly coming to the same conclusion. "But what if..."

I leaned down to where our mouths were only an inch apart. *What are you doing? Back off now before you kiss her.* "No buts. No what ifs."

Her little, pink tongue snaked out to lick her bottom lip. I wanted to taste her right then and there. Unfortunately—or fortunately, depending on how you wanted to look at it—Alex interrupted us. "I'm sorry for the intrusion." He inclined his head towards Aimee and then held my gaze. "We have a situation, Nik," he announced.

"Now?" I inquired with irritation.

"Afraid so." He had the decency to look apologetic.

"Okay." I turned my attention back to Aimee and declared, "We'll work out the details in a little while, alright?"

She half-smiled. "I'll see you when you're finished."

I stepped away from her and followed my brother into the study. If I went by his purposeful stride, along with the staid look on E's face when I entered, this was not something I wanted to hear. *Ah, shit. What now?*

Chapter Twenty
Aimee

For all intents and purposes, I was getting married in the very near future. Put a whole new twist on "for better or for worse" when I considered the circumstances. Should I really marry a man I hardly know? Again with the niggling sensation in my gut, that, somehow, some way I did know Nik Strand. Well, duh. I mean, we had shared some intense moments. Doubtful the image of him pleasuring himself would ever truly disappear, not to mention him talking me through my own escapade. Yeah, I did know him intimately. Although I felt as if there were more, like I was missing something crucial. But what? Once more, I searched my memories, trying in vain, to figure out just how and/or where we could've met before. Nothing. *Gah, how frustrating!*

As I approached the guestroom, the memory of his almost kiss began to haunt me. What would it feel like to have his sculpted mouth on mine? Better yet, to have those lips on my most private ones. Warm liquid pooled low at the thought. Clearly, I was not going to be able to stay away from him. If he really thought we could live without sex for any length of time, he was sorely mistaken. That smile of his nearly brought me to my knees right there in front of his brothers. Yes, we seriously were going to have to revise that part of our agreement. No way would I keep my hands—or anything else, for that matter—to myself.

It was quite the challenge to avoid touching myself as those thoughts danced through my head. I searched for a diversion and decided it was time to call my parents. The conversation went very well, all things considered. How often did your only daughter call and announce she'd be home soon with a bridegroom in tow? As always, my parents conveyed nothing but love for me, along with respect for my decision to marry a man they'd never even heard of before today. Mom concluded, "We can't wait to meet the man that's finally swept our girl off her feet."

Shoot. How to counter that without giving anything away? "I'll let you know the details once we have everything hammered out here. I love you both."

Dad ended our call with, "We love you more, sweetie."

If they only knew. No, that could never happen. I needed to remind Nik not to inform them of the truth about me. Goodness, they'd never recover from that info. And to think, I would have let Caleb tell the whole world. Truth was, I still would if that was what it took to get him to leave me alone. Well, didn't make a difference anymore. Yet I wondered for the hundredth time, who did he think I was impersonating? Geez, the look on his face was pure malevolence. Like the devil himself had marked me as his target. Ooh, that thought caused a horrid chill. What I needed at the moment was a hot bath. My mission as I entered the bathroom: locate soothing salts. Before I called Renée or faced off with Nik once more, I definitely had to get my head on straight. After I put my iPod on shuffle, I sunk into the almost too hot tub of water. As I lay back and closed my eyes, Jae Camilo's "Under My Spell" began to play. Yeah, if only that was the case with Nik. Then my problem would be solved.

I relaxed until the water was cool, then climbed out and wrapped a towel around my body. When I padded into the room to search for something comfy to put on, the song "How To Save A Life" by The Fray began to play. Instantaneously, I lost it. The song always reminded me of Cheryl, even though it didn't release until four years after her death. Still, after all these years, I couldn't believe she was gone. While I fell onto my knees in the middle of the room and sobbed for my dear, sweet cousin, I wished with all my heart I had known how to save *her* life. Lost to my pain and grief, I didn't hear anyone enter, but suddenly, I was engulfed in thickly hewn arms.

"Hush, now," Nik crooned gently. "I'm here."

His words belied his very stature. How did such a large, muscled, dangerous man, speak so softly and with such compassion? Most of the time, he appeared apathetic. Yet there were times—*like these*—when he was anything but. I sank into his embrace and let go. He sat behind me and pulled me onto his lap while I cried. As the tears began to subside, he kindly asked, "Wanna talk about it?"

Yes, actually, I did. Though I wasn't sure why I felt the need to share. "Remember when I told you about my cousin's suicide?"

"Yeah." He ran the pad of his thumb along my cheekbone, removing the moisture. "Is that why you're so upset?"

I attempted a watery smile. "Doesn't ever get easier, y'know?"

He nodded. Whether he ever chose to share the entire story about Rachel with me, I knew he very much understood loss. I gathered the courage necessary and forged ahead, "She was bullied mercilessly. She tried to tell her parents how bad it was, but they didn't understand." I shook my head. "I don't think any of us really had a clear picture of the hell she endured, day in and day out."

He stroked my back and waited patiently for me to go on with my story. I took a fortifying breath and continued, "You see, it wasn't only the traditional BS that goes on in the hallways, at the lockers, in the gym, on the bus, and so on. No, those girls were ruthless." I choked back another sob before I progressed, "They haunted her every waking moment through technology."

"Did she report them?" The concern in his voice was almost my undoing.

"She'd changed her passwords, user names, cell numbers, et cetera many times. Still didn't change a damn thing. Somehow they always got a hold of her info again. Everyone's hands were tied. The police couldn't help, no one could. It was unbearable. I tried every way in the world to help her, but she slipped further and further into depression."

"What'd your parents have to say?"

"Well, as much as anyone else. You know things like: 'Stay positive.' 'This too shall pass.' 'You're better than them; don't stoop to their level.' " I tugged on the towel that was precariously slipping to an indecent position and sighed heavily. "Looking back now, it was stupid. We should've done *more* for her. Got her some kind of help." I shrugged. "I don't know, *something*."

"Hey, don't blame yourself. You were just a kid. Even the adults didn't know how to handle the situation."

"Didn't change the outcome." Tears began to slide down my face once more. "She called me right before she took those pills. She told me how she couldn't live one more day like that. I just didn't understand." The sobs began again.

He soothed me with his hands and kissed the top of my head. I courageously let the rest out. "The call came around midnight. My parents rushed me up to the hospital. By the time we arrived, it was too late. She was gone."

"I'm so sorry, Aimee. Really, I am." When I looked up, his brows were furrowed, as if he couldn't quite grasp how much he understood my loss. Why was that?

I exhaled loudly. "Like I said, it was a long time ago. That song just brings back the memories."

"Is that really the *only* reason?"

No. But did I feel the need to confess that? "I doubt you want me to bear my soul here."

A ghost of a smile played at the corners of his mouth. "I asked for it."

I did grin at that. "Fair enough. I confess, I'm overwhelmed by all of this." I waved my hands for emphasis.

"You mean the wedding?"

"Well, yeah. That and"—I squirmed figuratively—"the expectations of our marriage." There, it was now out in the open.

"I see. Are you referring to the no sex agreement?"

I petulantly replied, "I don't recall being in favor of that."

His brow arched. "What exactly would you suggest?"

As I bit my lip in consternation—*in for the penny, in for the pound*—I persisted, "I'm not asking you to fall in love with me, Nik." When he tried to speak, I placed my fingers over his mouth. "I think we could be great friends. We already have a level of respect for one another. Thus, adding sex to the equation shouldn't be a big deal."

163

He actually chuckled. "Honey, having sex with *you* will most definitely be a big deal."

I blushed, which made no sense whatsoever. "So what are we waiting for?" To make my point perfectly clear, I wriggled on his lap. The greeting I received against my bottom was all the invitation I needed. I turned into him and kissed the sinews of his shoulders, working my way across his clavicle. There was just *so much* of him. He was gloriously muscled. After a few moments, his hands fisted in my hair and pulled my mouth from his body, then, he descended. His lips unfortunately did not meet mine. Instead, he reciprocated my moves. He licked and nipped his way along my neck, then suckled the hollow spot beneath my throat. I mewled in response. The next move he made caught me completely by surprise. He stood with me in his arms, like I weighed nothing at all. Once he placed me on my feet, he slowly backed away from me.

"It's late. You've had a long and trying day. Get some rest," he commanded softly as he made his way to the door.

I shook my head in disbelief, but I'd be damned if he'd see my disappointment. I pivoted and walked away from him to put as much distance as the room would allow between us. While I stood in front of the window, over my shoulder I called, "I'll see you tomorrow."

Not waiting to see if he was gone, I dropped my towel and sighed. Would he ever touch me intimately again? Or were those last couple of times all I would ever get of him? I ran my hands through my hair out of pure frustration and tried to get lost in Snow Patrol's "Just Say Yes" as I swayed to the music. I startled suddenly when I felt a presence behind me. I peeked through my hair, and there he was. Hunger blazed in his eyes. I could see his arousal pressed painfully against the seam of his jeans. With half hooded eyes, he closed the distance between us. As I began to turn fully towards him, he stayed me with his huge hands. "Don't move," he demanded.

No worries there, I was his.
There was no denying it.
Not now.
Not ever.

Chapter Twenty-one
Nik

When I stepped into Aimee's room, I had every intention of conveying—lock, stock, and barrel—what I had just learned, as well as our suspicions where Reynolds was concerned. But all preconceived notions left my brain once I saw her there sobbing. My only concern at that moment was consoling her anyway possible. She was so caught up in misery. It broke my heart. *Wait! Heart? WTF is happening to me?* Yet nothing could have stopped me from enfolding her in my arms. Did I actually think her merely beautiful? She was beyond that, utterly and completely stunning. And, right then, so damned vulnerable. After she had poured her heart out, I knew I had to get away from her. For if I stayed one moment longer, I was going to make her mine. She was pissed; that was clear. But she didn't want me to know it. Worse…I'd hurt her deeply. *Had she begun to care for me the way I do her?* No, surely not.

When I turned to close the door behind me, I could not believe my eyes. The towel fell with such ease, and I doubted she was aware I was watching. I strode up behind her with deliberate purpose—she was mine.

Mine to have.

Mine to take.

And, damn it all to hell, I was done holding back. The song that played on her iPod vaguely caught my attention. The irony not lost on me as I commanded her not to move. Question was, where did I start? My dick throbbed. There was nothing I wanted more than to push her onto her hands and knees. Then take her with the violence rising in me rapidly. With all of my self-control, I leashed the beast. Barely.

I placed my hands on her shoulders in an attempt to maintain some form of sanity. Thanks to the considerable height difference, I had full view of her luscious body. Ah, those incredible tits begged for my mouth. And the sexy as hell landing strip beckoned for pleasure. Holy shit! I was going to blow my load, right there, just from the peepshow.

Without any forethought, I began to rock my hips into her curvy ass to the beat of the music. She moaned as my hands ran down the sides of her body and rested on the flair of her hips. We began to dance, slow and rhythmic. A prelude to what was yet to come. I interlocked my fingers just above her pelvic bone and pulled her as close to my groin as possible with jeans on. In case there was ever a doubt to how much experience she had, she ground into me with precision and caused pre-ejaculate to wet my fly. Crap. Any minute I would fully come. Not going to happen. Yet.

I decided, then and there, that until she screamed my name in pleasure I wouldn't take mine. Against her ear I directed, "Get on your hands and knees for me."

She groaned, "Can I take your clothes off first?"

"No," I growled.

I could smell the onslaught of her arousal as she said, "There's something sinfully naughty about that."

I chuckled, low and dark. "Baby, you have no clue as to how dirty I can be."

"Oh," she gasped while she obeyed.

The sight before my eyes was a wet dream come true. I fought the urge to yank down my zipper and pound into her dripping sex. I went to my knees and leaned over her perfect ass. Then I licked and nipped her nape, shoulders, and back as I worked lower. Before I ravished her rounded globes, I moved to her tiny feet and mapped my way up one, and then the other leg. I purposely avoided any of her hot spots and focused on the neglected erogenous zones. Behind the knees was one of my favorites.

While I was not a man that frequently dined on a woman, something about *her* made me want to overindulge. I kissed each cheek of her ass and suckled where they met the backs of her thighs, occasionally blowing along her seam. Awarded with her mewls of pleasure, along with the juices which slid along the inside of her upper legs. There was no more restraint left in me. I moved my head into position between those lovely thighs, and then, with a growl of possession, I pulled her slick pussy onto my face.

Ah, she was sweet. Like nothing I'd ever tasted before.

The little voice inside my head reminded me *that's not true*. Hold on. I took one long lick from her perineum to her clit. Sure enough, her flavor was an awful lot like... *No, it couldn't be, could it?* Her thick honey was distinctly similar to the mystery woman from a few years ago. Was it possible for two women to taste the same? Wouldn't seem feasible, yet there was no denying it. At that moment, I couldn't have cared less. No way would I ever get enough of Aimee and her sweet, sweet nectar. I buried my tongue in as deep as possible, plunging in and out of her wet core. She didn't let me down and rewarded me once again with her cream. When she began to writhe against my mouth, I lost it and ravished her with: nose, chin, lips, tongue, and teeth.

She released while she screamed my name, which did nothing more than ramp me up another notch. No, I wasn't letting her go with only one orgasm. By time I finished, she would be well past spent. The desire to erase all men that'd been here before me was a force to be reckoned with. I intended to make damn sure no other man would ever bring her the pleasure I could. So I dove deep with two fingers, all the while I sucked her tight bundle of nerves at the top of her slit deep into my mouth. I had to hold her hips with my other arm—tight—to keep her from bucking away from the erotic torture. As I growled approval, she screamed again.

"That's right, little one," I encouraged. "Let me hear you. Tell me how good it feels."

"Omigod, Nik. You feel amazing." Her breath suddenly hitched with a ragged "Y-yes!" Then she squealed, "Just like...that," while she squirmed to get more friction. Finally, her voice broke on a sob of ecstasy.

Party time.

The action, along with her response, had inflamed me to the point of no return. I was on edge, a hairsbreadth from losing all control. Something I hadn't done since my first time. Annnnnd that thought began to sober me, bringing me back to the here and now. What was I doing? *Tongue fucking the sweetest pussy known to man, dipshit*. Yeah, there was that. Before I knew it, I was lost once again between Aimee's feminine folds. As I devoured her, images of that night at the masquerade began to flash in my mind's eye. Holy hell, Aimee even sounded the same. Talk about coincidence.

She pulled me from my musing when she pleaded, "Please. Nik, I need you inside me."

I shook my head. "Uh-huh," I purred, causing her to come yet again. Oh, hell yeah.

Without any forethought, I arched my hips and came on a guttural grunt. Where I should've felt embarrassed, all I could feel was the need to be inside her. The longing to feel her wet heat milk my still semi-erect cock was not something I could ignore any longer. I slid out from underneath her and then turned to caress and kiss her lovely ass, as I worked my way up. She collapsed onto the bed with a delicious whimper of a well pleasured woman.

Unable to fight my grin, I whispered, "I want to be inside you."

"Mm," she replied.

But before I could strip off my clothes and bury myself deeply, she was lightly snoring. Maybe I should've been pissed; instead, I curled up next to her while I pulled the blanket up to cover us. I lay on my side just watching her sleep, which brought an ache to my chest I couldn't name. Although, try as I might, on a soul deep level I had recognized her from the get-go. Why was that? Could this be the woman from the masquerade I had searched high and low for? If so, how? As she nuzzled my chest, I encircled her. My final thought was, *I never, ever slept in the same bed with any woman I had gratified.* Not since Rachel. Yet for whatever reason, Aimee felt right. I tugged her in closer and inhaled deeply. Mine.

*****

The dream was as vivid as the actual event:

"Give me your hand, Niky." Rachel beamed while she tugged my free arm over to the slight bump in her belly.

"Oh my God, is that her?" An awe I'd never known before swept through me as I felt my daughter move inside her mother's womb.

"Uh-huh. Amazing, isn't it?"

"You could say that again."

She bit her lip. "Yes, simply amazing."

I gave her a sidelong glance, not wanting to take my attention from the road for too long. The storm blew in with a fury unlike any I'd seen in the two years I'd lived in the Sierras. I looked back over and held my wife's gaze as a tear trickled down my cheek. At the same time Celine Dion sang, "Because You Loved Me." Rachel joined in with her angelic voice and held on to my hand while she serenaded me.

Unable to hide my joy or my love, I teased, "Bit sappy, don't y'think?"

She wiped the moisture on her cheeks and confessed, "Not at all." Then she continued to sing.

Grateful for Rachel and our baby girl on the way, I sang right along with her.

All of a sudden, there was a doe standing right there in the middle of the curve. Rachel screamed, "Watch out!"

I swerved and pumped my brakes, but they wouldn't catch. I tried not to panic, as I continued to hold the slide of the truck. It was no use. Without my brakes, we had too much speed. When we hit a patch of black ice, I lost my hold. The truck pummeled until it hit the huge pine tree. I blinked several times and tried to clear my vision, realizing there was blood running down my face. I looked over to the passenger side and saw my broken wife fighting to breathe. I unbuckled my seatbelt and leaned over to her.

"It'll be okay, Rach. Hang on."

She gasped, "Hurts."

"I know, baby. I know," I cried out.

I grabbed my cell and placed the 911 call. After I disconnected the call, I vowed, "I love you so much, Rachel. Just a few more minutes and help will be here."

She groped for her belly, and my hand went right there with hers. I could feel the baby kicking. Rachel's gaze became glassy and unfocused as she squeezed my fingers. "I...l-love...y..."

She never did finish her declaration. Her breath shuddered and then *nothing*.

I howled, "NOOOOOOO!!!"

I shot straight up in bed, yelling at the top of my lungs. Aimee stared at me, not sure what to do or say. She jumped off the bed as fast as possible. And I left the room like a bat out of hell.

Shit! How could I possibly think my life would go on normally? Happiness and falling in love were *not* options. Lest I forgot that, the night terrors would always remind me. As if Rachel was staking her claim from the hereafter. Though I knew that wasn't fair to Rachel. She would never haunt me. No, this was all on me.

I was so full of darkness that light couldn't reach me.

Now, Aimee just had a taste of it. She didn't deserve to be saddled with a bastard like me. But God help me, I still wanted her with every ounce of my being. And didn't that just make me the world's biggest asshole. For I knew, sooner or later, I *would* have her: heart, mind, body and soul. Even though the fact remained I couldn't give them back in return. But it would not stop me from taking.

What the fuck?!

I cranked the shower on as hot as I could stand it and stood under the spray to wash off the cold sweat left behind from the nightmare. I braced myself against the wall and willed myself not to cry. I would not give into tears, ever again. That'd been a lesson learned in the joint. I ran my hand over the brand that lay on the side of my neck just under my hair line. One of the many reasons I wore my hair long. Although there were no regrets for joining LD—hell, if I hadn't I would be dead—because the affiliation helped me make my first million. Still, what got to me the most was how I had ever ended up in prison in the first place. Dear God, if there were a way to turn back time, I never would've driven up that mountain road during a snowstorm. But I was young and thought we were invincible. Never once, did I stop to think about the danger we were in that fateful night. I ran my hands through my wet hair and tugged it harshly, as I fought in vain to erase the worst night of my life.

Warm, small hands came to rest on my shoulders. "Wanna talk about it?"

There were no words, so I shook my head once. Everything inside me wanted to bury my head in the cradle of her neck and release all these emotions that were rearing up on me like a tsunami. Again, I was struck by how much she'd come to mean to me in such a short time. Although I was a wreck, my blood still heated at her nearness. Her touch. She was a balm to my torn soul. As I resisted with all my might, I barked, "Leave." And hoped like hell she'd heed my warning. At the same time, I wished she wouldn't go. *Fuck!* If I didn't push her away now, I wasn't sure I ever could.

She inhaled sharply. "I don't think you really want me to." As she stroked along my back, she wrapped her arms around my waist. "I think you're hurting, but you don't want me to see just how much." She moved around my body and stood in front of me. Next, she rested her hands on my chest and began to trace the tattoo over my heart.

My breathing hitched as I stilled her hand and trapped it against my pec. "Don't," I warned.

With anguish in her eyes, she replied, "You can't keep locking away your grief, Nik. Living like this is going to kill you." First, I tried to push her away. But she fought me. Instead, I reached up to place her hands on either side of my face and tilted my head down towards hers. She whispered, "Let. It. Go."

I closed my eyes tightly and barely strangled out, "I can't."

She encouraged, "Sure you can. I'm right here, I promise."

I meant to shove her back—to run from the pain like I always had—but when I looked into those amazing eyes and saw the compassion, along with understanding, I finally gave in. Once I lowered my head to her shoulder, I let out a sob. And that broke the dam I'd had in place all these years. I actually crumbled from the weight and hit my knees, dragging her with me to the shower floor. While she held me tightly against her body, I buried my head between her breasts and cried until there were no more tears left.

After the onslaught was finished, she shut off the water and wrapped a towel around me. My feet were heavy, yet somehow we made it to the bed. She stripped off the drenched robe and climbed in beside me. I fell asleep cradled in her warm embrace. And I knew, I had just found my anchor.

The knowledge that emotions like this were a calling card for disaster should've made me fight the feelings off. Yet, I just couldn't do it. As much as I wanted to deny it, she was becoming important to me. Necessary. I very well may not deserve a moment of peace. But damn it all, for this moment in time, I was going to revel in it. Tomorrow, I'd put back on the mask and be the cold-hearted dickhead I was notorious for. But for tonight, I would pretend I was whole. All was well in my heart. In my soul. And I was capable of giving her all of me. *Pipedream.* Possibly. Yet even the worst of us deserves a reprieve every now and then, right? *Keep telling yourself that.*

Chapter Twenty-Two
Aimee

Awakened by the cold, I groped for the mountainous male body that had been next to me. Nada. Where could he have gone? I found one of his t-shirts lying on the floor. Once I donned it, I began to search for Nik. As I roamed the halls of the penthouse, I heard the haunting strains of that song once more. Dear Lord, was this his song to Rachel? I backed away silently and left him alone with his grief. I wondered if one ever got over losing their spouse. Probably not. I mean, was I over the loss of my cousin? Definitely, no. So the question was, could I live in the shadow of *her* memory? For a good man like Nik, yes, I could. I didn't live in Neverland and was fully aware I couldn't ever take her place. Yet surely he was capable of loving another. Not the same way. I wouldn't want that for him or myself. For the hundredth time, the little voice in my head asked, *"What makes you think a woman like you deserves love?"* I didn't. But the fact remained, I wanted it.

Since going back to my room seemed the wiser choice, I crawled back in bed and curled under the covers, letting sleep have its way with me. Unfortunately, I didn't rest well. Haunted by images of a gorgeous woman I could never even hope living up to. It was odd; my vision of Rachel looked an awful lot like me. As I tossed and turned, my thoughts were: *I need to find a picture of her*. Also, I yearned for the whole story of that fateful night. Maybe, if I understood what was caught in Nik's memories, I could help ease them.

*****

Later that morning, distinct male voices could be heard. As I sat up and hung my legs over the edge of the bed, the argument escalated. There was no way to decipher the exact words; however, I recognized my name more than once. Crap, just what I didn't need. I figured a shower would help wash away my worries.

Afterwards, I searched for something to wear and made my way into the kitchen. My stomach growled loudly to make itself known. As I rounded the corner, Nik sat at the breakfast bar with a cup of coffee in hand.

"That smells heavenly. Is there any more?"

"Sure, have a seat. I'll get it for you." He stood and walked over to the pot resting on the countertop.

"I am capable of pouring myself a cup."

He shrugged. "I want to."

I shook my head. "Okay."

He asked, "Cream? Sugar?"

"Both, please," I replied.

Once he handed me the coffee, I took a sip and then said, "Thank you."

"No problem." He sauntered back to the barstool and sat facing me. "We should talk about last night."

Uh-oh. Never a good sign when someone said that. "We don't have to."

He raised a brow. "I think we do."

I sighed, "Look. I don't expect anything."
Now his other eyebrow shot up. So I explained, "Am
I attracted to you? That's a no-brainer. Do I want a
physical relationship with you?"

He held his hand up to stop me. "We both
know it'll happen. That's not what I was talking
about."

We did? 'Cause I had no idea he was willing
to have sex with me till a moment ago. "Hold on. We
will?"

He fleered, "Never said I was happy about it.
But let's face it; I want you as much as you want me."

He couldn't have made me feel more like a
whore if he'd tried. I huffed, "Nice to know you think
so damn highly of me."

He snorted, "Don't start, Aimee. I haven't the
time or the patience to put up with a temper tantrum."

"I beg your pardon?" My brows furrowed as
my eyes narrowed. *Cocky SOB.*

"Enough," he commanded. While I fought the
urge to slap his rugged, handsome face, he continued,
"I'm leaving in the next hour or so. The episode last
night will not be repeated."

Was he trying to convince himself or me of
that? "I'm sorry you feel that way. I, for one, thought
it was kind of nice to see the more human side of
you."

He held my gaze intently. "If you think I'll
lose my grip again, you're sorely mistaken. Besides,
I'm not human. I've told you before I'm a cold-
hearted bastard."

My eyebrows reached my hairline. "Really?
Last time I checked, 'a cold-hearted bastard' didn't
rescue a whore in distress." I stood and placed my
hands on my hips. "They don't give a rat's ass that
some wealthy, powerful douchebag wants to harm
her." Then, I got right in his face. "And they damn

well don't offer marriage as a way to protect her."

He sneered, "Believe what you want. I'll meet you in Missouri the night before our wedding." His last statement sounded like he had a doctor's appointment he didn't want to keep.

FML. How had it come to this? "No," I whispered.

He grabbed me by the shoulders. "What'd you just say?"

I looked up into his furious eyes. "You heard me."

He held on firmly, but he didn't hurt me. "Aimee," he warned. "We're getting married next week. What's your problem?"

I lifted my chin and snarled, "You."

"Come again?"

I spat out, "You are my problem."

He leaned over me. "That's beside the point."

"Like hell it is," I growled.

Low and dark, he rumbled, "It's happening one way or the other."

I squared my shoulders and held firm. "Not if *I* don't want it to."

"This isn't a matter of want to. It's the only way to keep Reynolds at bay."

"So, what about Caleb?" I asked indignantly.

His eyes widened as his nostrils flared. "He wants to harm you, you stubborn woman. Matter of fact, I've no doubts he wants to kill you."

Now that shocked me. While I admit Caleb was one scary-ass bastard, never had murder crossed my mind. Oh, I knew he wanted to cause serious pain, but not end my life. "Why do you think that?"

"Honey, I know the look a man gets when he has homicide on the brain. Trust me, if he gets his hands on you again, you *won't* walk away."

My shoulders slumped from that little piece of

information. But it didn't change anything. "I'm not marrying a man that doesn't respect me."

He hauled me into his massive chest. "Who said I didn't appreciate you?"

"Uh...hello, you just did," I said frankly.

He shook his head. "You baffle the hell outta me. I never said that. Nor will I ever say such a thing." He blew out a breath. "Any woman who could stand her ground in the face of disaster deserves not just my admiration, but everyone else's as well."

You could've knocked me over with a feather. I inhaled deeply, which brought my breasts in direct contact with his pectorals. And wouldn't you know, the action brought on a wave of lust—my nipples hardening instantly. I wanted him with a ferocious desire. His pupils dilated as his breathing hitched. Oh, yeah. He felt it, too. "I still can't marry you," I choked out.

"Yes, you can," he claimed as he nuzzled my neck.

"I..." Unable to complete my thought, I mewled. What was it about him that made me weak in the knees?

He suckled the sensitive spot below my ear and then susurrated, "Say it."

There was no denying this man anything. I submitted, "I'll marry you."

"Good girl," he crooned as he fisted my hair and yanked my head back, all the while ravaging my throat.

Lost to his ministrations, I arched my hips into him and purred, "Take me, Nik."

He growled, "Hell, yes," and lifted me onto the bar.

We began to tear at each other's clothing. There was no foreplay. Not a trace of gentleness between us. And I was fully aware he was going to fuck me hard. That knowledge made my juices flow. He grabbed a condom from the drawer beside us and rolled it onto his sizeable member. As he positioned himself at the opening of my core, he groaned, "Ready?"

"Please," I begged.

In one furious thrust, he buried himself inside me. Never had I felt so completely taken, and, oddly enough, I reveled in it. Only wanting more—all he could give me. I commanded, "Harder. Oh yeah, like that. Faster, Nik."

He moaned, "Bossy little thing, aren't you?" Then proceeded to show me just who was in charge.

He was magnificent.

Raw.

Primal.

My nails marked his back as I came, screaming his name. He followed with a sexy grunt and leaned into me heavily. While we tried to catch our breath, he murmured, "You are amazing, little one."

I jolted at the endearment as another deep, raspy voice echoed in my mind. I could've sworn they were one in the same. "So are you," I complimented.

With an expression of reluctance, he pulled out of my heat. I mourned the loss of him instantaneously. He grabbed a towel and gently cleaned me before he removed the condom and took care of himself. Such a sweet gesture. I watched as he pulled his slacks back into place and remembered him saying he had to leave town. He was definitely dressed in business attire. As if he read my mind, he answered, "I have some business to take care of in Chicago. I'll meet you in Missouri."

I bit my lip, wondering if he went to Chicago often. Aware he was in a hurry, I decided to ask at another time. I smiled, "Alright. I'll make the flight arrangements for Renée and myself."

He graced me with a half-smile. "Silly, girl. My jet will be available tomorrow for your use."

"Oh," I gasped. "Guess that'd make more sense."

He playfully tousled my hair. "I'll see you soon."

"It's a date," I grinned as he turned and left the kitchen.

*****

Afterwards, I put myself to rights. I decided to call and check on my best friend, knowing she'd been released from the hospital yesterday. So once she was ready to travel, we could leave for my hometown to prepare for my wedding. OMG! I was actually doing this.

Shortly after Nik had departed for the Windy City, Renée showed up. Squee! Once all the excitement was down to a low roar, we hugged again and then sat down on the sectional in the living room to chat. Oh, how I had missed my BFF. She looked good, all things considered. Though there was one thing I wished she wasn't so attuned to. "Spill it. Was he any good?"

Geez. How did she do that? "Yes."

"I knew it. You can just tell when a boy's got swag."

Holy crap. As if I would tell her all that had happened between Nik and me. Weird for a prostitute to be embarrassed, *but it is what it is*. My face heated as I nodded.

"Girl, you got nothin' to be ashamed of. I can't believe it took this long to tap that." She shook her head in disbelief. "I'd have been all over him from the moment I set eyes on that man."

I had to laugh. "Never said I didn't fantasize. Just wanted to wait for the right time, you know?"

She chortled, "Aims. I'll be the first to admit you were never cut out for the *business*."

Boy, did she call that correctly. But then, she knew the ins and outs of why I decided to sell my body for profit. With those thoughts came a deep sense of melancholy. Not that I'd do anything different, just wish the situation had never come up. The one saving grace, my daddy was healthy now. *Thank you, God.*

Renée snapped me out of me reverie. "Yoohoo, you there?" She waved her hand in front of my face.

Man, I must've really been out of it. I offered her a half-smile and explained, "Sorry. My mind's in other places right now."

She playfully smacked my shoulder. "Would you please get your head in the game?" She reached over and lifted my hair up off my neck. "Yeah, I think an up-do will be perfect."

I shook my head slightly. "Seriously? 'Cause I was thinking down and curly."

"That'd be pretty, too." She shrugged one shoulder. "Not like you won't be breathtaking—whatever you decide will be spectacular." She chuckled at my embarrassment. "Always humble. I'm a firm believer in, you got it flaunt it."

I threw my head back and laughed from deep in my belly. No matter what, she could make me feel better. I spontaneously hugged her, hard. "I love you. You know that, right?"

She pulled back to wipe a tear from her cheek. "That's enough with the mushy crap." Then she stroked the side of my face. "I love you, too. Now, have you picked out a dress?"

I bit my lip as I nodded. "It's online."

"Did you order it?"

"No. I just wasn't sure, y'know?"

"Yep, I get it. However if you're walking down that aisle in a week, we need to do some serious shopping."

"Are you saying…?"

"Definitely. Get off your butt. We're going to the West Village."

There was no containing my excitement as I squealed, "Yay!"

She linked her arm with mine. "Let's go see what we can find."

*****

As we entered the parking garage, I didn't miss that we had a tail. Neither did Renée. She waggled her fingers at one of Nik's security guys. He gave a curt nod, but continued to follow us. I glanced sideways and whispered, "Sorry."

She smiled, "I'm not."

Nonplussed, my brows rose. "Really? Why's that?"

She answered, "Means he cares. And I, for one, like that about a man."

Never had I let that thought cross my mind before. Yet she had a point. It was rather nice to know, that while away, Nik was still making sure I was protected. Yeah, being Mrs. Strand was not going to be a hardship—whatsoever.

Chapter Twenty-Three
Nik

Chicago messed with my head, in more ways than one, as thoughts of that masquerade grew stronger. Of course, staying at the same hotel as I had five years ago probably didn't help curtail those memories. Then again, meeting with one of my lead executors and personal friend, Franco D'Arpino, didn't help matters, either.

When I stepped into Franco's opulent foyer, the sights and sounds of that particular night nearly blew me away. His wife, Gina, welcomed me with open arms. It had been her benefit for abused children which had brought me to this very house on the said night. Since Franco and my connection go all the way back to our time with LD's corporation—a.k.a. gang—there wasn't anything I wouldn't do for him. And that also meant for Gina. I embraced her warmly. She had always been a beauty, and the years had been kind. Her lovely raven hair with just a hint of silver, flowing down to her shoulder blades, was just as eye catching now as it was then.

Never one to hold back, she asked, "Where is your bride to be?" Her gorgeous Italian accent still warmed me.

I smiled, "Busy preparing for *our* wedding."

"Ah, I see."

I continued, "Will you two be able to join us?"

"But of course," she replied, "We wouldn't miss it."

Franco gave her a meaningful look, and she politely excused herself. He turned to me. "Let's talk in the study."

I inclined my head as I followed him.

Although this meeting hadn't been on my radar, ironically it felt good to be back around "family." Once you are a part of LD—Lorenzo D'Arpino—it was forever. I had done everything within my power to turn the corporation into a legit powerhouse. But it didn't change the facts: The ties were strong. Not to mention the only way out was through death. I had made sure there were no new recruits and kept everything legal. Franco had been instrumental in assisting with that venture. He was Lorenzo's nephew; therefore, the one—through tradition—who should've inherited it all. But Lorenzo wanted new blood at the helm, and Franco was more than willing to bring that into fruition. Hence, once my debt had been paid for the help in prison, I took over. With the blessing of Lorenzo before he died, I renamed it Strand Industries. Franco was my lead man in Chicago. Unfortunately, he'd hit a stumbling block with a long, lost cousin, and it was time to handle things before the law got involved. Thus, the little cleaning house mission I was on.

After all the deets had been laid out, we made our collective decision on just how and where to deal with the wayward family member. I must admit, if only to myself, gratitude I wasn't on the receiving end of that meet-and-greet ran thick. Been there, done that. On more than one occasion. *Yeah, being the head honcho had its perks.*

Once business was settled, we went into the

dining room for dinner. Gina, as always, was a stupendous hostess. I actually looked forward to Aimee and her meeting officially, along with my team. The more I thought about it, the more I liked the idea of Aimee joining ranks. She had a good head on her shoulders, and I knew we could put it to great use. As the food disappeared and the wine flowed, I decided to make an inquisition. "Gina?"

She glanced over. "Yes, Nikko." Few people ever called me by my given name. And she was one of them.

I cleared my throat, not knowing just how to broach this topic. But it had been eating at me enough I knew I had too. "That masquerade you threw a few years back... Do you remember your guests? Or, by chance, still have the list?"

She beamed, "Why, it just so happens I keep all of my guest lists. Give me a moment; I'll go find it for you."

This was hopefully going to answer my question, once and for all.

We'd moved into the living room by the time Gina had found the particular list I was looking for. As she handed it to me, I tried to be nonchalant. But she knew me all too well. "Who are you searching for?" she queried while she sat next to me on the couch.

I did my best to avoid being forthcoming and replied, "I'll know when I see the name."

She had been raised around the Mob, therefore didn't persist. "Let me know if I can be of any help." Franco grabbed his wife's hand and lifted it to his mouth. She giggled like a teenager and then excused herself. Once she had left the room, he picked up the discarded sheets I'd set aside. "What's the name?"

I shook my head. "It wasn't BS, my man."

He shot me a wry grin. "So, a female."

Geez, was I that transparent? I would neither concur nor deny. He chuckled, "Will you confide in me if you find her?"

Again, I didn't capitulate. As I scanned the list of guests for Aimee's name, there was nothing. A couple of names did stick out above the others: Ann and Jack Dubois. If memory served me correctly, they ran an escort service. *And look at that*, next to their names in parenthesis was: (guest A. Lockhart.) All of a sudden, my heart began to pound so hard I could hear nothing else. Could it really be? Surely, I would've remembered. *You did, dipshit. You've known all along*. I stood abruptly, the list scattering at my feet. Franco's eyes widened. "Are you all right?"

"I'm sorry. I need to go," I announced while I strode quickly across the room, almost knocking Gina over. As she entered with dessert on a tray, she inquired, "You're leaving so soon?"

I bent to kiss her cheek. "Another time, I promise."

"But..." She set the tray down on the coffee table and then ran after me. She placed her hand on my forearm. "You found who you were looking for," she confirmed. "Is there any way we can help?"

Franco joined us at the front door. "Nik, whatever you need."

Still in shock at my discovery, I nodded, "Thank you. I'll be in touch." With that, I rushed to the rental car and sped back to the hotel.

*****

When I entered my suite, only one thought went through my mind, *I found her. Finally*. While part of me was elated, the other was horrified. The former was from years of searching for my mystery woman. With the latter, also came the question: How had I been intimate with Aimee and not been able to identify her? I would've sworn that was impossible. Yet, somehow I had missed it. And didn't that suck ass. Geez, I hadn't even made love to her. No, I fucked her in my kitchen and then left town. What a shithead. *Now, what do I do with this information?*

It definitely changed things.

Dammit.

I fell onto the bed as my knees gave out. Either I didn't make as big of an impact on her that night as she did on me, or she hadn't recalled it was me yet. Which was it? As I lay there, realization hit me like a ton of bricks—didn't matter one way or the other. While I would be the first to confess, that night had been a game changer for me. Plus there was no denying the fact, each moment I spent with Aimee *only* made these feelings grow stronger. Problem still remained: My soul had been shattered. There wasn't anything but pieces to share with her. Would it be enough? Didn't she deserve a man that could completely give his heart to her? Yet now that I'd found her again, there was no way I was letting go. *Selfish MOFO.*

*****

The dream of the masquerade gave me some hope until it morphed into the repetitive nightmare of the accident. Of course, that did not help my confusion with Aimee. Then the damn thing switched again, and I was back in prison. I awoke because of a blood curdling scream—*oh, that was me!*—and looked around frantically as I tried to get my bearings. Fuck. Who in their right mind would want to be saddled with a loser like me? Was there another option I hadn't seen? As I stumbled across the room, I felt a chill. I glanced down at the sweat drenched shirt and realized just how much those nightmares screwed with my head. I peeled off my clothes and climbed into the shower, all the while thinking of another solution to the whole damn dilemma. I came up with…zilch. What the hell?! There was surely some other way. Though the harder I contemplated the options, the more I surmised: This was the correct course of action. Annnd didn't that bite. Big time.

Truth was, marrying Aimee didn't bother me one iota, although she deserved so much more. At that moment I made a vow: I would do everything in my power to be the best husband possible. Not that staying faithful was going to be a challenge. Hell no. The problem was, only a shell of a man had been left. However, if she would have me, then she'd have *all* of me. As for telling her what I'd discovered last night, not going to happen. Besides, I'd much rather she put two and two together herself. And if she never remembered, fine by me.

Yeah, I could live with that.

For the hundredth time since I had removed my mother's wedding ring from the safe, I sat there staring at it in the light. A family heirloom and a remarkable piece of jewelry: with a round, brilliant-cut diamond in the center and six smaller diamonds on the sides; two carats total weight and set in textured platinum. Yes, I could easily afford bigger and flashier. But this one was sentimental. I was optimistic she would feel the same way. Even without the knowledge of whom I was from the masquerade a few years ago. Let's hope so, at least. For me, now that I knew exactly who Aimee was it meant so much more.

*****

After I tied up all of the loose ends with Franco—as well as making sure Gina received my apology bouquet—I headed for the airport. Time to do this. By tomorrow evening, Aimee would be legally mine. Damn, if I didn't like the sound of that. I did a mental fist pump, with a *hell yeah* tacked on for good measure, and boarded the company jet.

"All set, Mr. Strand?" the pilot asked.

"Yes, thank you," I answered as I strapped in to the leather seat.

Once the plane took off, I made quick work of finding a perfect honeymoon location. We hadn't discussed it. Until that moment, truthfully, I had not planned on one. Lucky for me Strand Industries owned several resorts. Yes, she was going to love my surprise. And heaven help me, but an honest to goodness smile broke across my face. The very thought of sharing everything I had with her made me an extremely happy man. I suddenly felt lighter, as if a heavy fog had just lifted. Peculiar. Not in a bad way, though. *Nah, it's all good.*

Chapter Twenty-Four
Caleb

One of the things I loved most was working off my frustrations. Yes, a good hard workout would definitely do the trick. After I arrived at the warehouse—which was owned by me, via a dummy corporation—I confirmed the area was locked down tight.

"All's well, Joe?"

His smile was pure malevolence. "Yes, sir."

Damn. The man was as into this as I was. From time to time I let him participate. Sometimes, I let him finish the job. But tonight I was in rare form. That bitch, Aimee, had put me in a mood. And it was time to get my head on straight.

When I walked into the locker room, I stripped down and took a much warranted shower. I had to get the feel of that *woman* off my skin. Yes, she was going to pay for deceiving me. However, she hadn't been the first to pass herself off as my beloved. And I would deal with her appropriately, along with that bastard, Strand. I had had it with his knight in shining armor routine. As if my beautiful Rachel had ever been in danger from me. I could never, would never, have harmed her.

"You were the one who killed me, Caleb." Rachel's voice reminded me.

"We've been through this, my love. Nik was supposed to die that night, not you. Never you," I appealed for the millionth time. Yet, she refused to listen. That was a woman for you—always had to have the upper hand in any given argument. "I love you," I avowed. In my mind, she sat on the lovely chaise lounge and shook her head with disapproval. Someday, I knew, she would believe me.

As I rummaged through my assortment of clothing, I wondered what my colleagues would think if I brought them here. The deviant ones were aware of my proclivities as they, too, shared in their own debauchery. But I meant, the holier-than-thou crowd. They were the ones who not only supported my reform on prostitution, but gave generously to the cause. Little did they know, I thoroughly and utterly enjoyed beating such girls. While the thought brought on a fierce arousal, I turned to the man I often shared pleasures with.

"Tonight you will only watch. If you masturbate, I will whip you. Are we clear? Speak, now," I commanded.

"Yes, Mr. R," he replied with a wicked glint in his eyes as he bowed his head in deference.

By the way he stood there; I knew this night was going to be a twofer. Holy hell, I was going to come. I quickly brought my baser self under control and slid on a pair of leather pants. There was no need to bother with a shirt, for I knew my body was well defined. Since I waxed all body hair, they especially loved to touch. I put on the leather mask and gloves to insure there would be no DNA left on her body. Doubtful that my prostitute would live through the events about to unfold, most just couldn't handle my ways of seduction. But every now and then, I found one who could. And, oh, the fun we had. Matter of fact, afterwards, those specific whores searched for a repeat session. Joe always shared the finite details of his performances with them long after I had finished. He had informed me that they always requested Mr. R's return. *Naughty sluts*. Before the real entertainment could begin, I was going to have to get off—judging by the weight of my erection. As I adjusted, over my shoulder I called, "Stay in the suit. Make it look like you might rescue her."

"I hope she begs for it." He licked his lips methodically. "Love watching them realize I'm not here for that."

Had I mentioned his depravity? It was why we worked so well together. I winked as we entered the main warehouse.

Show time.

*****

My God, she was exquisite. After I had worked her over for three hours, she was still cognitive. "Please," she lustfully begged, "I need more of you."

With a low and deep chuckle, I queried, "How do you need me, baby?" I stroked her sweat covered hair away from her big, gorgeous hazel eyes.

She looked up at me through hooded lids. "Use the whip."

"Now, now, beauty." I cupped her perky, lacerated breasts to make a point. "Your body can't handle that, again."

She whispered, "May I lean into you?"

I gave her the go ahead with a nod. As her slick, warm body cradled into mine, I couldn't resist holding her. Which made no sense—usually after four releases, I was beyond spent. But there was *something* about her that drew me in. Images of her writhing beneath me flooded my vision. Abnormal. Never had

I fucked one of *my* girls. The thrill, the high, came
from full control of them. The knowledge I could do
whatever my heart desired to their bodies, and they
could do *nothing* to stop me. Which was why, I kept
them restrained in the shackles and chains hanging
from the steel beam above. Not her. I had even lost
the mask and gloves about an hour or so ago. *Why
was that?*

I purred in her ear, "Tell me your name."

"Marissa," she panted.

"Lovely name for such a breathtaking
woman," I complimented.

When her cheeks flushed, I swatted her ass,
hard. As she bit her lip to keep from crying out, I
growled, "If I pay you adoration, you will not ever
blush."

She lowered her eyes and waited for my
permission to reply. *Yes, I like that.* "Good girl." I
patted the top of her head. "You may speak."

"I'm sorry. It won't happen again," she
declared.

"If it does, I'll have to spank you with
something other than my hand."

At that, her breathing increased. And the smell
of her arousal hit my nostrils. Yes, I would have this
one for a while. She certainly was not leaving here
tonight—*maybe not ever.* I was beginning to think
Joe, Viviane, and I had just brought on a new partner.
As if the thought brought Joe back to consciousness,
he moaned deeply. We watched his swollen, bruised
body as he came fully back online. When he searched
my face, I commanded, "Go." Once he stood, I
grabbed a towel and threw it at him. "Clean yourself
up. Rest. I have no more use for you this evening."

Without a reverential response, he lumbered
to the locker room. This time, I would forgive the
error. Matter of fact, a reward was necessary. He had

truly outdone himself. From the selection of Marissa, to his stamina through the lashing I gave him. The man was spectacular in his demonstration of male restraint. Slowly, I escorted my girl over to the table. As I bound each wrist and ankle with the leather cuffs, she bled. I licked each and every droplet before I stepped back to admire her spread eagle form. Yes, time to really work her over. Hopeful she would survive it, I set the clamps to her most obvious erogenous zones.

For some unknown reason, about halfway through my paces with her, I stopped. There were spots where she was bleeding profusely, which brought on an unnamed emotion. I shook my head to clear it and began to nurse her wounds. Bizarre. I'm not a caring man. Cold, dangerous, violent, but never one to give a damn about anything or anyone except myself and how another person could benefit me. I released her bonds and slowly eased her into my arms. What was it about *her* that brought out a side I never knew I had? I leaned in to suck on her split lip and then released it, but never pulled away from her face. I whispered, "You're incredible, Marissa."

She blinked several times in rapid succession and replied, "I still want you."

When her brows furrowed, I could see the confusion in her eyes. Yes, it was a bit disconcerting to yearn for the one who had only brought you extreme pain. Yet I understood the longing completely, even though I had been the one to torture her for almost five hours straight. I began to care for the wounds that were open and stated, "We need to be careful. You don't want an infection."

As if she comprehended what I had just alluded to, she glanced down at the torn, raw flesh of her womanhood. How pretty it was now that it was free from all the pesky pubic hair. I licked my lips at the memory of the straight edged blade I'd used. When I swiped the towel between her legs, she arched into my hand.

"You *are* horny," I uttered as I rubbed her clit with terrycloth. A vision of a piercing through the hood had me adjusting myself. Definitely happening next time. What the hell?! Not only was I planning on fucking her in the next few minutes, but apparently there would be another round. I wondered why that was.

All thoughts disappeared when she moaned, "Can I come now?"

"No," I barked.

There was no reply from her. She just laid there and patiently waited. I would have tested her. But, at the moment, I wanted to bury myself deep inside that stunning cunt. Once I stripped off my leathers, I mounted her quickly and surged forward with enough power to move her to the front edge of the table. Damn, she was tight. You would have thought that impossible with the trade she was in. As her inner muscles squeezed tight, I began to pound mercilessly. She latched her legs around my waist and held on for the ride. Wasn't long before I came, and she surprised me by following suit. *Finally, I've met my match.* Wait! Where did that thought come from?

Our gazes locked while I tried to regain some composure. I had lost all sense of her. Myself. The whole situation at hand. And when she pulled me against her, I knew it wasn't going to happen any time soon. As her hands moved down to my ass, I was undone. We began again, although this time slow and easy. I should've been scared shitless by that, but, somehow, it just felt too damn good to fret about. There would be plenty of time to figure out the details. Later.

I released on an "ah, fuck," as I bent to take

her mouth with mine.

Afterwards, I pulled out of her body and stood. When I walked over to grab another towel, I tossed it to her and declared, "You're not leaving. Ever."

She held my gaze and vowed, "Never."

With that I left the warehouse, only one thought raced through my mind: *I now have my partner*.

A tiny voice responded, "What will you do with me?"

I sank down on my haunches in the locker room. What was I going to do about Rachel? Aimee? Nik? Not to mention my pastime, which I truly did not want to give up. Was Marissa worth it? Only time would tell. And fortunately, there was plenty to go around.

Chapter Twenty-Five
Aimee

"Mom, this is amazing," I gushed as I took in the surroundings from every angle.

The church I grew up in was filled with lavender, hydrangeas, freesia, and purple roses. The pièce de résistance was the altar draped in silvery-white gossamer accentuated with two large, pewter and crystal candelabras on either side of the ornate Bible. Still, I was in awe of how she and her friends had turned the simple, quaint sanctuary into something otherworldly. The guilt began to overwhelm me as the little voice in my head reminded me, *this isn't a true marriage*. Not to mention the shame that went with the fact, I had *sold* my body for money. I bowed my head and stepped away from everyone.

In a small, silent corner I sank down to my knees, having a moment of reflection. Could I really go through with this? I knew my parents would never have the 411 on my past, or how Nik and I ended up together. Part of me felt awful for the prevarication, yet what other choice was there? While I sat in a place where truth, grace, and forgiveness should overflow, I wanted to retch. Lies. And I was trapped with no way out. All of a sudden, a quote from Sir Walter Scott came to mind. "Oh what a tangled web we weave, When first we practice to deceive!" And didn't that just sum it up, right there. Renée placed her hand on my shoulder; meanwhile, I was mentally kicking myself in the butt.

"You have a visitor," she announced.

As I wiped the tears from my cheeks, I glanced across the room. There—taking up almost every inch of the threshold, with a bouquet of yellow roses in hand—stood Nik. What a sight. A tingle of warmth began to blossom deep in my belly. His rugged, masculine beauty took my breath away. He narrowed his eyes and strode towards me. I rose to my feet and greeted, "Hey."

Once we were toe to toe, he tilted his head to the side and reached up to capture a tear that escaped. "What's wrong, Aimee?" he asked with deep consternation etched in his face.

I shook my head and lowered my eyes. He wasn't tolerating my obvious attempt at hiding. Gently he lifted my chin with his forefinger, and our gazes locked. "Talk to me, please."

Before I could answer, my mother approached. I half-smiled at him and then grasped the hand on my face. I turned us towards Mom and introduced them. Nik was so gracious with her, handing the bouquet over, which caused her to flush. At that moment my dad walked in. When he reached us, he wrapped an arm around my mom's shoulders and jokingly queried, "Now, how did you know my wife's favorite flowers?"

Nik cleared his throat and stammered, "I...uh...had no idea, s-sir."

Never would I have imagined such a powerful man struggling for words. Somehow, it made him more approachable. Let's face it; his size alone was a helluva intimidation. Therefore, witnessing his very normal reaction to meeting my father for the first time, made me love him just a little bit more. Did I just say love? *Gee, shocker*. Time to be honest, with at least myself; I was falling in love with him. Scratch that. I am in love with him. Annnnd didn't that just fan the flames more. While I was actually marrying him for the right reasons, I knew it wasn't reciprocated. Subtext: This was the real source of my previous mendacity. My biggest fabrication was, he thought I would only go through with it for protection. What a farce. Somewhere, in midst of this mess, I had developed very deep feelings for this wounded, yet honorable man. Go fig.

While I came back from my reverie, my dad said, "It's a pleasure to meet you, Nik."

As the men shook hands, my mom smiled, "If you gentlemen will please excuse us."

I squeezed Nik's hand and began to step away. He tugged me into him and hugged me hard. Then he leaned into my ear and whispered, "I'll see you soon, sweet Aimee."

I blinked several times in an attempt to get my bearings. That was so unlike him. As I pulled out of his embrace, I called, "See you at dinner," over my shoulder.

He flashed a genuine smile, and my step faltered. It was enough to make a woman weak in the knees. Realization hit, staying out of his bed tonight would test my self-control in more ways than one. For some reason, I wanted to follow tradition. How sappy. All too aware of his effect on me, he winked. OMG, I wanted him. *Right here. Right now*. I walked outside with my mother and Renée reluctantly. All the while I fought the compelling urge to march back inside and demand he take me. Phew! This was going to be one looooong night.

Mom turned towards me in the parking lot. "Oh my!" She fanned herself for emphasis. "That is one massive hunk you have there, Aimee."

I attempted to suppress my giggle—and failed miserably, I might add—and confirmed, "Yeah, he's pretty amazing."

Renée chimed in, "Girl, please. He's a major hottie. And you know it."

I blushed furiously and bowed my head. Then added, "Hard to believe he really wants to marry me." Uh-oh, that was a little too close to the truth for my comfort. Although my bestie understood completely, my mom was in the dark. And there was no way, unfortunately, I could shed any light. It was for her well-being, as well as protection, if she never knew the ins and outs of Nik's and my relationship. Gah, I abhor falsity. Yet in my heart of hearts, I knew there were no other options. All of a sudden my blood ran cold; I wrapped my arms around my torso tightly.

Of course, Mom didn't miss it. "Are you chilly, hon?"

"Just a bit," I affirmed.

She rubbed her hands up and down my arms to generate some warmth, which made me feel like crap. I held back the moan of despair and glanced sideways. Renée caught my gaze and held it intently. With her eyes, she silently asked, "You okay?" As imperceptibly as possible, I shook my head. Code for: Help me out here! Not skipping a beat, she said, "Mrs. Mitchell, do you mind if I take Aimee back to your house?"

Mom smiled, "Of course not. I'll see you soon." She kissed my cheek as she made her way over to her car.

Once she was out of earshot, I disclosed, "Thanks, Ren. I don't know what I'd do without you."

She scoffed, "Oh, you're going to start talking. C'mon." She tugged on my arm, practically dragging me to her rental car.

I made the mistake of looking towards the church. Nik stood there watching me. A look of concern crossed his face, along with some unnamed emotion. Huh, what was that about? Then I mentally scolded myself, *don't go reading into things. You're already in way too deep with the man.* Yeah, I was. And honestly, I didn't think there was a way out now without shredding my heart to pieces in the process— which very well might happen in the long run. Too bad we couldn't control who we loved. Or who we shared sexual chemistry with. Life would be so much easier if we got a say in such matters.

*****

As we drove, I did my best to sidetrack Renée. "So, how's everything with Keshaun?"

"Great." She shot me a wry look. Darn, she didn't buy it. Should've known better than to try and pull the wool over *her* eyes. Once she cleared her throat, she pointed out, "Stop beating around the bush. What's going on?"

Weary and sick to death of covering my true feelings, I decided to let 'em loose. "I'm in love with him."

"Are you, now?"

I laughed with no humor. "Hell, yes. And it's really complicating things."

She inquired, "Such as?"

I exhaled heavily and then proceeded, "For starters, he doesn't feel the same about me."

She quirked a brow at me. "Really?"

"Of course, really," I stated exasperatedly.

"Looks to me like you're wrong 'bout that."

"How so?"

She reached over and patted my hand, which

was resting on my thigh. "Trust me. I just know these things."

Truthfully, she was almost never wrong on the feelings between a man and a woman. Yet I couldn't help but think, *there's a first time for everything*. No matter what, I wouldn't hold my breath on this one.

As we drove around, she continued to milk me for info. "Why don't you think he could feel the same way about you?" She arched a brow. "Has he said something?"

Awesome. As if I would ever divulge Nik's secrets. *Like you know them*. Well, I knew enough of them to know he was still very much in love with his late wife. Oh, he craved me as much as I did him. But that was not love. I answered, "Not in so many words. Call it female intuition."

She pulled over beside a park and faced me. "Cut the crap. What's really goin' on here?"

I got out of the car and began to walk. She strode beside me as I organized some of my thoughts. I finally stopped mid-stride and challenged, "Do you think I should go through with the wedding?"

Her eyes widened with surprise. "Little late for that question, don't ya think?"

I shook my head. "I don't know what to think anymore." I threw my hands up in the air and pointed out, "This is the twenty-first century."

"Um…'kay." She countered, "What the hell does that have to do with anything?"

Frustrated, I replied, "This is what women did in centuries past."

"Not sure I'm following your train of thought here, Aims." Her face was pinched in confusion.

Dammit. How to articulate it? I sighed, "What I mean is, women don't get married this day and time for protection."

"Alright, I see where you're goin' with this.

You mean in the past it was status quo, right?"

I emphatically nodded. "Exactly."

"But *you* love him." She added, "So, I'd say you're marrying him for all the right reasons."

I marched away from her, too angry to speak at the moment. As she followed, I queried, "Shouldn't he love me in return? I mean, aren't I lying by omission if I don't tell him my true feelings?"

She grabbed my shoulders and turned me towards her. "You listen to me, Aimee, and listen well. He *does* have strong feelings for you. Give him time to realize just how magnificent you truly are."

I pulled out of her grasp and scoffed, "I can't, Renée."

She shook her head. "I appreciate the fact you're humble. I do. But you deserve happiness. More than *anyone* I know." She grasped my hands. "I have a feeling he does as well. I think you two were made for each other."

"I'm not so sure about that." I could hear the sadness in my voice. Would she?

"Which part? His happiness or being made for one another?"

It was my turn to grab her by the shoulders. As I declared, "No one deserves happiness more than *Nik*."

Her brows rose to her hairline. "What aren't you telling me?"

"Not my story to share," I conveyed.

"Fair enough," she ceded. "You actually believe in coincidences?"

"No. You know better than that."

"Then there you go. You were meant to be," she reiterated.

I shook my head and slightly chuckled, "Your way of reasoning leaves a lot to be desired."

"Yeah, well, you can't argue with me. Can

you?"

No, I really couldn't. And the last thing I wanted was to stand there and fight over something like that. Instead, I threw my arms around her. "I love you."

She hugged me hard. "Right back attcha."

We began to stroll back towards the car. Once we were back inside and traveling to my parents' house, I said, "Thank you for everything, Ren."

"Not a problem, Aims."

*****

A little while later, we walked into the house I'd grown up in. I couldn't help but notice all the people I had known since childhood were there. My eyes widened in surprise as I leaned in and whispered, "Renée, did you know about this?"

"Nope. Looks like your mom and dad wanted to throw a little party for you."

When we rounded the corner, I smacked right into my fiancé. I studied his face to see if there was anger there and then greeted, "Hi."

"'Bout time you got here," he declared as he cupped my face with his hands.

My heart was beating so hard I could barely hear anyone in the room. What the?!

Without warning, his lips, strong yet gentle, were on mine. Oh, boy. That was our actual first kiss, although it ended way too soon. I stared up at him breathless. His smile reached his eyes as he murmured, "I missed you," against my ear.

Dazed and confused, I stood there blinking like an idiot for a few moments before I finally responded, "Did you, now?"

His chuckle was deep and low. "Ah, Aimee. You have no idea," he seductively proclaimed.

I bit my lip. Goodness he was sexy as hell like this. I swallowed hard. "Well, we're together now."

Before he could answer, my mom walked up with two glasses of champagne. She gave each of us one as she glanced over at my dad and nodded. Dad announced, "May I have everyone's attention."

Everyone turned collectively to look at us. He continued, "Here's to our lovely daughter, Aimee, and her soon to be husband, Nik. Cheers."

With that everyone toasted. Then Nik whispered, "Game on," so low only I could hear.

I almost spat my drink out. Once I recovered, I quickly and playfully retorted, "Bring it."

He shook his head and then bent down to place his lips against mine. Without pulling away, he suggestively stated, "Mm, what *I* can bring *you*."

Well, hell. When I vowed not to jump him until our wedding night, he just had to go and say that. He would pay dearly for getting me all hot and bothered like this. As he grinned at me, I knew he was well aware of my inner turmoil. Yep, pay backs a bitch. I smiled demurely and took another sip. Game was most definitely on.

Chapter Twenty-Six
Nik

My feelings for her were unmistakable. Aimee was witty and playful, and the sexiest woman I'd ever seen. By this time tomorrow evening, she would be mine. Mine forever. Reality hit hard, I really wanted this. I waited a beat to see what my head had to say about that. Nothing. A strange peace settled over me with the insight. While my heart still ached for Rachel, it was amenable with the feelings I had developed for Aimee. I knew now I was in love with her. How would I *convince* her? She knew how much I had loved my late wife—still did actually. Would she believe I could love them both? Guess my job from here on out was to make sure Aimee *knew* I was more than capable of cherishing her for the rest of our lives.

As I looked up, my brothers entered the room. I smiled while I strode towards them. They both stared at me like I had just grown another head when I hugged each one in turn. I chuckled, "What?"

Alex quirked a brow. "Nik, everything all right?"

E chimed in, "Who are you? And what have you done with my brother?"

At their inquisition, I threw my head back and laughed hard. Once I got myself under control, I replied, "I'm great. Last time I checked, I was still Nik." I wrapped an arm around each of them. "Thank you for being here with me."

E recovered first. "You're really okay with all of this, aren't you?"

"Yep, sure am."

Alex shook his head. "I'll be damned. You're fessing up to your feelings for her."

It wasn't a question, but a statement of fact. And there was no way I would deny it. "Weren't you the one who noticed it first?"

"Yeah. But still…"

E stated, "No one thought you'd realize it."

I put my hand over my heart playfully. "Ouch. That hurts."

They both grinned.

Alex affirmed, "We're happy for you, Nik."

"Seriously. We are," E confirmed.

"Thanks." I gazed at them intently, holding back the emotions that tried to emerge. "I owe you both an apology." I shook my head. "No. I owe so much more than that. But I'll start there. I'm sorry."

I watched both of my brothers fight their own emotions, which was difficult. But the knowledge that I'd caused it, downright unbearable. In unison they answered, "Apology accepted."

And then, my knees buckled. They were right there to hold me up. Just like always. What would I have done without them? They had been my foundation for so long now. I'm not a man of many words. Though I knew actions would speak louder. Once again, I hugged them hard. In front of all those people, I was actually thawing. No longer full of ice. My brothers were all I had left. And like a fool, I'd wasted so much time pushing them away. Silently I prayed, *thank you for them. Thank you for second chances.*

As Aimee approached, I knew she belonged in my family. I embraced her with all I had, nuzzling her hair. *Man, she smells good.* She whispered, "You okay?"

I couldn't answer her, so I nodded. Then my brothers shocked me as they wrapped their arms around us.

Alex whispered, "Welcome, little sister."

E continued, "Nice to have a girl in the family."

We all began to laugh.

It felt good.

It felt right.

Rest of the night was a blur. There was no way I would remember all the people I'd met at the party. One thing was certain, Aimee was well loved. Made me understand why she couldn't tell them the truth about herself. I had every intention of making sure her secret stayed safe. Not wanting anyone to accidentally stumble upon what her occupation had been for the past few years. And I definitely didn't want Reynolds to leak the info. Alex would make sure no one would ever connect the dots. Paid to have an attorney for a brother.

When I stood back and watched my fiancée with her father, my heart melted. I got it. I really did. There wasn't *anything* I wouldn't do for my family. The realization only made me love her more. A small voice in my head whispered *you deserve happiness*. I couldn't agree with that. Though, I shouldn't have been surprised I could still hear Rachel after all this time. She had made sure I knew she was at peace with me moving on long ago. I didn't quite see it that way at the time. But now...I did.

Once Aimee broke away from her dad, I beelined towards her. "How're you holding up?" I asked as I put my hands on her waist and pulled her close.

She sighed, "Good, but tired." She wrapped her arms around my middle. "How 'bout you?"

"Better, now."

She narrowed her eyes as she inquired, "How so?"

I leaned down to speak in her ear. "I'm holding you. Nothing's better than that."

She blinked several times. With her eyes shining, she responded, "What changed?"

Should've known my smart girl would put it together sooner rather than later. "Would you believe me if I told you, I had a wake-up call?"

"From whom?"

"Let's just say, you're not the only one who can put two and two together," I replied.

Her eyes narrowed. "Did something happen in Chicago that you'd like to share with me?"

I rubbed my nose against hers. "Sort of." She pulled back and stared at me. So I expounded, "I'll have to show you myself. If that's okay?"

She nodded and snuggled into my chest. It felt right to have her against me. I kissed the top of her head. I was about to drop the L-bomb when Renée interrupted.

"Hate to bother you guys, but it's time to leave, Aims."

"Give me just a sec," Aimee replied.

Renée politely stepped back out of hearing range.

Aimee looked up at me. "I'm sorry I have to go."

"So am I." I hugged her a little tighter and fought the urge to haul her off in my arms. *Possessive much?*

"I have my cell phone if you wanna text me."

I raised an eyebrow. "That's allowed?"

She giggled. And it was the most beautiful sound I had ever heard. I stared in awe. She reached up to stroke my face and answered, "Sure it is."

I murmured, "Are we permitted to have phone sex?"

She smacked me. "No!"

I pouted. She pressed a chaste kiss to my lips. There was nothing I wanted more than to deepen the kiss, but I knew if I started, I wouldn't stop. I replied, "You better go."

She grinned, "Alright. I'll see you tomorrow," she said while backing out of my embrace.

"I'll be the guy in a tux, standing at the altar." I winked.

Over her shoulder she called, "I'll be the girl in a white frilly dress." Then she blew me a kiss on the way out.

How will I ever make it through the night?

When I turned around, my brothers stood there eyeing me with an expression on their faces I couldn't quite name. "What?"

They shook their heads as Alex clapped my back. "Nothing."

I narrowed my eyes. "Bullshit."

E chuckled, "It's just nice to see. That's all."

"Speak English," I demanded.

Alex elaborated, "To see you happy. Relaxed. More yourself than you've been in years."

Oh. Well, I was all those things, and so much more. Chagrined, I responded, "Look, I know I've been a real hard-ass. I really am sorry—for all of it."

E replied, "Over and done, my brother."

Alex nodded, "Yes, it is." Then he added, "No more apologies, okay?"

I shook my head as I wrapped an arm around each of them. "Fair enough. I'll stop, for now."

E asked, "You ready to blow this Popsicle stand?"

"Hell yeah, I am." I stepped back. "Let me go say goodbye to Aimee's parents. I'll meet you by the car."

Alex called, "sounds good," over his shoulder.

After a little chitchat, I said my farewells to Mr. and Mrs. Mitchell. *Down to earth* was what went through my mind as I turned to leave. They really were wonderful people. Aimee came from a great family. I strode outside and thought; *now, she'll be part of mine.* She had already wormed her way not just into my heart, but my brothers as well. Somewhere deep down I knew my parents would've loved her, too. Not knowing how or when I did anything worthy of such an amazing woman. But I did know, I'd move heaven and earth to deserve a fraction of her love. Yeah, I wanted to be a better man. She needed that. And if I were being truthful, so did I. E was right, the past was over and done. No amount of could've, would've, or should've was going to change that fact. Time to move on. Something told me, the best was yet to come. Damn, I could really use that. So could Aimee.

*****

Actually excited about tomorrow, I was concerned I wouldn't get much sleep. Then I saw my brothers standing outside of a stretch limo. Ah, shit. As I approached, the laughter grew more raucous.

E handed me a bottle of Heineken. He tapped his against mine and said, "Let's get this bachelor party started."

Alex hooted and then boisterously yelled, "Damn straight."

Once I climbed inside I saw the "ladies" that

were waiting. My eyes widened in surprise as I looked over at my brothers, crawling among the *entertainment*. "Fuck a duck," I exclaimed.

E wiggled his eyebrows in a devious way. "You can say that again, Nik."

Alex leaned over with his hand on a taut female ass. "We don't expect you to partake in the festivities. Enjoy your beer."

At that moment, E lifted his head from a bouncy breast. How he had managed to tie her wrists with her bra straps, I would never know. *Kinky bastard*. He smirked, "Don't worry. We'll enjoy these lovelies for you." There was nothing more said for a while. His mouth was a bit occupied.

I rolled my eyes heavenward. I had only *thought* I was horny earlier. As I sat there watching live porn, I realized this would test my self-control in ways I'd never imagined. But then, Aimee's beautiful face and delectable body came to mind. After that, all I could think of was how spectacular making love to my wife was going to be the next evening. Yeah, those desirous images would hold me. She was well worth the sacrifice. I leaned back, closed my eyes, and fantasized of *only* Aimee.

Chapter Twenty-Seven
Aimee

In front of the lighted mirror, I sat in the chair and watched the stylist work my hair in an intricate up-do. Wow, if only I could ever copy such artistry. Not going to happen. But a girl could dream, right?

Renée pulled me from my reverie when she said, "Seriously, your hair looks incredible."

I winked at her in the mirror. There was no way I was turning my head to look at her. So I could see the back of her hair as well, I motioned for her to turn around and then replied, "Yours is pretty spectacular, too."

She grinned, "And look"—bending down in front of me so we were eye level, she pointed to her face—"all evidence of my bruising is gone!" she exclaimed.

Really, there wasn't a trace of a mark anywhere. "Too bad Keshaun had a game today. He'd be speechless if he could see you now."

"Oh, he's seen it. I sent a pic a lil' while ago." She waggled her eyebrows at me mischievously.

I shook my head imperceptibly. "I don't even wanna know when you did that."

As she sashayed over to the coffee bar, she answered coyly, "Couldn't've been when I was in the changing room, now could it?"

One thing about it, she was a flirtatious Domme. Not sure if that was the norm, because I didn't know any other ones. Thank God for that! Renée and her antics were all I could handle. I did my best to ignore the visual which came to mind every time I thought of her penchant for BDSM and replied, "You're incorrigible."

"Yeah, I am that." She sultrily added, "And then some."

While I was happy she felt more herself, it was not what I needed when my stomach was tied in knots. Still unsure if the wedding was truly in my best interest.

Eventually, I heard Renée talking. "Hello. You in there, Aims?" She stood in front of me waving her hand.

Gee, how long had I been caught up in my musings? I cleared my throat and responded, "Yeah, I'm here. Sorry."

She shook her head. "You're still worried about this, aren't you?"

I sighed heavily. "How could I not be?" I bit my lip and then continued, "I mean, theoretically, you say 'I do' forever."

"You're right. But I thought we settled that."

"So did I."

She nodded, "You'll see. He's completely beguiled by you." She grasped my shoulders. "Didn't you see it yesterday?"

I shrugged timidly. "I saw something different. But what if…"

She interrupted, "Uh-huh. No you don't." Then she sternly commanded, "You will not second guess him, yourself, or this wedding. We clear, here?"

Ah, Ms. Take-Charge had spoken. "If only it were that easy, Ren."

"It is." She tugged on my hands to pull me out

of the chair. "Now, let's go finish getting ready."

I smiled, "Alrighty. I'm sure Mom's wondering where we are."

*****

The church was already halfway filled when we arrived. *Oh, crap.*

Renée wrapped a reassuring arm around my waist. "Come on. Everything's going to be okay."

I nodded as we went in through a side door to enter the bridal dressing room. Not convinced she was right about that, but knew it was too late to back out now. Was Nik this nervous? I wanted to speak to him, but tried to keep with the tradition of not seeing my groom before the ceremony. I inquired, "Do you think the guys are here yet?"

She chortled, "Let me check."

I squeezed her hand. "Thanks."

"No problem." She winked on her way out.

I began to strip out of my clothes and then wrapped a silk robe around me. As I sat in front of the mirror, I decided to put my make-up on. Most brides would've let the ladies at the salon do it, but I like to do my own. I found it relaxing in its own way, plus, I enjoyed watching the subtle transformation. Me, only better. There was a light rapping on the door. Without forethought about who was on the other side, I answered, "Come in."

I heard a male clear his throat. Then a deep, raspy voice replied, "I'm not sure that's allowed."

"Nik?" I queried shyly.

"Yes, Aimee," he confirmed. I was standing by the door to hear him better when he asked, "You doing all right in there?"

Unable to hold it back, I confessed, "I am,

now."

A low chuckle responded. "I'm glad to hear that."

I bit my lip. "You are?"

He assured, "Yeah, I am. You ready for this?"

"As long as you're sure, then, yes, I'm ready."

"No cold feet on this side."

I giggled, "That's a good thing." Then I proclaimed, "None on this side, either."

He took a deep breath and exhaled, "I'll see you in a few minutes."

To clear the fog of joy from my head, I shook it and answered, "See you soon." I leaned against the door for support. Just the sound of his voice did things to me—like make me giddy. And then there were the *other* things. Oh, my. I fanned myself. Someday I would put my theory to the test. I was going to learn if he could make me come just by talking to me. I went back to finish putting my face on when Renée and my mom entered.

Mom directed, "Renée you get dressed first. Then you can help me get Aimee together."

Renée grinned, "Yes, ma'am."

That in itself was funny, because usually she didn't take orders. From anyone. Mom continued, "Come over here, Aimee. You can leave your robe on the chair."

I smiled, "Okay."

She gazed at me. "Am I doing it again?"

"Yeah. But it doesn't bother me."

Renée called out, "Me, neither."

We all laughed as I dropped the robe. My mom gasped, "Oh dear. Those are some really fancy undergarments you have on."

I blushed. "It's only silk and lace, Mom."

She shook her head. "Still, with those garters and stockings it's quite a package."

I stepped into the dress she was holding for me. "I just want to look nice for him. Know what I mean?"

She grinned, "He'll be very pleased," and then added, "No need to worry."

I licked my lips. "I hope so."

As she did up the back of my gown, Renée stepped out. I whistled. "Look at you!" I exclaimed. "Grape is definitely your color."

She spun in a circle so I could see it from every angle. The dress was simple: off the shoulder and form fitting. And she looked lovely. She began to adjust the sweetheart neckline on me—not an easy task with my ample chichis—while Mom continued with the back.

When they finally finished, both of them oohed and aahed for a couple of moments. I decided to take a peek and walked over to the full length mirror. The dress was extraordinary with the high, low look. The corset torso with the organza skirt looked amazing, sliming my waist while it showed off my legs. And the intricate jeweled belt, sitting at my natural waist, completed the effect.

Mom gushed, "You look like a million bucks."

Renée commented, "I haven't seen you look this gorgeous since that masquerade years back."

At the mention of that charity ball, my stomach did a little flip. Not like I would ever forget that evening. Again, I had to wonder, what happened to Mr. Mysterious? Mom pulled me back in the moment. "Well, I didn't see that dress. But this gown is absolutely breathtaking."

I smiled and hugged her, hard, then whispered, "Thanks, Mom, for everything."

We were interrupted by a knock at the door. Renée answered it. After a beat, my dad entered. He looked so spiffy in his suit. Such a handsome man, even with all the chemo had put him through. He embraced me, and I could hear the emotion in his voice when he spoke, "You look beautiful, Aimee."

Again, my face flushed with color. "Thanks, Dad."

Mom was dabbing a tissue under her eyes with a huge smile on her face.

Renée took control. "All right, folks. If we don't get moving, there won't be a wedding."

I mouthed, "Thanks."

She winked. "Are we good to go?"

We replied, "Yes."

*****

While Renée walked down the aisle, I waited for my turn in the foyer and listened to the beautiful, classical music that played. It relaxed me in ways I couldn't put into words. Dad came over and escorted me to the doors. "Ready?"

Unable to speak due to the emotions racing through me, I nodded.

The music changed when the double doors opened. I was not sure I heard it clearly. Was that Luther Vandross and Mariah Carey singing "Endless Love?" I blinked back tears as I asked, "Dad, who picked this song?"

His eyes were a little teary when he answered, "Nik."

"Oh," I gasped.

Then Nik came into my line of sight, and I could no longer hold back the waterworks. Once we reached the altar, dad placed my hand in Nik's. I leaned in so only he could hear me and whispered, "Nik, you picked this?"

"Yeah, I did."

I bit my lip. He gently tugged on my chin, so I would release it. Meanwhile, he brushed away my tears with the pad of his thumb. It was such an intimate gesture. And suddenly everything and everyone ceased to exist. There was only us, lost in one another's gaze. Renée had been right; love *did* shine in his eyes. He leaned down and murmured, "You ready?"

I breathlessly replied, "I am."

Although our song was not the traditional "Wedding March," our vows were. I was still processing Nik actually loved me. No, he hadn't said the words. But it was in the song, as well as written all over his chiseled, masculine face. Our kiss was far too short and, once again, chaste. Afterwards, we were bombarded with hugs and kisses—a bit overwhelming, and yet so wonderful. We had to step into the office to sign our marriage certificate. E and Renée were there as well to sign as our witnesses. I looked over at Nik.

"E spells his name E-v-e-n, not E-v-a-n?"

He chuckled, "It's the Norwegian spelling."

I glanced down again, and that was when I noticed Nik's given name was not Nicholas like I had thought. I whispered, "Nikko?"

"That'd be me," he replied with a slight bow.

How I loved a sense of humor. "Fitting," I declared. He raised his brow. So I explained, "Sensual name for a sexy man."

He growled in my ear, "You think I'm sexy?"

As I licked my bottom lip, I met his gaze and nodded.

His smile was downright sinful.

Oh, boy. The promise of seduction his eyes held made me squirm.

Alex broke the spell when he poked his head

in and inquired, "Everything all right in here?"

Nik answered, "We're good to go." With that, we all walked out to the front steps of the church.

*****

Bird seed was thrown as we made our way to the waiting limousine. Once inside, I thought for sure I would finally get a more passionate kiss. Unfortunately that wasn't the case. A few seconds behind us, Alex, Even, and Renée climbed in to share the ride over to the hotel for our reception.

I glanced over at Nik and thought: *I want to kick them out and have my wicked way with you.*

As if he read my naughty mind, he leaned in so only I could hear him. "Later," he said with seductive promise as his tongue roved over his sculpted bottom lip.

Oh, fucking, my. Wet heat pooled between my thighs. Yeah, I was more than ready to consummate our marriage. And I had no doubts our lives would be filled with love and passion. I softly kissed the side of his mouth. His hot gaze captured mine, and I damn near spontaneously combusted.

E snapped out, "Stop that." We both looked over at him as he continued, "I refuse to sit here and watch the two of you go at it like monkeys." Then he rolled his eyes. "Besides, that vanilla crap is so prosaic."

Alex added, "That's what your honeymoon is for." His face grew stern as he looked over at Even. "And *you* need to put a cork in it. No one here wants to hear about your preferred methods." He shook his head and made a face of mock disgust.

Hmm, what was that all about?

Renée's eyes locked with me. "You have no clue, do you?"

"Uh?" I responded unsure of where she was going with this.

I didn't have to wait more than a few moments when she remedied my naiveté.

"Do you know what Even does for a living?"

I regarded E. "Sure. He runs a high-end night club."

Alex chuckled, "Well, half of it is."

I gave Nik a sidelong glance. "There's more?" I asked him.

He squeezed my hand as Renée proceeded, "You know how you *hate* for me to talk about my sessions?"

My eyes narrowed as my brow furrowed. "Yeah."

"Who do you think taught me the tricks of the trade, so to speak?"

I paused. Then, suddenly, it all became clear. "OMG!" I looked directly at Even. "You're *the* Master?"

He bowed his head. "That'd be me, sister dear."

Beyond dumbfounded, Nik leaned down and queried, "You've heard of him before?"

Renée answered, "Who hasn't? He's known in at least six States."

Still, I sat there with my mouth gaping open and stared in shock.

Alex added, "Yes. It's questionable if the clubs are legal."

Even fired back, "That's what I have you for. To make sure I toe the very gray line."

I finally found my voice. "So, you're the teacher?"

I attempted to process what I had just learned as my eyes darted between E and Ren. Of course, I knew about her *lessons*. I'd seen the welts and bruises first hand. I studied Even closer. He didn't seem like the type of man to enjoy hurting a woman. Granted, he was dangerously handsome with his almost platinum hair and silver eyes; still, I couldn't wrap my brain around the contradiction. Then I recalled what Renée had told me once before: *It's not like that, Aims. I wasn't grasping what I was supposed to do. He didn't hurt me for the joy of it or on purpose. Only to show me what I needed to know so I understood.*

Even pulled me from my reminiscence. "Correct," he answered.

Nik turned my face to his. "Don't worry." He vowed, "That's not my thing."

I bit my lip. "Then, what is *your* thing?"

He purred, "You."

Renée chimed in, "Told you so."

I giggled as Nik queried, "What?"

"Tell you later," I whispered

He grabbed my hand and kissed the palm while he gazed at me. "I'm gonna hold you to that."

Both of his brothers made mock gagging noises while Renée chortled at their antics. So this was what life was going to be like. Honestly, I couldn't be upset with that. I really did love them already—different preferences and all.

Cue the warm fuzzies.

I laid my head on Nik's shoulder and sighed in contentment. Life as a Strand would never be boring. That's for sure.

Chapter Twenty-Eight
Nik

Nothing would've made me happier than to kick everyone out of the limo, so I could properly kiss my wife. 'Course I knew good and well that would lead to more promising things. Damn. I shifted my legs to somehow disguise the raging erection tenting my tailored Fioravanti's. We arrived at the hotel, thankfully, before I embarrassed myself.

I climbed out and offered my hand to escort Aimee. Once we entered the ballroom for our reception, the DJ officially introduced us. "Ladies and Gentleman, may I present Mr. and Mrs. Nik Strand."

We made our way to the front of the room to a standing ovation. Unable to stop my memories, Rachel's and my wedding suddenly played through my mind as flashes went off from cameras and cell phones.

It had been a simple ceremony. Our witnesses were the older couple who owned and operated the tiny, wedding chapel in Reno. There had been no reception. Her family hadn't attended—of course, Alex had been there for me—nor any of our friends to wish us well. We had spent our wedding night in a motel just up the road from the chapel. Inside the tiny room, we had danced to Michael Bolton's "When a Man Loves a Woman" until we fell on the bed, laughing. Then we had made love for our very first time.

I was suddenly back in the present, trying to make sense of my surroundings. My brothers stood in front of me while Aimee had her arm wrapped around my waist. Once I recalled where I was and why, I cursed under my breath. Immediately I apologized, "Aimee, I'm so sorry. I…"

She interrupted, "Don't. It's not as if you can control when that happens."

I wanted to confess this time it wasn't PTSD, but, at the moment, it didn't seem appropriate. Alex held my gaze for a few beats before he appeared satisfied with what he saw.

E clapped my shoulder. "No one even noticed but us," he confided.

As I took in the room, I realized he was accurate. What had felt like hours, in reality had only been a couple of minutes at best. I nodded my acknowledgement. Words refused to surface at the moment. Then shock became the only thing I recognized when Aimee reached up to wipe the pads of her fingers along my cheeks. She pulled her hand away, and I saw the moisture on them. Dammit. I had been crying like a big-ass baby. Once I politely excused myself, I went to pull my shit together in the men's room. My brothers entered while I splashed water on my face.

Alex didn't hold back. "What the fuck, Nik?"

E added, "We know that wasn't your PTSD making its appearance."

After I turned off the water and dried my face with a paper towel, I leaned my hip against the counter. "No." I concluded, "You're right, that's not what it was."

They both stood there with brows raised. I took a deep breath and disclosed, "Just remembering mine and Rachel's wedding."

E was the first to respond. "Ah, hell."

Alex grabbed my shoulders and looked me in the eye. "You okay? Not having any regrets, are you?" His question was laced with concern.

"No." I shook my head for emphasis. "Nothing like that."

E narrowed his eyes. "You're still in love with Rachel, aren't you?"

I blew out a breath I didn't realize I was holding. "I'll *always* love her."

When we all heard the high-pitched gasp, we ran out the door. Aimee stood there against the wall with her hands over her mouth and tears streaming down her face. I instantly turned towards my brothers and suggested, "Give us a minute, would ya?"

They made a respectful departure, as I lifted Aimee's chin and gazed into her eyes. "Don't do this," I beseeched.

She began to babble, "I-I wasn't trying to eavesdrop."

I tugged her into my chest and attested, "I know that."

"You do?"

"Yup."

She continued, "I was worried about you. I swear, I only wanted to check on you."

"But instead, you heard me confess to loving my late wife," I answered self-deprecatingly.

She went stiff in my arms. I grasped her face in both my hands. "A man can *love* more than one woman."

"Yes," she sighed. I could tell she was attempting to grasp what I said. "The heart is capable of many *types* of love," she affirmed.

No, that was not what I meant. But my ability to convey that left much to be desired. Thus, I simply

nodded and gently brushed my lips against hers.
Before things could heat up, Renée interceded,
"Erghm, I hope I'm not interrupting anything. But the
two of you are needed at the table."

I smirked, "We're on our way."

She nodded and then walked away.

Aimee shook her head, looping her arm with
mine. "Shall we?"

*****

We ate dinner, enjoyed several toasts, and
then cut the cake. After that, there was the bouquet
and garter toss. Aimee didn't want to part with her
beautiful, deep purple calla lilies, so there was a
smaller bouquet full of all kinds of flowers for her to
throw. It was no revelation when Renée snagged it.
The big surprise was when E not only caught the
garter, but then flaunted it in Alex's face. I tried my
best not to bust a gut at my brothers' shenanigans, as I
tugged Aimee onto the dance floor. Once there, I
inclined my head at the DJ for him to begin the song I
had specifically picked for our first dance.

Aimee inhaled sharply when the soulful voice
of Adele filled the room. "Oh, I love "Make You Feel
My Love." It's my favorite song by her."

I grinned, "I wasn't aware of that." Then
admitted, "But I think the words sum up my
feelings."

As we danced around the floor, I whispered
the words that conveyed everything I wanted to tell
her and vowed those lyrics to her. Did she understand
what I was saying? When our eyes met, hers were
shimmering with unshed tears. Yeah, she got it.
Thank God. I held her just a little closer as the song
came to an end. We shared another chaste kiss before
we danced with her parents.

By the end of the evening, I was worn out, yet overjoyed. Still, trying to process emotions other than anger and guilt was new for me. Yet whenever I looked at my wife, I knew I wanted to be the best I could be. No, I would *never* deserve her. But I'd be damned if I would give her up now. For all it was worth, she had what was left of my splintered heart. Although, truth be told, due to her love and light those pieces were reattaching themselves. Sure, the scars would always be there. Though, somehow I knew, that only made the fusion which was going on better. More complete. The things I felt for Aimee went far beyond the remnants of the love I'd had for Rachel. I was aware I needed to tell her all of this, but unable to put it into words. I vowed to myself, *I'll find a way.*

*****

As we made our way to the penthouse suite of the hotel, I gave her a little information. "We're only here for tonight. In the morning, we'll fly out on the company jet to the most romantic getaway I could pull off on such short notice."

She squeezed my hand. "Anywhere is fine as long as I'm with you."

Humbled, I took a deep breath before I replied, "Same here. Unfortunately, we won't have but the weekend." Her eyes widened as I continued, "I have business that cannot wait. I'm truly sorry."

She bit her lip in consternation. "I'll go back to New York alone?"

Man, she's adorable. "No. I was hoping you'd join me."

She smiled, "I'd love to."

Once we reached the suite, I picked her up and made our way across the threshold. The door clicked shut, and I ensured it was locked before I turned back to her. She had a wicked grin on her face. I stepped forward, but she held her hand up and commanded, "Stay right there."

I'm not a man who normally took orders. But something about her made me comply. When she reached back to undo her dress, the front fell to her waist. And there, peeking through soft, gray lace and begging for my mouth, were the most attractive dusty rose nipples I'd ever had the pleasure to look at. Who was I to deny them?

Yeah, she *thought* she was running this show.

Fuck.

That.

I prowled—like the predator I was—forward and captured her by the nape of her neck, drawing her supple curves into my hard planes. Perfect damn fit. My mouth seized hers in a devastating mating, and, for a moment, I was lost to her sweet, wet recesses. Exploring. Dominating. I took everything she was willing to give. My God, she was luscious. As that tongue of hers dueled with mine, I knew I would soon be undone.

My lips traveled down her slender throat, across her collar bones, and further down to those hard peaks pleading for attention. I rasped, "So fuuuuuucking sweet."

She arched into me on a moan.

I reached behind and undid the hooks on her lacey bra, which was keeping me from her taut nipples. Once freed, I continued my torture. And enjoyed every sigh and gasp she uttered. A little rougher than I meant to, I shoved her up against the wall and laved my way down her stomach, paying homage to her oh-so, sensitive navel. I could feel her orgasm climbing, but I wasn't ready for her to go over. Just yet. I traced my way along the silky edge of her thong and worked down to the garters clipped onto her stockings. I looked up her body while she watched my mouth. Hell, yeah. "Play with your breasts," I commanded.

Her brow furrowed for a moment. I wasn't sure if my bossy side turned her on, or pissed her off. When she complied, I had my answer. With a little satisfied smirk, I continued, "No, not small circles." Her palms stilled while her lustful eyes held mine. "Use your thumbs and forefingers. Yeah, like that." As she rolled and tugged those beautiful nipples, I went to work on her core. I used my fingers to hold her panties along the side; meanwhile, my tongue plunged into her slickness with gusto. She came all over my face, screaming my name. I. Fucking. Loved. It. So to bring her again, I switched my attention to her swollen clit and took her up and up and up. Then, I pushed her over on a hard suck of the sensitive nub.

She went boneless in my arms. Once she was somewhat coherent, I stood and devoured her sexy as hell mouth. I wanted her to taste herself on me, so I dove deep. She moaned a protest when I picked her up and made my way to the bedroom. No matter how sexed-up I was, I would not take her against the wall for our first time as husband and wife. I would do this properly. I laid her on top of the bed while she looked up at me and whispered, "Your turn."

I stepped back and gave her a show. Slowly I removed my clothes, gazing into her eyes. When my boxer briefs hit the floor, she sat up and gripped my painful erection. "Oh…yes…just like that," I approved.

She worked me from root to tip, and back again and again. I stilled her hand and then crawled over her body. She was more than ready for me, spreading those lovely thighs wide so I could see her sex glisten. That sight alone was enough to send me over the edge. With deep concentration, I held back. Just. I settled my large, heavy body over hers, feeling like the brute I was. She looked so tiny underneath me. Then I entered her and reverently praised, "So damn tight, little one."

She hissed as I sheathed my dick inside her. I had died and gone to heaven. For a moment, I held still to get myself under control. That was when she locked her legs over mine to rub her clit against me. *Oh, I can take a hint.* I pulled myself up a little further, so the top of her head was under my chin. Then I began to pump, knowing full well that in this position, my cock rubbed that sweet, little nub. And as she gasped, "Oh, yes, Nik," I knew I was hitting her just right. That was when I fully unleashed, and pounded into her with all I had. I took her over the precipice once more, before I followed.

I slumped against her and nuzzled into her silken hair as I whispered, "I should move before I crush you."

"Don't you dare," she warned while she wrapped her arms around me.

I chuckled, "Baby, I could stay like this forever."

Her satisfied, "hmm," said so much more than words ever could.

I reluctantly pulled out of her wet heat and then lay on my side, tugging her onto my chest. I stroked her back, up and down, soothingly as we drifted towards sleep. The last thought I had was, *my wife forever.*

Chapter Twenty-Nine
Aimee

I was still not sure how many times Nik had woken me up through the night to make love. When my heavy lids lifted, there he was staring down at me, humming. I stroked his shadowed jaw and mentioned, "Aero Smith. We like a lot of the same music." I propped myself up on one elbow and kissed the corner of his mouth, then reached over for my iPod. Once I hit one of the play lists, I directed, "Sing for me." He winked as he sang along with "Don't Want to Miss a Thing." Yep, his deep, raspy voice alone could absolutely send me into eternal bliss.

I had put the song on a loop. So once it ended that first time, I mounted my husband and sank down on his sizeable penis. Sure, I was sore, but I couldn't have cared less at the moment. Afterwards, I gently eased off of him and made my way to the bathroom. He followed, swatting my butt as he said, "Hustle up. We have a plane to catch."

I grinned, "What, you're not going to join me in here?" I let my fingers travel down to my wet sex as I held his gaze.

On a growl, he joined me in the shower. Once we were temporarily sated, we cleansed one another. I had a feeling, no matter how many times either of us orgasmed, we were never going to be completely satisfied. Fine by me. There was nothing in this world I wanted more than my body joined with his. While those thoughts passed through my mind, I licked my lips. His eyes met mine in the mirror. "We have the plane as well as the entire weekend to make love, insatiable wife of mine."

"It's your own damn fault."

He cocked a brow. "How's that?"

"You're just too fucking good at making me come."

His grunt of satisfaction, along with the deep grind of his hips into my backside, was all I needed to know I'd just made him a very happy man. Then he kissed the side of my neck and murmured, "Goes both ways, little one."

For some reason, him calling me "little one" brought back the masquerade. Why did Nik remind me so much of my mystery man? What was the connection? I had planned to ask, but suddenly my mouth was invaded by a most persistent tongue. All thought left, in a whoosh of sensation, as he devastated me once more with his oral talents. Hot damn! The man's expertise knew no bounds.

*****

We were late arriving to the plane. Not that it mattered. I mean, Nik owned the darn thing, so it wasn't as if we held up other passengers. Once onboard and seat-belted properly, we took off. Tired, I closed my eyes as Nik's thumb rubbed soothingly along my wrist. My intention was to make love to my husband on our five hour journey; however, sleep prevailed. I didn't budge until we landed in St. Lucia.

I awoke to gentle lips on mine and whispered, "Hi."

He chuckled, "How was your rest, Sleeping

Beauty?"

I blinked several times to clear the fog from my brain. "I suppose it was fine." When my stomach grumbled, he smiled, "We'll eat as soon as we arrive at the resort."

My eyes widened as I leaned forward to look out the window. "Crap. I slept the entire flight here?"

"To be fair, so did I."

"No way!" I exclaimed. "Some honeymoon couple we are."

He nuzzled my nose with his. "We barely slept last night," he purred. "I think rest was foremost this morning. Besides, we'll be busy later."

Oh, my. The promise that went with the statement was unmistakable. I brushed my lips against his softly and declared, "Then, I think we better get there. Like, now."

He stood and proffered his hand to assist me.

*****

The spectacular island made our drive beautiful, at times breathtaking. But Jade Mountain itself was phenomenal. The galaxy sanctuary was remarkable. It was one thing to take in the fifteen-foot high ceilings and the eclectic furniture; however, the awe-inspiring infinity pool, where the fourth wall should've been, was nothing short of magnificent. A full two-hundred-and-seventy degree view of the Caribbean Sea was not a sight I would soon forget. If ever.

When hard, muscled arms enveloped my waist, I leaned back and enjoyed the feel of his body pressed against mine. He whispered, "You like?"

I turned in his arms and locked eyes with him. "Nikko Mathias Strand, you have outdone yourself," I praised. "This place is incredible." I pulled his face to mine. "Just like you." Then I proceeded to show him exactly how appreciative I was.

Once we came up for air, he murmured, "I love the sound of my full name on your lips." To prove his point he licked his way around my mouth.

Wow, his attention to detail could not be matched. As if he needed to show me just how meticulous he could be, he began to work lips, tongue, and teeth down my body. All the while, his equally gifted fingers undressed me until I stood fully nude: he remained clothed. Now that was freaking hot! He laid me down gently on a chaise lounge as he fell to his knees, and then continued his sinful ministrations over and around my core. The orgasm crested, strong and proud, as he proceeded to show me my body was more than capable of multiples. Good Lord, I wasn't sure I would survive. Oh, but the la petite mort was so damn worth it.

Once I'd recovered from the dizzying climax, my stomach rumbled. Embarrassed, I laid my hand over the loud beast. Nik shook his head and announced, "Right, time to eat."

Well, it looked as if my plans for him were going to have to wait. *That's fine*. Later, I would show him he was multi-orgasmic as well. A sly smile played at the corners of my mouth, which caused Nik to question me. "Now, what is that expression all about?"

While I slipped on a sundress, I replied, "For me to know, and you to find out."

He placed his hands on my shoulders and growled, "Don't tempt me, woman."

I bit my bottom lip and then teased "Or what?"

He spun me around so fast I would've lost my balance if he hadn't pushed me up against the wall and held me in place with his hard body. As he licked my ear, he cautioned, "You're playing with fire."

Holy crap. Torn between my angry stomach and the desire to push him further, I wasn't at all sure which one I wanted more.

He made the decision for me when he stepped backwards and chuckled, "We need food to keep our strength up. Let's go." Then he tugged me out the door.

As I looked at him sideways, I confirmed, "You're right." Then I promised, "Afterwards, I have plans for you. Wouldn't want you passing out from all I'm going to do to you."

"Oh, little one, I can't wait to see you try," he rumbled.

*****

We ate alfresco beneath the romantic canopy overlooking the exquisite Caribbean Sea. I inquired, "Will this be all we see of this beautiful island?"

His brow arched. "If you would like to explore, I'm fine with that. If not, I'm more than okay. The decision is completely yours." He grabbed my hand and brought it to his mouth, where his wicked tongue began to dance along the sensitive skin between my fingers.

Wow, it was as if those spots had a direct line to my clitoris. Never had a man been able to arouse me like Nikko. Hmm, I wondered if he let me call him that. 'Cause honestly, the name was as sexy as the man. Time to find out. I whispered, "Ah, Nikko, you're beyond insatiable."

As he rested his forehead against mine, he groaned, "Say it again."

Along the seam of his mouth, I breathed, "Which one?" Even I could hear the desire drenched quality to my voice.

He licked the outside of my lips before he answered, "My name."

I susurrated, "Nikko."

His hand fisted my hair as he took my mouth with a hunger I so easily matched.

Our server interrupted us, "Erghm. Would you like dessert?"

Nik broke our kiss, keeping his eyes on me. "Yes. But not here."

She blushed profusely as she answered, "I see. Then I will take my leave, sir." She winked at me. "Ma'am."

Once she left, we did as well.

*****

Intention didn't always mean follow through. In other words, we were headed for our sanctuary, but our passion refused to wait. Exhibitionism had never been something I'd aspired to. Although when the obscure hammock presented itself on our walk…well, you could do the math. And, yeah, I admit, my curiosity regarding sex swings had just ramped tenfold. Goodness, he was buried deeper inside me than ever before. No wonder those things were so effin' popular. Thankful we had just climaxed and were fully clothed, because we were suddenly not alone. After quickly putting ourselves to rights, I buried my head in Nik's chest as he greeted our intruders. "Hi."

The other couple stared wild-eyed for a moment before the guy responded, "I hope we didn't…"

Nik was fast when he replied, "No, not at all. I apologize if we have embarrassed you."

The guy expediently answered, "'S all good, my man."

Nik gave a self-satisfied grin. "Yes, it was."

I gasped as I caught the other man's gaze go from the hammock to his woman, and back again. Oh, looked as if we weren't the only ones who would enjoy exhibitions alfresco.

As we walked away, I stifled a giggle.

Nik reproached, "Stop that." Then he smiled.

Dear me, would I ever grow accustomed to that heart-stopping grin of his. No, probably not. I reached over to caress his sculpted lips.

He cocked a brow. "What?"

I honestly answered, "I can't believe you're mine."

He stopped and hauled me against him. "Always." Once more, he took my mouth with his. After a few moments, he whispered against my lips, "And you are *mine*."

The possession was an aphrodisiac. I clasped his hand and drew him along the walking path. "I need *more*," I stated when he shot me an inquisitive glance.

He responded on a growl, "Fuuuuuck."

He really had said it best. That one word meant a dozen different things at the moment.

I coyly replied, "And then some, baby."

All of sudden, I was in his arms, and then he began to jog back to our own private haven.

Chapter Thirty
Nik

Good God, I wasn't sure I could've gone another round. We'd been at it for hours. And I had lost count of how many times I'd come—which, that right there, was a damn miracle in and of itself. Before Aimee, I had only managed to climax twice in one night. But my siren had me fully erect and ejaculating on command. So. Fucking. Hot. Spent and exhausted, sleep finally won the battle.

The next day when we awoke, it was well past lunchtime. After we grabbed some food, we headed out to do some snorkeling. Although I would much rather have been buried inside her welcoming body, I was glad to enjoy a couple of hours of fun. We were still getting to know each other in many ways, so having some downtime was necessary. Unfortunately, we had a plane to catch. Though, I mentally made plans to come back here for at least a week, soon. Very soon.

*****

Before Aimee fell into a deep sleep on the flight back, I informed, "We're stopping in Chicago for about twenty-four hours."

"Hmm. What for?"

"The business we spoke of earlier."

"Together?"

"Yes, my little one. I plan on us staying together."

She smiled before fully losing consciousness.

While I hated that Franco was unable to handle his cousin, and that the situation had escalated, I was excited I would be able to tease Aimee's memory. Silently I prayed, *Please, let her remember me from that night at the masquerade.* Somehow I knew, once she connected the dots, things would be much better between us. Not that they were bad. Oh, hell, no. On the contrary. But I hated having knowledge about something she didn't. It felt like lying. And the last thing I ever wanted to do was lie to her. Never her.

I glanced over at my precious wife. No, she wasn't perfect. By far, she was too good for me. Yet, something about her lit up my soul in a way no other ever had or would. To cherish her would never be a burden. I gently kissed the top of her head and then drifted off myself.

The nightmare was not one I could wake from. Terrifying. No, this was not a memory like all the others. Still so frickin' vivid, I could've sworn it was happening in real time. I saw my beautiful wife lying in a mangled car against a huge pine tree. No movement, body broken and bloody, just as Rachel's had been in my work truck all those years ago. Same damn curve on Highway 89, and like before, I was impotent. All I could do was scream as something or someone restrained me. If I could only turn my head slightly, I would be able to see who or what had my arms wrenched behind my back. But no, it was as if my head were being held in place, forcing me to watch her die. I woke on an ear-splitting howl that scared the hell out of Aimee.

"Nikko?" she gasped, "What is it? What's wrong, baby?"

As she rubbed her hand up and down my arm, I pulled her onto my lap. I buried my head in her hair and breathed deeply. "Dream," I uttered. "Sorry I frightened you."

She caressed my back and asked, "Another memory?"

"Nah. It was nothing."

She pulled back and held my eyes with hers. "Bullshit. Talk to me, please."

I shook my head. "I can't. Not yet, anyway."

She stroked my jaw and then leaned in to brush her lips against mine. I held her a little tighter as I tried to slow my heart rate. If I lost her, I would never survive it. And that knowledge made me want to whisk her away. Protect her. Make sure no harm ever came to her. But I knew that wasn't even an option. Aimee wasn't the type of woman to let me go all caveman on her. It was actually one of the traits I admired most about her. I closed my eyes and emptied my brain of the horrid nightmare—reminding myself, *only a dream, Nik. Just a dream.*

Before I drifted off again, I heard her say, "I love you." She ran her fingers through my hair and reassured, "No more nightmares. Rest. I've got you."

She really was a godsend in more ways than I was willing to count.

*****

We awakened as the plane was making its decent. Aimee moved from my lap to her seat, and cinched the seat belt around herself. As she clasped my hand with hers, she asked, "How're you feeling?"

I pulled her hand to my lips and kissed her

palm. "Better, thanks to you." I laid her hand on my face. "You always have a way of taking the sting out of my nightmares."

She leaned her head against my shoulder. "If I could take them away completely, I would."

I kissed her beautiful blonde hair and admitted, "I'm fully aware of that, lille."

Since it was late, I'd informed Franco and Gina we would stop by the next day. Of course, that meant we had the entire evening to continue our explorations of one another's bodies. Discover all the ways to bring each other pleasure. Yeah, this was a very good thing indeed. Aimee glanced over at me in the limo and caught my hooded, lustful eyes watching her. Deliberately her tongue darted out and slowly worked its way across her full bottom lip. On a growl, I attacked her mouth and showed her just how much I hungered for her, as I swallowed every gasp and moan that escaped her. Oh, she tasted so damn good. I suddenly wanted my mouth all over her. Drinking. Feasting. Until she writhed underneath me and pled for my mercy—which would never happen. I wanted to show her heights she hadn't imagined existed. Against her mouth, I breathed, "It'll never be enough," then declared, "I won't *ever* have my fill of you."

"Me, either," she replied. "No matter how many times you take me, I will *always* want more."

Our tongues dueled for the entire ride to the hotel. And, still, I needed more.

*****

The elevator ride was a journey through the seventh circle of hell. Every ounce of my control was tested as I fought the urge to ravage her. *Right here.*

Right now. There was no way I could keep my mouth off hers. As the car traveled to the top floor, I pinned her against the wall and ground my hips into hers harder than I intended. She cried out my name when I spread her thighs with my knee and placed my monstrous quad right between her legs. I rubbed back and forth, causing friction up against her clit. As she released, I bit her, in that super sensitive spot, just below the ear.

She panted, "Oh, Nikko. I *need* you inside me."

My breathing was heavy as I answered, "I know, little one. Hold on to me."

Her small arms looped around my neck while I swooped behind her knees, and then carried her down the hall. Once we reached the door to the suite, she reached inside my front pocket for the keycard and decided to play with my cock for a few moments. "Wicked imp," I growled.

After she'd had her fun, she worked the card into the slot. And I whispered, "I'm going to take you on every surface inside that room."

Her purr of approval was all I needed.

The door closed behind us as I shoved the front of her into the wall. While I licked and nipped along the nape of her neck, I tugged her blouse from her skirt. Her back arched in response, which brought her ass right up against my swollen dick. Then and there I lost my patience, tugging her slightly away from the wall and ripping her shirt apart. Tiny buttons flew across the room. She groaned when my rough hands drew the cups of her bra down her breasts, freeing them, so I could stroke her hard peaks. When her hips gyrated against my crotch, I damn near came from the glorious torture.

I hiked her skirt up to her waist and pushed her lacey boy shorts down her lovely legs. What tiny thread of self-control existed vanished the moment I slid my zipper down and freed my weeping cock. I knew this would be hard and fast. She did, too. As she spread her legs wide for my entrance, I slammed home. I tweaked her nipples while I pounded her luscious body like a deranged maniac. Never in my life had I been so hot and bothered. It was as if each time I took her only made me crazed to have more. So much more. On a shout, I came. And she followed on a scream.

I held her jaw fast in my hand as I turned her for a deep, penetrating kiss. Our breathing was still ragged from fucking. Really, there was no other word for what we'd just done. When our pulses slowed, I eased out of her and murmured, "Stay put. I'll be right back."

She whispered, "Hurry up."

I chuckled while I strode across the suite to the huge bathroom. Once there, I ran a washcloth under warm water, wrung it out, and then walked back to where I had left her. She'd turned around, and was now leaning her back against the wall. I stopped short as I took in the sight before me: Her tits all trussed up from her bra. The skirt rucked up around her middle—her panties around one ankle and her stilettos still on. I rasped, "You. Are. So. Damn. Fuckable."

She glanced up at me from under her long, lush lashes. The look she gave me was hot. Heady. Then her eyes slid down my body and held on the fly, where my dick still hung out. She licked her lips as she pushed off the wall. Once she stood toe to toe with me, she went down on her knees. Without preamble, her warm, wet mouth encircled the head of my cock. I groaned as I watched her work my semi-erection into a full one with a hard suck. Reaching up, she finished undoing my pants and yanked them, along with my boxer briefs, down my legs. I toed off my shoes, and then she pulled everything away from my body.

"My God, you're so beautiful on your knees like this with my dick in your mouth," I purred.

She tugged away on a *pop* and directed, "Take off your shirt."

I held eye contact with her, and did what she told me to.

Next she instructed, "Lie down," she patted the floor in front of her, "right here."

I raised my brows, but complied.

While I reached for several cushions off the nearby sofa, she stripped. I stilled and growled, "I *need* to be inside you."

She shook her head flirtatiously as she crawled between my legs. Then she went back to work on my cock. As she swirled her tongue along the sensitive underside, her cheeks hollowed and her throat relaxed, so she could take me all the way to the root. Her hands joined the party. And that was when I arched off the floor. With one hand she pumped me. The other was at my balls, where she stroked and gently squeezed my sac. I came on a grunt. Damn, the woman could give head like no other.

We eventually made it to the bed, making love again and again. If we hadn't been exhausted, we would've gone all night long. Instead, we fell asleep well sated and spooning.

*****

The six o'clock wake-up call was not welcomed. After I answered the call, I leaned over and kissed her mussed up hair. "You don't have to go with me. I can handle this while you sleep."

She stretched and groaned a little. "No. I want

246

to be with you."

"Alright. Grab a few more minutes of sleep while I jump in the shower."

She rolled over and sleepily replied, "'Kay."

As I showered, apprehension filled me. What if she didn't remember the masquerade? What if she did remember, and ends up pissed off I didn't tell her? What if that night didn't mean the same to her, as it did me? All of those negative thoughts plagued me throughout breakfast—which did not go unnoticed by Aimee.

"Are you going to tell me what's bothering you?" she asked before sipping her coffee.

I shrugged. "Nothing to worry about, Aimee."

Her brow arched. "Really? Because you sure seem anxious."

Could I hide *nothing* from her? I took a deep breath and found a calm I didn't feel. "I'm good," I replied, "Please don't concern yourself with my moodiness."

She only stared at me. I knew she didn't buy my act for an instant. As I wiped my mouth with the linen napkin, I stood and inquired, "You ready?"

She met me across the room. "I don't give up so easily, Nikko."

I half-smiled at that. "Don't expect you to, lille."

When she placed her hand on my chest, she tiptoed to kiss the corner of my mouth. "So you know, you speaking to me in your native tongue won't change a thing." She kissed the other side of my mouth. "No matter how freakin' sexy it sounds."

With that, she sashayed out of the suite. I followed her swaying ass with my eyes, and thought, *I'll never pull one over on her*. No clue why I even tried. I gave myself a mental shake and placed my hand on the small of her back, as we made our way to the waiting limo. When I opened the door for her, she smiled up at me. "I do love you."

In return, I smirked, "Good thing for me. 'Cause I would hate for you to havta kick my ass."

Once I crawled in beside her, I noticed she was laughing. Wow, I would give anything to hear that every single day for the rest of my life. Someday, I really needed to tell her just what she did to me. I squeezed her hand and didn't let go on our ride through town. She really was the most incredible woman I had ever met. The fact that she was mine humbled me in ways I was still learning. My heart swelled with that knowledge. Somehow, someway, she had calmed the beast in me. Brought him to heel. And in doing so, she thawed out a side of me I thought I would never see again. I guess it was true: All things *were* possible. Not so long ago, I would've argued: but not probable. Now…well, I knew differently. And wasn't that saying something about the power of what true love could do. Yes. Yes, it was.

Chapter Thirty-One
Aimee

When Nik had accused me of being able to "kick his ass," there was no holding back the belly laugh that erupted. As if! The man was nothing but a slab of muscle and sinew. So freaking masculine it hurt to look at him. Every part of him was a bulging display of male anatomy—right down to that sexy as hell V, which led to his all impressive, long and thick, cock. My husband could give a porn star a run for his money in the ample penis department. Yet while all those thoughts ran through my head, I couldn't help but notice the adoring look in his eyes and the loving expression on his face. Were those feelings for me? Or was it due to the fact, we were visiting old friends of his?

Once he began to rub his thumb on the inside of my wrist, I was moved to some serious distraction. Why did that calming move not have the appropriate effect? It definitely caused a most sexual response, like he was stroking the ever-throbbing hot spot between my legs. Oh, hell. At this rate, I would mount him and have my wicked way with him.

As we turned the corner, my lustful gaze took in the sight in front of us. The Tudor mansion set back from the street. We stopped at the security gates before we were allowed to enter. Why did it all look familiar? The closer we got, the more déjà vu it felt. Odd, that. Something teased my memory, but refused to reveal itself. Nik kissed the side of my neck, effectively bringing my attention back to him.

"Where'd you go, lille?" His low voice rumbled, sending sparks of desire through me.

I reached between his legs and stroked his erection, as I replied, "Was thinking of all the naughty ways I could have you—here and now." I licked my lips to drive my point home.

He growled, "Later, you're goin' to show me."

Before I could act, the door opened. Well, there went that seduction. I inwardly sighed because it was time to put on my new-bride-smiley-face and pretend to be interested in spending the day away from him. He proffered his hand to assist me out of the limo. I laced my fingers with his once we were on the sidewalk. As we approached the front door, it opened wide to welcome us in. A beautiful Italian woman stood there with a huge smile on her face. Without letting go of my hand, Nik leaned forward and kissed her on each cheek.

"So good to see you again," she greeted him with a glorious accent.

He returned, "You, as well," and added, "Though I would've preferred if it were under better circumstances."

She looked chagrined as she stated, "Yes, I would have to agree with that."

Nik turned towards me, tugged me forward and addressed, "Gina, this is my lovely wife Aimee. Aimee, this is Gina D'Arpino," he introduced.

I held my hand out and announced, "It is a pleasure to meet you, Gina."

She drew me into a hospitable hug. "Oh, you are a beauty." Then she gestured for us to enter.

"Please, come in."

Once inside, a dark haired gentleman met us. "Nik," he greeted—with the same accent as Gina's, but not as thick—while they shook hands.

"How's everything, Franco?" Nik requested.

He replied, "As well as can be expected." Then he looked at me and smiled, "Ah, this must be your *splendida sposa*." He stepped in front of me.

Gina introduced, "Franco, this is Aimee. Aimee, my husband Franco."

With that, Franco hugged me tight and kissed each of my cheeks. I did my best not to pull away from the affection, as I replied, "Pleased to make your acquaintance, Franco."

He put his hand over his heart. "Nik, she's as polite as she is beautiful."

Gina playfully smacked her husband's shoulder. "Don't scare her off."

He grinned when Nik took a possessive hold of my waist. Nik leaned in to me. "Don't let him fool you, he adores Gina."

"He better," she replied, "If he knows what's good for him." Her eyes narrowed on her husband.

Franco grabbed his wife, dipped her over his arm and planted a sound kiss on her mouth. When she stood, she blushed—which was impressive, considering her olive complexion.

After a few minutes of small talk, Franco turned to Nik. "Shall we handle this so we may return to these *belle signore*?"

Nik kissed me softly and then said, "I'll hurry."

I smiled, "No worries. I'll be fine," I assured.

Gina stepped forward and clasped my hand. "She's in good hands, Nikko."

I shot her a surprised look, having never heard someone say his full name—well, with the exception of me, that is.

He bowed his head before leaving the room with Franco.

*****

Without preamble, I probed, "Why is it, that only you and I use Nik's given name?"

Her brow arched. "If you'd prefer me not to, I will honor your wishes."

I shook my head. "It's not that. I was only curious."

"Well, by all means, let's have breakfast. You may ask all the questions you wish about Nikko."

I grinned, "I would like that, a lot."

While we sat at the table, in an extraordinary gourmet kitchen, Gina poured me a cup of coffee and queried, "So, what all would you like to know, Aimee?"

There was a warm sparkle in her eyes, which instantly made me feel like I belonged. It was comforting, especially considering I was unsure of my reception into Nik's world. I mustered up some courage—time to get to the bottom of exactly *who* my husband was. "How 'bout we start from where you all met."

"Ah, those were trying times." She sighed heavily. "Of course, Lorenzo brought Nikko into the fold."

My eyes narrowed as my brow furrowed. "You have me at a loss. Who's Lorenzo?"

"I see Nikko is as tightlipped as always."

I shrugged one shoulder. "In his defense, it's not like we've had a lot of time to get to know each other."

She bobbed her head. "Yes. How are things

with the senator?"

I blew out a breath. "Not sure. I mean, we haven't seen or heard from him since the threat he made when he took me to the hotel."

"Oh, dear. I had no idea he had made other threats."

"Yeah, well, let's just say the man is beyond unstable. He seems to think I'm impersonating someone."

She gasped, "How horrible!"

"And then some," I agreed.

She refilled my cup and then hers. "I suppose I should give you a little back story to Nikko and Lorenzo."

I half-smiled at that. "Anything you feel comfortable sharing would be wonderful."

She continued, "Lorenzo came to this country at the tender age of seventeen. Quickly, he connected with old families which had relocated here." She paused and glanced out the window, then proceeded, "See, these families had left Italy for good reason. They were, how do you say, crooks. Therefore, they were run out of our town after someone of great esteem was murdered."

My turn to gasp. "Wow. That must've been quite a scandal."

"Oh, yes. Thus, when Lorenzo reacquainted himself with these men, his family disowned him."

"How could they?! I mean, no parent wants their child to take the wrong path in life. But I would think *love* could overcome a bad decision."

"I wholeheartedly agree with you on that point." She sighed, "Unfortunately, not all see things our way."

I shook my head in disgust. Admitting only to myself, *and this is the reason you have never told your family that you were a prostitute.* Yeah, well, there was that fact to contend with. Fear, shame, and guilt, kept my skeleton locked tight in the closet. In a way, it seemed fitting I carried those feelings with me—a self-imposed punishment, as it were. Not something I would ever recommend one do, albeit, I would make the same choice all over again to save my dad.

"What happened next?" I inquired, desperately tamping down my morose feelings.

She shrugged. "As you can imagine, Lorenzo did not work within the law. But soon he established his own customers, and quickly made *a lot* of money." She smiled, "Wanting to begin anew, he also ran legal companies. He desired for all of his companies to eventually be above board." She exhaled heavily. "Others did not agree, unfortunately."

"Oh, no!" I exclaimed. "What happened?"

"While on business in California, he was set up. But it wasn't all bad. That's where he met Nikko." Her words belied her expression of true despair.

I swallowed hard—truly unsure if I wanted to hear anymore—and queried, "How exactly did they meet?"

Her big brown eyes grew serious as she replied, "They were in the same prison at the same time."

My mouth popped open on an O of shock. Yes, I knew Nik had done time—thanks to the Internet. Yet I didn't know what for. The knowledge that I was about to learn this information tied my stomach up in knots. *Maybe, you should wait for Nik to tell you this part?* Instead of stopping her, I inclined my head for her to continue. *Stupid! Don't say I didn't try to warn you.* Gah, sometimes I really hated that voice in my head!

Gina went on, "Lorenzo saved Nikko's life."

Unable to stop the surprise, I gasped, "What the?!"

She nodded, "Prison is a dangerous place. Not where a mere child should be put. Especially…" She paused. "Well, that's not really my story to tell. Anyhoo, for protection, Lorenzo did what he *had* to do."

"Which was?" I bit my lip, hard.

Her eyes widened. "Why, to bring him into the gang, of course."

Gang? WTF?! My husband was in a gang. Holy crap!

She clasped my hands with hers. "You didn't know."

I fought the tears and whispered, "No. But I'd like to understand."

"There's not much to it. You need someone to have your back when you're in the pen. Lorenzo genuinely liked Nikko, so it wasn't a tough decision." She chuckled, "Besides, it was how he groomed the perfect CEO."

"Come again."

She beamed, "He saw the potential in Nikko. Plus, he knew the distraction was needed. Hence, your husband got his degree, along with one-on-one tutelage from a very successful business man."

"Oh, my! That's incredible." Seriously, I sat there in awe. To think he took a horrible situation and turned it around to something remarkable. Were there words for that?

"Needless to say, once they were released, Lorenzo brought Nikko home to meet those of us who were ready for a change."

"Change? You've lost me again," I affirmed.

"You see, Lorenzo wanted all of his companies legal. Traditionally Franco, being his nephew, should've been the one to take over when he stepped down. But my Franco is a wonderful assistant, not a leader. Therefore, Nikko took the reins. And as they say, 'the rest is water under the bridge.' "

Incredulous, for a moment, I couldn't speak. As I processed all I had just learned, I took a sip of my coffee.

Gina stood and stretched. "Would you like to see the rest of the house?"

"Yes, thank you. I'd love to."

With that, we began our tour.

*****

Each room was lovely, old world money mixed with modern tradition, which made for a welcoming environment. I took mental notes, wondering if I would have a chance to decorate a home for Nik and myself. Were we staying in New York? Moving here? Guess it was time I inquired. As I took in everything, that same niggling sensation of familiarity filled me. What was it about *this* home? Why did I have the sense I'd been here before? We rounded the next corner, and I stopped short. I had long lost what Gina was saying as we entered the ballroom, which brought back memories of the masquerade like nothing else ever had. While I took it in from every angle, the night replayed through my head with crystal clear clarity. I could see the band, Michael Bublé center stage, the elegant ladies and debonair gentleman in their exquisite masks. The smells were even there in my recollection—all brought to the forefront as soon as I had walked into this ballroom.

Gina finally pulled me from my reverie. "Aimee, is everything all right?"

I shook my head and pivoted towards her. "Do you have many festivities here?" I inquired.

Her puzzlement was obvious as she answered, "A few. Why do you ask?"

I swallowed the huge lump in my throat before I replied, "You have an annual masquerade for charity." Not a question. Somehow, I knew I was accurate.

She grinned, "Yes, we do. We've been hosting that event for abused women and children for ten years now."

"Oh my God," I gasped as my knees buckled.

Before I hit the floor, strong arms enclosed my waist. A deep, raspy voice spoke low in my ear. "Breathe, little one."

With my head spinning, I barely whispered, "It was *you*."

"Are you okay, Aimee?" Gina frantically questioned, "What can I do? Nikko, what's wrong?"

Nik responded, "Could you give us a minute, please, Gina?"

"Yes. Of course I can." Before leaving the ballroom, she said, "I'll bring some water."

"Thank you, Gina," Nik answered.

*****

Once we were alone, Nik turned me towards him, and held my chin as he held my gaze. "What was me, Aimee?"

"Th-that…n-night," I stammered, "Y-You were there." I gasped, "You're *him*." Shock overwhelmed me as I covered my mouth with my hand to keep from screaming out.

"I'm who, exactly? What night are you speaking of?"

How could I have not known before now?

We'd been intimate so many times, and, still, I hadn't recognized him. *That's not true. Your body has always known his.* I blinked back the tears and answered, "You were at the masquerade here five years ago." He nodded, fighting a smile. I confirmed, "You're Mr. Mystery."

Now he laughed, "Mr. What?"

My eyes suddenly narrowed. "The name I gave you since I didn't know your name at the time."

"Clever."

I stepped back aghast. "You've known? All along you knew who I was. And you didn't say a thing!" I yelled.

He laid his hands on my shoulders to placate me.

To. Hell. With. That. I shrugged out of his grasp. "Did I not mean anything to you, is that it? That night was nothing more than a one-night stand!" I exclaimed as anger boiled through my veins.

"Aimee, let me explain."

That did it. He had just confessed not only to knowing who I was, but how we had first met. I took a step forward and slapped his face with all I had. "Bastard!"

He rubbed the red mark I left on his cheek, then grabbed my hand and hauled me against him. "Let. Me. Explain."

I shoved against him. "No!"

Wisely, he released me. I unfortunately had too much momentum and lost my balance. When I fell on my butt, he tried to catch me—which naturally pulled him on top of me. I grunted from the force. His huge body held me to the floor as I panted, "Get off me."

He held my face between his hands. "No. Now, listen." As he smoothed my hair away from my forehead, he looked into my eyes intently. "I only *just* figured it out myself."

I huffed, "When was that?"

His mouth curved up on one side. "When I was here before our wedding." He shrugged. "There really hasn't been the right time to bring it up. Besides, I wanted you to put it all together without my assistance."

I shoved him away, so I could breathe and get some space. "Any time would've worked," I hissed.

He shook his head as he moved to stand, grabbing my hands to pull me with him. "You're wrong." Before I could interrupt, he placed his fingers over my mouth. "*That night* changed my life. I searched frantically for you, all to no avail. You had disappeared."

The tears began to slide down my cheeks. "Jack and Ann got wind of an investigation into their business. So, for our protection, they sent us to D.C."

He ran his hand through his hair. "That explains a lot."

I glanced up at him, not fully understanding the emotions that played across his face. Anger. Frustration. Disbelief. Sadness. Oh, my poor, broken husband. I went to him and clutched him tightly to me. Then I stood on my tiptoes, cupped his handsome face and pulled him down to me. I kissed him with all I had, letting my mouth say what I couldn't speak: I love you. I've loved you since the first moment you spoke to me.

At first, he returned the kiss tenderly. But somewhere, in all of the pent up emotion, a beast was released. All of sudden, I was against the wall. His mouth devoured mine, full possession, as he poured out all of his longing for me.

I moved my lips to his ear and whispered, "I *need* you, now."

As I wrapped my legs around his waist, I

reached down to free his engorged cock. His eyes rolled back while I stroked him. Then, he eased my skirt up a little higher and moved my panties to the side. When he entered me on one full thrust, we both groaned in pleasure. We knew we had to be quick, because Gina would return any minute. He drove into me, hard and fast, releasing on a grunt. I followed right behind him. At the same moment, we heard Gina, and quickly put ourselves to rights. She walked in as he turned towards the door.

"Oh!" she gasped. "I hope I'm not interrupting anything."

I stepped out from behind Nik and smiled, "No, you didn't."

She walked over and handed me a glass of water. "Well, you look better."

I took the glass and downed it. After I finished, I said, "I feel better, also." I shot Nik a knowing glance and continued, "Thank you for the water."

She grinned, "No problem."

Franco strode into the ballroom. "Why is everyone in here?"

Gina chortled, "No reason, caro. Come," she motioned to us, "we must go tour the gardens."

I laced my fingers with Nik's and gazed up at him. "Yes. Let's do that."

I winked as we all left the ballroom, which had forever altered my life. Nik was the man I dreamt of every night since that masquerade. He was my Mr. Mystery. And I was grateful destiny had brought him back to me. *Finally*. No matter where we were, *he* would always be *my home*.

Chapter Thirty-Two
Nik

The rest of our afternoon was extreme torture. There was nothing I wanted more than to make love to my wife until morning. But that wasn't going to happen. Once we received the call we had been waiting on, Franco and I left the ladies again to finalize the arrangements for his cousin. Back in the day, the man wouldn't have lived another twenty-four hours. While a part of me could appreciate the completeness in that, I wasn't going to murder someone in retribution. No matter how much I wanted the problem gone.

Before we were able to leave, we had dinner with Gina and Franco, promising we would return under better circumstances. Then, we headed back to the hotel. Sometime soon, I needed to inform Aimee of our change in living arrangements. But I was unsure of exactly how to handle it. Instead, I gave in to the lust that had been burning inside me since our interlude in the ballroom.

Inside the limo, I hauled her onto my lap—so she straddled my knees, facing away from me. "Let me show you how much I missed you today," I murmured.

She gasped when my fingers unbuttoned her

blouse. While I circled her taut nipples with my thumbs, she leaned her head back against my shoulder. That sweet move gave me full access to her throat. Aimee really had no idea just how breathtaking she truly was. Her curves were enough to make a man weep with joy. At that moment, I decided it was time to make her cry out in pleasure. I spread my legs, effectively opening her to me.

As I moved one hand to the inside of her thigh, stroking up to her drenched panties—*Fuck, yeah!*—I praised, "I love how you're always ready for me."

"Hmm," she moaned, "Only for you."

I nipped her ear as my thumb skated underneath the edge of her thong and entered her moist heat. Next, I massaged her inner walls and, with my other fingers, teased her swollen clit until her orgasm hit. She sat trembling on me while I continued my sensual assault of her sweet pussy. Unable to hold back a moment longer, I released my painful erection and traced it along the seam of her ass. Images of taking her there, in positions I was totally unsure were feasible, danced in my head. Holy Kama Sutra Batman! She rubbed herself up and down my dick, only fueling my fire more. When she leaned forward to grab the seatback in front of her, I slid home inside her core.

She began to ride me hard. After a few minutes, I grabbed her luscious hips and thrust up into her. She was so close. As soon as I felt her walls grip me, I inserted my thumb to the first knuckle into her asshole. Her scream of pleasure was my undoing. My seed spewed as I growled, "Ah, fuck."

She leaned back against me and turned to kiss my jaw while our breathing slowed. I met her lips with mine and then declared, "Someday soon, I'm taking your gorgeous ass."

She whimpered, "Please."

Well, shit. If I'd known she was down with anal play, I would've been happy to oblige. Though I should've known she would be up for just about anything. I mentally shook my head to clear the images of her with other men. It wasn't that I blamed her, nor was I disgusted by the fact she had sold her body. How could I be? I'd long ago lost count of how many women I had used to ease my loneliness. Their faces and bodies all blended together. I didn't even remember their names. How sad was that?!

Aimee shifted off me and smiled, "I think we're here."

To bring myself back to the here and now, I blinked hard and glanced out the window. Damn, we had arrived. I gave her a slow, wicked smile as I stuffed myself back into my pants and zipped up. She held my gaze with a naughty glint in hers. Oh, yeah. Tonight would be one wild ride after another. Once she was decent for other's eyes, I opened the limo door. After assisting her out, we walked into the hotel hand in hand. Somehow, I had to keep our clothes on until we were privately enclosed in our suite. Shit. Talk about a lesson in self-control. Something I'd never had a problem with before. But with Aimee, that went to hell in a handbasket.

*****

Unable to keep our hands to ourselves, we put on quite a show for the other hotel guests and staff. Once safely enclosed in our penthouse suite, I directed, "Take off your clothes."

Her lips pursed before she challenged, "You first."

Oh, ho. So that's the way she wants to play this. Fine by me. I stalked forward until I towered over her. Then skimmed my hands under the collar of her blouse and pulled, effectively spewing tiny buttons across the room. Her eyes widened in shock as she calmly said, "I can't believe you just tore my blouse."

I grinned wolfishly and countered, "Should've listened."

An elegant brow rose as she tugged on my tie. While she wrapped it around her neck, she backed up and proceeded to put on quite a show. After she was fully naked—well, except for my tie—she sauntered towards me. Once we were toe to toe, she unzipped my pants while she glanced up at me with hooded eyes.

"Uh-huh, babe." I stilled her hands and turned around. "This is my scene."

Her brows rose. "Says who?"

I shook my head while I reached back and tugged on my tie, which dangled between her tits. "Don't challenge me, Aimee," I warned as I yanked on the tie with her behind me.

She resisted—I knew she would—as she stamped her little foot, with a hand on her curvy hip, and hissed, "I do not take kindly to be ordered around." Then she jerked the tie out of my hand. "I'm neither a dog nor your *submissive*."

I fought back the laugh that threatened to erupt. I quickly schooled my expression and met her eyes. "I don't want a bitch. And for the record, I don't play the games my brother does. Hence, I'm not your *Dom*."

She narrowed her eyes and replied, "I wouldn't't've married you if that were *your* thing. Although be forewarned, you will not tell me what to do."

I chuckled, "Hell yes, I will." With that, I threw her over my shoulder and carried her into the bedroom. When she squirmed and kicked, I swatted her ass, bringing forth a yelp. "Stop fighting me, Aimee," I cautioned. "You and I both know you get turned on when I take control."

She tried to deny it, but when I slid my fingers between her wet folds, there was no more to be said on the subject. As I stood there and toyed with her pussy, for a moment, her next squeal was one of pleasure. "Mine," I growled as I eased her body down mine. "And don't you *ever* forget that."

While she held my gaze, she licked her lips and cupped my nads. "Just as *you* are mine," she countered.

I threw my head back when she began to stroke my length, before releasing me into her warm hand. After a beat, she began to undress me. As soon as I was naked, I spun her around, so she was facing away from me, and ran my hands all over her delectable body. I would *never* get enough of her.

I eased her down to the edge of the bed—now she was on her hands and knees—and whispered, "Spread your legs as wide as possible."

Without question, she did as I had directed. The temptation of taking her gorgeous ass was damn near irresistible in that position. Also, the desire to put my head between those lovely thighs and dine made my mouth water. But what stopped either of those actions was my too engorged cock. Instead, I placed the head of my dick into her slick core and thrust home. After a couple of hard pushes, I eased back and began to watch the erotic show. Then, I remembered how she had slapped me in the ballroom and decided it was time to repay her. On the next withdrawal, I held only the tip inside her as I smacked her right ass cheek.

She howled, "What was that for?"

In response, I buried deep and pulled back

again. This time, I went for the left side.

She exclaimed, "Ouch!" When I soothingly rubbed my hands over both sides, she moaned. I thrust forward, once again, and then repeated the actions several times until she was dripping wet and groaning. "Please, Nikko," she begged.

"Please what, lille?"

She backed into me. "Harder," she commanded, "Fuck me hard while you spank me."

I growled, "Hell, yeah." I continued to do as my wife demanded. It was the single most erotic thing I had ever done. While I watched her ass redden, I pounded into her until we both climaxed, which went on and on.

Once we both came back to earth, I exclaimed, "Now *that* was hotter than hell!"

She had fallen face first on the bed while we were catching our breath. I sidled in next to her and drew her onto my chest. As she gently stroked my pecs, I played with her silky hair. Eventually I suggested, "Would you like to take a bath with me?"

"I'd like that, a lot," she answered sleepily.

"Stay here while I get the water warmed up."

After I poured some bath oil into the tub, I sauntered out to see why she hadn't joined me yet. All I needed to hear was her light snore, to realize what had happened. I chuckled as I covered her luscious body with a blanket. Not wanting to let the bath go to waste, I decided to stretch out in the oversized tub.

I awoke to slender fingers caressing my jaw. "Hey," Aimee greeted as my heavy lids began to lift.

"Hello," I rasped while I tugged her into the tub with me.

She squealed when the tepid water met her body. I leaned forward and turned on the hot water to rewarm the bath. After it met her approval, she shut the water off and then turned to face me. I pulled her astride my erection and grasped her face with both hands. Our joining was slow and rhythmic, all consuming. With no hurriedness, like the times before, we eased into our climax. Once we had disengaged, we took turns bathing each other. It had been a very long time since I'd simply enjoyed the pleasures of pampering a woman, or being pampered by a woman.

Aimee stroked my face, with a look of concern in her eyes, and whispered, "Is everything okay, Nikko?"

That was when it finally registered; I had tears on my cheeks. There had been a time when I would've called myself a pussy for showing my softer side. But I didn't do that this time. Instead, I tenderly kissed her and poured out all the love I had with actions, not words. Though I recognized she should hear me say it, so I murmured, "I love you, lille."

She traced the outside of my mouth with her tongue. "I love you, too, Nik."

We made love again on the vanity of that bathroom before calling room service for a midnight snack.

I knew it was time to talk about our move, so I hedged, "Tell me…did you really want to live in California?"

One elegant brow arched. "Yes. Why do you ask?" she inquired.

Man, my wife was not an easy person to fool. I liked that, a lot.

While I fought the smile that threatened, I replied, "We own a home there."

That got her attention. Her eyes widened. "What're you saying?"

I casually shrugged one shoulder. "The business I had to handle with Franco involved my San

Fran companies."

She began to bounce with excitement, like a little girl on Christmas morning. And it was that very moment in which I realized, there wasn't anything I wouldn't do for her just so I could see that reaction time and time again. There was no hiding the shit-eating grin on my face. My damn cheeks ached it was so frickin' big. She was suddenly in my arms. "Seriously? We're going to San Francisco?"

I chuckled, "Yes, Aimee, my love. That's what I'm trying to convey."

She exclaimed, "OMG!" Kissing me over and over again, she gushed, "I love you, so much. Thank you."

Had I really been concerned with her response to our move? There was obviously nothing to worry about. Honestly, I couldn't have been happier. Although California held many ghosts for me, to see my wife that elated made me more than ready to move forward. *Time to put those ghosts to rest.* And maybe—just maybe—it was time to share it all with Aimee. Her enthusiasm was downright contagious. So to show my gratitude, I brought her to the height of pleasure, over and over again, until she begged me to stop.

A-fucking-mazing. Night.

Chapter Thirty-Three
Aimee

Elated was not a strong enough word to describe my feelings with regards to living in San Francisco. If you had told me four-and-a-half weeks ago I'd be married, and fulfilling my dreams of residing in California, I would've called you a bold-faced liar. Now, all of my hopes and dreams were coming true. I fell more deeply in love with my husband each and every day. Not to mention the sexual chemistry between us was out of this world! To help calm me down on our plane ride to the West Coast, he exhausted my body with one pleasure after another. The man was a damn sex god. I was willing to bet his brother Even had nothing on him. All right, maybe E had kink down in spades, but Nik knew how to truly *please* a woman. His ministrations were quite successful, and I eventually gave in to a blissful sleep.

I awoke to soft, firm lips on mine. Nik announced, "We land in about twenty minutes. I thought you might like to freshen up."

I smiled up at him. "Yeah, I would. Thank you."

"Anytime, lille."

Oh, how I loved when he spoke in his native tongue. That accent of his did something to my insides. I leaned forward and grabbed his face, kissing him deeply, before I left the bed. When his hands began to slide over my body, I stilled them. "You're going to have to wait till we arrive at our home, big boy." As I said that, I stroked his very large, very aroused penis.

He reared back out of my reach and rasped, "Go on, now. Before I change my mind, and take you."

I sashayed across the room. He abruptly stood and was behind me in three long strides. Then he smacked my ass and teased, "I'm gonna punish you for tempting me like that."

Over my shoulder I called, "Promise me."

As I closed the door, I could hear his low, sexy rumble of a laugh. I probably shouldn't have challenged him like that. Ah, hell yeah, I should. One thing about it, Nik was extremely ingenious. The thoughts of all the ways he could pleasure—I mean, punish—me were interminable. *Crap. Now I'm all hot and bothered.* I splashed cold water over my overheated face to get my thoughts under control—all of them were on how I would ravage him next time. Soooo naughty. Yet there was no denying how much I wanted to see him completely unhinged. When did I plan on doing this? Duh, as soon as I possibly could.

My grin had not abated as I met him in the main part of the plane for landing. As I strapped myself in—just in time, I might add—Nik shot me a wary glance. "Pushing it a little there, weren't you?"

"I made it, didn't I?"

"Barely," he grumbled.

Aw, my sweet husband was concerned for my safety. I cajoled, "So protective."

He seriously replied, "Always."

I laced my fingers with his and softly chortled, "I like that about you. A lot."

He grinned as he brought the back of my hand to his lips, tenderly kissing my knuckles.

His actions were once again incongruous with his size.

*****

We entered Pacific Heights just as the fog had cleared. The enchanting Golden Gate Bridge was to the north as we turned into the driveway of a spectacular Georgian Mansion. I gasped when the Bentley came to a stop at the side entrance.

"Are we visiting someone?" I asked hesitantly.

Nik climbed out of the backseat and stretched his large frame, chuckling. How he compressed all of that height and bulk still fascinated me. He held out his hand for me.

We made our way inside a very modern kitchen.

"This is your home?" I was still a bit discombobulated. Yes, I knew Nikko was an obscenely wealthy man, but…

"No, little one. This is *our* home."

"Oh." Really, what was there to say? I mean, sure, I'd been around money and power for a little over five years. And while his Fifth Avenue penthouse was astounding, it had nothing on this exquisite home.

Nik snaked his arm around my waist, effectively placing me in front of him. When I wouldn't meet his gaze, he gently raised my chin with his forefinger and stared intently. "You don't like it?" His hesitant question caught me a bit off-guard.

I swallowed the lump in my throat before I answered, "It's not that," while I blinked back tears that threatened to fall.

He cocked his head to one side, studying me. "Then, what's wrong?"

I pulled free and began to trek through the house, stopping at the floor to ceiling windows off the living room. I had an unobscured view of the bay. I shook my head, still incredulous to what I saw. Nik came up behind me, coiled his arms around me and rested his chin on my shoulder. "Tell me, Aimee. Please," he implored.

Unsure if it was his concern or the mansion itself, the tears I tried so desperately to hold back slid down my cheeks. Hell, maybe it was the fact my dreams were actually coming to fruition. I leaned into his warmth and strength. "You're crying?" he asked appalled.

I nodded, but refused to let him turn me around in his arms when he tried. Sure, he could've forced the issue, yet he didn't. And that was what made me start talking. "I'm overwhelmed at the moment." Before he could question me again, I continued, "It's everything I ever wanted—and more. So much more that I'm having a bit of trouble processing it all."

His voice rumbled next to my ear. "I'm glad you like it. I wasn't trying to bewilder you. For that, I apologize."

I bit my lip and turned to gaze up at him. "Yes, I like it. I know you didn't mean to, which makes it more confounding." I held my hand up to keep him from interrupting me. "Having said all of that, you should know I *love* you." With that, I stood on tip-toes and brushed my lips against his. It would've escalated if we hadn't been interrupted.

"Erghm, sorry. I'll just be in my office."

I leaned to the side to get a better look at who had just spoken, and saw Ray standing in the doorway. I smiled at him. "I knew I recognized that voice."

He inclined his head. "How are you doing, Mrs. Strand?"

While I held Nik's hand, I approached Ray. I felt like we had bonded in the hospital when Renée had been laid up. However, Nik stiffened at the familiarity I used towards his lead security guy—and if I wasn't mistaken, friend. I respectfully held back from hugging his right-hand man. Something unspoken passed between the two men. Suspicious I inquired, "What's going on?"

"Nothing to worry about," Nik appeased. "Would you give us just a moment, Ray?"

"Not a problem, sir. I'll meet you in the office." He turned and left the room.

I let go of Nik's hand and stated, "Start talking."

He shook his head in disbelief. "You do realize no one speaks to me that way, right?"

"I'm not just anyone," I huffed. "I'm. Your. Wife."

His brow quirked. "Which is why, I let you get away with it," he pointed out. "But don't confuse my willingness to have an open conversation with you for weakness. Clear?"

Ooh, his bossiness was enough to make my blood boil. I bowed my head. "Yes, sir," I retorted and stomped away.

He tugged my arm, halting my progress. "What is this about, exactly, Aimee?"

Could he really be that clueless? Well, he asked for it. "You keep hiding things from me, Nikko. I won't tolerate it any longer."

His brows hit his hairline. "I beg your pardon!" He blew out an exasperated breath. "I'm not hiding anything."

To which, I stamped my foot and met him toe to toe. "Liar!" I accused.

He grabbed me by the upper arms and warned, "Watch it."

My chin jutted out in defiance. "Or what? You'll take me over your knee."

This time, he stepped back and ran both hands through his long hair. "If that's what it takes, I'll do it," he declared.

"Like, hell," I growled.

He spun and swept me into his arms. I beat his chest and demanded, "Put me down."

He dropped me unceremoniously onto the sofa. Before I could scramble away, he tugged me onto his lap. "Now, stop it. Or I will turn you over my knee and spank your sweet ass."

Crap! Those words shouldn't have caused the low ache deep in my belly. I spat out, "Pervert."

He half-smiled. "As I recall, you seemed to have enjoyed it the last time."

My lips pursed. "In pleasure, I do. Not the way you mean right now."

He ceded, "Fair point." He held his finger over my lips, so I wouldn't interrupt. "Listen, I wasn't lying to you. I may be guilty of protecting you, but not hiding things."

My eyes narrowed. "There's a difference?"

He sighed, "Of course there is. Hiding would imply, I have no intentions of ever telling you what's going on."

I petulantly queried, "And that's not what you and Ray just did?"

"No, lille. It's not. I was protecting you. Last time I checked, that was a husband's job," he said insistently.

I sighed heavily. "This is about Caleb, isn't it?"

"Yes," he confirmed. "But I wasn't hiding that fact."

"So you were going to tell me, when?"

"I was hoping I wouldn't have to," he confessed.

"Why's that?"

He stroked my hair and replied, "Well, it wasn't him, per se. And I really didn't want to worry you needlessly."

"I'm confused," I admitted. "What wasn't him?"

"A couple of his henchmen have been spotted a few times since the wedding."

I gasped, "And you not telling me sooner, wasn't hiding?! How do you figure?"

He leaned his forehead against mine. "I didn't hide it, Aimee. I wanted to *protect* you."

"Alright," I acknowledged, "I refuse to keep going around this bush. Protect me, how?"

"Until we knew for sure, I didn't want to cause you any anxiety. Nothing was going to happen to you. If I had felt you were in grave danger, I would've told you and taken action."

I grasped his face with both hands. "Swear to me, you won't go after him."

He shook his head in denial. "I can't make a promise I don't intend to keep."

I stood. "So that's it, then," I shouted, "You'd spend the rest of your life in jail over that shithead. What about me?"

He approached cautiously—*wise man*—and proclaimed, "I never said I was going after him. However, if he comes after you, I will handle it," he vowed as he clutched my shoulders. "I have no intentions of going back to jail, Aimee. But I won't let him endanger the woman I love."

His mouth came down on mine furiously. I

could taste his fear. His anger. His insecurity. I fisted his hair and yanked him more firmly to me. Then devoured his mouth with mine, pouring every emotion I had into the kiss.

Once we pulled away, we were both panting. "You better go," I insisted. "Ray has been waiting for a while now."

He nodded and strode to the threshold, where he paused and over his shoulder inquired, "We okay?"

"Yeah, we're fine. I'll see you when you're finished."

He winked before leaving the room.

What the hell was I going to do about Caleb? The dickhead obviously wasn't giving up.

*****

While I contemplated everything, I went into the kitchen for a drink of water. There, stood a rather pretty woman in her late thirties at the stove cooking. She smiled and greeted, "Hello. You must be Mrs. Strand."

I bobbed my head as I replied, "Please, call me Aimee."

"Well, Aimee." She inclined her head. I'm Mary Alice, your housekeeper."

I grinned, "And cook."

"Yes, and cook," she nodded.

As Mary Alice poured me a large glass of ice water, we talked a little. She was very nice and efficient. I liked her. Also, I learned she wasn't just a cook, but an actual pastry chef. And the piece of information that really floored me, she was Ray's wife. Wow. I had so many questions, but knew it was inappropriate to ask. Bummer. 'Cause I highly doubted Nik would know. Men just weren't as interested in the details of other's lives the way women were.

Before too much time had passed, Nik had found us chatting. Mary Alice's demeanor instantly switched to professional. Nik politely spoke to her as a boss, not a friend. Then he excused us, and escorted me into the hallway. "Have you seen the rest of the house?"

I smiled, "No. I was waiting for you."

He uncharacteristically swung me around before he placed a reverent kiss on my lips. "Well, Mrs. Strand, let me show you around our humble abode."

I couldn't quash the giggles that had erupted. Oh, how I loved this playful side of him. I only wanted more. So I vowed to myself, *I'll do whatever needed to make him truly smile and laugh at least once a day.*

When we walked back towards the kitchen, I was more sexually frustrated than I had ever been. I thanked Mary Alice as she made her way out of the dining room, so we could enjoy our dinner. Still, I grappled with the fact I now owned a home with an indoor pool, library, wine cellar, and entertainment room. The house had six bedrooms, each with its own bathroom, and of course a master suite, which was the size of my childhood home. *WTF!* Did two people really need this much space? Although I knew, Alex and Even spent a fair amount of time here as well. The brothers were not usually in residence at the same time; however, it did happen occasionally. That didn't upset me as much as I thought it would, ironically. Since we were a newly married couple, you would think I'd want every minute possible alone with Nik, yet, somehow, having his brothers around felt like family. Let's face it; the place was big enough to find privacy—and then some.

As we sat down, the images of all the ways Nik had just teased my body with his danced through my brain. I had half a mind to swipe the dishes off the table and have mind-blowing sex with him—*here and now*. Arrogant bastard knew it, too. He sat there watching me intently; fully aware he had aroused me to my limits. Almost. Granted, I barely held on to my desire, but I was holding on. Fine, he wanted to play. Then, so be it. It was my turn to drive him insane with lust. I smiled impishly as I took a bite of lasagna.

Let the games begin!

Chapter Thirty-Four
Nik

Every cell in my body screamed out for release. I had pushed our bodies to the edge. One little nudge and we would both go over into a pleasure abyss. Aimee knew it, too. The wicked glint in her eyes told me the tables were about to turn. A part of me wasn't sure I should give her any leeway. The other, was about to expire from anticipation of what she could— correction, would—do to me. The fact she had more knowledge of carnal penchants than any other woman I had ever been with was a huge turn on. My arousal was downright painful as I shifted, trying to find some kind of relief from the pressure. Shit. Wrong way! I then tugged my crotch violently with the hopes I wouldn't blow my load right there at the kitchen table. I let out a long breath to find some sort of control.

Rotten little imp was completely aware of my condition. She smiled seductively, and then slid the last bite of tiramisu between her lovely lips. The erotic image of her wet mouth as it worked my cock almost undid me. She finished her Maury red wine, and that pink tongue of hers darted out to catch the last drop. That did it. I stood and held out my hand to her. When she glanced at it implacably, I cautioned, "Don't push me, Aimee. Take my hand. It's time."

With mock innocence she responded, "Time for what, exactly, Nikko?"

Done! I held her gaze with predator intensity and growled, "Playing coy doesn't suit you, lille." I grabbed her by the arm and tugged her out of the chair, which effectively brought her magnificent body against mine. I moaned, "Come. Now."

She grinned devilishly. "No, surely you didn't," she said in mocked horror.

What?! Ah, I got it. "Saucy, bitch," I teased before I laid claim to her mouth with mine. "You're so fuckin' sweet."

She mewled, "Hmm. You're not half bad yourself."

While I lifted her gorgeous ass into my hands, I rubbed my erection along the seam of her slacks. I fought hard not to explode, barely. I tried my damnedest to focus on anything that would give me some form of control; consequently, I began mentally working financial stats. Once I knew I wouldn't lose it, I drew her up the stairs to our bedroom. The one room I had purposely not shown her on our earlier tour.

As we entered the room, she gasped. I couldn't help but feel a little smug. The one thing I'd taken great precision in doing was to learn the fine characteristics of my wife. Her tastes. Her likes. Her dislikes. Her favorite things. All of which, made her who she was—*my* Aimee Grace. I leaned down to speak directly in her ear and whispered, "You like it?"

She bit her lip as she nodded. Then she walked over to the oversized, mahogany four-poster bed and ran her a hand over the thick plum duvet. "It's so luxurious." She began to finger the intricate detail of the bedframe. "Where did you find this marvelous antique?"

Pleased she recognized quality, I apprised, "This belonged to my parents, a wedding gift from my grandparents."

Her eyes widened. "You mean this came from Norway?"

I approached her with the stealth of a panther and snaked my arms around her middle from behind. Then I nuzzled into her golden hair—it always smelled of oranges with a hint of cinnamon. "Yes, it was custom made," I confirmed as I caressed her hairline with the tip of my nose.

She leaned back and tilted her head, which gave me full access to her neck. I licked, suckled, and grazed with my teeth until she cried out, "More, please."

I pushed her forward onto the bed and followed. Then I inched my hands under her hips to undo the clasp, and slid down the zipper on her linen slacks. She assisted by rising up, effectively bringing the curve of her bottom into my groin. I groaned. As I glided her pants down her lovely legs, I used my feet to finish removing them. Grateful, that neither Aimee nor I wore shoes when we were inside our home for any length of time. I did the same with her silky panties. Next, I removed my trousers and boxer briefs. I placed my hand between her thighs to check and see if she was ready for me. She turned her head towards me and asked, "Is there any lube in the nightstand?"

Fuck! My mouth now dry, I swallowed before I spoke, "Let me check."

After I found what she had requested, I needed no further instructions. I rubbed a generous amount along the crack of her ass, working forward. Next, I moved my fingers along her folds, and concentrated my efforts on her most sensitive spot at the apex. Once I felt her orgasm begin to ripple, I eased my dick into the rosebud of her ass. She screamed, "Yes. Oh, just like that."

I continued my ministrations and eased two fingers into her core. I could feel my own fingers working her g-spot against my cock. Unable to hold back another second, I came on a roar. While our breathing settled back to normalcy, I made love to her mouth with mine. Our tongues tangled, just as our bodies had. With no desire to break our connection, I stayed buried inside her body. Eventually I eased out of her, rolled over onto my back and pulled her on top of my chest. We, then, continued to mate with our mouths.

*****

We must've fallen asleep. I awoke to her warm tongue on my balls. *Ah, what a way to be greeted*. Her warm, wet tongue traced the underside of my cock before her mouth captured the head. She licked along the crown, causing me to fist her hair and arch my back. "Hmm," she hummed, bringing forth a burst of moisture. After that she went to work, and took me all the way to the back of her throat. She used one hand to fist my shaft while she followed her mouth. With her other hand, she stroked my sac. I had no desire to come—*just yet*—so I gently pulled her off.

She licked her lips as she tilted her head to the side. "Something wrong?" she asked seductively.

"God, no," I declared, "It's just that I want you to climax with me."

She grinned before turning her body around and straddling my chest. "Much better," I praised and then ran my tongue along her feminine folds.

She groaned in response. Against her core I spoke, "So fucking beautiful," before I licked her perineum. A tremor traveled along her body.

Next thing I knew, she imitated me along the same muscle on my body. Her one hand went back to work, stroking my rod from root to tip. There was suddenly something very wet applied to my asshole. *Oh, shit. She doesn't plan to…* Her tongue was assisting with the lube along my sensitive seam. I wasn't sure about this. Never had I let *anyone* touch me there. Not since that horrible almost rape at the God forsaken prison, in which, the only other person with that knowledge was now gone. Matter of fact, I was generally pretty damn squeamish when it came to anal play on me. Yet, there was something so erotic about what she was doing. And I would be a liar, if I said it didn't feel unbelievable. Her hot, little mouth began to softly suckle my balls, once again, joining her hand that was busy stroking me off. There was no way I could hold back the orgasm. I dove with my tongue as far into her core as possible, and, with my fingers, gently plucked her clit. No way was I coming without her. I felt my lower spine tighten as the pressure ramped up in my gonads. When she slid her forefinger into my rosebud—far enough to caress my prostate—I erupted fiercely, taking her right along with me.

I held on to her bucking hips with all I had as we fell to our sides. And that was when I lost control of my emotions. There was no containing the sob that broke. Aimee suddenly climbed my body and held me tightly against her breasts. They were wet and sticky from me, yet I didn't care. I let out all the fear, anger, and frustration of the incident all those years ago. It was just one of the many nightmares I wished I didn't have.

She softly crooned, "It's okay. I've got you."

As I blinked back the tears, I looked up at her. "You've no idea what that means to me."

She caressed my hair and coaxed, "Why don't you tell me what this is all about."

I straightened up, placing some pillows behind my neck and shoulders for support. Then I eased her onto my lap, facing away from me. Next, I pulled the covers over us and bared my soul. "I was almost gang raped while in prison."

"Oh my God," she gasped, "I didn't know." She tried to turn around, but I held her firmly to me.

"I know that," I answered self-deprecatingly. "No one does. Well, except Lorenzo. And he's not telling anyone from six feet under."

She composed herself and inquired, "Is that how he saved your life?"

I shrugged. "Yeah, I suppose it is. That damn gang was going to make sure they abused me every which way before they finally offed me."

She swallowed hard. "Did they...*touch* you?"

I shook my head emphatically. "Not there. They'd just beaten the crap out of me, and managed to get my pants to my ankles when Lorenzo and his gang arrived on the scene."

"I'm so sorry, Nikko. If I had known..."

"Shh, lille," I reassured. "It was a long time ago. Like I said, nothing else happened." I scoffed, "Well, not of that particular variety. That was the night I was brought into the fold and branded."

She exclaimed, "What?!" Then she turned herself around so she was facing me. With her knees on either side of my hips, she held my face in both hands. "You said 'branded.' What do you mean by that?"

I ran my fingers along hers as I eased my hair back on my right side to expose the LD brand that was there. Tears slid down her cheeks when the fingers of her left hand traced the mark. "How come I never noticed this before?"

I was fairly sure she asked herself this question. But I went ahead and answered, "It's not very obvious. Plus, I make sure it stays hidden."

She leaned forward and kissed the puckered skin. "I thought it was a scar. I never once thought to investigate it further."

"Nothing you could've done differently—it is what it is."

She began to trace the initials with the tip of her tongue. Then her right hand slipped between our bodies as she positioned the head of my cock inside her. Easing down, she rode me softly and tenderly. It was exactly what I needed—sexual healing. I captured her mouth with mine, kissing her, with all the reverence I had for her. This climax was slow and easy. And the sleep that followed was peaceful and nightmare free. Aimee was the balm to my wounded soul. And *she* owned me—like no one ever had or ever would. Forever.

*****

The next morning I was edgy with anticipation. Not wanting to blow my surprise for her had made me slightly punchy. Poor thing couldn't move fast enough for me. Once we were in the car, she read me the riot act. "Knock it off, Nik! I have no idea what has gotten into you, but you have to stop acting like this. Enough, already."

I grabbed her hand and brought it to my lips. "I'm sorry, lille. I'm a bit excited, is all."

Her brow arched. "And why is that?"

I smiled, "You'll see in due time."

She gave me a petulant *huff,* but didn't say anything more. Good. I wasn't completely sure I could keep a lid on it for much longer.

We arrived downtown, and I parked the Aston Martin AM 310 Vanquish. On our ride up the elevator, she queried, "Is this where your offices are located?"

I half-smiled. "This is my building. So, yes, my main cooperate office for the West Coast division is here."

"Oh." She shot me a wary glance, but didn't say anything else.

I leaned down and kissed the tip of her nose. "'S no big deal, Aimee. Relax. You'll be fine."

She shook her head and said, "So *you* say."

I chuckled as the doors opened. As I placed my hand at the small of her back, I escorted her to my assistant. "Hello, Emil. Could you please make sure my nine o'clock is comfortable? I'll just be a few minutes."

"Yes, sir," he replied.

Before I forgot, I introduced Aimee and Emil. Then we made our way to the back corner of the floor. When I opened the door wide, I motioned her to precede me. She entered the elaborate office, turned and inquired, "Is this yours?"

I ran my hand through my hair and closed the door behind me. "No."

She walked over to the feminine black desk and looked out of the floor to ceiling windows. "If it's not yours, Nik, then whose is it?"

I walked up behind her and coiled my arms around her waist. "Yours," I whispered in her ear.

She spun in my arms, clutched my shoulders and sputtered, "What...did you just say?"

I cupped her face in my hands and stated, "You heard me."

She held my gaze with intensity as moisture glistened behind her lashes, but didn't fall. "I don't understand."

I brushed my lips against hers gently and expounded, "My gift to you."

"What exactly are you giving me, Nikko?"

"Your own division," I apprised confidently.

"Of *your* company?" she inquired cautiously.

I pressed my forehead against hers and explained, "You're in charge of *our* hotels."

"Our h-hotels?" she gasped, "W-What do you mean, 'in charge'?"

"Congratulations, Mrs. Strand. You are the new head executive of our remarkable hotel division. Last count, we owned about twenty-five world-wide."

"Is this some kind of joke?" She had an incredulous look in her eyes.

Man, I loved that she had never once anticipated this. "No, lille. It's all very real—and yours."

She blinked several times, hard. Then, I watched as the gears clicked into place. "I'm in charge. I'm the boss. You've just given me what I would've had to work a good ten years for."

I kissed her again. "Yes. That about sums it up."

She squealed with joy. The next thing I knew, she was in my arms and her lips were locking with mine. After a few moments, she murmured, "Thank you," over and over again against my mouth.

Now that went better than I had planned. I returned her impassioned kiss before the intercom buzzed in. "Mr. Strand, your nine o'clock is enjoying coffee in your office as we speak."

"Thank you, Emil. I'll be right there."

I held Aimee's hand. "I need to go. Have a look around. Your PA will be in shortly."

She stood on tip-toes and pecked me chastely on the cheek. "I love you, Nikko Mathias Strand."

I beamed as I strode to the door, opening it

wide. Over my shoulder I called, "That's a mighty good thing." I winked before closing the door behind me.

All the way to my office there was a spring in my step, and I didn't give a damn who noticed. I was a man *madly* in love with his wife. Together, we would make one hell of a team—at home and in the cooperate world. Happy didn't even begin to cover how I felt at that moment. I knew full well that my commitments, along with my work, kept me away from home. This was the perfect solution. Bonus was, Aimee had the education to pull this off without a hitch, and I would have her close by. Win-win, if you asked me. She would hopefully see it that way, too, because the thought of being away from her for twelve-plus hours a day would not work for me. Ever.

Chapter Thirty-Five
Aimee

While I stood by the elegant desk, I took in my spacious office. It was decorated in a feminine, yet classic way—with shades of violet accented with grays, brushed silver, and black. Honestly, I couldn't have chosen better if I had done it all myself. The man knew me too well. I smiled as I gazed out at the incredible view of downtown San Francisco—incredulous that my husband would think to give me something so extraordinary. The mansion was magnificent, yet it had been his all along. He could've bought me my favorite car, but I really didn't care what I drove as long as it was safe. No, he knew the one thing I'd always dreamed of was my own company, and/or running my own hotels. Unbelievable. After such a short time, he understood me better than most.

As I stood there lost in my musings, in walked an impeccably dressed tall, thin man. He held out his hand and introduced, "I am Adrian, your personal assistant, Mrs. Strand."

I was utterly speechless for a moment; finally, I shook hands with the man. "How do you do?"

After the awkwardness passed, Adrian brought me up to speed on the projects at hand, along with the meetings I had scheduled for the next day. I was apparently to take a look-see of our hotel down by Fisherman's Wharf in about an hour. Once he left, I sat down, feeling a bit overwhelmed. Unsure if I could pull this off with no hands on experience behind my belt. Yet if I was anything, I was tenacious. Time to dig my heels in and make things work. And that was just what I began to do.

When Adrian buzzed in and reminded me of the tour I was supposed to take of our local hotel, I was surprised. Thankful I'd had the presence of mind that morning to wear business attire; subsequently, I donned my Dona Karan blazer and left the office. *Time to take the bull by the horns*, I thought as I made my way to the waiting Bentley.

*****

There was no hiding my exultance over this city. I took everything in on our drive down to the wharf. The tourists were thick, but not like they would've been during the right season. We pulled up in front of the valet, and I was instantly greeted by the manager, Mr. Greenfield, who escorted me from the car and inside to the lobby.

As I entered the extravagant hotel, my breath stopped for a moment. I looked around furtively for a name of the grandiose structure; finally, I spotted the name over the splendid registration area. Not surprised in the least to see the Strand name, big and proud, in elegant script of gold filigree. My curiosity could no longer be held at bay when I turned to Mr. Greenfield and queried, "Has this always been called The Strand?"

"Why, no," he replied. "We recently underwent a name change."

"I see." As politely as possible I inquired, "Is this, by chance, the old Fairmont?"

290

"Yes, it is. However, it has undergone many improvements since Strand Industries purchased it."

I knew it! While I kept my emotions in check, I continued, "And, how long ago was that?"

His smile was a bit bewildered, but he answered, "About a year now."

Thank you, Jesus. For a moment, I thought Nik had acquired the property once he knew where I was supposed to be working. That was before the whole Caleb debacle altered my life forever. Of course, it was hard to be upset about that when it led me to Nikko. I glanced down at my diamond wedding ring and smiled. The knowledge that he hadn't changed a thing since his mother wore it made me happier than I thought possible. Nik's sentimentality and his strong connection to family was some of the things I loved most about him.

Mr. Greenfield pulled me back from my reverie when he stated, "I was hired on when an unexpected change caused the *would be* manager from accepting the position."

I hid my knowledge of just *who* that was supposed to be. "You don't say? I do hope it wasn't anything terrible," I said in mock innocence.

"Oh, no, ma'am. Although I was not privy to the details, I was reassured all was well with her. It was simply a change of plans."

"Thank goodness. I would've hated to hear otherwise." Again, I offered up a prayer of gratitude that no one had been talking behind my back. The only thing they were told was pertinent information.

"As would I, Mrs. Strand." I could see the sincerity in his eyes. He gently motioned for me to precede him. "Shall we continue our tour?"

"Yes, please," I responded with genuine enthusiasm.

After about an hour or so, I had seen all there

was to offer of The Strand. It truly was a marvelous, five star hotel. Mr. Greenfield had been most accommodating with each and every detail to the place, as well as the surroundings. Though my plans had been severely rearranged, the reality was that, now, I was in charge of this lovely place and others like it. My heart soared with the knowledge. I couldn't wait until that evening to thank my husband properly.

*****

Later that afternoon, I arrived back at the spectacular office building. Once I was ensconced in my office, I took my time going over reports. So when Nik stood there, his huge shoulder leaning against the doorjamb and his massive arms crossed over his muscular chest, I startled. "Is it time to leave already?" I asked surprised.

He grinned, "No." My brow arched, so he clarified, "It's past time, lille."

I glanced down at the time on my computer screen and gasped, "Eight o'clock. Where has the time gone?"

Nik sauntered in, closing the door behind him. "You've been a busy bee today."

"Yes. Well, I do have to earn my keep." Conspiratorially I whispered, "You see, the boss is a tyrant."

The desire in his eyes caused his pupils to dilate. His nose slightly flared while he continued to stalk towards me. His voice, low and deep, rasped, "I hear he really knows how to *ride* your ass."

My breath hitched as I bit my lip. Holy hell. We were going to get *busy* in this mostly glass office. I had never really been one for exhibition sex—wait, have I said that before?—but the thought of it with

Nik did things to my insides. *Oh, we had come close to getting caught on that hammock in the Caribbean, but not like this.* My core was molten lava as he went to his knees in front of me. While I held his gaze, I seductively responded, "Yeah, he does. Though I'd be a liar, if I said I didn't like *his* style."

He grunted as he took my mouth with his. Not in a sweet, tender way either, no, it was violent with unadulterated hunger. My nipples strained to reach his chest. His hands roughly traveled up my skirt. When his fingers located my garters, he growled from deep in his throat, causing me to moan. If there was one weakness I'd always had, it was sexy undergarments. With impatience he unsnapped the first one, and then the other.

My silk stockings tore under his demanding fingers. The lacey thong really didn't have a chance in hell of surviving his ardent pursuit to my slick womanhood. Once I was bare from the waist down, he buried his head between my thighs. His wicked tongue wreaked havoc over my feminine folds. He lifted his head, and I could see my juices coating his lips. He ordered, "Put your feet against the desk."

When I complied, he purred, "Yeah, just like that."

He went back to work on my core and rapidly brought me to a soaring climax.

The next thing I knew, he hauled me up out of the chair and commanded, "Bend over the desk, Aimee."

Omigod! We didn't have lube. Was he going to…? When he entered my core on a fluid thrust, all my questions disappeared. He was absolute power as he fucked me, hard and fast. He bit down on my shoulder as he came, insuring no one could hear us. Although whether he realized it or not, he'd just marked me. Doubtful he even understood what that meant; however, it took me right over the edge. We eventually put ourselves back to rights and left.

*****

Sleep wasn't on our agenda when we arrived home that night. Instead, we made love in the shower. Afterwards, we went to find our dinner waiting for us. Mary Alice wasn't just a master at desserts, she was a remarkable cook no matter what she chose to make. And I admittedly was a bit jealous. I actually liked to cook. Even though I knew I couldn't hold a candle to her expertise. Nik noticed the change in me as he inquired, "What is it?"

I laughed without humor. "Nothing."

He reached forward and ran the pad of his finger between my eyes. "This frown is not 'nothing.' Tell me, please."

While I really liked his bossy side, the politeness always won me over. "It's silly." I shook my head.

"How do you know I'll think that if you don't tell me?"

Well, he had a point there. I shrugged. "I like to cook. But there's no way I can compete with Mary Alice's brilliance."

"Ah, I see. You're feeling a little jealous."

"Yeah, I guess I am."

He stood and scooped me up into his arms, kissing my cheek, jaw, and then my lips. "I'd love for you to cook for me."

Still a tad breathless from the unexpected ardor, I panted, "You would? Why?"

He nuzzled my nose with his. "Because it would be an act of love. Mary Alice does it for a living. Yes, she enjoys it. But it is still her job." He began walking through the house and up the stairs to our bedroom.

I held on to his neck and kissed his stubbled jaw. "I think I get what you mean," running my tongue along his sculpted bottom lip, "For all intents and purposes, I would be doing it to *bring* you pleasure."

His breathing was ragged, causing him to half-growl out, "Precisely."

And that was the end of our conversation for the evening, as we proceeded to make love well into the wee hours.

*****

The next couple of weeks were insanely busy. I was learning the business by trial and error while Nik worked on a merger. Therefore, we didn't spend more than the evenings together. But we made the most of our time. We were an active newlywed couple, so there wasn't one night we didn't make love. Sometimes, it was a few times a night. Okay, maybe we were a bit *overactive.*

As I looked back now, I continued to question if what happened next was necessary. Though life didn't come with do overs, there were times I truly wished it did. Having said all of that, that particular night had gone like the others before it. I couldn't recall the exact moment it all changed. Completely. As if you were watching the speeding train head directly for the stalled car on the tracks, and there was not a damn thing you could do to stop the impact. You knew it would be bad. Aware, there was no chance of escape. A smart person would've screamed, at least closed their eyes, but, no, I chose to watch in abstract horror as my life altered, once again.

*****

We were snuggled under the covers enjoying the aftermath of tremendous sex. By far, one the best experiences we'd ever had. I lay on his chest tracing the brutal, yet beautiful tattoo over his heart. The dagger was downright ferocious in its dark black ink. Though it was the red hearts with the darker crimson blood teardrops I had always wondered about. I felt exceptionally close to my husband, especially at that moment, so I dared to ask the question: "What does this tatt mean to you?"

He instantly stiffened underneath me and gave me an indifferent, "Nothing."

Bullshit. I knew better and countered, "Don't be so enigmatic with me. I am your wife; hence, I have a right to know."

Well, that pissed him off royally—if the look he shot me was anything to go by.

"I don't have to tell you shit about me or my body." His voice was implacable. "Drop it," he demanded as he sat up, turning away from me.

Oh, hell no. He was not avoiding me on this. I placed my hand on his shoulder and continued, "Stop evading me. I really don't see what the big deal is."

He stood and began to walk away. There was no way I was going to tolerate such an action. I darted in front of him, effectively blocking his path. "Tell me," I demanded. Hind sight, I should've been gentler—more understanding. But damn it all, his attitude had pushed me too far. There was no backing down, now.

When he grasped my shoulders, I could feel the tremors wracking his body. Was it temper, or something else? I would never know. "Why can't you just accept that I'm unable to discuss this with you?"

Exasperated, I blew out a breath. "Because your behavior doesn't make a lick of sense."

His nostrils flared as his eyes narrowed. "That's your perspective. I make perfect sense when it comes to this issue.

"You don't share crap with me, Nik!" I roared. "So don't stand there playing all high and mighty with me." I yanked out of his grasp and held my ground. "I know the dagger was done in prison. You've at least told me that much. What's the rest of the story?" I queried while I placed my hand over the hearts the tip of the dagger pierced.

He recoiled from me like I had burned him. Then nastily he snorted, "You don't touch me without my permission."

That did it. Bastard had some serious audacity. I spat out, "Fuck you and the horse you rode in on!" With that, I left the room and stormed down the hall until I reached a guestroom, where I planned on staying. It would be a cold day in hell before I'd go back into the master bedroom with that asshole.

I heard the door slam and then Nik's heavy footsteps on the stairs. *Good. I hope he doesn't sleep tonight.* Finally realizing he was somewhere in the huge mansion cooling off, I crawled under the covers and fell into a fitful sleep.

*****

Later, I awoke discombobulated. It took me a few moments to recognize where I was. All of a sudden, I remembered the horrible fight we'd had earlier and decided it was time to make up. I hated sleeping without Nik's monstrous arms wrapped around me. Let's face it, I missed him. So I did the most logical thing, I grabbed a robe from the closet and went in search of my wayward husband.

As I walked down the stairs, I could hear the guitar. I padded towards the sound, instantly recognizing the sorrowful tune by Tim McGraw being played. When I peeked in through the crack in the door, I froze.

The sight before me would forever be etched in my mind. Nik sat strumming his guitar while he stared, with tears streaming down his cheeks, at a picture. From where I stood, I couldn't see who was in it. But when the song changed to the haunting, mournful melody I'd heard him play once before, I had a pretty good idea. Crap! It seemed no matter what I did I would never hold a candle to his dead wife.

I eased away from the room and crept back upstairs. After I carefully closed the door to our bedroom, I grabbed a bag and began to pack a few changes-of-clothes, along with my toiletries and makeup. Once the task was completed, I wiped my tear stained face and then went back to the guestroom I was using. As I composed the note, I once again broke down and sobbed. I pulled myself together and set my iPod on the song by Lunatica. It was as much for him as it was for me.

I made my escape cautiously. The fog matched my mood as I walked along the deserted street. I eventually found a cab, making my way to the airport. There was only one place I could go where no one would know to look for me. And I had every intention of staying there until I could face life *without* Nik. Because that much was clear, I couldn't compete with a ghost, nor did I want to try anymore. I was done. No matter how much it broke my heart; I wouldn't be second best. Even if that meant being alone for the rest of my life.

So.

Be.

It.

Chapter Thirty-Six
Nik

The hardest thing I had ever done in my life was say a final goodbye to Rachel. As the tears rolled down my face, a sob broke through. Though I knew it was time—well past time, actually—it still tore me up. I relived every moment I had ever shared with her. All the way to the untimely end I had brought about, which was the very reason why I still couldn't explain the tattoo over my heart. On cue the spot began to ache, and I rubbed it profusely. The knowledge that it was time to bare my soul to Aimee didn't make any of this easier. Really, who wanted to hear their spouse was a killer? Hell, I sure wouldn't. Why would Aimee be any different? Yet through the avalanche of those uncontrolled emotions, I could hear Rachel's last words: "I love you, Niky." All the while the damned song "Please Remember Me" played, loud and clear, on the radio that fateful night. How did the song mysteriously come out of that busted radio? I would probably never know the answer to that.

Fact was, rehashing all the could'ves, would'ves, and should'ves, wasn't going to bring her back. Although it pained me to say that, I wasn't sure it was what I wanted. Please, don't misunderstand me. I would give anything to have Rachel and my daughter alive and well. It wasn't that. What I meant was, my feelings for Aimee ran deeper. Wider. More all-consuming. Did I feel like shit for admitting that? Hell yeah, I did. But it didn't change the facts: I loved Rachel. But I love Aimee more.

Now it was time she knew that. Rachel was my past, and a part of me would always love her. But Aimee was my present, my future. I would tell her everything about me, and I'd start with the damned tattoo. After I put my guitar aside, I went over to the wet bar and grabbed a towel to dry my face. *I'm sure I look like hell.* There, I decided a little liquid courage couldn't hurt. I finally got my shit together and headed back to our bedroom. *Don't you dare wimp out here. Man up. No pussyfooting it, either.*

Before I opened the door, I took a deep breath. Huh, it was strange she wasn't in bed. I peeked in the bathroom—no Aimee. What the fuck? A chill ran down my spine as I cautiously approached the walk-in closet. Shit! Some of her things were missing. I went back to the bathroom and inspected it closer. Yep, her stuff was definitely gone. My fist went through the wall before I marched out of the bedroom.

Over and over I yelled her name; as I threw open every door. Wait, was that music I heard? What the hell? I knocked before I entered, just in case I had blown this out of proportion. No. Such. Luck. The song "Who You Are" was playing on a loop. With a beastly roar—I didn't recognize—I began to destroy the room and everything in it. In a haze of rage, I almost missed the letter lying on the pillow. I ran both hands through my hair, pulling at it profusely, until I found some kind of control. Barely. Ticking time bomb was an accurate description of how I felt at that moment.

I fell onto the edge of the bed and grasped the neatly folded piece of paper with my name written in beautiful script. For a minute, I simply traced over her handwriting. Scared shitless of what I was about to read, yet I knew I had to. I would've paid an enormous amount of money to not read her words to me. Though being a pussy was never something I had ever been before. No sense starting now!

My dearest Nikko,

    First and foremost, you need to know how much I love you. More than I ever thought possible. You are my everything. Which is why, this is much harder than it should be.

    I don't understand your reticence towards me. Maybe you're like that with everyone. Though it appears you're not with your brothers. Could be I've misread that. Still, your reaction tonight was abhorable. I realize that sounds a bit cruel, but dammit, it's how I feel. I thought your body was mine? Just like my body is yours. I guess I misunderstood that.

    Once I calmed down and slept on things, I realized I didn't want to be without you. So, I came looking for you. But what I saw and heard sealed the deal. Your tribute to Rachel was beautiful. I wish you could feel that way about me. It's obvious you still love her very much. FTR, I never wanted you to stop loving her. I just thought you had room for me, too. Again, I suppose, that was just my wishful thinking.

    Here's the thing, Nik. I thought I could play second fiddle. I really did. But I can't. That's not your fault. I don't blame you. You need to know, I didn't leave because I'm angry. I left 'cause no matter how much I love you, I can't take the backseat to another woman. I'm truly sorry. I thought I could.

    I won't compete with a ghost.

I wish you well. I hope you find happiness.

With all my heart,
Aimee

As I shook my head and moaned out my sorrow, the words to the song caught my attention: it was all about not feeling or healing until you found yourself. Well, hell, didn't that just about sum me up?! Oh, she was good. I would give her that. Problem was, I had finally figured it out. While she was up here writing this blasted letter to me, I had come to terms with everything, everyone, myself and her. I slammed my fist down to shut the fucking iPod up, and then I strode downstairs.

She.

Wasn't.

Leaving.

Me.

Come hell or high water, I would find her.

When I walked into the lower level hallway, I banged on Ray's door. I would give him credit, he never batted an eye as he opened the door and said, "What's wrong, sir?"

Thank God, someone had presence of mind. I howled, "Aimee's gone."

He quirked an eyebrow. "I'm sorry. What did you say?"

I swear, at that moment, I could've hit the guy. "I think you heard me loud and clear."

"I-I meant, I have twenty-four hour surveillance outside of the mansion," he stammered. "I don't understand how she slipped by my guys?"

"Well, neither do I. But she has."

He grabbed his radio to double-check with the security team. Sure enough, James confirmed, "I had her, sir. Then somehow she gave me the slip."

"Fuuuuuuck," Ray growled back.

Yep, my sentiments exactly! My brows rose at him. "See." The "I told you so" left unspoken, *for now*.

*****

The next few hours were spent gathering any intel possible on Aimee's whereabouts. We still hadn't come up with jack when my brothers entered the stressful scene. They knew me well, and didn't mince words.

"What've you got so far?" Alex inquired.

"Nada. Zilch. Nothing whatsoever. It's as if she fell off the face of the earth."

E, in his general sarcastic tone, fired off, "Maybe she snuck through a portal and is now in another realm."

I threw the glass I was holding right at his head. Luckily, he had the reflexes to lean away from the flying object. While that pissed me off at the time, later on, I was damned grateful I hadn't hurt my baby brother.

Alex, being the forever peacemaker, stepped between us. First, he scolded E: "That, bro, was uncalled for. And you know it." He then turned to me. "Second, Nik, what the hell were you thinking? You could've killed him if that had struck just right." We both received a stern look that was so much like our mother's I paused. He continued, "Now, you two, cut the crap. We have a wife to find." He used his utmost lawyer voice.

Bastard had a point. Not that I would tell him so. Hell, no. Never admit defeat had been my motto for years. And the reason I was successful at business. Although I concede—at least to myself—it didn't work very well in a marriage. I ran my hand through my hair, and then extended it out to E. "I'm sorry, man. Tension's a bit high right now."

"Yeah, I get that. I apologize, Nik. I really don't mean to be a dick."

Alex messed up his hair. "We know you don't. You just can't help yourself."

Without heat he growled, "Up yours."

After a few more moments of my brothers banter, we got down to the nitty-gritty. "Here's what we know so far," I informed them. There really wasn't squat to go by. We had no idea where she went. No trace that Aimee had rented a car, bought a plane or train ticket.

Alex piped up, "So, we're back to square one."

"Unless I've missed something here," I countered as I laid out all the documentation and surveillance photos we had of her.

E sighed, "What a clusterfuck."

I began to pace as I responded, "Yeah, it is."

"And then some," Alex added.

With a fine tooth comb, we went through every single thing we had. And still we had no direction on her whereabouts. Frustrated, I spat out, "Damn it all!"

That was when the door flew open with no preamble. Ray strode in purposely and threw a manila envelope down on the desk. "We may have something," he said implacably.

I motioned for him to continue.

"A ticket agent at the airport thinks she recognized Aimee from a photo."

Alex chimed in, "But?"

Ray nodded, "But the woman she saw had

dark auburn hair."

With no humor I chuckled, "Clever girl."

E caught on fast. His gaze held mine as he stated, "She wore a wig."

"Apparently." Ray continued, "At least it looks like that's what she did. Plus, she made the disguise complete with old clothes and no makeup." He stroked his jaw. "She's damn good, I'll give her that."

Alex queried, "Let me guess, she paid cash for the ticket?"

Ray confirmed, "Yep. Oh, and get this, she changed planes four times, yet we don't have a destination."

Before I could, E asked, "How's that possible?"

"Simple," Ray answered, "She didn't continue on. From what we could gather from the airline, she didn't board the flight in DFW."

"Well, hell," I snorted. "She could be anywhere."

Ray confirmed, "Yes, sir." Then, "There's no record of her renting a car."

Alex scrubbed a hand over his face. "She found another mode of transportation."

That was when Ray dropped the bomb. "And altered her appearance, again." He jabbed his finger at a security camera photo of Aimee in the getup she left San Fran in. Then another photo was of a very well-dressed woman walking away from the camera. She had dark brown hair styled in a sleek bob and wore dark sunglasses.

I swear the woman was going to be the death me! I snarled, "Get the plane ready, Ray." Once he left the room, I made eye contact with both of my brothers. "Well, boys, looks like we're goin' hunting."

E smirked, "In Texas, no less."

Alex clapped me on the back. "Don't worry, big brother. We'll find her."

I exhaled a breath I didn't realize I was holding and pointed out, "Hopefully before Reynolds finds out she's unprotected."

"Fuck a duck," E growled, "I hadn't even thought about that."

Alex nodded, "Then we better get our asses in gear, gentlemen. Looks like the race is on."

*****

Unfortunately, Texas was a bust. We were still no closer to finding Aimee than we were in California. We decided to regroup, rest, and get some food. Therefore, we called it a day around ten that night. Beyond any coherent thought, I fell onto the bed and passed out.

At the loud knock on the connecting door to the suite, I came to. I stumbled groggily to open it. Alex marched in with a scowl on his face. "Talk," I commanded.

"We found one of Reynolds's men," he advised.

I growled, "Where?"

"St. Louis."

E entered the room. How the hell did he get a key card? Crap, I really didn't care at the moment. Alex continued, "You've spoken to her parents?"

"Yeah," I answered exasperatedly. "I told you that already."

E added, "What about Renée?"

I blew out a "yes."

"All right, so no one she's close to has heard from her, either," Alex confirmed what we already knew.

"Correct," I answered.

"So why St. Louis?" E inquired what I had been wondering myself.

"Your guess is as good as mine," I conceded.

Alex walked over to the room phone. "Let's get some coffee."

I grabbed my cell phone. "I'll get the plane readied for the next leg."

E clasped my shoulder. "He won't find her first," he vowed.

When I glanced up into his intense eyes, I knew my brother would kill to make sure he kept his promise. Fact of the matter was, he'd have to get in line and take a number. Because if Caleb laid one finger on my wife's beautiful head, I would tear him limb from limb. Not an exaggeration, I *would* do it—and never once regret it. I laid my hand over his. "Thanks for having my back, E." Then I turned to Alex and said, "You, too."

They both nodded in unison and answered, "Always."

Not for the first time, I was eternally grateful for my brothers. They were always willing to lend a hand whenever I needed them. There was no doubt I could count on them no matter what the circumstances. How the hell did I repay them? I didn't know, but what I did know was that I would, somehow, someway. That, I could guarantee.

Chapter Thirty-Seven
Aimee

The tiny cabin had a spectacular view of the Lake of the Ozarks, not too far from Eldon, Missouri. My childhood memories were of Osage Beach at this same lake. No one knew I owned the little place. A purchase I had made about three years ago. I'd paid cash for it, and had asked the previous owner to keep the title in his family name for me. Of course there was some legal documentation locked in a safe place, but, for all intents and purposes, it didn't appear to be mine. I had bought the cabin when I needed a time-out from a tough breakup with a man I *thought* I would marry. Ironic that it was now a breakup which had led me back here, once again. This time from the man I *did* marry. Life was full of surprises.

This time of year, there were no tourists. And very few residents remained. It was exactly what I needed to lick my wounds and have myself a grand pity party. No, I'm not proud of that. *But it is what it is.* Unable to face anyone at the moment, I entered my small abode. It was a bit dusty and needed to be aired out. Definite must. I began to open some windows, and then quickly realized I should light a fire. Good, gathering firewood kept my mind off things—*for a little while, at least.*

As the fire raged, so did my emotions. I ran

the gamut from anger to sorrow; finally, grief overtook me. My biggest regret: I wasn't carrying Nik's baby. I knew it was impossible since I was taking a birth control shot, but, still, I felt the loss of what could've been. For about a week or so, I did nothing but cry. Not sure I ever ate or truly rested. I would sob myself into a stupor, and then wake to do it all again. My whole world had ceased to exist. There was no point to any of it anymore.

*****

Honestly, devastation almost won until the sweet, elderly lady down the road paid me a visit one afternoon. To say I was in no mood for company would've been a vast understatement. However, I shuffled to the door and answered the incessant knocking. And to this day, I would forever be grateful for the angel here on earth by the name of Nan. If I had known how short my time with her was going to be, I would have spent every second possible with her. Have you ever met someone like that? A kindred spirit I believe was what they were called. My only solace was that someday I would see her again as we walked the streets in heaven.

Some snow blew in, blinding me for a moment, when I answered the door. Once it had cleared, an older woman stood there with a basket in hand.

"Hello, honey," she greeted. "I'm sorry it has taken me so long to make it up here." She put the handle in my hand. "I made these for you. Oh, goodness, where are my manners?" She held out her other hand to me. "I'm Nan—your closest neighbor."

I shook the proffered hand and introduced myself. "A pleasure to meet you, Ms. Nan. I'm Aimee."

"Just Nan. May I come in?" she asked as the cold and snow caused her to tremble.

"Oh, dear, of course. I'm so sorry." I held the door wide for her to enter.

She took in the sight before her with kind eyes. Needless to say, I hadn't exactly been keeping a clean house. I quickly tried to tidy-up, but she stilled my busy hands. "Honey, I don't mind a bit of mess. It's what makes you real. Please, don't feel like you need to clean for me," she said gently. "Besides, I came to visit *you*, not the cabin."

I nodded, fighting back tears. One would think I'd have been tapped out at that point. "May I get you something to drink?"

She smiled, "Coffee or tea would be wonderful."

After I made us both some herbal tea, we sat by the fire to enjoy each other's company. Curiosity had the best of me, so I peeked into the basket to find homemade muffins and cookies. My stomach growled loudly, reminding me I hadn't been taking very good care of myself lately.

Nan urged, "Please, help yourself."

I politely laid the goodies aside, and did my best not to scarf down the treats. "Delicious," I praised once I gobbled a wonderful cranberry and pumpkin muffin.

She offered another as soon as I finished, and I gladly accepted.

We sat and made small talk for a while, getting to know one another. I really liked her spunk. If I had memories of a grandmother, she would've been just like Nan. I unfortunately never had a chance to meet either one of mine. They had both passed away by the time I had been born. What I loved most about older women was how they spoke their minds no matter what. Nan was no exception. "So, what did *he* do?"

Caught off guard, I stammered, "I…uh…I'm sorry, what?"

She inclined her head towards the CD player, where I had Sarah McLachlan's "Wintersong" playing over and over again. "Seems to me, that's a song of heartbreak," she stated knowingly.

I sighed heavily. "Yeah, I guess it is."

"Did he cheat on you?"

"No," I answered a bit appalled. "Why would you ask me that?"

She ignored my question and persisted, "Did he take your money? Shoot your dog? Call your mother an unforgivable name?"

I shook my head as I half-smiled. "No, none of those things."

"Well then, apparently he *can* be forgiven. Or, oh my, did he hurt you?" she gasped. "Hurt someone else you love beyond repair?"

"No. He hasn't harmed anyone, even me," I clarified, "At least, not physically."

"I see. Will you make peace with him by Christmas?"

The tears began to trickle down my cheeks. "I don't think so. You see, I'm the one who *left* him."

"Hm-mm, I gathered that. Do you love him?"

I shrugged my shoulders. "Doesn't matter how much I love him, he can't reciprocate."

"Ahhh, now it's becoming clear." She rubbed the pad of her thumb over her bottom lip, as if deep in thought. After a beat, she inquired, "Do you know that for sure?"

"Unfortunately, I do." I wrung my hands, knowing, I really didn't want to expound on the subject.

She continued her inquisition, "So you've talked it over, and that was his confession."

"Not exactly," I apprised, "It's very complicated."

"Well, maybe, I can help uncomplicate the situation."

I bit my lip and then confessed, "I wish you could."

She stood and grasped my hands. "Don't give up on love, Aimee. It's too priceless a gift to just throw away."

I gave her a watery smile. "If only that were true, Nan. Seems more and more people are willing to toss it aside instead of fight for it. But sometimes, even when you've fought, you lose," I admitted.

"It's just a battle, dear," she countered. "There's still a war to be won."

Now how did I argue with that?!

She walked to the door and opened it. Over her shoulder she called, "I'll be by in the morning."

"I don't mean to be rude, but why?"

"Church, of course. Tomorrow is Christmas, after all."

Oh, no! How did I tell her that church and a former call girl did not mix? Though lightning hadn't struck me down at my wedding, hence, I figured I would be safe. So reluctantly I accepted, "I'll be ready."

She grinned, "Good. See you then."

The door closed behind her, and all I thought was, *what in the world have I gotten myself into?*

Still, I couldn't believe I had somehow forgotten the next day was Christmas. Under normal circumstances, it was my favorite day of the year. And I was more than thankful I'd had the presence of mind during my stealth departure from San Francisco to mail my parents a Christmas card with a little note, so they wouldn't worry. With those morose emotions churning inside me, I curled up by the fire, and, once again, let the tears fall.

*****

The next morning was clear and cold. Grateful for the body heat in the little church that was not even a mile away from my cabin. Nan sat and held my hand as we listened to the service together. She didn't let go when we stood and sang old Christmas songs. Yes, she was a bit off key, but I liked how she sang for the joy of the Lord, not for others. I knew I needed to remember that—this was between myself and God, no one else—as I realized it was time to repent and make peace with my past. Nothing I could do would ever undo the choices I had made. But somewhere down the road, there would be beauty from the ashes. For that, I was positive.

After service Nan invited me over for Christmas lunch, and I gladly accepted. I had to smile at the Big Band music playing over the old stereo system. It was then that I heard her story: "You know, Aimee. I lost my husband nearly fifty years ago, and I still miss him like it was yesterday."

I swallowed hard; this must be how Nik felt about Rachel. "I'm so sorry, Nan."

"No, don't be. We had a beautiful love that I wouldn't trade for anything."

I inquired, "How long were you married?"

"Ten short, yet amazingly joyous, years."

"And you never remarried?" I hoped I wasn't being too presumptuous.

"When you've had the *best*, there's no need to."

Huh, I wondered what that meant for Nik. Then, I was thrown for a loop when Julie London began to sing "I Left My Heart in San Francisco." I had to excuse myself and take a walk out on her front porch. Sure, I knew the song wasn't about the lost love between a woman and a man; still, it resonated deep in my soul. Could a heart possibly break anymore? Not to mention, my eyes burned from all the darn crying I had been doing lately. How I still had tears was a conundrum!

When I reentered her cabin, I proceeded to tell her about Nik and Rachel, along with how I couldn't live in *her* shadow. Nan surprised me when she slammed her wrinkled fist down on the table. "That's a copout!"

Excuse me?! Just who did she think she was? "I beg your pardon?" Astonishment coated my voice, for I was taken aback.

"You love him. Therefore, you fight for *him* and for *you*."

"How do you suppose I battle a ghost?"

"Show him you're alive and well—a flesh and bone woman worthy of his devotion, as well as his love."

"But…?"

"No, Aimee. There's no but when it comes to true love." She held her hand up to silence me. "You see, love is the greatest gift of all. It doesn't die or go away. Not true love, no, now that is eternal. It only knows to fight, to hold on and sacrifice daily."

"While I hear you loud and clear, what if the other person doesn't see it that way?"

"Then it wasn't true. Love is action, not pretty words." She gave me an all-knowing wink. "Though pretty words are nice, and they make us feel special, even cherished."

Well, I couldn't deny that. "Nik isn't a man of many words, Nan."

"Taciturn. Yes, my dear, sweet Clive was the same. But he had his moments of real romance." She beamed at the memories I could tell were floating through her mind.

"What do you think I should do?"

"I've already answered that for you," she explained.

"Fight?" I replied.

"Yes. With *all* you have."

I stood and began to pace. "How?"

She tried to stand up, but lost her footing, and fell back into the chair with a huff. I went to assist her. While she held eye contact with me, she imparted, "Stinks getting old." I smiled, but didn't reply. "Thank you for your help, dear. Now to answer your question: you *know* your husband. Only *you* know what's needed in your arsenal."

Once I knew she was all right, I let go and grabbed my coat. I nodded with a determined set to my jaw. "You're right. I do know."

I bent over and hugged her tight. "I don't know when I'll be back to see you again. Will you be okay?"

She squeezed my hand. "Aimee, you're a smart girl. Surely you know, I won't be around much longer," she stated matter-of-factly.

As I pulled her close, I begged, "Please. Don't talk like that."

She looked up as she tenderly wiped the tears from my face. "Dying is a part of living. Besides, I'm ready to go *home*."

I held back the sob and then confessed, "I hope I see you again here on earth before you go. I know it sounds selfish, but that's how I feel."

She kissed my cheek. "Sweet, sweet girl, I'll see you again. Don't you worry about me. You have a man and love to *fight* for."

I smiled as I took my leave. I knew now what I had to do. It was time to get some answers, or as Nan would say, "load my weapons." No, I wasn't going to let this be the end of Nik's and my story.

*****

Before I could head back to California, I was awakened by the local sheriff. It seemed Nan had passed away in her sleep that night. I stayed for the little funeral, and was gladdened to meet so many people Nan had touched. Lives changed for the better. Although her children had passed away years ago, she managed to stay encouraging and helpful to others. I instantly recognized how the good Lord had used her in a mighty way. My life would never be the same after having the privilege of meeting her. And I could rest assured, she was singing with the angels at that very moment. She was right, I would see her again. My last words to her were from Mathew 25:21. I bent over the casket and whispered, "Well done, good and faithful servant," before I kissed her cold cheek. Then silently I prayed, *Lord, no matter the outcome, please, help me to remember you can still use me to serve others.*

*****

As I entered the town of Eldon to gas up the old truck I had bought, I thought I recognized the man in sunglasses and ball cap. If I didn't know any better, I would've sworn he was one of Caleb's goons. No, surely, I was mistaken! Yet when I pulled back out onto the highway, there was no disillusionment I was being followed. Well, crap! I guess Caleb hadn't given up on me, after all. Fine. I knew this area like the back of my hand. Confident I would lose the spy in no time. Afterwards, I headed to Lake Tahoe to find the answers to all my questions about Nik and his past.

For better or for worse.

Chapter Thirty-Eight
Aimee

The first stop I made, once I reached South Lake Tahoe, was the court house. Nik had paid a lot of money to make sure his information stayed private and off the internet. I was positive he had made sure his offers were grander than what someone could make over disclosing the case. Although, no matter what, the fact remained it was a matter of public record. And I was bound and determined to find what I quested for. Going through case after case from nearly fifteen years ago, was a daunting task. I eventually came upon what I had been searching for; though, there was no victory dance in what I discovered that day. Also, there was no doubt my husband was a very wounded man. Not that I hadn't already known this, yet somehow, seeing it in black and white made it all too clear.

As my heart broke for him, I read every line word for word. He was too damn young—only nineteen-years-old—to have gone through such a tragedy. And I confess, I was pissed off at the system for charging and convicting him. The knowledge that it happened every day to so many people didn't quash my anger. Yet, there it was written for anyone to see: sentenced to three years for involuntary vehicular manslaughter. I learned he only served a little over a year of that sentence. Still, I didn't give a rat's ass what anyone said to me about the incident. It. Was. An. Accident. But according to the police report, he was driving too fast for conditions. Though it was noted he complained of "having no brakes," but I couldn't find any documentation on the car itself to verify his claim. Odd.

Once I made it back to my hotel, I had another crying spree for Nik, Rachel, and their unborn daughter. Life really was cruel. I couldn't even fathom how a person lived through such an ordeal. Yet Nik had. Even though he was cold, and could be heartless at times, now, it all made sense. Surely the survival guilt was horrendous, not to mention the damn PTSD that I had witnessed firsthand. I had to wonder if it was the reason he didn't open up to me, or others. I guess I couldn't blame him for not getting too close to people. Just meant you weren't devastated when they left your life—one way or the other. *Hello, you left him, too. Oh, shut the fuck up!* What a sad way to exist. Let's face facts; it was an existence, not living. Now, more than ever, I wanted to hold him close, and let him know I was there for him. Always.

*****

For the next few days, I learned the area and found Nik's old house, plus the high school he and Rachel graduated from. Everything and anything I could find on him, I devoured. I eventually worked up the courage to go to the library and look up old newspaper articles of the accident. Once again brought to tears, especially, when this time, there were photos. Needless to say, those images would forever haunt me. Though in some strange way, I was glad I had them. Somehow it made me feel closer to

Nik. Maybe it helped me understand him a little bit better than I had before. What I did know was that I missed him terribly. But I wasn't sure if I was quite ready to reach out to him, just yet.

As if reading the articles hadn't been traumatic enough for me, I then decided to go see Rachel—well, her grave at least. I believed, with everything in me, she joyfully walked the streets of heaven with her daughter in her arms, and possibly was having a cup of tea with Nan. The thought brought me a great sense of peace, along with a smile. For that I was beyond grateful, and offered up a silent *thank you* for such a beautiful image.

For some time, I sat in the cemetery deep in thought. A beautiful, pixie-like woman, with flowers in hand, came up to me. "I haven't seen you here before. Was Rachel a friend of yours?" she inquired.

I met her gaze and confessed, "No, ma'am."

Taken aback for a moment, she knelt down beside me and continued, "I don't understand. It's obvious you're crying. If you didn't know her, then…"

I admitted, "I know her husband."

She gasped, "Oh!" She quickly regained her composure and held out her hand. "I'm Joanna Burns," she introduced herself, "Rachel's mother."

Well, crap. This could be bad. Should I tell her exactly who I am? As I shook her hand, I proceeded, "Aimee Strand."

Her eyes widened at my last name. "Are you married to one of the Strand boys?"

"Yes, ma'am." I decided it was poor manners to withhold the information she was seeking, so I conveyed, "I'm Nik's wife."

"I see," Joanna replied. After a pregnant pause, she apprised, "I come out here as often as possible to visit them." She ran her hand over the tombstone—where Nik's unborn daughter's name, Miley Faith Strand, was underneath her mother's name, date of birth and date of death. Without forethought, I clasped her hand. When her tear filled eyes met mine, she expounded, "You should know, I *don't* blame him."

I bit my lip, hard. I had meant to bring her comfort, yet here she was offering it to me. "That means a lot. Thank you."

She shook her head. "I never did. I liked Nik. It was my husband who couldn't deal with any of it."

I queried, "What couldn't he handle?"

She sighed, "Everything. He hated she had married a boy he didn't approve of. For a while, he managed to keep me away from her. But what he could never accept was that a mother's love never goes away—no matter what her child does." She grabbed a tissue from her purse and offered me one from the small packet as well. Then she went on with her story: "He also sorely underestimated the power of young love. God rest his soul. He just never understood."

While I tried to grasp the information she'd just revealed, I offered my condolences. "I'm sorry for your loss."

"Oh, honey, thank you for that. He's been gone six years now," she imparted. I didn't know what else to say, so I sat there quietly. She continued, "I hope he found peace on the other side."

I assumed, "So, he never forgave her for marrying Nik."

She exhaled, "No. Unfortunately, he did not. Which was a darn shame, Nik went through enough." She held my gaze intently. "It was my husband who used his money to make sure Nik went to jail. As if the poor boy hadn't suffered sufficiently. Those were very *dark* times."

I gasped, "But why? I mean, the whole accident was horrible enough as it was."

"I agree with you wholeheartedly. I think he was hurt and wanted to hold someone accountable."

I shook my head. "No offense, but that's awful."

"None taken, dear." She patted my knee. "What I never understood, was why Mr. Reynolds felt the need to help pay for the investigation that convicted Nik."

"Excuse me? Are you saying Caleb used his money and power to punish Nik? How? Why?" I knew I shouldn't be firing all those questions at her; therefore, I laid my hand over hers and apologized.

She nodded, "Your frustration and confusion is understandable." She stood up. "How about we have a cup of coffee? We can discuss this further."

"Yes. That's probably wise since the snow has begun to fall again."

"Ah, life in the mountains. I'm used to it, but I doubt you are."

I bobbed my head and then walked back to the rental car.

*****

We met at a small coffee shop I never would've found if she hadn't led the way. Once inside, she picked up where she had left off: "It wasn't Caleb that provided the funds. It was his father."

"Why would Mr. Reynolds care so much?"

"Well, he and my Richard were best friends since college. They had decided long ago that Rachel and Caleb should marry."

"Omigod, now I get it!" I exclaimed.

"Hm-mm. Really, I don't know what either

man was thinking." She shrugged. "I mean, Rachel liked Caleb, but not that way." She sighed, "Unfortunately, Caleb did love her, which caused all kinds of issues."

My eyes widened as I finally put two and two together. Caleb still loved Rachel to the point of utter obsession. Now his accusations made sense to me. Fact was, I'd seen the photographs of her, and we do look enough alike to have been sisters. Oh, this was bad. Really bad. "He stalked her?"

She waved her hand dismissively. "I don't know about all of that. He was quite upset when she fell in love with Nik." She rubbed the back of my hand that was resting on the table. "I mean no disrespect towards you."

I half-smiled. "That was years ago. I accept Nik has a past."

"Good. I'm glad you didn't misunderstand me."

I really didn't want to get into Nik's past too much. Fact was, it hurt a little. Even though I knew Rachel was gone. So I said, "Well, I should let you get on with your day." I hoped she didn't think I was being rude.

"Yes, I still have some errands to run." Good, she didn't think that at all. She grabbed a piece of paper out of her purse and wrote something down. Afterwards, she folded it and handed it to me as she stood. "Let me take care of this." She had the check in hand before I could stop her.

I stood as well. "Thank you for everything. It was a pleasure to meet you." I meant what I said, I was glad to have the puzzle in place. And she really was a nice lady.

Joanna surprised me when she hugged me tight and whispered, "Rachel would've liked you. You take care of yourself and Niky."

With that I pulled back, a little shocked to hear my powerhouse husband once went by Niky. Not that I had a problem with the name, it just sounded so young. Then again, I guess when she knew him he was.

"Take care of yourself as well, Joanna."

*****

Once I left Mrs. Burns, I opened the folded piece of paper in my hand. Her address and phone number were written on it, along with: call me anytime. I smiled as I tucked it inside the front pocket of my jeans. As I pulled away from the restaurant, I decided it was time to visit the spot where it all happened. I followed the directions on my GPS, and easily found where Highway 89 and U.S. 50 split.

Due to the fact I was driving in the opposite direction, I had to turn around where Highway 89 intersected with Highway 88. Then head back the way I had just came from, to really see everything clearly. With the sun starting to set, it made the scene more surreal. Since I planned on stopping, I made sure to take the turn slower than usual. However, I didn't see the SUV until it was right up on my bumper. There was nowhere to pull over. My intention was to cross over to the other side, but the jerk smacked right into me. I did my best to keep control of my vehicle. But I overcorrected and caused the car to flip. There was a horrible scream—*oh, that's me!*—and a loud crunching noise as the car careened out of control. And then, there was nothing.

Chapter Thirty-Nine
Caleb

The bitch had evaded my hit man. How, I would never know. The imbecile was of no use to me any longer. Viviane had phoned and informed me Joe had terminated him. Good riddance. I knew good and well Joe was not sloppy with disposing bodies; thus, focusing on my task at hand would be much easier. I had neither the patience nor the inclination to deal with inadequacy. Which was why, I had always been able to avoid the long arm of the law. Did that make me arrogant? Hell, yes. Most were beneath me, and I never tolerated stupidity in anyone. Of course, my constituents were a different story. But let's face it, they needed someone to guide them, show them the error of their ways. They weren't obtuse, per se, just ignorant. And I was more than willing to educate them. Not that any of them would understand the depths I must go to in order to insure all was well in their world. For example: ridding our streets of prostitution. What the simple-minded could not grasp, there was a place for whores. Granted, it was not the streets, which was why I had devised the task force in the first place. No one wanted to see scantily clad drug addicts, flaunting their assets. Especially when, they strolled through the streets, arm in arm, with their children in tow. Revolting.

Then there were the traitorous, deceitful posers like Aimee Taylor Strand, who made my damn blood boil. She shouldn't ever be allowed to breathe the same air with the rest of us. I would remedy that, soon enough.

"But Caleb, I don't think…" Rachel whispered from the corners of my mind.

"Hush now, my lovely. It's my place to handle such women. Go and rest. I'll take care of her," I assured my precious angel.

She really couldn't handle the punishment that must be dealt to those who tried to impersonate her. Oh, some succeeded longer than others, but, eventually, their lies caught up to them. I would be the first to admit, Aimee fooled me longer than any other, notwithstanding she still revealed her true colors. Now, she would pay.

I was sick and tired from the failure of others; therefore, I decided it was time to take the bull by the horns. Besides, I had an extra special treat for Mrs. Strand. Marissa had some grand ideas on how to inflict the most pain possible before Aimee's life ended. Not that I didn't have my own ways of dealing with her. Although I must say, the combination would be positively horrific. I reached down and rubbed my engorged erection those thoughts brought me; yes, soon I would have my revenge on Mrs. Nikko Strand. My only regret being, he would not be here to enjoy the festivities. Pity, that.

Locating Aimee had not been the easiest of chores, yet not insurmountable by any means. She honestly had made it quite simple on how I could get my hands on her. Then, there would be no mercy. My only hope was that the darn wench didn't die in the crash. Though it couldn't be helped, I needed her incapacitated. When the opportunity presents itself, one must act quickly.

Her rented Lexus didn't stand a snowball's chance—pardon the pun—against my Cadillac SUV. Really, it didn't take much effort at all to run her off the road. With her unfamiliarity with snow and ice, she had made it easy. Too easy. Dammit! Once her vehicle had come to rest halfway around the huge pine tree, I exited mine. The smell of gasoline was thick. Which made me wonder, how long did I have before she went up in flames? I grinned. How wonderful would it be to see Nik's face when he received that news?! Yet again, I adjusted my arousal as I realized a quick end to Aimee was not at all what I wanted, or needed. Hence, I made my way down towards the wreckage.

When I reached her, I could see blood dripping from the windows. Shit! Please tell me I hadn't actually killed her with a little bump from a car. With gloved hands, I immediately attempted to pull open the driver's door, all to no avail. She was most definitely trapped. I made my way back to the SUV to grab the tools necessary to free her. And that was when I heard another vehicle approach. Not good. I stayed in the shadows of the trees and watched the Hulk like figure approach her. Once I heard him yell her name, I knew who was there. Nik. *Well, isn't this an interesting twist of fate.* Recognition of where he was must have hit him. Because he suddenly dropped to his knees, in the throes of, what appeared to be, a panic attack. This was the very spot where my beauty, Rachel, had lost her precious life at the hands of the man who was now in a vulnerable position. I clutched the crowbar tightly as I made my way towards him. Yes, tonight he would lose his life, too. Poetic justice—*if you asked me.*

Sirens were incessantly blaring, and I had to cover my ears to help block their harsh sound. At that moment I knew full well, I couldn't stick around for the three-ring circus. Thus, I went back to the rented Cadillac. "Fuck," I roared once inside. As I banged the steering wheel with my fists till they ached, I knew a choice had to be made, immediately. *How had this happened?* Either I stayed in town for the aftermath, or I went back to my cabin in Kirkwood and attempted retribution at another time. Decisions, decisions. Which was in my best interest? On cue, my cell phone vibrated.

The text read: **I found a positively sinful device while shopping today. Can't wait for you to try it out. Yours, M.**

Attached was a photo of what looked to be a leather condom with metal spikes all over it. For a moment I didn't understand, then the image I had made it all too clear. The condom—for lack of a better word—was meant to be used as a torture device. *Debauched little whore.* Question was: did I use it on her or someone else? Funny, because I knew I had told her before I couldn't usually have sex with my playthings. Well, she would be disciplined for her lapse in memory. Even though I couldn't stop the grin spreading across my face, she would like that as much as I would. And *there* was my answer—time to go home and wait for a better opportunity to present itself. Aimee couldn't avoid me forever. Her death would come in due time. Patience was just one of the traits I had in spades—*if I do say so myself.*

*****

I made it back to the cabin with no complications, which put a genuine smile on my face. Marissa liked pain and perversion as much as I did. Therefore, when I found her bound and waiting for me—*now that's priceless*—I came instantly. And then I railed, "Just look at what you've made me do."

"Do tell," she whispered huskily before she licked her lips.

I approached her spread eagle legs and thrust my fist inside her. She bit her lip from the intrusion, arched her hips up and begged, "Again."

I noticed the blood from where her teeth had just punctured her lip. It was the only evidence that my fist had caused her any discomfort whatsoever. Damn. The woman simply didn't have a pain threshold. Huh…maybe it was time to find it. As fast as possible, I yanked my clothes off and then went to the closet to grab a thick leather belt. When I walked back into the bedroom and made eye contact, she began to writhe. "Oh, yes, Master. I've been soooo naughty."

"Hell, yes, you have," I agreed.

After thoroughly lashing her body, I had to be inside her. She was covered in welts—some angry and bright red. Her face was tear-streaked, and her wrists, along with her ankles, were raw from pulling against the restraints with each blow to her delectable body. Pain was her aphrodisiac. And I had every intention of seeing just how much she could endure. I licked her swollen, bruised breasts and then latched onto her nipple, biting down hard until she screamed. "Yeah, just like that, whore," I approved before I repeated the action, over and over, until my mouth was smeared with her blood.

When our gazes met, I could see the lust in hers. Holy hell, she was amazing. She glanced over to the bedside table where her newest purchase set. Uncertain if I should try this particular brand of torment at the moment, I inquired, "Are you sure, Marissa?"

"Please," she pleaded, "Rip me apart."

I nodded as I donned the condom with the

wickedly sharp spikes. There was going to be some extreme damage. I stared down at her and affirmed, "I happen to like this cunt." I pinched her folds tightly, bringing forth a groan of agony. "Don't you dare refuse me later, due to infection or healing wounds."

"I won't," she vowed.

As I entered her slowly, she let out an earsplitting scream. Her body in complete paroxysm, therefore, I held still and let her move when she was ready. She begged, "More."

I refused her request. "No." I explained, "I have no intentions of killing you."

I pulled out of her and released the restraints with every intention of mounting her again, sans torture device. So when she yelled, "Bastard!" I was shocked.

"Come again?"

She then proceeded to strike me with her fists, again and again, as she wailed, "How dare you! I told you what I wanted. You refused." I held her wrists so she couldn't hit me anymore. She spat out, "You're spineless. All you think about is your revenge on Aimee. Not to mention your damn Rachel. Who *you* refuse to accept is dead and gone. "

That did it! All I saw was red as I hit her, over and over, until my rage finally subsided. In my haze of fury, unfortunately, I had latched my hands firmly around her tender throat—which effectively killed her.

To this day, I didn't remember the precise moment she gasped her last breath.

*****

To dismember a body wasn't anything new to me, though it was unbelievably messy. Not something I relished doing. That was more up Joe's alley. As the fire roared, I sat quietly and watched the last of Marissa's body go up in flames. There were no tears, just silent commiseration for a woman I had thoroughly enjoyed. Where would I find another like her? Did I want to? At the moment, I wasn't completely sure if I did or not. What I was sure of; Aimee was to blame for the whole damn thing. And she would pay for it. Dearly. For that, I could ensure.

Chapter Forty
Nik

Excitement filled me as I made my way to Lake
Tahoe. Alex as well as Even had voiced their
opinions, loud and clear, about me returning to this
place. Although I understood their concerns for me, I
was insistent that I would be the one to locate Aimee.
Emotions ran high while I drove along the familiar
road. My first and foremost thought was to tell Aimee
how *much* I loved her. She had to hear me out and
comprehend beyond a shadow of doubt that I *needed*
her. *My* key to survival was *her*. She meant the world
to me, as if she were the very air I breathed. There
was no other option than for us to be together.
Forever.

A cold chill of foreboding ran up my spine as
I traveled the fateful highway. Damn, I really hated
this road! I tried with all my might to keep the past
from colliding with the present, so I focused on my
surroundings. Did I just see...? Wait! Was that
smoke? No! It couldn't be. Surely that was not the
same ominous tree. Even when I glanced around to
ensure I was definitely at the same curve, my brain
just couldn't quite wrap around it. Until I recognized
the car that fit the description, to a T, of the one
Aimee had rented. The only misstep she had made
since she left me nearly two weeks ago—instead of

cash, she used a credit card. No one was more grateful for that than me.

Alright, Nik. Pull your shit together here, buddy. If that's your wife in the car, she needs you. You're a man, not a pussy; I reminded myself when my legs trembled beneath me as I got out of the vehicle. Holy hell, was there a white SUV parked down the slope? Not that I had time to contemplate what it meant if it were. Now was the time for action. Even if it wasn't Aimee wrapped around the tree, whoever was in there needed help. Fast.

I made my way down the snow covered slope. My breathing accelerated as I gazed upon the wreckage before me. My God, it was a complete reincarnation of what my truck had looked like all those years ago. As I took in the sight, for the first time, I realized how I had walked away and Rachel hadn't. The entire passenger side of the car was coiled around the huge tree, almost as if they were embracing. I got down on my haunches to peek inside. What met my eyes took my breath away. Blood was everywhere. The beloved face of Aimee was hardly recognizable against what was left of the air bag. Her grayish-green eyes stared into the unknown. My knees gave out, then and there, as my mind raced to keep up with all the images flashing through it: Rachel telling me she loved me before she took her last breath. The haunting dream I had of Aimee dying, which seemed to be a premonition as the current situation played out. I would never survive losing another woman, another wife, I loved this way. No, that was just too damn cruel. Even for a bastard like me.

I attempted to pull myself together—yet failed miserably—and placed my head in my hands. If I lost it now, there would be no coming back. I stood on the cusp of sanity, barely holding on. Then, over the high-pitched sirens, there was a faint moan. At first, I thought it was my imagination—wishful thinking—until our gazes locked. Tears slid down my face as reality hit with the force of a freight train. *She's alive!* Aimee had survived the crash. I crawled towards her, not aware of the glass shredding my knees, and breathed, "Lille." Then louder, "Hang on. Help is on the way."

When she reached for my hand, a sob of elation broke free. There was suddenly horror in her eyes as she looked over my shoulder. "What is it?" I asked while glancing back; however, I couldn't see anything to cause such alarm. Yeah, there seemed to be a shadow, but, honestly, I couldn't make heads or tails of it. A man, maybe? Of course, that didn't make any sense. If someone were there, wouldn't they offer to help? I shook my head to clear it, grasped her hand and assured, "It's okay. You'll be out of there in no time." *God, please let my words be true.* Granted, I'd stayed mad at *Him* for years, yet, at the moment, prayer was all I had.

The smell of gasoline was ripe. And yes, I was aware you're not supposed to move an injured person; therefore, I began to pray more fervently, promising to take my sorry ass back to church if *He* would help her. *I will do* anything, *even die in her place*, I avowed. As long as she was all right, I really didn't care about the particulars.

I was taken aback when Aimee groaned, "Stop that."

Crap. I hadn't realized I'd spoken aloud. "Those weren't words for your ears." I half-smiled.

She snorted, "Then you probably shouldn't've been talking so loud."

I shrugged and asked, "How can I help?"

When she tried to lift her head, she cried out, "Get me out of here. It hurts, Nik."

Fuck the not moving her rule. I began to tug on the door, but it wouldn't give. Next I reached into the car to see if there was a chance, I could pull her through the broken window. No such luck. The steering column held her in place. Visibility was poor due to the setting sun; therefore, I couldn't tell if her legs were crushed. The thought caused a grimace to cross my face. She hadn't missed it, either. "What?" Her voice was full of panic. "Why are you looking at me like that?"

Shock would set in soon, so I calmly stroked her jaw where there was no injury. "Hey. Hear that?" I announced, "They're here."

All of a sudden, we were blinded by the bright lights that shone down on us. Someone yelled out our location. Then several uniformed people made their way down to us. Thankfully they silenced the shrieking sirens. The entire scene was covered in a myriad of blue, red, and yellow flashing lights, which made it a mishmash of abstract horror. As I leaned in, I gently pressed my lips to her head and declared, "I'm not leaving you. But I need to get out of their way."

"Please," she appealed, "I just want to hold your hand."

I looked up at the firefighter assessing the car. "For now," he approved.

Soon EMS was checking Aimee over; consequently, I had to release her. "No!" she screamed, "Don't leave me!"

The terror in her voice froze my heart.

The medic addressed, "Ma'am, he'll be right here. Let's get you out of this mess."

She finally agreed by nodding her head, yet her eyes held mine. Every ounce of pain she endured I could see in her gaze. Even though it about killed me to watch her go through it, I never lost eye contact. She needed me. And I'd be damned if I would let her down.

Once she was freed from the wreckage, they placed her on a stretcher to get her up the steep incline. I approached the ambulance when an officer stopped me to ask the required questions. Afterwards, they let me ride with her to the hospital. She had lots of cuts, but seemed to be all right—all things considered. However, I would feel better once a doctor confirmed that.

*****

While the doctors and nurses worked to patch Aimee up, I called my brothers to inform them of what had happened. They loved her, too, and their concern was a balm to my soul. We agreed they would be there in the next twenty-four hours.

Aimee was eventually moved to a private room. When I entered, she was asleep. So I sat in the chair next to her bed and held her hand. A nurse came in to check her vitals. I had already been apprised of her condition by one of the ER doctors. There were lots of bruises and lacerations, along with a few stitches in the deep gashes, in addition to a mild concussion. Otherwise, she would be sore for a while, but fine. They were holding her overnight for observations. As long as she did well, I could take her home. I knew she wouldn't be up for traveling any time soon. Besides, E had agreed to let us stay at his home here at the lake. He kept it since snowboarding and rock climbing were his two favorite sports. Well, actually, sex was probably at the top of that list, but my brother's erotic tastes were none of my concern. I was grateful, yet again, that one my brothers had come through for me. What they did in private flat out didn't matter to me. They were good men, even better brothers. I loved them, demons and all. *Huh, wonder if that's how they feel about me?*

There was a squeeze on my hand that effectively pulled me from my musings. I looked up and met Aimee's gaze. "Hey," I greeted. "How're ya feeling?"

She licked her dry lips. "I've been better." I glanced over at the water glass on the bedside table and reached over to get it for her. She drank the entire thing greedily.

"Easy, lille," I cautioned. "You don't want to make yourself sick."

When she bobbed her head it brought about a wince, along with a frown, and then she cried out, "Ow!"

"Yeah, you have a couple of stitches on your left eyebrow," I imparted.

"Oh," she gasped. "Do I have any more?"

Softly, I stroked her cheek where a burn from the airbag left its mark. "Yes. You have a few on your right bicep, compliments of flying glass."

She half-smiled. "I see."

"All in all, you're in pretty good shape," I apprised.

She attempted to sit up as she said, "Good. Then let's get out of here."

I pushed her gently back against the pillows. "Not so fast," I warned. "You have to stay tonight for observation."

For a moment, she studied me before she asked, "Why's that?"

"You have a mild concussion," I informed. "And in case you've forgotten, you were just in a major car accident."

"Better safe than sorry?" she inquired.

"Precisely," I confirmed as I leaned in to kiss her nose.

"Can you stay with me?"

"Is that what you want?"

Tears threatened to spill over as she replied, "More than anything."

I maneuvered my overlarge body into the small bed with her, and then positioned her head so she lay across my wide chest. The nurse did not approve and stormed out of the room. But when she returned, there were no more complaints. I had to assume whoever was in charge set her straight on who was in the room. While I didn't come back up to the area frequently, I did make generous contributions to this hospital. After all, it was where Rachel and I had been brought all those years ago. And though there had been no help for her—since she had died at the scene of the accident—they had helped me. Besides, there was a children's wing named after my unborn daughter, Miley Faith. This was just one of the things Aimee needed to know. There would be *no more* secrets. Time to lay it on the line, all of it, and trust she still wanted me afterwards. Because if she didn't, I doubted I would survive without her. I held her, as close as possible, with the knowledge it could be the last time she was ever in my arms.

*****

Once we arrived at E's place, she had something to eat. Then I offered, "Would you like a bath?"

She smiled, "I'd love one."

"Wait here while I go and draw it for you."

She nodded as I left the room.

After I ensured the water was the right temperature and filled it with soothing oil, I set up some music, lit the candles, and made sure the bathroom had become a relaxing spa like environment. I wanted her comfortable. No more pain.

I assisted her with disrobing in the connecting bedroom, swept her into my arms and carried her into the bathroom. Although I was aroused, this wasn't about sex. It was all about her comfort. I eased her into the bath and knelt beside the tub. She tugged my arm and queried, "Aren't you joining me?"

I stroked her face tenderly as I explained, "Not this time. Let me take care of you."

She leaned back and let me do just that. I began to wash her hair, careful not to get any shampoo on her stitches. The song I had wanted finally began to play. As if she understood the cue, she listened intently before she whispered, "Secrets."

I agreed, "Yes, I like One Republic." After I rinsed her hair, I soaped up the pouf and washed her sore body, as I confessed, "That's not why I chose this song, though."

"Mmm," she hummed as she fully reclined, and let me pamper her. She surprised me when she inquired, "Then, why did you?"

"Seemed fitting in many ways," I stated matter-of-factly.

That got her attention. She sat up too quickly, which caused water to lap over the edges, soaking my jeans. "Oh, no!" she exclaimed. "I'm so sorry." She tried to reach over and assist me, so I stilled her hands.

"Hey, it's just water," I said as I grabbed a towel, proceeding to dry off myself and the floor. While I did that, I started, "We didn't always live here in Lake Tahoe." She sat there quietly and let me spill my guts. "We moved here the summer before my senior year of high school." I clarified, "We were previously in San Diego. But after my dad was killed in an accident, we relocated here."

She swallowed hard and then asked, "How did he die?" She added, "If it's too hard to talk about, I understand."

Always putting others first, I was in awe of her for so many reasons. Once I finished with the towel, I went back to washing her. "He was a zoologist. There was an incident with one of the elephants. When he entered the enclosure to check things out, the elephant panicked and trampled him. He died instantly."

"How awful," she gasped. "I'm so sorry."

I shrugged. "It was a long time ago. My mother always loved this place, because it reminded her of Norway. So she packed us up and brought us here."

She grasped my hand. I half-smiled as I continued, "My brothers and I decided to go mountain biking at one of the resorts once we had finished unloading the moving truck for Mom. That was when I first met Rachel." I expounded, "Her parents owned the ski resort, and she had been working that day." I ran my knuckles along her cheek. "I won't tell you those details, Aimee. It wouldn't be fair to *you*, or to her memory."

She held my hand against her face and nodded.

I went on, "Needless to say, we hit it off instantly and dated our entire senior year. We were married right after graduation. And she got pregnant our first night together."

Aimee titled her head and stated, "On your wedding night."

I exhaled loudly before I replied, "Yeah. We played by the rules and waited until we were married. Little did we know how short our time together would be."

There was no controlling the tears that slid

down my face, but I persevered, "Rachel's dad was really angry about our marriage; hence, she hadn't seen her mother since graduation. You see, they were really close." I suddenly noticed a strange look pass over Aimee's face. It was gone before I could put a name to it.

I continued, "Anyhow, Rachel was thrilled when her parents invited us to dinner that night." I barked out a humorless laugh. "She couldn't wait to tell them about the baby. Although I had pulled a double shift that day, I just couldn't tell her no." I paused and took a deep cleansing breath. "Unfortunately, Rachel's car was out of gas. She'd been so sick and hadn't made it out that day. For that reason, I thought it best we stayed home. But she refused. So we took my work truck instead. We knew a storm was coming in, but, quite frankly, we weren't concerned. Since Highway 89 was more convenient to her parents' house, we took that route instead of Kingsbury Grade." A sob broke, and I had to pause for a few minutes.

Aimee chimed in, "You don't have to do this. I know what happened next." She climbed out of the tub and onto my lap. I don't know how long we sat there like that—her holding me while I broke down completely.

I eventually brought my emotions to heel, picked Aimee up as I stood, and carried her to the bed. Once there, I stripped out of my wet clothes and spooned up against her, careful of her injuries. I knew full well I had to confess the next part if we were ever going to move forward. I grasped her hip tightly and admitted, "The night you left I was saying goodbye to her."

She peeked over her shoulder, her eyes narrowing as she listened. I continued, "In order to cope with my loss, I wrote a song. Music is therapy

341

for me in many ways. I know you must've heard me playing."

She inhaled sharply and then confessed, "That wasn't the reason."

"To let her go, I needed to also play *her* song." I clarified, "Not the one I wrote. The one that was playing as she died in my arms."

She choked out, "Please Remember Me."

I snorted, "Yeah. That radio was busted all to hell. How it was able to play, I'll never know. But it did, and that was the song."

She turned towards me and held my face. "She was saying goodbye to you."

I shrugged. "Possibly."

She began to kiss the tears that were falling freely, but I couldn't let her think I loved Rachel more. Therefore, I drew in a breath and conveyed, "Yes, I loved her very much."

She tried to pull back, but I held on and clasped her face between my hands. "I love you *more*, lille."

As she blinked back her own tears, she looked into my eyes quizzically. "What'd you say?"

I brushed my lips against hers and affirmed, "*You* mean more to me. I don't know how to explain it. Everything with you is just... You are my light. My world. My all. I cannot be without you. I have never needed someone as much as I *need* you." I brought her hand up to my heart and held it there. "This tattoo represents my past. I'm the dagger. The larger heart is Rachel's. The smaller one is Miley's." She traced her finger over the tear shaped blood drops." I expounded, "Their blood shed by me."

"Nik," she gasped. "That's terrible, yet beyond beautiful at the same time."

Apparently, I still wasn't getting through to her. Thus, I brought her hand up to the brand against my hair line behind my ear. "The outside of my body may be forever marked by my past. But you…You, Aimee, have branded my heart. My soul. They are completely yours for as long as you want them." A sob broke as I implored, "Please, don't leave me again."

She clasped my face in her hands and reverently kissed my cheek bones, jaw line, and then mouth. All the while she whispered, "I love you with all my heart. Never will I leave you. I promise."

With that I deepened our kiss, mindful that I couldn't make love to her at the moment, but needing the connection. So when she reached between our bodies and guided my cock to her core, I argued, "Lille, we can't do this."

She rubbed her wet folds along my painful erection and countered, "Yes, we can. Please, Nik. We need this."

There was no more talking as I entered her as gently as possible, rocking slowly. Healing sex. Yet, it was so much more. The bond between us grew stronger with each stroke, and then we eased into completion together. I knew from that moment on, nothing would tear us apart again. We would weather whatever storms came our way. Together. Though I'm not a fool, there would be plenty of passion and, more than likely, some fighting. But in the end, we would be just fine.

Once, I had thought you had to be a lover *or* a fighter. Thanks to Aimee, I now realized how wrong I was. To be a *lover* you must also be a *fighter*. Because to truly love, you had to be willing to fight for it at all cost.

Nothing was more valuable.
More rare.
More precious.
And I would never again sit on the sidelines.

No matter what, I would stay in the fight. Always.

Epilogue
Aimee

Two weeks later.

We were finally back in San Francisco. Lake Tahoe was spectacular, but the memories it carried for Nik would always be bittersweet. Before we had left the lake, he insisted we stop by the cemetery. Not wanting to be an intruder, I suggested I should stay in the car. He wouldn't hear of it. Together, we made our way over to Rachel and Miley's grave. There were many tears, as well as more things he chose to share with me. I no longer viewed Rachel as a ghost to compete with for Nik's love. I knew now he loved us both, yet in different ways. And that was more than enough.

Our biggest shock came when Joanna showed up at the graveside. I was grateful they could finally make amends. It was what Nik had needed the most: forgiveness. Yes, he craved it from Rachel's mother. But he needed to forgive himself even more. While the former was important to his emotional state, the latter was key to his freedom. And being a witness to those chains breaking was immeasurable.

I thought Nik would never agree to go to church with me; therefore, no one was more shocked than I when *he* suggested it. We went to the church he had attended with his mom and brothers all those years ago. When the same pastor remembered him, it was like a coming home. I still get teary every time I think about it. Beautiful. Healing. There was nothing I could've wanted more for him. Needless to say, we left the area different people than when we had arrived. Free. Forgiven. The world our oyster. And I, for one, couldn't wait to start living instead of just existing.

*****

Since we weren't together for Christmas, we planned a family dinner a few nights after New Year's. I believe it was referred to as Twelfth Night. The "boys" were as funny as usual with their brotherly banter, and, this time, Nik had joined in. That was such a magnificent thing to witness. At first, I think Alex and Ev were a bit taken aback. Though it didn't take them long to welcome the camaraderie. Even Ray had joined in from time to time. And I must confess, having Mary Alice there as a guest, not an employee, was wonderful. With all that testosterone, it was a pleasant treat to have some female companionship.

I couldn't help but notice throughout the evening that E seemed a bit off. Unable to put my finger on what exactly it was. Yes, my brother-in-law was inappropriate on a good day and downright crass on the others. But I loved him all the same. So when he sat silently brooding while he stared out the window, I had to wonder if there was a woman involved. Not feeling it was my place to intervene— *for now*— I didn't inquire, yet. I did vow to myself I would get to the bottom of things, one way or the other. Yep, I would definitely be keeping my eye on him.

Anticipation of our night together, once Alex and Even left, had me a bit distracted. Nik had been so careful, treating me like a delicate object since the accident. Now, I had the green light from the doctor. While I thoroughly enjoyed slowly making love to my husband, I was ready for a little *more*.

*****

As everyone else said their goodbyes, I snuck away to put the final touches on my assault—I mean, outfit. I stripped out of my designer jersey dress and slipped on a naughty little ensemble. The red leather skirt was so short if I bent over, the whole world would see my lady parts. Albeit the blouse—if that's what you wanted to call it— revealed just as much. It was black and sheer, making sure his eyes were drawn to the lacey bra underneath. The said bra had no support whatsoever, but it did push my boobs up in a tantalizing way. For a full view of my assets, I kept the blouse unbuttoned down to my navel. And speaking of ass, mine was clad in an almost nonexistent thong, which barely covered the entrance to my core. Adorned in fishnet stockings held on by a garter belt, I slipped on my five inch CFMPs. Hell yeah, I looked downright edible. Of course, that thought brought forth liquid heat between my thighs. The final touch was the music—Alicia Keys' "Fallin'" was on a loop. That particular song made me want to bump and grind all over my husband. *Damn, I have it bad for the man.* The Cheshire cat grin spread across my face, because I knew it was reciprocated.

When Nik entered the room, I pushed play on the remote and began to swivel my hips to the beat. His eyes widened as his nostrils flared. He looked sexy as sin with the top button of his silk dress shirt undone along with his tie, which simply draped around his neck. Oh, yeah, I was going to use said tie in a while. As he approached, I sauntered forward while I watched his pupils dilate with desire. I used him as a stripper pole and began to do some provocative moves against his body. The eroticism of the moment urged me on. Now his eyes were hooded, and his arousal strained against the zipper of his trousers. Poor baby. Really, I should do something about that.

Unable to stop myself, I knelt before him and tugged the zipper of his pants down with my teeth. All the while, my deft fingers released the clasp and freed his magnificent cock—which already wept for me. I traced the tip with my tongue. That brought forth a groan from him as he fisted my hair. What was it about having such a strong, powerful man at your mercy that brought out the bad girl in us all? And, ooh, my naughty side wreaked havoc up and down his enormous erection. With one hand, I fisted his thick shaft at the root. With the other, I cupped his weighty balls. Then, I used my mouth to lick, suckle, and lightly nip until he erupted down my throat. Ah, his taste was salty, pure male. Yet with Nik's unique flavor added to it. Mmm, an intoxicating elixir.

I worked my way back up his body as he struggled for control. I shook my head while I pushed him back into the strategically placed winged chair. His eyes widened in surprise. I licked my lips slowly, catching the remains of his zest on my tongue. He watched in rapt fascination and reached for me again. This time I cautioned, "Not until I tell you to." Of course, he ignored my warning. A sultry chuckle bubbled out of me. "Just remember, you asked for it."

I drew the tie from his neck and draped it around mine, then proceeded to rub it across my already hard nipples. He leaned forward, and, once again, I went to my knees. Next, I patted the arm of the chair and instructed, "Give me your hand."

His brow rose as he complied. I wrapped one end of the tie stealthily around his wrist and then the front leg of the chair. Once I ran it underneath, I fastened his other hand in the same fashion. I knew full well if he wanted out of his predicament, all he had to do was flex his deliriously huge muscles. But he didn't. Instead, he watched me continue to lap dance for him.

First, I pulled the cups of the so called bra down, releasing both breasts. I aptly bounced them in front of him until he captured a nipple. Before I let him take me any higher up the mountain of ecstasy, I leaned back to release my breast from his mouth, causing a *pop* from the suction. I then turned so that my ass was in his face. He playfully bit a cheek, which brought forth a *yelp* from me. As I continued down the path of naughtiness, I placed my bottom against his face. This time he didn't play. No, he got down to business and laved me from the seam of my butt all the way forward to my swollen clit. "Oh, that feels sooo good," I purred.

His deep chuckle vibrated against my opening, nearly sending me over the edge. I controlled my orgasm—barely—and eased away. Then, as sexy as possible, I disrobed for him. Once I was completely bare, I sat astride him. He knew where I was going with that move and slouched down into the chair. I grasped his now throbbing penis and used my own juices to lubricate, before inserting him inside me. On a groan, he straightened his legs while I leaned back on them to hold my weight on my hands, which were placed on his shins. Next, I put my feet on either side of his head, giving him a full-blown show.

He growled, "So fucking beautiful." Then he arched his hips.

After a few minutes, I released his hands. With my knees bent, he held my ass. Now that my hands were free to roam, I caressed his massive bicep with one. With the other, I reached between my spread legs and pleasured myself for him. All the while I held his gaze. His eyes were so dark they looked black. As he picked up the rhythm, he lifted me and thrust deep until an earth shattering climax ripped through our bodies. Both of us cried out each other's names as wave after wave of pure ecstasy crashed over us.

We made it to our bed eventually, where we continued to explore our naughty sides together. He had once told me that I had "branded" him. But the truth was—it was he that had *branded* me.

Heart.

Mind.

Body.

Soul.

Play List

When this story came to me, I wanted to quote the song that went with the scripture in the front. Due to copyright laws I was unable to do that; however, the song is: We Fall Apart – We As Human

I've Got You Under My Skin – Michael Bublé

We'll Meet Again – Johnny Cash

One Solemn Hour – Within Temptation

Pushing Me Away – Linkin Park

Before It Began – Olivia Somerlyn

How To Save A Life – The Fray

Just Say Yes – Snow Patrol

Because You Loved Me – Celine Dion

Endless Love – Luther Vandross & Mariah Carey

When A Man Loves A Woman – Michael Bolton

Make You Feel My Love – Adele

Don't Want To Miss A Thing – Aerosmith

Please Remember Me – Tim McGraw

Who You Are – Lunatica

Wintersong – Sarah McLachlan

I Left My Heart In San Francisco – Julie London

Secrets – One Republic

Fallin' – Alicia Keys

You can listen to this play list on Spotify here: https://open.spotify.com/user/loraannr/playlist/538F2MMkgUC1ZHcMEZ4Iwg

Preview from

Bound
(Strand Brothers Series, book 2)

Prologue
E

What a hellacious week. The need for a little alone time was a must. I loved my brothers and my new sister—well, sister-in-law, to be exact. Aimee was a Godsend for Nik. Never had my brother been so flippin' happy, that in and of itself was a sight to see. But I needed an escape. No, what I needed was a warm and willing woman. They were a dime a dozen, and, quite frankly, I was bored with them all. The only action I'd seen in the last few months was at Nik's bachelor party; even then, I only played around. Yes, I made sure she was satisfied, yet there was no fulfillment in it for me. Oh, she offered more than once, but I couldn't. It was a sad state of affairs when the man who taught others the art of pleasure could no longer find any for himself. That'd be me.

So there I sat back in the shadows to the left in one of my numerous clubs, ruminating over what all of that meant for my future in the business of instructing BDSM, when the dancer on stage caught my eye. Damn she was a knockout, with a body like Tyra Banks—back when she modeled for Victoria's Secret—and waist-length black hair. If I wasn't mistaken, those were mahogany highlights shining in the stage lights. Hello, any red-blooded male would have a hard-on with just that image shimmying in his brain. But it was her moves that held me captive.

Fuck. If she swiveled her hips like that again, I would come. She had Christina Aguilera's dance moves down pat as "Genie In A Bottle" blared out through the sound system. I murmured under my breath, "Sweetness, I promise to rub *you* the right way."

As if she heard me, her eyes met mine. Like her body in motion wasn't bad enough, her face was beyond stunning. For a tall woman, she had a delicate, heart-shaped face. What I could do with those full lips made me groan with anticipation. Seemed I wasn't out of the race, after all. This beauty was doing things to my body no other woman ever had. Without forethought, I stood and prowled towards her, not once breaking eye contact. The electricity actually hummed as our bodies drew closer to one another. Unbidden, my tongue snaked out when I finally reached the edge of the stage. She didn't miss the implication either. I placed my hand on the edge about to hop up and join her when several other dancers assembled with her on stage. Apology was in her eyes before she turned towards the other girls.

Holy hell. I wanted her so much my dick actually hurt, yet there wasn't a damned thing I could do about it now. The realization I needed to vacate the premises immediately became crystal clear. If I stayed any longer I would have her, and I didn't play with the help. It was my number one rule, and I enforced it fiercely with my managers. There would be loss of respect, not to mention obedience. That, I wouldn't tolerate. I firmly tugged on my slacks to find a more comfortable position before hightailing it out of there. Unbelievable, I had never run from a female in my life. Nor had I willingly walked away from a sure thing. And let's be honest, I would've taken her without an ounce of hesitation on her part. I knew it. She knew it, too. It was best for both of us if

I continued towards my car and never looked back.

*****

A week had passed since I had left the breathtaking beauty at my club up in Lake Tahoe, and still I was hard for her. This was supposed to be a celebration, our family Christmas party, yet my mind wouldn't let the mystery dancer go. Every cell in my body wanted her, needed her, in a way I didn't comprehend. Without a single taste of her, I was hooked. She had become a drug to me. And damn it all to hell, I had to have another hit.

Of course, my intuitive sister-in-law knew something was off with me. Hell, I didn't want an interrogation. There really wasn't anything to share even if I had wanted to, which I didn't. For now, I wanted to brood in peace. Though, the knowledge I wouldn't be able to resist much longer truly pissed me off. I was the *master* of control, *master* over my body and anyone else's I chose to be. So the damn ache inside made me meaner than a snake. I had no desire to take it out on Aimee. No, until I either found relief for my ever throbbing cock or broke down and drove back up to the lake, I was not good company for anyone. My brothers were fully aware something was up, but they were wise enough to give me space. After I slammed back another glass of Grey Goose, I said my goodbyes. Alex was right behind me. I wasn't so preoccupied I hadn't noticed the looks Aimee had been shooting towards Nik. Time to leave the newlyweds to their evening.

As Alex and I walked to our cars, he affirmed, "When you're ready to talk about whoever she is, E, I'll be here to listen."

"Fuck you," I said without heat as I climbed into my Veyron Bugatti.

He grinned and smacked the roof of my car before I drove off.

I had no idea how to get the woman out of my system, but I had no intentions of giving in—yet. I found myself at my club in downtown San Fran. Yeah, maybe what I needed was to get laid. With that, I strode with purpose into the club bypassing the main floor. Nah, I needed something rough and knew just who could satisfy all of my power hungry demands.

I rapped on the door twice before it opened. She hit her knees instantly and stared at the floor. When I stroked her head, she purred, "I've missed you, Master."

I back kicked the door closed as I grabbed her hair in my fist and yanked so her eyes met mine. "I'm glad to hear that. This will be a night you won't forget any time soon."

Bound ft. Even Strand (Strand Brothers Series, #2)
US: http://amzn.com/B00RY777O4
UK: http://amazon.co.uk/dp/B00RY777O4

Contact the Author

Website
http://www.loraann.com

Amazon Author Page
https://www.amazon.com/author/loraann

Facebook Author Page
https://www.facebook.com/lora.ann.books

Strand Brothers Series page
https://www.facebook.com/strandbrothers

Google +
https://plus.google.com/u/0/+LoraAnn

Pinterest
https://www.pinterest.com/loraannbooks/

Goodreads author
https://www.goodreads.com/author/show/419
700.Lora_Ann

Twitter
https://twitter.com/Loraann_

Tsū
https://www.tsu.co/LoraAnn

About the Author

Lora is a Missouri native who relocated to California as a teen. She spent several years as an international flight attendant for a major airline, before taking on her greatest job ever, a stay-at-home mom. Now she resides in Kentucky with her family, and has taken on her newest adventure, writing.